As she reached the door, Arinna called, "You're not leaving now, are you?" Snarling malevolently, she stretched her arms above her and said gleefully, "We're just getting started!"

The arms came down, casting all Arinna's wrath across the room. The first strike of blue fire hit hard enough to rock Kali within her sphere of shields. Trembling and sweating, Kali clutched her side and ended up on her knees. The second strike flattened her, and the shields shimmered an amber shade, almost, but not quite collapsing.

Kali lay there, wheezing, vulnerable. Surely, the next blast would destroy the shields completely, and in the minutes afterward, she would be made Arinna's slave. Determined to resist to the end, Kali shakily drew her knife, preparing to finish herself in the last free-thinking seconds that remained.

Other Books by Jean Stewart:

Return to Isis

Isis Rising

WARRIORS
OF ISIS

Jean Stewart

Rising Tide Press
5 Kivy Street
Huntington Station, NY 11746
(516) 427-1289

Publisher's Acknowledgments:
The publisher is grateful for all the support and expertise offered by the members of its editorial board: Bobbi Bauer, Adriane Balaban, Beth Heyn, Hat Edwards, Pat G, and Marian Satriani. Special thanks to Joyce Honorof, M.D., and S.E. Hutchins, Ph.D., for their excellent technical assistance. Thanks, also, to Edna G. for believing in us, and to the feminist and gay bookstores for being there.

First printing January 1995
10 9 8 7 6 5 4 3 2

Edited by Alice Frier and Lee Boojamra
Book cover art: Evelyn Rysdyk

Library of Congress Cataloging-in-Publication Data
Stewart, Jean 1952-
      Warriors of Isis/Jean Stewart
          p.cm

ISBN 1-883061-03-2   LC 93-087-606

Dedication

For Susie,
Gaea's unexpected gift to me.

In loving memory of Mandy

Acknowledgments

As always, thanks to SJH for the proofreading and allowing me to endlessly bounce ideas off her.

And my everlasting gratitude to Alice Frier and Lee Boojamra of Rising Tide Press. Ladies, through your love of community and hard work, you provide a grand platform for a host of voices that might otherwise go unheard.

1

Kali's heart was racing. Another cold trickle of nervous sweat chilled its way down her spine, and was quickly absorbed by the thick poly-fiber of the bodysuit she wore. She glanced over her shoulder, and saw nothing but the fir trees and granite boulders that bordered the narrow cliff edge. Anxiously, she returned her uneasy scrutiny to the twisting trail ahead.

In the murky dawn light, the trail which led up to the mountain pass seemed quiet and harmless. All the same, her psychic antennae were screaming *Danger!*

She had been picking her way cautiously, stumbling over stony ground for nearly an hour. At last she was closing in on the area that satellite surveillance had pinpointed as Arinna Sojourner's base of operations. Arinna was the fugitive from justice already responsible for two deaths; a woman who would not hesitate to kill anyone else who got in the way of her dreams of a personal empire. Kali knew that hours earlier she should have been intercepted by some sort of security patrol. Instead, she had succeeded in penetrating deeper and deeper into hostile territory, without being challenged. Which could only mean that a deadly trap awaited her somewhere just ahead.

As Kali stepped forward, her boot skidded on a loose stone, throwing her momentarily off balance. Simultaneously, at the edge of her vision, she saw two huge, uniformed men leap from behind the boulders two meters to her right.

Recognition of the green uniforms hit her; a silent inner wail broke loose. *Regs! They're Regs!*

Desperately, Kali lurched backward, trying to regain her footing as the brawny Regulator in the lead bore down on her. Her foot slipped again and she was suddenly on her hands and knees, scrambling frenziedly. She saw the Reg above her, his short, rounded staff raised in his hand. It was too late—the Reg was snarling, the thick, wooden club was descending, and she was paralyzed beneath it, watching her doom unfold.

Suddenly, a shrill computer tone sounded, seeming to go on and on. In a helpless mix of terror and frustration, Kali groaned and sank against the stony trail. Above her, the fir trees, and then the fierce fascist soldiers of Elysium, disappeared as she tore the ARC band off her head and abruptly emerged from the computer-generated world of virtual reality. The bright halogen ceiling lights nearly blinded her. The jarring alarm ended and was followed by a courteous, well-modulated female voice, which to Kali seemed even more insufferable than the alarm.

"I'm sorry," the disembodied voice soothed. "The projected opponent of choice has made contact in a manner which renders unconsciousness. The Seeker is captured, and thus loses round 24 of ARC Training."

It's only a simulation session, Kali reminded herself, trying to center herself. *They weren't real Regs.*

Still, here she was lying on the platform of the Artificial Reality Centrum, defeated and badly shaken. All because Danu's amazing new training device had unexpectedly brought Kali face to face with the creatures of her worst nightmares.

Sighing, Kali lifted her head and looked up. Above the vast ARC Platform, she could see Styx standing by the floor-to-ceiling windows of the enclosed observation deck. Styx's arms were folded disapprovingly over her chest, and her weathered Mayan face wore a stern frown. At her side stood a stranger, a young woman of Japanese heritage dressed in a Freeland Warrior's uniform. The shoulder insignia on her burgundy jacket marked her as a lieutenant, and her impassive, dark eyes seemed to be taking Kali's measure.

Disconcerted by the presence of an observer, and feeling strangely defensive about it, Kali protested, "Regs?! There wouldn't be *Regs*!"

She gripped the ARC headband in a clammy palm, carefully folding protruding pieces—the eye visors and holophonic filaments— tightly to the thin plastic circumference. Shakily, she slipped the device into its small protective case and then pocketed it.

She stood up quickly and marched across the simulation field. Beneath her climbing boots, the adjustable molecular density surface began rapidly abandoning its appearance of rocky terrain and twisting trail. Recklessly, Kali stomped across the shifting surface, her ability to keep her footing faultless as the flexible-plastic composite layers steadily flattened out into a smooth, hard plane. When she reached the end of the platform, Kali hopped over the edge, dropping the two meters to the hardwood floor with the supple grace of a cougar.

The observation deck intercom carried Styx's unruffled reply to Kali. "We didn't build this Artificial Reality Centrum," Styx counseled patiently, "in order to stock the opponent file with images of villains you feel *comfortable* fighting against."

Raising her chin obstinately, Kali countered, "The Regs are in Elysium, enclosed safely behind the electromagnetic force field screen we call the Border. Right?!"

Styx said nothing, but instead exchanged a brief, indecipherable look with the warrior beside her.

Her face felt hot, and Kali mentally cursed her fair skin for its ready betrayal of emotion. "Before we locked down the Bordergates two months ago," Kali reminded Styx, "we determined that no trace of Arinna's DNA had registered in any of the Bordergates, which led everyone to agree that Arinna's still in Freeland—somewhere." Using what she thought to be classic logic, Kali continued, "Now, since the Regs are all safely corralled behind the Border, in Elysium, and I'm going to be looking for Arinna in Freeland, where there are no

Regs...tell me why I'm wasting my time and energy, tangling with Regs in my combat exercise!"

Tossing her blonde braid over her shoulder, she suddenly noticed Whit leaning against a wall about seven meters away, her serious, gray eyes leveled on Kali with that familiar intensity. Taking a deep breath, Kali fought to get her emotions under control. In a strained voice, she finished, "For Gaea's sake, you should have warned me, Styx."

With a noncommittal grunt, Styx left the observation deck and came down the stairs, followed by the young lieutenant. Pushing up the sleeves of her loose, wheat-colored pullover, Styx came steadily closer, the concern in her ebony eyes cooling the last of Kali's anger.

The stranger beside Styx spoke up then, her respectful tone not masking the fact that she expected a truthful answer. "Deputy Leader, you panicked—am I right?"

All at once ashamed of herself, Kali's gaze dropped to the polished hardwood floor. "Yes," she managed, her throat closing on the reply.

"If you are to survive a confrontation with a mind-power like Arinna Sojourner, you cannot allow yourself to panic—no matter who or what you meet on your mission." Again the lieutenant's tone was mild, but when Kali looked up, disconcertingly perceptive eyes probed her own. *The eyes of an exacting teacher*, she realized.

Dejectedly, Kali stood there, considering how to explain the overwhelming terror that even now pounded in her blood, making her clench her hands into fists in order to mask the fact that she was still trembling. One look at a Reg and she was like a deer in a raging forest fire, unable to think, able only to run.

"Ever face a real live Reg, Tor?" Whit's husky voice called, saving Kali from trying to explain the unexplainable.

The stranger turned and watched Whit push off from the wall, advancing on them with that distinctive, long-legged stride. The click of Whit's polished boots sent echoes through the huge chamber that surrounded them. Her gleaming dark hair glinted with strands of auburn and the high-cheekboned face seemed to shine with an austere beauty. Kali noted, for the hundredth time since last month's election, how magnificent Whit looked in formal Leader's attire. Today it was a long scarlet coat with intricately embroidered shawl lapels, draped over a high-collared black shirt and tight black pants.

The lieutenant gave a slow smile, as if conceding a point. "No, I've fought every kind of tough guy, but I must admit I've never had the dubious pleasure of encountering an Elysian Regulator."

With a nod at Kali, Whit said, "You've heard all about the Deputy Leader, I suppose."

Kali was trying to figure out who this woman was, and realized she could actually *feel* the weight of the lieutenant's keen appraisal as it passed over her, examining, registering details of Kali's outward appearance. *Who is she?* Kali wondered. She looked to be only in her early twenties, but the patience and wisdom in that face belonged to an elder.

"Oh, yes," the woman stated, "I've heard of Kali Tyler, the warrior who survived both the Fall of Isis and ten years' internment in Elysium." Stepping forward, with a look of sincere respect, the woman bowed, while Kali sent a puzzled glance to Styx.

Pushing her hands deep into the pockets of her khaki trousers, Styx shifted her big-boned frame and made introductions. "Kali, this is Lieutenant Tamatori Yakami, of the colony of Morgan. Lieutenant Yakami is both a martial arts expert and a seasoned Wiccan." Flicking a look at Whit, Styx explained, "I asked Whit to petition the Eight Leaders Council, so that Tor could be reassigned to military duty here in Isis. We wish her to assist us in your training."

Extending her hand, Kali murmured, "Welcome to Isis, Lieutenant."

With a composed smile, the woman returned, "Call me Tor, and I won't call you Deputy Leader, okay?"

Relieved, Kali nodded. The title still made her feel awkward. She clasped Tor's hand firmly, and looked searchingly at a pair of serene eyes in a very attractive face. Oddly enough, Kali found that her natural ability to mind-read was being blocked. Although she listened with all her might, she was unable to pick up any images or feelings.

With a cool smile, Tor began removing her wine-red dress-uniform jacket and western string tie. Handing the clothing to Styx, Tor went on to roll up first one starched white shirtsleeve, then the other. With a deft twist of a barrette, she pulled her long black hair away from her face, neatly out of her line of vision. Abruptly, she motioned for Kali to move over to the closed door that served as the main entrance into the room.

"Let's review some basic ways of handling a surprise attack," the young lieutenant began. "In a minute, I'm going to put you on the other side of that closed door. I'll dim the lights in here, then when you're ready, you'll open the door and enter this room."

Kali shot a questioning look at Whit.

In answer, Whit winked, then grinned like a rogue.

Beside Whit, Styx cocked her head sideways and sent a telepathic remark: *Listen to her. Yakami holds every hand-to-hand combat award a warrior can earn.*

Tired and discouraged, Kali licked her lips, wishing she could at least get a drink of water. That last nerve-racking session on the ARC Platform had left her parched. Normally, they ended these sessions around four in the afternoon and then had a meal while they checked the latest air-search reports. But tonight, whether for Tamatori's benefit, or because of this unusual visit by Whit, the combat training session was dragging on and Kali's wristcom indicated that it was well after six.

Tor was still talking, going through a slow-motion example of how she expected Kali to react to a surprise attack. "Once you've lost your footing, for whatever reason, drop your weight and roll *into* your opponent." As she spoke, Tor dropped to the floor and rolled sideways, until she bumped against Kali's shins.

Licking her lips again, Kali concluded for her, "And the attacker's momentum makes them trip and fall over you." Frowning slightly, Kali offered, "I'm a Freeland Warrior. I know this move."

"But do you know this?" Demonstrating the roll again, Tor added a surprising variation. At the end of the roll, as her boots hit the hardwood floor again, Tor leapt up, one arm poised in a half-cocked punch, the other close to her face, acting as a shield. "Attack immediately,"

Tor instructed, and just in time Kali leapt aside as Tor began a series of windmill strikes, her arms and legs almost a blur of motion.

"Mother of Earth," Kali breathed, retreating still further away, trying to see exactly what martial art technique Tor was using. As suddenly as she began, Tor stopped. The smaller woman took a deep breath, then spread her arms out and up in a smoothly powerful stretch. "I am here to teach you to balance ki, to direct the flow of inner energy, which is your life force." Stepping closer, Tamatori pressed her palm against Kali's flat stomach. "Feel ki here. Direct ki into each kick and each punch. When you kick, kick through your opponent. When you punch, send the ki through the first two knuckles of your fist." Tor moved away again, studying Kali's face.

Staring back at her, bewildered, Kali thought, *I have a vague memory of this. Was it from one of Baubo's trance teachings?*

Motioning toward the door, Tor finished, "Let's try it."

Again, Kali checked her friends and caught Styx and Whit exchanging what was definitely a conspiratorial grin. *So they've taken me up on the demand I made last week,* Kali thought ruefully, remembering her complaints to Styx and Whit.

In a fit of impatience, Kali had snapped that the past month of memorizing Wiccan lore and sweating through a daily fitness regimen was doing little to develop her natural, latent psychic abilities. Fearing that she would still be unprepared when they finally discovered Arinna's location, Kali had demanded that her training be speeded up, demanded to be "challenged without mercy, pushed to the limit of my abilities." *I suppose using the Regs against me was just the beginning,* Kali realized glumly.

Knowing she'd asked for this, that she truly *needed* it, Kali examined her opponent. Though shorter than Kali by several centimeters, Tor had the broad shoulders and firmly muscled thighs of a lifelong athlete. She looked relaxed and eager, as if she were anticipating this opportunity to tear someone apart.

Reluctantly, Kali walked past Tor and through the doorway. Once outside, she paused a moment, studying the panel of the door as it slid closed. Nervous, she bent over, massaging her aching thighs. The clinging material of the gray bodysuit beneath her hands was hot and uncomfortable. However, since the electrical leads that cued the ARC program were implanted in the suit, signaling her kinesthetic reactions and thus feeding her responses to the advanced interactive program, she had no choice but to wear the suit and suffer.

Goddess, what I wouldn't give for a drink of water, Kali thought wearily. She looked longingly down the hallway. There was a water fountain just outside the bathroom. *It would only take a minute if I hurried.*

Squinting against the slanting rays of the late September sunset, seventeen-year-old Danu slowed her mountain bike at the end of Cammermeyer Street. Surrounded by mountain meadows, at the edge of the city limits, an immense, dark building loomed against the red-lavender blaze of western sky.

With the eyes of an experienced architect, the young genius surveyed the huge structure before her. Externally, Navra Recreation Hall was a completed structure, its rainbow-hued, vinyl-concrete slabs marking it as one of the most striking buildings in Isis. Yet within, Danu knew the edifice housed a series of vast, empty rooms, defined by retractable walls. Though it was presently devoid of decor, carpets, and furniture, one day Navra Rec Hall would be a luxurious gymnasium complex. But at the moment, the only comfort in the place was the high-tech plumbing. As the ARC Platform was assembled within this structure, so were the only two completed rooms: one consisted of rows of enclosed toilets and a counter of sinks, the other consisted of showers surrounded by heat lamps.

In fact, after the newly constructed Leader's House had been destroyed in mid-August, there was only one reason why work crews had been allowed to finish Navra Rec Hall at all: Whit had seen Danu's design for the ARC Platform. While most work crews were reassigned to clearing the debris of the Leader's House and starting over at that site, the best computer designers and craftswomen in the colony had been quickly gathered and asked to assist in building the ARC Platform. And there was only one place in Isis with a chamber big enough to house such an immense mechanism. Navra Rec Hall had been given top-priority status simply to provide a home for the ARC.

The computer grid alone had taken up the entire section of wall below the eight-by-three-meter observation deck. High ceilings and huge areas bordered by retractable partitions created an inner "outdoor" feel. And in order to amplify the desired impression of continuous space, the flexible-plastic composite platform was forty square meters . Scenery, additional characters, unexpected events— all unfolded after the Seeker placed the ARC band upon her head. The eye visors were a snug fit, the holophonic fibers caressed both the upper ear cartilage and the audio-sensitive bone behind the ear. A wired bodysuit provided kinesthetic feedback, and the flexible composite platform made any landscape feel utterly real. Danu had succeeded in creating an incredibly vivid artificial reality system, run by a specially enhanced super computer that measured its data in terabytes, its capabilities in teraflops,

Dismounting with a rangy swing of her leg, Danu trotted her bike to the main entrance and parked it. Casting a surreptitious glance around, she reached for the DNA lock plate, keying the restrictive lock which allowed her to tug open the heavy oak door. She passed from the bright, autumn sunlight into a dimly lit hall, but as the architect who had conceived this building, and in fact most of Isis, Danu knew her way. Her soft sport shoes were soundless on the smooth hardwood floor as she jogged along.

Danu hesitated before the door of the chamber where the ARC Platform was contained, her hand hovering near the crystalline DNA lock plate. Another hallway intersected this one, leading on either side to a pool of darkness. Turning her head, Danu listened intently to a faint noise.

Water? she wondered.

Straining her ears, she lost the sound. After another moment, she uneasily ran a hand through her lengthening crop of red curls, then decided it was nothing. She opened the door, stepped into the near darkness, and reached for the panel of light controls.

The next thing she knew, someone grabbed her reaching arm and yanked, tossing Danu head over heels to the floor. She landed hard, felt a flicker of shock that this was happening, then responded with moves she had been honing each night for nearly a month.

With a swift sweep of her leg, Danu brought the figure hovering over her down to an equal level. Immediately lunging forward, Danu's hands grasped someone squirming in the dark, someone smaller than herself, someone agile and quick. Danu clambered over a warm, thrashing body, using her longer limbs to wrestle it down.

The lights came on. Danu found herself astride a young, dark-haired woman. Blinking, disconcerted, they stared at each other for a moment. Then Danu saw a lieutenant's insignia on the ripped shoulder of her attacker's white shirt—the shirt of a Freeland Warrior. Releasing the woman's wrists, Danu leaned back, breathing hard, unconsciously settling her slim weight fully on the firm hips beneath her thighs.

Wide-eyed, the lieutenant rasped, "*Who* the hell are *you*?!"

Confounded, Danu got off her, and staggered to her feet. Nearby, Whit and Styx were staring at her in disbelief. And then Kali came to the open doorway, brown eyes wide, wiping from her chin the last traces of the water she had just drunk.

With a laugh, Whit shook off her amazement and advanced on Danu. "Don't tell me they taught you that in those progressive university courses you mentioned!" she joked, grabbing Danu's hand and shaking it heartily.

Ignoring Whit's jest and scrutinizing Danu thoughtfully, Styx asked, "What are you doing here? No one expected you."

Flustered, Danu yanked her hand free of Whit's grasp. "I come over every night and use the ARC Platform," she muttered.

Whit turned to Kali in surprise. "Did you know this?"

Calmly earnest, Kali reasoned, "Danu invented the ARC. It's hers to use if she wants to, don't you think?" When no answer but a glare came from Whit, Kali went on, "Danu's been coming in alone for the past three weeks, ever since we started my training. Since I'm on the thing in the day, and she's on it at night, there's no conflict...."

Her voice sharp with disbelief and aggravation, Whit interrupted, "No conflict?! She's been doing combat sessions alone in here! She could have been hurt!"

"How?" Kali demanded. "It's artificial reality!"

"Well, there's no reason for her to be in here!" Whit stubbornly insisted. "You're in training, Danu's not!"

"Danu's got her *own* demons, Whit," Styx counseled softly.

Unappeased, Whit glowered at Kali until Kali rolled her eyes in exasperation, then looked away. And though Whit didn't speak, her feelings ran high enough for Styx, a lesser telepath than Kali, to hear the projection of her thoughts. *Damn! She's not telling me things. When I try to be included in these training exercises—or in any of the plans regarding how she's going to take on Arinna Sojourner—she acts like I'm getting in her way!*

Kali no doubt heard Whit's thoughts, too, but seemed aware that Styx was monitoring them both. The blonde gave Styx a cool gaze and allowed her to read nothing.

Meanwhile, Tor was brushing herself off and getting to her feet. Looking over Danu's attire of a navy knee-length tunic over a gray feeder-wired bodysuit, the puzzled young lieutenant guessed, "You're a warrior?"

Still vaguely incensed by the rough attack, and equally offended by the Tor's imperious appraisal, Danu grudgingly admitted, "No. I intend to enlist, though, as soon as my duties here in Isis conclude."

"What duties?" Tor inquired, ignoring the frostiness of Danu's reply.

"I've been Architectural Director all summer, and...I became Chief Builder, as...well, after Lupa...died." Danu stopped and swallowed, her sky-blue eyes suddenly falling away from Tor's.

"You fight creatively," Tor commented, trying to distract the young woman from the piercing pain she had glimpsed. "We could use someone like you as a sparring partner for Kali. The holograms can only do so much. We'll need a solid body, and I ought to be in a position where I can observe and instruct, rather than be a combatant."

Her face lit by a flash of hope, Danu returned, "I'm willing."

With a firm nod, Styx sent Tor her approval.

They all looked to Whit for confirmation, but her gaze was resting on Kali, and it was full of consternation.

"How about it, Leader?" Tor prodded.

Sending a hand through her dark, glossy hair, Whit thought a moment. "The Leader's House is nearly finished," she decided, "so until the better weather next spring, Danu's duties are her own to choose." Then, with a keen look of concern, Whit added, "Let's call it a night and get some dinner, shall we? Kali looks ready to drop."

As if on cue, Kali broke into an enormous, unstoppable yawn, causing them all to laugh. With a weary, good-natured smile, she shrugged, and then led the way down the hall.

2

Moments later, Whit was walking between Kali and Styx, as they all strode purposefully down Cammermeyer Street. The sky overhead was rich with the deepening blue of twilight. They passed a sentry posted on the corner of Achtenberg Avenue, who, in spite of the poor light, recognized Whit and snapped to attention. The sentry thumped her hand to her heart in a brisk salute, and then held the salute as she noticed Lieutenant Yakami walking with Danu a couple of meters behind.

Saluting in return, Whit reflected on the highly visible military presence in Isis these days. *With so many sentries posted all over the city and the airfield, it feels like a siege is imminent. But at least Arinna Sojourner won't come marching down Cammermeyer Street without a fight.*

Behind her, Whit could hear Tor saying something to Danu about the mud-spattered mountain bike Danu pushed along. Half-turning her head, Whit discreetly eavesdropped.

Tor politely inquired, "Do you ride for fitness training?"

"No," Danu explained. "I've been traveling all over the colony, rushing from one job site to another—for much of the past month. I guess I was kind of in demand for a while there...but most of my buildings are finished now."

"Your buildings?" Tor quizzed.

Discreetly glancing back over her shoulder, Whit watched Danu bend her head, bracing herself for prejudice. "I'm a Think Tank Innovation—enhanced intellectual abilities—especially in architecture." Taking a deep breath, Danu finished, "I designed this city and helped coordinate its construction."

Without comment, Tor immediately began scrutinizing the sleek, modern compositions of wood and granite they were passing on either side of the road. Anxiously, Danu cast several furtive glances at Tor, obviously concerned about how the news of her Think Tank identity was being received. Tor, meanwhile, seemed more interested in Danu's buildings than in anything else.

As they approached the meal hall, Whit asked the other four women if they wouldn't mind making a quick stop, and then continuing on to the Leader's House. Readily agreeing, they were soon jostling through the crowds of women to the serving line and then carrying thick sandwiches away with them. Outside again, they noted that the night had grown considerably darker.

They strolled along Cammermeyer Street in the yellow light beneath the street lamps, eating as they pressed on toward the Leader's House. The night air was chill with autumn, and wood smoke was a sharp fragrance in the air. Whit noticed that Kali almost wolfed down her wheat bread and grilled salmon, while Tor savored her sour dough and scrambled eggs with small sighs of appreciation. Styx chewed as if eating were more habit than pleasure, and her troubled eyes kept wandering to Kali.

She's worried, Whit perceived. *And after Kali's reaction to the Reg holograms, so am I. Kali ought to stay right here and wait for Arinna to come after her. I don't understand this crazy insistence on going out there alone—searching the wilderness for a cunning killer!*

A mixed-breed dog trotted by, out for his nightly jaunt. With a whistle, Danu hailed him. Leaning the bike she had been pushing against her hip, she summarily handed over most of her veggie-soy pita pocket to the dog.

"You hardly ate anything," Styx remarked mildly.

"Not hungry," Danu mumbled.

There's the one we ought to be worrying about, Whit decided. *She's shutting down emotionally—from what I hear—not eating or sleeping or even talking much anymore. That chat with Tor was the most I've heard out of her in weeks.*

As they passed the Leader's House, Whit gestured for them to follow her and set off across the vast garden area to the large granite and cedar building. At the door, she watched Danu park her bike, the somber blue gaze turned inward, as usual. Nearby, Tor was subtly looking Danu over, the spark of interest in her dark eyes indisputable. Automatically, Whit filed the information for future reference.

The brightly lit structure was not officially opened for use yet, and looked it. Inside, the Great Hall they traversed was a phenomenal mess. The tile floor was covered with a jumble of painters' cloths, and they had to carefully wind their way through an obstacle course of tall metal frames and stacks of paint cans. High above them, the network of scaffolding hid what Whit knew was under creation: the roof and walls were going to be covered with murals of legendary Amazons. At present, the conceived likenesses of Semiramis, Lysippe, Andromache, Hippolyte, Antiope, Candace of Ethiopia, Trung Trac, and Trung Nhi were going to grace the near section of the ceiling, above the door. On the surrounding walls, Aetheflaed, Aife, Mebd, Tomoe Gozen, Long Meg, L'Angevine, Natalie Barney, Eleanor Roosevelt, Grethe Cammermeyer, and Franco Stevens had already been painted, all of them in dynamic action.

They moved along the far wall of the hall, to a corridor that led toward the rear of the building. Weaving around stacks of thick madrone paneling and rolls of yet-to-be-laid carpet, they eventually came to a wide steel door.

Above them, on the second floor, Whit could hear the power-hammers and electric saws of the night crew racketing through the quiet evening air. Squads of warriors were laboring here almost around the clock. Since it was late September, and Isis was in a mountain valley, everyone knew it could snow any time now.

The group waited as Whit paused before the steel door, keying the DNA lock plate. Setting the discriminator chip in the unit to "record," she asked each of the women to step forward and touch the plate, thus entering their DNA code into the lock memory. Once this was accomplished, Whit ushered them all into a large, freshly outfitted room.

Within, a slender figure in a white jumpsuit turned to face them, a motorized panel rachet still in her hands as she stepped away from the wall. Strands of her lovely, silver hair had escaped the chignon at the back of her head and her wise face was smudged with dust.

"Lilith," Whit groaned. "You were supposed to let the technicians take over hours ago."

"I did," Lilith returned, her bright blue eyes innocent as Styx moved forward and placed a greeting kiss on Lilith's forehead. Lowering the panel rachet to the floor, Lilith defended, "There were just a few last-minute adjustments I wanted to make. You know, circuit-chip orchestrations are so variable these days. I wanted to try out a new pattern—try to boost the power base a little."

With a sigh, Whit introduced Tor, "This is Lilith, legendary Leader of Artemis, recently retired and now acting as my Deputy Leader while Kali's involved with apprehending Arinna Sojourner."

Smiling, Tor shook Lilith's hand, then leaned around her to get a better look at the instrumentation Lilith had just finished adjusting.

Danu, who was eager to examine the complex computer system built into three of the four walls, began prowling the perimeter of the room, her eyes riveted so intently on the hardware that she didn't even notice Tor doing the same thing, circumnavigating the room from the opposite direction. With a chuckle, Styx nudged first Lilith, then Whit in the side, so that they all three saw the two young women softly collide.

Startled, Danu froze in the circle of Tor's arms, blushing furiously. Tor looked up into Danu's intense gaze, raised her eyebrows, and then without a word, backed away, retreating to the other side of the room.

So, Whit thought.

After a brief smile, Lilith knelt and began disassembling her panel rachet, packing it into its carrying case.

Styx whispered into Whit's ear, "Why don't you do something about that?"

Tempted, Whit checked to see Kali's reaction, but her lover was over by the door, peering at the experimental solar-powered crystal unit that would drive this massive computer system.

There was a sharp rap on the outer steel door, and Kali involuntarily started. The intercom unit mounted on the wall above her broadcasted, "Captain Razia reporting."

After Whit's nod of consent, Kali touched the inside DNA lock plate and opened the door.

A husky, rugged-looking woman entered, dressed in a crisp, gray warrior's uniform with captain's bars on the collar of her jacket. Her short brown hair was slicked back. Intelligent dark eyes hinted at what Whit knew to be a keen mind.

Whit returned her salute, then said to Tor, "This is Captain Razia, our new Chief of Security."

Tor, who had come to attention when the officer strode through the door, saluted. When Captain Razia returned a murmured, "As you were," Tor visibly relaxed.

Moving past Styx to the plush, leather-covered compu-chair, Whit seated herself and called the others over. The women gathered around behind her, looking expectantly at the large wallscreen encompassing one end of the rectangular room.

"I want all of you to know how to use this unit," Whit announced. "A large part of our mission will be dependent upon the computerized surveillance this facility has been designed to provide. By the way, I call this the Watch Room, and I'll show you why."

Punching in a series of commands, Whit activated the wallscreen, bringing up footage shot earlier in the day from a jetcraft patrolling the length of the Cascade Range. "First of all," Whit asserted, "using patrol-craft films or satellite scans will probably be the only way we'll ever be able to locate Arinna's hideout." With a glance at Kali, Whit added, "And secondly, it will be the only way to circumvent Arinna's threat of returning to Isis, to seize both Kali and the Think Tank Project files."

Briefly, Whit noted the way Kali stood aside, her brown eyes blinking with that slow stubbornness that betrayed how hard she was fighting the need for sleep.

Then, in careful detail, Whit went on to explain the fundamentals of this specially designed tactical operations office. Soon, she was punching in commands for one satellite-search scan after another. Before them, the wallscreen displayed a series of augmented photos from space, each one a sectional photograph of Freeland. As she spoke, Whit also noted that Lilith was enraptured, her blue eyes sparkling, her lips parted, like a youngster with a new toy.

I don't think she'll be satisfied until we soup up a jetcraft and point it toward the stars! Whit thought, almost laughing.

And yet, despite using both heat-seeking and human-DNA indicators, the sophisticated equipment pinpointed only those citizens who were already listed as residents on the more distant farms situated around each of the eight colonies. The scans turned up no evidence of Arinna or Loy anywhere in Freeland.

Wherever Arinna is, Whit reflected, *she's hidden herself and her captive, Loy, very, very well. But eventually, she's going to show herself, and with the aid of this high-tech search facility, we're going to find her.*

Mildly discouraged, Whit terminated her search command, then patiently began instructing the women around her in how the computer was to be used. She wanted all of them to be able to run both jetcraft and satellite-surveillance programs, any time they desired.

Shortly afterward, Whit informed the group that a squad of warriors, all highly trained intelligence specialists, had been organized under the command of Captain Razia. These specialists would be monitoring the Watch Room night and day, on three consecutive eight-hour shifts. Agreeing to participate in the evaluation of the compiled data, Tor, Danu, Kali, and Styx briefly practiced running the various indicator-scans, then congratulated Whit on the complex design.

"Don't congratulate me," Whit chuckled. "This is Lilith's work."

"I didn't know you were so skilled in this field," Kali commented.

"When I was a pilot, I learned a great deal about air surveillance. And, after all, I was Maat's partner for twelve years," Lilith teased. "I was always learning new tricks, trying to keep up with you two...."

Kali suddenly broke into a long yawn and Lilith quietly said to Whit, "I think we've seen enough for tonight, don't you?"

Agreeing, Whit began shepherding them all out of the room, then paused to lock the steel door behind them. Captain Razia courteously excused herself, and then hurried away, intent on returning to her many official concerns.

As they wandered down the corridor, Whit draped an arm tenderly around Kali's shoulders. Aiming a shrewd wink at Styx, she asked, "Lieutenant Yakami, where will you be bunking while on assignment in Isis?"

"I was supposed to stay in one of the hostels," Tor answered, "but a sergeant at the airfield told me both buildings are full. I ended up just leaving my gear in a hangar locker and catching a lift over to the Rec Hall on a supply truck." Laughing ruefully, Tor concluded, "I'll bunk any place you can fit me."

"Hmmm," Whit hesitated, appearing engrossed in thought. "We still have four hundred Freeland Warriors stationed here on construction duty. With Arinna such a viable threat, I don't dare let any of them take the usual reassignment to new postings. Every warrior's departure leaves Isis more vulnerable to attack."

There was a short pause, during which Whit convincingly rubbed her chin and studied the ceiling overhead.

"*I know!*" she suddenly proclaimed. "Danu is alone in a two-person room. You can bunk with *her*, Tor!"

"*What?!*" Danu demanded.

Making eye contact with Whit, Kali gave a slight shake of her blonde head, clearly signaling, *No*.

Ignoring Kali, her tone mildly reproachful, Whit cajoled, "Danu, there's a housing shortage and you have an empty bunk in your room."

Obviously feeling cornered, Danu shot Tor a tense look. "I work odd hours," she grumbled. "Late and early, I'm an architect and I work on designs. When you least expect it, the lights will go on and I'll start tapping away on my keyboard."

"That's okay," Tor said agreeably. "We've all got our own set of objectionable habits. I myself can be pretty messy..."

Danu shrugged, accepting that.

"...And I listen to Blaster Rock," Tor concluded.

Her eyes growing wide, for a moment Danu stared at Tor in sheer horror. Gulping, she forcibly pulled her stunned gaze away.

Blaster Rock! Whit thought, casting a surprised glance at Tor. *That new variation of Rock and Roll has to be the loudest and most obnoxious music I've ever heard!*

"Yeah, I know it's kind of extreme," Tor hastened to add, a mischievous light in her eyes, "but I'll wear earjacks—most of the time."

Studiously not meeting anyone else's eyes, Whit remarked, "That sounds reasonable enough."

Danu's shoulders sagged.

Silently, the group snaked around the scaffolding which blocked a clear exit through the Great Hall. Once at the doorway, they all filed out into the darkened garden in front of the house.

Before they broke up to head to their separate places of rest, Whit ordered brusquely, "Danu, before you turn in, how about helping your new roommate fetch her gear out of that airfield locker."

Without reply, Danu nodded, snatched up her bike, and moved away toward the street. Tor's smaller, more compact figure hurried to stay at her heels.

Grinning, Whit turned to Styx and whispered conspiratorially, "Now, we'll just have to see what comes of that, won't we?"

"I don't know if ol' Sappho can get around Blaster Rock," Styx warned, though her dark Mexican eyes danced in the glow that fell from the lamp above the door. "Particularly when Danu listens to Beethoven and Mahler!"

"What are you two up to?" Kali demanded in a soft, irritable voice, though she frowned at Whit alone.

"Lupa would never have allowed her to get like this," Whit began.

Scowling now, Kali muttered, "You're meddling."

And though Lilith and Styx raised their eyebrows, surprised to see this side of good-natured Kali Tyler, Whit was in fact quite used to it. Giving Kali a testy sideways glance, she pretended she didn't hear the words. Instead, attempting a distraction, Whit declared to Lilith and Styx, "I can't tell you how glad we are that you two decided to move out here to Isis for a while. Between Lilith helping me prepare fiscal and mercantile policies for my first Council sessions, and Styx helping Kali..."

"Haven't you given enough speeches today?" Styx joked, taking Lilith's arm and starting toward the street.

"The only thing better would be if you built a house out in the country, next to ours," Whit pronounced.

"We listen to Blaster Rock," Styx jibed.

"Then never mind!" Whit returned, holding her hands over her ears. "Mother, that stuff's so loud and raucous! Poor Danu!"

"Tomorrow at seven—let's go over your strategy for the economic committee," Lilith decided, as the two partners moved into the shadowy garden.

"Thanks, again, Lil, for covering for me," Kali called.

Waving, Lilith reassured her, "Glad to do it. We all know you've got enough on your mind right now, without trying to carry the load of a Deputy Leader."

With a final good night, Whit took Kali's hand and started back into the building. "Don't worry about it, Kal," she soothed, recognizing Kali's fretful expression. "Truthfully, Lilith's help is a gift of the Goddess. You wouldn't believe the things she's teaching me—things it would've taken me years of leading to learn on my own."

"But still," Kali insisted, "I shouldn't bear the title of Deputy Leader if Lilith is actually doing the job."

"All anyone really cares about at this point," Whit reminded her firmly, "is what's being done to counter Arinna Sojourner's threat. You're the best option in that department...."

"Much as you hate to admit it," Kali mumbled under her breath.

Needled one time too many, Whit swung around to glare at her. They were back inside now, standing in the clutter of the Great Hall, both of them tired and cranky and certainly on the verge of another quarrel if this kept up. *What's happened to us?* Whit wondered with annoyance and despair. *We never used to be like this....*

"Can we go home now?" Kali griped crossly.

Above them, Whit could hear Marpe's elderly, ladylike voice ordering, "Ten o'clock! All work details dismissed!" A chorus of cheers erupted from the construction crews working upstairs. One by one, the power tools that were sanding, pounding, and whining in the distance fell silent. A few voices exchanged remarks and then gradually, a steady stream of women clumped down the stairs. Hearty voices saluted first Whit, and then Kali. Finally, the women slammed through the heavy oak doors into the night.

"I told Marpe earlier that we would select the color schemes for her tonight," Whit abruptly confessed, altogether sorry now that she had agreed to do any such thing. Judging by the groan Kali gave, this was not going to go well at all.

"I spent most of the afternoon at Cleopatra's Palace," Whit continued, "looking at furniture ensembles." She wrinkled her nose, then sighed. "I know this is a pain, Kal, but they *are* handling everything for us. The least we can do is pretend to be interested. Gaea knows, neither one of us has the time or the expertise with decor to oversee this job properly."

Upstairs, Marpe could be heard calling her partner, Samsi. A few more warriors jogged down the stairs, pulling on their gray uniform jackets. They exchanged pleasantries as they passed Whit and Kali, but once the door had closed behind the workers, silence again descended.

At last, Kali folded her arms across her chest and gave Whit a long, level stare. *Uh-oh*, Whit thought. *I know that look.* She immediately began running through the day's events, wondering just what she had said or done to set off the reprimand that was no doubt about to unfold.

"Why are you making Danu share her room with Tor?" Kali demanded.

Trying to appear both serious and prudent, Whit countered, "Because Danu's becoming far too solitary."

Bristling, Kali's hands went to her hips, a classic stance. "She's always been a loner," she protested.

"She's living like a recluse," Whit returned, the heat rushing up her neck, into her face.

Fuming, Kali asserted, "You don't always know what's best for everyone, Whit!"

"I know *you* shouldn't be so hot to go chasing around after Arinna Sojourner," Whit retorted, "when you can't face a Reg holo without falling on your face."

"I did not!"

"You did, too!" Whit barked. "That Reg *captured* you!" She fixed Kali with a hard stare, then burst out, "Arinna will know what you fear! She'll use it against you!"

Giving an angry wave of her hand, Kali flashed, "And is sitting here waiting for her to come back for me any better?!"

"She won't dare. I've got armaments in place now, and a standing army—to say nothing of that computer surveillance system I just showed you...."

"She'll come back, Whit!" Kali nearly yelled. "Your fanciest technology won't stop her! And she won't come alone! She's an enhanced intellect with a capacity for evil the likes of which none of us has seen before. The longer she's out there, the more dangerous she's becoming!" Blowing out a breath, struggling for self-control, Kali sighed raggedly. "I have this weird, unshakable feeling that she's creating an army of superwomen as we speak."

Whit came closer, took her by the arm, gray eyes wide with alarm. "You said she'd need the Think Tank files to create those DNA innovations she warned us about."

"She's a computer genius, with enhanced psychic abilities," Kali reminded Whit wearily, rubbing a hand across her eyes. "She's capable of just about anything."

Whit suddenly realized that the twenty-six-year-old woman standing before her was young and frightened, enmeshed in the lingering visions of a bad dream. Kali stumbled as Whit pulled her into a loose embrace.

Her voice raw with anxiety, Kali declared, "Arinna will do whatever she has to do in order to get what she wants."

"Well, she won't get *you!*" Whit responded, wrapping her arms protectively around her lover. "Not you," the husky voice murmured into Kali's golden hair. To Whit herself, the words sounded more like a plea than a promise.

And then, hearing a slight shuffle above them, they both looked up. At the top of the winding, freestanding staircase, Marpe and Samsi hesitated, clutching their books of colored swatches in their arms. By the gleeful look in Marpe's eyes, Whit knew the two biggest gossips in the colony had managed to overhear every word.

Tor carried her heavy backpack on her back and mounted the hostel staircase easily, two steps at a time. Behind her, Danu parked her mountain bike by the side of the porch, then grunted as she took on the full weight of the cumbersome duffel bag she had been carrying on the bike seat.

"Want to switch?" Tor asked softly, for perhaps the fifth time.

"No," Danu wheezed, still carefully avoiding Tor's eyes.

Cool and composed, Tor stood on the porch, watching, as Danu climbed the stairs, struggling against the combination of gravity and the duffel bag's awkward shape. At last, breathing heavily, Danu reached the top step and marched across the porch. Tor fell in step beside her, her dark eyes gleaming with barely contained laughter. If Danu noticed Tor's amusement, she grimly ignored it.

They crossed the hostel lobby and headed for the corridor at the far left hall of the large, E-shaped structure. As they entered what Tor assumed was Danu's corridor, two young women jumped up from a long, low bench near the comline units.

"Where've you been?" the small, wiry, dark-skinned one burst out, her voice mild and yet accusatory at the same time. "I've been waiting for you for over an hour." She wore a Healer's patch on her magenta jumpsuit and had the look of a woman who didn't wait long for anyone.

Beside the Healer stood a woman about Tor's own size, with long, shining brown hair and friendly eyes. The woman signed "hello" to Tor, then examined both Danu and Tor with a look of bold curiosity.

With a shrug, Danu swung Tor's duffel bag to the floor and swiped the DNA lock plate by her door. "Sorry, Neith. I got...involved in something unexpectedly." Her freckled face grave and set, Danu made a brief stab at introductions. "Neith, Albie," she waved a hand at Tor, "my new roommate, Lieutenant Tamatori Yakami of the colony of Morgan."

Albie smiled a welcome, then signed, *Good luck rooming with this clam.*

Neith was not as amiable. She regarded Tor with what seemed to be a mixture of jealousy and annoyance.

Oblivious, Danu's hands signed respectfully for Albie as she quietly informed Tor, "These are my closest friends. Neith's a Healer entering her fourth and last year of apprentice work. Albie's Forewoman of Utility Crews."

As Tor shook hands with both women, Danu signed to Albie, *I may need your help with the job load I'm carrying now. I've just been reassigned. I'll be spending a good part of each day working with Kali.*

Albie gave Danu an inquiring look, but signed back, *I'm no Chief Builder, but I can enlist the rest of the construction forewomen, get them to help carry the load.*

Signing her thanks, Danu grabbed the strap of Tor's duffel bag.

Excitedly, Albie continued signing. *Since the construction projects are slowing down and my part of the Leader's House is done, I took a mountain climbing group up to Mount Tahoma today. We had the greatest time on the Nisqually glacier....* Noting that Danu was watching her hands, but registering no interest, Albie's enthusiasm ended. Disconcerted, she stopped talking.

Without a word, Danu dragged the bag inside her room and propped it against the spare bunk. Then, with a sweep of her arm, she gathered the many blueprints that littered the mattress of what was now Tor's bed. She carried them to the opposite side of the room and tossed them unceremoniously beneath the other bunk.

Albie and Neith watched from the doorway, glancing at each other as if they were used to Danu's abrupt ways.

"Come, take a walk with me, Danu," Neith called softly.

Shaking her head, Danu mumbled, "I've still got some work to do." She briefly ran her hand over her face, betraying for the first time the deep weariness Tor had sensed in her from the first. A weariness no doubt born of weeks of little sleep and a grueling schedule of projects. "Maybe tomorrow," Danu mumbled, turning away and abruptly settling herself at her desk. In another moment she had turned on the computer and brought up an incomplete design. With a frown, Danu squinted at the screen, summarily withdrawing from them all.

Albie and Neith exchanged a glance full of unspoken meaning, then bid Tor a polite good evening.

Tor stepped inside, closed the door, and scanned the small, neat room. "Don't you have an office?" she asked, lowering her backpack to the floor. "As Chief Builder and Architectural Director, I would have thought..."

Danu answered distractedly, without bothering to turn from the design she was focused upon. "Um...last summer I used the Command Center, but security needs have become more important than construction blueprints." Finishing in a low voice, Danu disclosed, "My office has been turned into a communications headquarters for the sentries."

Finally, after a few minutes of surveying the room, Tor focused on one object to the exclusion of all else. Moving closer for a better look, she realized its significance.

On the desk shelf, above Danu's bent head, there was a holoplate of two women. In the depiction, Danu was smiling—a radiant smile—as she stood beside an elder whose eyes were aimed at Danu with a very warm and proud regard. Without having to be told, Tor knew this was Lupa Tagliaro, the famous Chief Builder of Isis, and Arinna's last victim. And from the expressions on both their faces, Tor had a sudden glimmer of understanding. Danu had lost a remarkable friend.

Unexpectedly, Danu glanced up and noticed Tor studying the holoplate. In an instant she had stood, grabbed the image, and thrust it into the recesses of a desk drawer.

"I'm sorry," Tor offered, not sure quite how to handle this thorny, yet obviously grief-stricken, young woman.

Advancing on her, Danu blazed, "Let's get one thing straight, Lieutenant!" With a graceless hop, Tor lurched backward and almost tumbled onto her own bed. "You are in this room," the redhead went on, "but you're *not* in my life!"

Amazed at the fire in those formerly shielded blue eyes, Tor stood there, mute.

Emboldened by Tor's lack of response, Danu placed a stiff finger on Tor's uniform jacket and punctuated every other word with a jab. "Stay on your own side!"

Narrowing her eyes, Tor swiftly grasped Danu's hand and yanked it off her chest. And though Danu tried to pull away, Tor held her grip, delivering a steadily increasing pressure to the sensitive, fleshy web between Danu's thumb and palm. Danu cried out and her knees buckled. Abruptly, Tor released her.

With a slight bow, Tor stated, "I honor your grief, and if this room must have 'sides,' then so be it."

Glaring, Danu straightened and edged back to her desk, rubbing her sore hand.

"But I will not be bullied," Tor maintained quietly, "nor will I be provoked into moving out. So you might as well get used to me."

And then, with a great show of calm, though she was seething, Tor turned her back on her roommate, opened her duffel bag, and began unpacking.

Lilith rolled over as Styx crawled beneath the covers. Styx nestled softly into her, sighing with contentment.

Chuckling, Lilith put her arm around Styx, but her mind was on other things. "You know," she confided, "working out the kinks in a new colony is endless trouble. I never fully appreciated the difference between Maat's role in Isis and my role in Artemis. Artemis had been around about sixty-five years before I ever took over as Leader, but Maat had to *start* the original Isis—from uniting a newly elected Council to conceiving trade policy. It's overwhelming...."

"But you're such a natural," Styx encouraged, nuzzling Lilith's long neck.

"No more so than Whit is," Lilith murmured, shivering as Styx's lips found that most sensitive spot. "She really just needs me to point out the subtleties and help her delegate responsibility."

"That's not what Whit says," Styx remarked.

"How do you like this Lieutenant Yakami you brought up from Morgan?" Lilith asked, twisting away from Styx's soft, distracting mouth, determined to satisfy her inquisitiveness before passion snuck up on them both.

"She's a cool one," Styx replied. "Danu walked into the combat challenge Tor had set up for Kali, and surprised us all—especially Tor, I think. It looked like suwari waza—you know, fighting from a sitting position—but I'm not sure. At any rate, Danu put Lieutenant Yakami on her ass, and then followed it up by actually pinning Tor with a brilliant wrestling hold." Laughing, Styx finished, "You should have seen Tor's face!"

"Danu can fight?" Lilith asked. "How? She's had no warrior training."

"She's been working out on the ARC Platform," Styx divulged. "And don't forget, she's a Think Tank Baby. Enhanced intellects are also gifted at mastering intricate physical skills."

"Incredible! Danu bested the current Freeland Martial Arts Champion," Lilith repeated, pondering what it meant.

"With ease," Styx answered, laughing softly.

"Danu wants vengeance," Lilith told Styx, her mind making one of those amazing leaps of deductive logic that always stunned Styx. "And she must be working like a cold-fusion engine to have advanced so far by herself."

"Yes," Styx breathed, "I suppose so."

"Well, we'll just have to keep an eye on her, Love," Lilith said evenly. "For all her genius, Danu's young and hurting. She may be contemplating something rash."

"I suppose that's why Whit assigned Tor to Danu's room," Styx observed, running her lips once more down Lilith's neck. Meanwhile, the broad, strong hand caressing Lilith's breast began teasing her in earnest, brushing over the nipple with delicate, circular palm strokes.

Groaning, Lilith acknowledged the answering surge of desire resonating through her. "So you think," she gasped softly, "that Whit has given Danu a watchdog?"

"Actually," Styx whispered, running her broad hand slowly down Lilith's stomach, "It's more like they've been given each other, if they're at all interested."

Fighting to continue her train of thought, even as her body quivered beneath Styx's seductive hands, Lilith said, "Danu has never taken a lover, you know." She groaned again as Styx's mouth claimed her breast. After several quick breaths, she panted, "And by the somber, haunted look of her now, I'd say Danu's hardly in the mood."

"As a matter of fact, she reminds me of you—before I got my hands on you," Styx whispered softly. And in illustration, Styx's hand skillfully dipped into Lilith's wetness, expressing her love with a cherishing, passionate touch.

3

Two weeks later, Kali aimlessly paced in front of the home she and Whit had built in the spring. Then Isis had been but a dream, not the energetic new city two kilometers over the eastern ridge. The autumn sun was warm on her back, and some of her blonde hair was blowing free of her French braid, lifting in the steady wind.

An impatient glance to the right revealed that Tor and Styx were still readying Danu for the complex attack drill. Tor was feinting through the moves she wanted Danu to employ, while Styx whispered words of caution in Danu's ear. Since Kali had been strictly instructed to concentrate on something else, so she wouldn't overhear their thoughts and ruin the exercise, she reluctantly turned away.

In an effort to comply, Kali concentrated on the house. It was a large, two story structure, constructed of granite block, with large windows and skylights. A broad wooden porch wrapped around most of the building, and stone masonry chimneys rose from the two opposite sides. Last winter, Whit had confessed to her as they worked out the design with Lupa, that she had spent much of her two years of undercover spying in Elysium longing for a home like this. "A porch in the summer and a hearth fire in the winter," Whit had said. "That's all I need." They had been living here only four and a half months, and already Kali had discovered that Whit needed far more than this house had to offer in order to thrive.

She's a born leader, Kali mused. *She loves to be in charge of things—all kinds of things—from making breakfast to making love.* Taking a deep breath, Kali faced the disturbing truth she'd been sidestepping for months. *And most especially, she likes to be in charge of me.*

It was an unsettling thought.

Beyond the house, stands of silver birches swayed in the brisk morning breeze, their bright yellow leaves shimmering and whispering ancient magic. In the east, the white vastness of Mount Tahoma dominated the crests of the great Cascade Range, while closer by, timbered ridges swelled. All around Kali, the tall, tan meadow grass was rustling with old secrets about winter's coming. Mesmerized, Kali sat down, closed her eyes, and just listened.

She was searching for an inner calm, breathing in long, even breaths. Steadily, she concentrated on reviewing the wing chun fighting style Tor had been drilling her in during the past two weeks. As part of the psychic preparation, Kali made herself concentrate on her breathing, channeling her ki as Tor was training her to do.

After a while, she noticed that the heat of the sun had taken on a strange, electric hum—as if a current were passing through her. The wind, too, seemed to enter her body and caress the very core of her being. And yet it all felt so natural, so fated, that Kali's conscious mind shifted. She relaxed and moved into another realm.

The wind spoke to her, soothed her in Maat's voice, then oh, so tenderly, enfolded her. The wind tugged at her to come along, and with a willing heart, Kali surrendered. She was lifted from her body, eased into the zephyrs that eddied above the meadow in invisible streams. On either side, she suddenly found seven huge golden eagles, their brown bodies and wings glinting with subtle yellow accents every time they stroked the air. Gently, Kali stretched out her arms, flexed her muscles, and was amazed to find herself carried through the mountain valley toward Mount Tahoma.

Up from the lowlands she stroked, the eagles gleaming in the sunlight on either side of her, until she caught the updraft and swept along the steep slope of the slumbering volcano. The eagles waited below as she rushed higher, feeling the wind cleanse her, purify her. At last, she reached the top and hovered there. At 4,433 meters above sea level, she surveyed the blue-green forest that stretched beyond the glaciers' reaches, as far as she could see. And the whisper came to her once more, speaking in her mother's voice, "This is your sacred trust."

When she opened her eyes again, the sun had shifted, and she knew without checking her wristcom that at least an hour had passed. Surrounded by tall meadow grass, Styx and Tor sat opposite her, their eyes intent and concerned. To her right, Danu stood, her face turned up to the sky. Tilting her head to see what Danu was staring at, Kali caught her breath. Above her, their outstretched wings flashing in the sunlight, fourteen huge golden eagles rode the autumn wind.

"They've been there for the last ninety minutes," Tor stated in wonderment. "Ever since you..."

Slightly overwhelmed by what seemed to have transpired, Kali sought solace in habit. Pushing through the dry grass, she placed her palms on the soil and pressed, then bent forward to touch her forehead to the dirt, finalizing the Wiccan grounding ritual Styx had taught her a short month ago.

Observing her, Styx stated simply, "You were working magic, then." Her dark eyes probed Kali knowingly as Kali lifted her face, then her hands, from the dirt.

"Uh, meditating, I think," Kali stuttered. She brushed her hands off, speaking slowly as she reconstructed events. "I was trying to not listen to you—concentrating on the house—then on the land and how much I love it. Then, while I was doing some ki exercises, all of a sudden, I was listening to the wind, and trancing...."

"Gaea called you," Styx pronounced, nodding thoughtfully.

"It sounded like my mother," Kali offered, her brow creasing with uncertainty.

"Why the eagles?" Danu asked softly, squinting up at the birds still wheeling overhead.

"Kali has been given a totem," Styx replied.

"A what?" Danu persisted.

"Sometimes it's a symbol, sometimes a protector." Tor spoke this time, her eyes running over Danu with a subtle, sensual hunger while the young architect's attention remained on the raptors in the sky.

Amused, Kali studied Danu, too. The red-gold curls had grown longer since summer, and swirled about Danu's freckled face in the constant breeze, a flickering fire against the blue sky behind her. Loose khaki pants and a large, russet-brown sweater hung on her strong, slender frame. Like Whit, Danu had a way of looking regal and fit, even in the simplest clothes. There was a new independence and sense of purpose about her these days.

Returning Kali to the topic, Styx prodded, "The Mother apparently summoned you. Why?"

Baffled, Kali lifted her eyebrows and shrugged, displaying how perplexed she was by the entire episode.

After a moment, staring hard at Kali, Styx rose and extended a hand to her.

Tor leaned forward and asked, "Shall we continue wing chun practice?"

With a nod, Kali grasped Styx's hand and let herself be helped to her feet. As Styx released her, Kali swayed, feeling light-headed. She was sure it was from sitting so long in one position.

"You're unsteady," Styx noted. "Let's wait. We can have our lunch and try this later."

Having gotten to her feet, Tor took Danu by the elbow and positioned her several meters away from Kali. "We've wasted a lot of time," she cautioned. "We're falling behind schedule."

"There's no need to force things," Styx reasoned, her voice taking on that deepening tone of authority.

All that flying around—for what? Kali pondered. She took several deep breaths, centering herself, then quietly assured Styx that she was fine. Looking very uncertain, Styx stepped away from her, as Tor moved away from Danu.

Silently, Kali and Danu eyed each other, separated by a mere five meters of knee-high meadow grass. They were about to play out a disarmament maneuver, and though Kali had repeatedly mimicked

Tor through the series of steps earlier this morning, she still expected to be blasted unconscious any minute. After all, there was a laser gun in the holster Danu was wearing, and this time, it was going to fire a low-range burst of live ammunition.

"Remember, concentrate," Tor urged.

Kali watched Danu put her left hand on the pistol handle.

"Ready?" Tor asked evenly.

Without thought, Kali felt her spirit lift up, poising in the air just above her body.

"Go!" Tor urged. "And remember to block and punch."

As if in slow motion, Kali watched Danu draw the laser gun from the holster around her waist. Like a hologram in stop-action strobe, the black pistol barrel swung upward on its path to a firing position. Kali was already reacting, darting to one side and then rapidly closing in. The flash of light meant Danu had discharged the first blast. Knowing she had successfully sidestepped the shot, Kali directed her flow of motion into a standard martial arts sequence. Chambering up her left arm, she rapidly closed the distance between them. With her right arm she blocked, sending Danu's left hand and the weapon clenched in it out, away from Danu's body, thus disarming her. Swiftly, Kali followed the block with a dim muk strike, driving her fist into Danu's solar plexus. Though she tried to pull the punch and only barely connect, the blow still landed with all of Kali's ki behind it, and Danu doubled over with an explosive gasp. The laser gun sailed to a resting place somewhere in the grass to Kali's right.

"Secure the weapon," Tor ordered.

Instead, Kali caught Danu as the young woman pitched over. "Oh, no," she cried. "I'm so sorry...." Going down on one knee, she lowered Danu to the grass. Mouth open, arms tight across her middle, Danu immediately curled into a silent ball.

Merciless, Tor advanced on them, commanding, "Secure the weapon, Deputy Leader—now!"

Nearby, Styx urged, "See the lesson through, Kali."

Distracted, Kali did as she was told, sensing quickly where the gun had landed in the field grass. She hopped up, grabbed the laser gun, and tucked it in her belt, snug against the small of her back. But she was still worried about Danu and returned to crouch beside her. Though Tor and Styx came to Kali's side, there was nothing any of them could do except listen to Danu's pained gasps for air.

Then, Tor bent over Kali, pulled the gun from her belt, and smoothly moved to Danu. Glancing at Danu's pained, beet-red face, Tor remained expressionless as she tucked the laser gun back in Danu's holster. "Why did you punch her so hard? Tor asked.

Her eyes wide with disbelief and then charged with anger, Kali exclaimed, "I pulled back on the punch."

"But not the ki," Tor returned, her eyes hard. "Your psychic energy makes you far more powerful than the average warrior. You must learn to restrain your life-force. Remember, dim muk is the delivery of precise deathblows. Even when you successfully check physical contact, your ki can still do damage."

Her face flushing, Kali placed a comforting hand on one of Danu's straining shoulders. "Enough coaching. She's hurt. Help her."

Tor asked serenely, "Where are you hurt, Danu?"

In answer, Danu shakily struggled up into a sitting position and tried to wave away Kali's solicitous concern.

"Answer me," Tor insisted.

Trying to speak, Danu ended up groaning, hunching over again, a series of spasms shaking her lean frame until Tor knelt beside her.

Gently placing a hand on Danu's hunched back, Tor spread her fingers across Danu's brown sweater, pressing gently into the straining muscles beneath the woolly fabric.

Acupressure, Kali noted.

"Blow out," Tor ordered. "Stop trying to breathe in—just blow out." She rubbed Danu's back as the redhead leaned against her, gasping helplessly.

Beside them, Kali watched, transfixed, as Danu's gasping for air gradually settled into a series of shuddering exhalations.

Shifting her position, Tor knelt behind Danu. Slowly, she moved her hands up either side of Danu's vertebrae, feeling for rigidity and then using her fingers to press and manipulate each particular muscle. Danu continued wheezing as her head lolled forward.

"This is because you stay up all night working on that damn computer," Tor muttered. "Muscle tension and exhaustion—a fine sparring partner you've turned out to be."

Eyes riveted on the two younger women, Kali rose and stepped back. Her psychic senses were positively tingling with the sexual energy she felt between Danu and Tor—an energy that stretched between their separate bodies like fine spiderwebs, glinting with morning dew in dawn sunlight. Amazed, Kali stared, acknowledging something she knew no one else was aware of yet, least of all Danu, or Tor herself. After two weeks of sharing the same room, and working together hours each day, they were still focusing most of their psychic energy on trying to completely ignore one another. And it was not working.

Roughly five minutes later, Tor's hands finally coursed up to knead the young woman's shoulders. "Better?" she asked softly.

Her blue eyes glazed, Danu looked at the flattened grass beneath her outstretched legs for a long, utterly perplexed moment, before whispering, "Yes."

Her hand still smoothing Danu's back, Tor turned to Kali and explained, "I do not wish you to 'pull the punch.' I wish you to refine your control of the power that is behind such a punch."

Mildly frustrated, Kali asked, "But how?"

"Magic." With a gesture to the golden eagles floating on outstretched wings above them, Tor finished, "You flew with them today. If that is not magic, I don't know what is."

Feeling sheepish, Kali pushed a few strands of yellow hair behind her ears, then fingered the unraveling French braid at the back of her neck.

"For you," Tor went on, "ki is an effortless extension of the self. Now you must become an artist in crafting its flow."

"I'm trying," Kali weakly defended.

"I realize that," Tor assured her, standing up and coming closer to Kali. Her dark, wise eyes pierced Kali with an unrelenting fervor. "But trying is not enough."

With a grim nod, Kali bowed. The Zen-master had spoken.

That same afternoon, across town, Whit was working beside Lilith. The loud din of the construction work going on in the Leader's House was a constant background noise. With a sigh, Whit realized how much that clamor was getting on her nerves. She was reading and rereading the fiduciary figures on the page in her hand, and never quite making sense of it.

She and Lilith were sitting at a table in one of the freshly completed conference rooms, surrounded by computer printouts of loan payments. Beyond the room's closed door, women were working, seemingly as noisily as possible, all over the house. Wood-polishing machines and assorted poundings penetrated through layers of newly installed carpets and drapes, and assaulted Whit's ears. Stoically, she focused once more on reviewing loan payments received thus far, making careful notes about each business's performance during the past month.

It was now mid-October, the population had grown to just over 3,500 women and children, and there were already several hundred private businesses functioning in Isis. Many of those businesses had applied for small, community loans in early September, when the colony had initially emerged from martial law. While the Small Business Office had processed those requests and awarded modest sums of money, final approval for the more substantial loans necessary for growth lay with the newly elected Isis Council members. On the computer printout sheets spread around Whit and Lilith, the accumulated credit data on every business in the colony was listed. And in a few more hours, it would be up to Whit to oversee her most politically dangerous Council meeting thus far.

It was essential that each business's records be presented to the Council members in an accurate and fair manner. Whit knew that quarrels about favoritism could paralyze her new government if the larger loans were not dispersed with care. Common sense dictated that in order to secure further investment, the business had to be showing a profit. It was just that simple. The community as a whole was still too new, and had too shallow a tax base, to be generously supporting a business which was operating at a loss.

Lifting her eyes, Whit caught Lilith staring at her. "What?"

"Would you mind if we put this aside a moment and pursued a private discussion?" Lilith asked, her keen blue eyes contemplating Whit.

Acquiescing, Whit placed the printout sheets she held on the table, then turned so that she faced Lilith. Calmly, Whit regarded the silver-haired, slender woman by her side. In a deep violet robe and pantsuit, Lilith had an undeniably noble bearing. The sixty-four-year-old former Leader of Artemis had had a retirement of exactly one month before she ended up volunteering to temporarily take Kali's place as Deputy Leader of Isis. Arinna's threat to their community had forced many emergency responses, but it still seemed unbelievable to Whit that she had ended up with an assistant who was one of the most gifted stateswomen in all of Freeland.

Without preamble, Lilith began, "I hear that you and Kali are having...trouble at home."

"You've been talking to Marpe," Whit guessed.

"No, to Styx—who heard it from Albie—who heard it from..."

"Oh, for Gaea's sake!" Whit grumbled. Dashing a nervous hand through her hair, she said, "It was just an argument. Kali gets short-tempered when she's tired."

"And you don't?" Lilith queried gently.

"Well, how am I supposed to feel about this self-appointed mission to find and subdue Arinna? Thrilled?"

In a firm voice, Lilith stated, "You cannot make this decision for her."

Feeling fractious, Whit looked down at the table. She pretended to give this some thought, and finally responded with, "I'll think about what you said." But in actuality, she truly believed she knew what was best for Kali.

❖ ❖ ❖ ❖ ❖

That evening, as Danu left the meal hall and headed back to the hostel, Neith sidled up to her and grasped her hand.

"The All Hallows' Masked Ball is only two weeks away," the svelte Healer informed Danu in an inviting voice. "What shall we go as?"

In the darkness of the street, Neith couldn't see the pained flinch that crossed Danu's face, but she had no doubts about the meaning of the very rejecting way her hand was released.

Feeling hurt, Neith whispered, "This has gone on long enough."

"I can't help it," Danu answered, trying to walk a little faster. "I just want everyone to leave me alone."

Desperate, Neith grasped Danu's arm and dragged her into the shadow of a three-story townhouse, pushing her against the cedar planking of its wall. "You cared for me!" Neith accused. "We were on the verge of being lovers, but you haven't even come near me since Lupa died!" Seeing Danu's formidable will steeling itself against this tactic, Neith abruptly switched to entreaty. "I know you're grieving— I know she was your friend—but let me in, Danu. It's time you let someone help you heal the pain."

With a half sob, Danu pushed Neith away. "I can't! I don't know why—I just can't."

"What's happened to you?" Neith demanded angrily. "You know, you weren't the only one who saw what was left of Lupa after Arinna blew up that construction site! I was there, too!"

The words slashed through the thick shields Danu had thrown up around her stricken heart. "Please, Neith," she breathed. "Don't."

"Don't what? Don't mess with your walls, huh?" Neith sputtered. "The famous architect knows all about how to make walls, doesn't she?"

In answer, Danu brushed past Neith, quickly moving away from the house and back into the street.

Behind her, Neith hurried to keep up with Danu's long, rangy stride. "Too bad," Neith asserted, "the architect has no idea how to make a bridge!"

Danu abruptly stopped and the small Healer almost slammed into her back. "I'm sorry," Danu rasped helplessly, turning to face Neith. "I don't know how to be who you want me to be."

"Bridges are what human beings are supposed to spend their lives making, Danu," Neith stated, her dark skin gleaming in the glow from the street lamp. "But if you insist on walling yourself up, there's really not much I can do to stop you, is there?"

Surveying the lovely woman who, in August, she had been intent upon taking to bed as her first lover, Danu made a hoarse confession. "I can't *give* anything to you, Neith." With a slight shrug, she explained, "You deserve to be loved, and the only thing I'm capable of now is hate."

With an angry shake of her head, Neith stormed away.

Shoving her hands in her pockets, Danu continued slowly down the street. When she reached the steps of the hostel, she dragged herself glumly to the top stair, then sank down on the wooden porch and looked out into the dark night. The afternoon warmth was long gone now, and Danu drew her jacket closer around herself, as she shivered in the chill evening air. Her breath was visible in small clouds as she sat there, feeling incredibly lonely and misunderstood.

Behind her, the hostel door opened. A form crossed in front of the porch light and cast a shadow down the steps. Looking up, Danu saw Albie hesitating by her side, as if unsure whether to stay or go. Brusquely, Danu made a motion with her hand, asking Albie to be with her, and Albie dropped her square, solid frame down beside Danu. A glance revealed that Albie was glaring at her.

You've seen Neith? Danu signed.

Fuming, Albie signed, *She ran by me. She was crying!*

It's better to be honest about this than to lead her on, Danu bitterly related. *It feels like my heart has turned to ice. I can't feel anything.*

Putting her fingertips to Danu's chest and pushing slightly, Albie gestured, *Ice has been known to melt when the heat goes up! What's the matter with you?! She's sassy, she's beautiful, and she really likes you!*

Pulling her eyes away, Danu retorted, *She doesn't even know me. I'm not the same person I was before Lupa died. I'll never be that person again.*

Albie sighed and reached over to Danu, slipping her hand under Danu's chin and turning her face. *I think I know why your heart is ice, Danu. All you think about is vengeance.*

Grimly shaking her head in denial, Danu stood up and Albie stood with her. Using her strong right arm, Albie blocked Danu's attempted retreat to the hostel doors. She signed quickly, *You're letting hate eat you alive. You'll be just like Arinna if you keep this up.*

Danu wiped her hand across her face, briefly allowing herself to feel the exhaustion she carried, before the fury surfaced. *If you think Neith is so wonderful,* she signed angrily to Albie, *why aren't you after her yourself?*

And then Danu pushed by her shorter friend and slammed through the hostel doors, leaving Albie standing on the porch with something to think about.

Tor sat on the edge of her bunk, reveling in the fact that she had some time alone in this room she shared with Danu. One thing about living with a workaholic—Tor had found she could rarely get a private hour to listen to her favorite music. And somehow, listening to The Maenads with wireless earjacks was just not as satisfying as feeling the whole room vibrating with the beat.

Eyes closed, Tor's hands punched the air before her in rhythm to the music. Harsh keyboards blared and an electric Welsh harp squealed, then a computerized orchestra picked up the theme and pounded it through the small speakers Tor had mounted in each of the four corners of the room. Feeling as if the harmonic, pulsating drumbeats were vibrating within her flesh, shaking her back to life, Tor let the rash abrasiveness of Blaster Rock take her.

Lately, she had begun to feel as if she were ready to explode. She was frustrated and discouraged and she wasn't even really sure why. She guessed it was partially because she was working to the point of mental and physical exhaustion each day. She was also far from her home and family, very lonely, and more than a little dismayed by the pressure of readying Kali Tyler for what undoubtedly would be a deadly struggle for Freeland's future. Aside from all that, she was finding that sharing both her daily work and her private quarters with the insular and intriguing Danu Sullivan was a feat in itself.

She won't talk to me unless she has to, Tor mused, punching the air in time to a spectacularly noisy beat. *So she doesn't like me. Why do I let it bother me so much?*

Opening her eyes, Tor suddenly noticed Danu across the room, sitting at her desk. Startled, Tor self-consciously leapt to her feet, reaching to the shelf above her bunk where her digital audio player rested. With a flick of the fingers, she turned the music down.

"Sorry," Tor offered. "I didn't know you came in."

Danu continued to stare at her computer screen, seemingly oblivious to Tor. Then, amazingly, without turning around, she asked, "What's the name of that group?"

"The Maenads," Tor replied, watching her.

With a nod, Danu urged, "Turn it up again, please."

"I don't understand," Tor answered, incredulous.

"It suits my current mood," Danu growled, and then leaned her elbows on the desk and put her head in her hands.

Thoroughly bewildered, Tor nonetheless obliged. She turned up the volume and the dissonant music once more pounded through the room and its occupants.

4

Lilith stood just inside, near the open doorway, watching the holiday crowd pour in from the chilly night. Masked women swept by her, jostling noisily into the shadowy expanse of Navra Recreation Hall. Miniature clowns and witches and skeletons scampered past each other as the children entered, squealing their excitement. She recognized a teenaged Marie Antoinette look-alike in a low-cut eighteenth-century ball gown and a powdered wig, then spotted an elderly, sensibly dressed Eleanor Roosevelt, feathered hat cocked jauntily on her head. Farther off, in a dark, relaxed-fit suit, complete with a cravat and slicked-back hair, Lilith admired a ripened k.d. lang. Smiling warmly, Lilith nodded to the costumed women who called out to her or waved as they paraded into the Great Hall beyond.

The retractable walls which normally defined each portion of Navra Rec Hall had been mechanically folded away and sealed into recesses in the walls, leaving a vast, woman-made cavern. Gazing about her in the purposely dim light, Lilith knew it would easily accommodate the roughly two thousand women expected. The colony's first Samhain in eleven years would be celebrated by all of them, together.

In the not-too-distant future, this space would become gymnasiums, weight rooms, martial arts and dance studios. But tonight, Navra Rec Hall had been turned into a ballroom. From the ceiling hung huge creations of papier-mâché wiggly-limbed brown spiders, black cats with poker-straight tails and angry green eyes, helium balloon ghosts billowing about in ghostly white sheets. Each of the four walls had been covered with recycled paper and painted with cartoon-like portrayals of a sinister black forest—as frightening a rendition as any Lilith ever hoped to see.

In the rear of the hall, a large stage had been set up, and as Lilith watched, a masked woman in black tie and long tails lifted her baton. Seated before her were thirty or so women with their musical instruments. Some were dressed in suits and ties, while others wore strapless, chiffon ball gowns. The bass drum read, "The Billy Tipton Orchestra." The conductor gestured a count, and together, sounding for all the world like a 1940s Big Band, the women swung into a lively rendition of "Blue Skies." And though the tune was over one hundred and fifty years old, it seemed that nearly everyone in the hall grabbed a partner and began to dance.

Styx, in a long, rainbow-colored robe and an outlandish headdress, approached Lilith through the crowd. As Lilith examined her lover's outfit more closely, she noticed that the skirt beneath the robe was constructed of what appeared to be hundreds of snake skins; the headdress, too, was a complex weaving of snake skins and numerous long, dark, bald eagle feathers. Coming to Lilith's elbow and seeing the questioning expression, Styx posed majestically and intoned, "I am Coatlicue, the Aztec Goddess."

A bit alarmed, Lilith asked, "Wasn't she rather bloodthirsty?"

"All the Old Ones were bloodthirsty," Styx informed her with a mock-evil grin, waggling her eyebrows. "That was the way in those days. But at least Coatlicue represented the fecundity of the earth— the original Mother Goddess for my people."

Suppressing a laugh, Lilith didn't reply, but instead inspected the brightly colored, hand-woven robe, with its small, red-and-black embroidered diamond shapes along the lapel and sleeves.

"You must have been working on this for months," Lilith commented, very impressed. "How did you keep it a secret?"

"You mean, how did I manage to keep it from you?" Styx reworded laughingly, then answered, "While I served as Herstorian for Artemis, the colony kids brought me everything under the sun."

With an accepting grin, Lilith stated, "That explains the snake skins and feathers. What about the robe? The craftswomanship is almost art." Stepping closer, Lilith fingered the embroidery on Styx's sleeve.

"I bought it at Cleopatra's Palace," Styx replied shortly, busily looking over Lilith's costume. "Samsi and Marpe have created some rather revolutionary textile programs. Their computerized looms are producing amazingly detailed cloth." Puzzled by Lilith's costume, Styx indicated that she wanted Lilith to turn about. "And who, or what, are you?" she prompted.

The corner of her mouth curling up, Lilith stood her ground, refusing to spin, so Styx walked around her, giving Lilith a lusty once-over that made Lilith's heart beat faster. "You ought to know who my heroines are by now," Lilith teased.

Slowly, Styx smiled. "Leather flight jacket, silk scarf, khaki pants, white, man-tailored shirt...." A low chuckle escaped her. "Of course. You're Amelia Earhart."

"Care to dance, Coatlicue?" Lilith invited.

Just as they moved together, embracing, they were interrupted by a breathless young voice.

"Lilith, Styx—have either of you seen Danu?"

They turned to find Neith Murray, dressed in a clinging linen shift, a bow and a brace of arrows slung across her slim torso. Large, gold hooped earrings and bracelets flashed against her deep brown skin and matched the thin band of gold that ran about her forehead and short, crisp, black hair.

"Ah, yes," Styx murmured appreciatively, "Neith was her name, too. A Goddess of Lower Egypt...."

"Goddess of the Hunt," Neith furnished, impatient.

Reacting to Neith's tone, Lilith answered, "I haven't actually seen Danu, but there's someone tall with red hair up there by the bandstand, right now."

Giving them a curt nod, Neith headed into the crowd, toward the distant stage area.

"She certainly has her heart set on Danu, doesn't she," Styx remarked, shaking her head sadly.

"I think Neith isn't used to being put off," Lilith observed quietly. "I'm beginning to wonder if it's her heart or her pride that's involved in this chase."

And then, as the band drifted into a sensuous, contemporary love song, Styx pulled Lilith against her. Slowly, they danced, and the need for words ceased. Their bodies were addressing each other quite nicely.

Pressed near the stage with at least a hundred other young women, Danu was moving unconsciously to the down beat, watching the musicians. She'd always preferred classical music, but a dance band was something new, something different, and it went to her head and feet like a tall glass of hard cider.

Suddenly Neith was at her side, capturing her hand and pulling her toward the women dancing farther away. Once they were in a more open area, Neith's arms encircled her waist and she began moving in a smooth, sensuous pattern. Following Neith's lead, Danu watched and emulated her friend, until they seemed to be floating together.

"You're good," Neith crooned, her fingers creeping into the curling copper hair at the nape of Danu's neck.

In spite of the romantic music and Neith's seductiveness, Danu abruptly found herself questioning her own feelings. Suddenly she felt incredibly confused and vulnerable, and dropped her hold on Neith.

"Don't, Danu," Neith commanded in a low, hushed voice.

"I'm sorry, Neith," Danu whispered, backing away. "I can't do this...." Turning on her heels, Danu plunged into the crowd of dancers. In her confusion, she made for the far wall, the only inner wall left within the otherwise-open expanse of the hall. She knew that behind this barrier, secured by a lock, was the ARC Platform.

After lurking near the wall for a while, blending into a group of elders, she found herself listening to one particular conversation. Several high-backed benches nearby were occupied by a coterie of clothing merchants, and they weren't talking about the spectacular costumes on display at this All Hallows' Masked Ball.

"...she practically *ran* from Neith, can you imagine!" Marpe disclosed, almost exulting in her news.

"She didn't!" This came from a robust attorney dressed as Blind Justice. With a distracted tug, the woman's symbolic blindfold dropped from its cockeyed perch on her nose. The metaphorical scales had already been stashed under the bench.

"I saw it," Marpe insisted.

"...and of course Albie's over there lending a shoulder for Neith to cry on," Samsi supplied, "since she knows all about Danu. Albie gave up on her two months ago...."

Looking suitably concerned, Marpe continued. "She's nearly eighteen and still uninitiated! I know she's Think Tank, but she *is* human, isn't she? She's got to have *some* sex drive."

Ominously, Samsi reported, "Even Loy Yin Chen didn't get her in bed, despite that scandalous campaign of hers last summer. One of the few times *anyone* ever succeeded in dodging Loy, I'm sure."

"Nonsexual," the attorney pronounced with a sniff. "It's probably a by-product of the Think Tank. Those enhanced intellects are just not like the rest of us, you know." Leaning toward Marpe, the plump woman confided, "Take, for example, Arinna Sojourner— brilliant, yes, but certainly a madwoman. And then there's Kali Tyler—all this paranormal exploration seems to have done nothing except put a strain on her partnership with poor Tomyris Whitaker."

"But Arinna and Kali are sexually active," Samsi pondered aloud, like a dog returning to a particularly meaty conversational bone.

Snickering, the attorney declared, "Maat Tyler knew how to create geniuses all right—but she left the spice out of the mix when she made Danu Sullivan!"

Covering their mouths with their hands, all three elders collectively burst into tittering laughter.

Embarrassed, her heart pounding wildly, Danu backed up until she stumbled over an empty folding chair. Unable to keep her balance, she fell against the wall. Then Danu heard Samsi's gentler voice proclaiming, "It's not the Think Tank at all. Danu thinks too much, instead of just allowing herself to feel."

Danu watched in horror as Marpe stood and began to turn toward her. Desperate not to be seen, Danu quickly reached out and slid her palm over the DNA plate that locked the door to the ARC Platform. Silently, the door slid open. Danu ducked inside, then hit the inside plate, closing the door behind her.

She stood there, thankfully hidden from view, in a dimmer light. She was breathing hard, dazed, caught in a familiar wash of emotions. She was mortified, she was indignant. But stronger than all the intense sensations slamming through her was the anguish. *Is it true?* she thought frantically. *Am I so different from everyone else?*

With a deep sigh, she decided to stay a while and settle herself. There was no sense going out into the crowd again until the hot blush faded from her face.

Deeply troubled, she pulled herself up the metal ladder attached to this side of the two-meters-high plastic composite platform. *What's wrong with me?* she wondered, her bruised heart aching within her.

And then, as she came up over the edge, she found herself face to face with Tor.

Sitting Indian fashion, with a flask in her hand, wearing what looked to be the clothing of a Samurai, Tor looked up in surprise, but recovered quickly and said, "Don't tell me...." As she studied the soft, brown deerskins Danu wore, she gestured for Danu to finish the short climb and settle herself on the platform next to her. "Let's see..." Tor guessed, "you're either Calamity Jane or Jemima Boone."

"Jemima," Danu breathed as she sat, not sure now if she wanted to stay or not.

"Not very herstorically accurate," Tor observed. "Daniel Boone's daughter probably wore a homespun skirt," she added, casting a skeptical eye at Danu's snug trousers.

"Who cares? She survived being abducted by a hostile Shawnee war party, didn't she?" Danu insisted quietly, not looking at Tor directly, trying to appear unruffled. *Did she hear those old gossips? Does she think I'm some sort of "nonsexual" mutation?* she worried. Breathlessly, Danu rushed on, "Then later, during the siege of Boonesboro, Jemima took a bullet in the shoulder while she was firing a musket on the fort wall."

Tor snorted softly. "Too bad that by the last half of the twentieth century, American men had forgotten all about Jemima and all the other courageous pioneer women. They were convinced females had to be kept at home and pampered. For over two centuries women weren't allowed to enlist as warriors."

As she leaned back on her hands, shifting her long, buckskin-clad legs out in front of her, Danu noticed the intense way Tor watched her. *Do I look like some sort of freak to everyone?* Aloud, perplexed, Danu asked, "Why in Gaea's name *didn't* Jemima wear pants?"

"Oh," Tor murmured, "one of those stupid expectations that comes from lumping people into categories."

Danu looked at her then. *Damn! Tor heard everything the elders said. Guess I was born into a category from day one, and I'll never escape from it.*

"Saki?" Tor asked, as if offering solace, and she passed Danu the flask.

For a moment Danu stared at it blankly, then accepted the thin metal container, and stared into Tor's wise, dark eyes. "Why are you up here?" she demanded.

"I don't like mobs." Tor looked sheepish, as if not used to conceding a weakness. "Sometimes I duck out for a minute."

Another long stare.

Tor broke the gaze first. "You want to be alone," Tor observed, unfolding her legs and readying to stand.

"Anxious to leave?" Danu challenged recklessly. "Could it be the company?" With a bitter look on her face, Danu took a deep drink from the flask.

Almost reflexively, Tor reached out and gripped the small flask, making Danu relinquish it before she was ready. "Saki has quite a kick," Tor warned.

"Maybe it's time I got roaring drunk," Danu countered. "Maybe it's time I did a lot of things 'normal' people are supposed to do."

"Hmph," Tor observed. "I don't think there's any such thing as 'normal' people...do you?" When Danu only sat there glowering at her moccasins, Tor softly elaborated, "Only lots of uniquely different beings, all just trying to find their own way."

A fleeting look of pain escaped Danu's control and she knew the expression had crossed her face before she managed to turn away from Tor. "What do you do when you...when you can't find your way, Tor?" Danu whispered.

There was a chuckle, then, "I listen to Blaster Rock."

Perplexed, Danu swung around and gazed at her.

"Rock and Roll has always been for, and about, outsiders," Tor explained. "And Blaster Rock is the same—only louder."

Grinning, Danu replied, "That explains it."

"What?" Tor laughed.

"I wondered why I was starting to like it."

Whit strode into Navra Rec Hall, arriving much later than she had intended. Impatiently, she peered about her, looking for golden hair. Kali was somewhere in this Samhain carnival, although she had kept her costume a secret and Whit had no clear idea just whom she was searching for. And with so many masks and elaborate disguises, the task was not going to be easy.

For some time she wandered through the multitude, rapidly checking out masqueraders, and just as rapidly dismissing them. She was beginning to despair of ever finding Kali when someone grabbed her arm as she passed.

She gave the woman a once-over. Not Kali—this woman was too broad across the shoulders and waist. But still, familiar. Whit noted the sandals, the serpent-skin skirt, and the rainbow robe. Styx lifted her ocher-colored mask and grinned.

Smiling back at her, Whit fingered the long feathers of the headdress. "Some sort of Mayan, I take it."

"A later Goddess of the Aztec tribe."

"Should I expect a human sacrifice at some point tonight?" Whit joked.

Solemnly, Styx retorted, "I've already eaten, thank you."

A slender figure clad in leather and khaki stepped around Styx, coming into Whit's view. The piercing blue eyes behind that small, tan half-mask could only belong to one woman. "Where've you been?" Lilith quizzed.

Casting another searching gaze around the hall, Whit confided, "I was with Intelligence in the Watch Room, running surveillance scans. One of the automatic satellite probes registered an anomaly and it triggered a full-scale grid evaluation. The computer recorded strange heat dispersions in the North Cascades—as if a good deal of power were being used and then vented."

Tensing, Lilith came to Whit's side. "Were you able to pinpoint a location?"

"No," Whit sighed. "All I know is that it's somewhere between Ross Lake and the Methow River. The satellite wasn't able to locate the heat source conclusively—some electronic artifact up there is obscuring the readings."

"So Arinna may be much closer than we dared to speculate," Styx remarked, watching Whit's deep, gray eyes travel restlessly over the crowd.

"It's certainly within striking distance," Whit commented. Then, casually, as if it were a minor concern, she asked, "Where's Kali?"

"We haven't seen her," Lilith stated. "We thought she was with you."

For the first time during the entire conversation, Whit's eyes snapped to the person speaking. Her tone hushed, the question slid out on one breath. "She's not here?"

Lilith opened her mouth to speak, but Whit was already moving. She hurried across the hall, sliding past bodies, heading for the door she had passed through moments before.

Maybe she's still at home.

Whit hit the cold night air outside the hall and ran down the street toward the Leader's House, where she'd left her motorcycle. She'd gone half a block when she glimpsed a woman passing her on the other side of the road, a woman whose shape and movement were instantly recognizable. Slamming to a standstill, Whit whirled around.

Beneath the streetlight, loose, golden hair floated behind the woman as she moved. In some odd, nonsensical corner of Whit's brain, it registered that there were silver-blue ribbons woven into the hair gathered at the back of this lovely beauty's head. And the ribbons matched the long, flowing, silver-blue Queen Guinevere dress that hugged her tight in the bodice and billowed out like a sail from the hips down.

"Kali!" Whit barked, furious now that her fears were allayed. Swiftly, she closed the distance between them as Kali turned, surprised, then nervously dropped her gaze.

Forestalling Whit's criticism, Kali held up her hand. "I know," she admitted, seeming contrite. "I'm late."

"Very late. I was worried," Whit accused. "The air-surveillance apparatus registered..."

"...an inexplicable heat source in the North Cascades," Kali finished. "And I couldn't pinpoint the exact location either." She pressed her fingers to her temple and rubbed her forehead as she began to walk alongside Whit.

Grabbing Kali by the elbow, Whit forced her to stop. "How do you know that?"

Sighing, Kali dropped her hand from her temple. "Gaea—I don't know how I know *anything* any more, Whit," she griped softly. "I was at home, rigging up this dress, and I...sensed Arinna. I reached out, tried to contact her." Kali gave an exasperated shake of her head. "She caught me and contained me, I think. The next thing I knew it was over two hours later and I was standing in our bedroom, in this stupid outfit, feeling grumpy and sleepy."

Disturbed by this frank admission, Whit snapped, "You tried to contact her? What are you doing *trying* to contact her?!"

"It's basic search technique," Kali retorted. "I'm a capable psychic—it's part of my work." Annoyed, Kali swung away, stubbornly walking toward the hall again.

"Capable!" Whit burst out, hurrying to keep up with Kali. "She held you, kept you in a psychic mind-net against your will for over two hours! Gaea knows what she was doing to your head during all that time!"

"She only kept me out of the way," Kali asserted. "She was engaged in some other process—I could sense the split in her power." They were nearing the door to Navra Rec Hall and Kali's quiet voice dropped even lower. "Believe me, I'd show the effects if she wanted to really *do* something to me."

"What's that supposed to mean?" Whit said, her tone flat.

Kali kept moving, past the women stealing kisses in the shadows by the door, through the large, open doorway, and into the crowded hall. Whit stuck close behind her, glaring at Kali's stubborn profile.

"You mean Arinna's stronger now, don't you?" Whit accused, sounding raw with frustration even to her own ears. "Stronger than you. Stronger than you could ever hope to be."

Kali didn't reply.

They were moving through a press of bodies. Their covert, yet evident, quarrel was drawing glances, causing others to step away from them as they passed.

Whit tried to speak more softly, but could not keep the commanding tone out of her voice. "Well, that's enough mind-magic! You're out of it, now! *I'm* taking control of this crazy enterprise. It was absolute nonsense to expect you, a novice Wiccan with a flair for telepathy, to triumph over a full-fledged sorceress like that damned Arinna Sojourner."

Slowing her steps, Kali turned to face her partner, her gaze ferocious. "Don't start, Whit. Not here," she hissed, while nodding and smiling at familiar faces.

The crowd around them seemed to move back. Whit was aware of the band, farther off, playing a lively twentieth-century jitterbug. She was aware of the noise of hundreds of revelers, talking and laughing together. High overhead, large papier-mâché spiders, cats, and ghosts danced, swinging in the breeze from the entranceway. Though it was cold outside, body heat from the crowd and the dancing was ably heating the entire hall. But the vague white light that seemed to pulse around Kali had nothing to do with the intentionally shadowy lighting of the hall.

Stubbornly, Whit challenged, "There's no sane reason for you to expose yourself to that psychopath." Drawing a breath, ignoring the attention focused on them, she blurted out, "I can't fathom why you insist on going out and hunting her down—like she's some sort of wild horse you're going to rope."

Dropping her gaze to the floor, Kali folded her arms across her chest and seemed to glow even brighter.

Whit darted a glance around, trying to discover where the strange light on Kali was coming from. Unable to discern the source, she indulged her nasty mood further and delivered what she thought was a very sensible suggestion.

"You should stay here in Isis," Whit advised, "where you can be shielded by trained companies of warriors and the most technologically advanced defense systems in Freeland."

Obviously at her limit, Kali's head snapped up and she made a guttural growl in her throat. "Mother's Blood," she swore, "you're just like an Elysian—wanting a *wife* to come home to and coddle!"

It struck Whit then that Kali wasn't just blazing mad—she was actually *blazing*—blazing with yellow-white light. Her entire body was illuminating the space around her like a huge synth-fuel lamp. But Whit was too angry to let that bizarre sight stop her own hot reply.

"*Me*! An *Elysian*!" Whit almost spat out. Conscious of the crowd around them, for an instant Whit tried desperately to check her reply, but then the defiant glare Kali aimed at her was simply too much. "Well, *you're* just like your mother! A prideful maverick who won't listen to reason and follows her own course, regardless of what anyone else thinks!"

"DON'T TALK ABOUT MY MOTHER!" Kali roared.

The entire hall was quieting, now. There was no music—the band had stopped playing some time back. Women in brightly colored costumes and elaborate finery silently ringed Whit and Kali, shocked at this exchange, apprehensive yet fascinated. Vaguely, Whit noticed Lilith and Styx about three meters away. They were pushing through resistant bodies, trying to get to them.

Kali clutched her head with both hands, and seemed to crumple a little. "I saw them all burn, Whit!" She took a ragged, sob-like breath, struggling to rein back her angry tears. "I was here eleven years ago when the Regs destroyed Isis—I *saw* what a surprise attack can do to a colony! I won't stay here and make Arinna come after me!"

Balling her hands into fists, Whit stepped closer to her and felt buffeted by pulsing waves of psychic energy emanating from her lover. "It won't be like that..." Whit began, trying for a more reasonable tone. She wanted only to reassure and soothe Kali now.

Kali dropped her hands and stared at her. With rigid lips, she said, "It *will* be like that...only...." Her voice barely a whisper, Kali ended the argument. "If Arinna comes here, determined to take me, she'll leave this place far worse than the Regs ever did."

Lilith broke through the periphery of the crowd and crossed the space to Kali. In one smooth motion she encircled Kali's shoulders and pulled the golden head to a maternal shoulder. Kali relaxed against her like an exhausted child.

Just as Styx reached Whit's side, the dim overhead lights began to flicker. Then, with a brief sputtering sound, they shut off and the hall was thrown into utter darkness.

Women's voices rose around them, calling in fear for loved ones, even as Whit blindly moved to the last spot she had seen Kali. It was but a couple of meters away, but it seemed to take an eternity before she felt the raspy soft material and knew it was the silver-blue dress Kali was wearing.

And as Whit's arms claimed her, Kali whispered ominously, "It's her—she's here."

In a panic, Whit shouted, "Arinna?"

Above the crowd, a reddish-lavender light formed, progressing from mere vapor to a clearly delineated figure, in a matter of seconds. The only thing that marked the figure as illusion rather than reality was the towering size of the womanly body. At least five meters tall and laughing, Arinna Sojourner hovered above the massed population of Isis.

In the strange light, Whit was briefly distracted by seeing the door to the ARC chamber slide open and Danu and Tor appear in the doorway

"Greetings, citizens of Isis!" Arinna proclaimed, her seductive voice quieting the multitude at once. "I have come to wish you wicked tidings on this All Hallows' Eve."

"Danu—she's on some sort of remote—keying the ARC circuitry," Whit called. "Go cut the power board interface!"

Immediately, Danu was moving, off the platform in a leap and thrusting past women in a determined dash to the observation-deck stairs. Tor, meanwhile, examined the image of Arinna, dumbfounded.

Lilith wondered aloud, "How can she be initiating a hologram? None of us are wearing ARC headbands—we're not carrying any sort of radio receptors."

"I don't *know* how she's doing it!" Whit answered. "But what other explanation can there be?"

As Kali shrank in Whit's arms, Arinna spoke in a melodious, mesmerizing lilt. "I am tiring of waiting for you, Kali. You know I am your fate. Why do you try to escape it?"

Slowly, Kali turned toward Arinna, listening despite herself. "Come to me, Kali," Arinna summoned.

In horror, Whit saw that half the women around them shuffled forward, enthralled with the call, even though Kali's name, not their own, had been used.

"Give yourself up to me," Arinna was sweetly entreating. "Only you can save the rest of these women. Pathetic though their lives are in comparison with our own, I will spare them if you help me."

With a shudder, Kali burrowed deeper into Whit's arms. "No," she breathed against Whit's neck, as if the muted refusal were an enormous effort.

"Hurry, Danu!" Whit shouted.

Flying up the stairs and opening the observation-deck door with a slam that echoed through the hall, Danu raced for the computer power panels at the back of the room.

The apparition intoned, "Kali, don't make me punish you."

Whit felt Lilith enclose both Kali and herself in a protective embrace, as if preparing to block with her own delicate body, any blow Arinna dared to strike. Styx was attempting to do the same thing from the other side.

Her voice thundering, Arinna commanded, "Come to me!"

The crowd surged toward her and Kali began fighting to free herself.

In the next instant the image was gone and the house lights went up to full power. Confused, women were turning to each other, murmuring in a belated panic.

A few minutes later, Danu jogged back to the ARC chamber doorway and into clear view. She waved a handful of circuit fibers in her hand as she shouted to Whit, "Power board down!"

A rush of noise filled the hall as everyone began to speak at once. Lilith and Styx held Whit and Kali an extra moment between them, then they all took deep, settling breaths.

Styx's brow furrowed as she studied Whit and Kali closely. Attempting to divert their attention and thus put the sudden terror behind them, she gestured at their costumes. "What are you, anyway? I never did figure out either of your get-ups."

Shifting weightier concerns aside for a moment, Kali and Whit surveyed each other.

Whit noted the small, cylindrical crystal on Kali's necklace, and all at once comprehended the Camelot style of the silver-blue dress. Not Guinevere, but Morgan, the true feminine power in the tale of Arthur. "Kali's a Wiccan Mage," she guessed, and was rewarded for her insight with a beautiful, loving smile.

Then Kali narrowed her eyes and took in Whit's gray bodysuit of lightweight armor, the white tunic that fell to her knees like a Knight Templar's. On her snowy chest was imprinted the Freeland symbol of matriarchy: a purple, six-pointed star with a leaping dolphin in the middle. The small, sheathed sword loosely belted to her side was ornamental, but the plastic pistol in her holster marked her for what she was in real life. "Whit's the Warrior Chieftain," Kali supplied.

"We came as our true selves, didn't we?" Whit asked, her gray eyes pensive. "Have we taken on the roles so seriously, then?"

Reaching out for Whit's hand, Kali sighed, "Well, we can hardly put them off now, can we?"

With a shake of her head, Whit pulled Kali close, once more frightened. Arinna had appeared in Isis—if not physically, then with enough psychic force to convincingly register her evil presence. Somehow, Whit felt she had come very close to losing Kali tonight.

Meanwhile the crowd noise had escalated and fear was written on many faces.

"Whit," Kali softly urged. "Our people need to hear from you."

Clapping Whit softly on the back, Styx agreed. Lilith sent Whit a supportive nod and then took her place beside Kali. Quickly, Styx led the way for her as they walked to the bandstand. Whit mounted the stage and held out her arms for quiet. She quickly got it. The women she was about to address anxiously pressed toward her, seeking reassurance and leadership from a woman they felt certain would give it to them.

All Hallows' Eve had unexpectedly fulfilled its reputation for being the scariest night of the year.

5

It was now mid-November. Two tense, rather uneventful weeks had passed since Arinna's surreal visit during the All Hallows' Eve Ball. And though they half-expected Arinna to make another attempt to draw Kali toward whatever trap she was setting, no further enticements were received. It left all of them—Kali, her training crew, and most of Isis—on edge. Winter was rapidly approaching, and they all seemed to be waiting, like a captive audience, for Arinna's next performance.

Meanwhile, all military personnel in Isis had been placed on red alert. In addition to the sentries already posted throughout the city and all over the airfield, five helijets had been dispatched to make continual forty-kilometer sweeps around Isis. The thud of copter blades had become a constant background noise in the routine of their daily lives.

Then, on the third Saturday of the month, a chagrined Captain Razia called Lilith to report gross inaccuracies in the Watch Room surveillance data. After meeting with the captain and her Intelligence team and thoroughly reviewing the flawed data, Whit and Lilith elected to investigate further by themselves. They hoped that, as the system designer, Lilith might be more efficient in tracking down and fixing the source of the problem. When Whit dismissed Captain Razia and the anxious members of the Intelligence team, their relief was evident.

Hours later, Lilith was still studying the wallscreen and rechecking her final figures. The readouts just didn't make sense. Initially, there was no sign of life in grid number 451 of the air surveillance. Then, one day, grid 451 contained the population of a small farming village. And then, two days later, grid 451 registered no one again. Either the satellite data was incorrect, or Lilith had made a mistake. Given the fact that the satellites were computer based, she had initially doubted her own reckoning, but she had gone over her stats at least ten times now.

"Whit," she called softly. "Something's wrong with the satellites."

Alarmed, Whit looked up from the auxiliary screen and terminal across the room, where she had been auditing another set of tally sheets. The Intelligence team had been entering this data after each satellite-surveillance operation for the past month, in exact sequence. Yet only when reviewed in random order did the program flaws become glaringly apparent. "I know," Whit answered. "This data is inconsistent, too."

Cursing softly, Lilith left the compu-chair and walked to Whit's side. "It can't be—I audited the first two weeks myself, and it was fine, then."

"You're right," Whit clarified. "The discrepancies start on All Hallows' Eve."

Lilith looked over the figures, quickly seeing what concerned Whit. "Do you think the satellites were the target of Arinna's attention that night—the night you and Kali both noted heat dispersions in the North Cascades?"

"By the Mother, I hope not," Whit returned, frowning. "Those satellites keep the Border in place. Part of the problem may be that those particular surveillance and Border-controlling satellites are in a relatively low orbit around Earth. The communications and weather satellites are occupying much higher orbits. It may be possible to use those satellites to control the Bordergates...I just don't know. The

Freeland Council will have to assign a few specialists to work on this problem."

Stunned into silence, Lilith considered the implications. Decades ago, Maat Tyler had discovered how to control the Border through the old NASA satellites, long abandoned in space. Elysium's own electromagnetic force field had been turned against them, as what was once the fascist state's fortress wall—their method of dealing with the AGH plague—became Elysium's own prison. Over the years, within the Border, the eastern half of Old America continued to degenerate in a brutal spiral of starvation, disease, and savage cruelty. And now, the only thing that kept Freeland from the grasp of the barbaric Elysian Regulators was probably in danger of collapsing.

"If the Border fails, we are all doomed," Lilith said simply. "It is imperative that we fix the satellites. But how?" she demanded, knowing time was now of critical importance.

Crossing the room to the compu-chair, Whit quickly coded an All-Leaders Emergency summons into the computerized comline network that linked all Freeland. As she waited for responses, she turned back to Lilith.

"We may be in luck," Whit disclosed. "Some of the scientists down in Lang have been digging around at the old NASA site in Houston, collecting and inventorying abandoned equipment."

"Yes, I read those 'For Leaders' Eyes Only' reports last spring," Lilith said. "They found enough usable salvage material to advance us into an era of limited space travel. The obstacle was locating a viable fueling agent. The reports established that rocket fuel had not survived the passage of time as well as NASA's hardware had...."

Whit cut her off with a wave of the hand. "Sorry," she murmured, but Lilith only grinned, pleased that Whit was growing more comfortable with exercising the authority associated with her rank, especially her rank over Lilith.

The comline started blinking as several of the Leaders reported in at once. Whit politely asked them to hold while the remaining Leaders were contacted and assembled for an emergency briefing.

Placing all comline channels on mute, Whit gave a shrewd glance to the crystal power unit in the rear of the room.

"We have limited quantities of usable rocket fuel," Whit conceded, "but what if I know of another source of energy to power the rockets?"

Lilith followed Whit's eyes and studied the solar-powered crystal unit, glowing within its casing as it powered the computer that made up this entire room. It was Lilith's own experiment, her dream. *Could the crystal do it?* she wondered, excited by the theoretical possibilities. *Could women rocket from the earth, into the endless sea of the cosmos, on the power of light?*

As the calls from other Freeland Leaders came in, Lilith left Whit to her task. Taking out her portable microprocessor, Lilith wandered over to the crystal and began calculating the specifications and energy requirements necessary to thrust a ship free of Earth's gravitational pull.

Across town, in Navra Rec Hall, Danu slid out of range as Kali went on the attack during martial arts practice. She successfully dodged two kicks, then executed a slap block and escaped a vertical punch.

Tor sat near the mat, evaluating the training session, while Styx observed from a short distance away. Though still erratic in her use of ki, Kali was becoming an incredibly dangerous opponent. Weaving and darting, Danu managed to avoid a relentless flurry of strikes, and even Tor was not quite sure how Danu had managed to do it. Like Kali, the young redhead was more than intellectually gifted, for an instinctual athletic prowess had been engineered into her gene base at conception. Watching them move before her, Tor realized she had never seen such easy and thorough mastery of skills she had spent much of her life developing. Once these two had created a few years of muscle-memory to draw upon, even Tor would be no match for them.

If the fugitive Arinna is found, Tor decided solemnly, *Kali is probably ready to meet her—at least on a physical plane.*

In the two weeks since the All Hallows' Ball, an uneasy silence had settled over Isis like an early winter snow. Outside Navra Rec Hall, Tor knew the mid-November wind was blowing harsh and cold, and the sky overhead was the sort of solid white which usually signaled an approaching snowstorm. No one was out on the streets. Most of Isis had gone quietly into hibernation, as if it wished to go to sleep and wake in the spring, having ignored the problem of Arinna Sojourner until she went away.

Since Arinna's appearance at Navra Rec Hall, Kali had been relentless in perfecting her skills in Wiccan spell-casting, martial arts, and controlling the flow of ki. Tor sensed that Kali had already made a decision and had moved on, out of Isis. There was a centered, detached quality about her now. Tor suspected that part of her was constantly engaged in listening for, reaching toward, Arinna. From her own studies, Tor knew enough about Wiccan spells to suspect that Arinna's call was like a lingering sensual ache, demanding satisfaction.

I had heard of her malevolent power, Tor mused, *but nothing prepared me for that sinister, five-meter-tall illusion, floating above the citizens of Isis, calling to Kali like a siren.* She had to admit, Arinna had frightened her like nothing else she'd ever encountered.

Tor's attention was snapped back to the mat before her as Kali landed a blow and Danu dropped like a Douglas fir—in a long, clean line—straight to the mat. They all went to her side, but she gasped, "I'm fine," and then stayed there, breathing hard.

Kali shot Styx a beseeching look and pointed to her bare wrist, where she usually wore her wristcom. When Styx smiled and nodded, Kali said to Danu, "That's enough for today, birthday girl." Grabbing up two small sweat towels, Kali tossed one to Danu.

Danu pushed herself up on her elbows and looked confused.

In answer to the unasked question, Kali tapped her forehead. "Forgive me—I heard you. Do you mind?"

"Oh," Danu breathed, still winded. For an instant, she blushed, possibly because she remembered some other things she must have been thinking about lately. Kali waited, watching Danu anxiously. At last, Danu seemed aware of Kali's concern, because with a dismissive shrug, she said, "It's okay."

"Good," Kali concluded. "Be at our house at seven, then."

"What?" Danu pushed herself all the way up, startled.

"It's your birthday, right?" Kali said with a smile, going to her backpack and sweatshirt, readying to leave practice. "We're all having dinner together—like good friends sometimes do when one of the friends has a birthday."

For an instant, Danu appeared so overwhelmed that Tor looked away, allowing the young architect time to regain control. When she looked back again, she thought she saw a tear glide down Danu's reddened cheek. But then Danu snatched up the sweat towel and lowered her face. After rubbing her face briskly, Danu emerged from the terry cloth more composed. "But I'm working on an important project...," she began.

"Oh, don't even start that hoary marmot-shit," Kali impassively informed her, pulling her sweatshirt over her damp bodysuit. "It's been planned for weeks and you're not allowed to ruin it by being compulsive."

Styx broke into a soft, genial laugh.

To Tor, Kali remarked, "Whit tells me you've spent some of your hard-earned warrior's pay on a salvaged motorcycle."

Tor grinned and said, "A 2004 Harley low-rider. My legs aren't as long as Whit's. It only cost me two hundred Freeland dollars and," Tor teased, "a promise to the cycle dealer to bring you around to shop for your own retooled bike."

With a smile, Kali yanked on a pair of sweatpants. "Why ride solo when I can ride with Whit?" she returned archly, then informed Tor, "And by the way, you're in charge of bringing the guest of honor. Just so she doesn't forget all about our dinner party while she's tinkering on her computer." Still grinning, Kali donned her mountain parka, hoisted her backpack, and made for the door.

Tor turned toward Danu—just in time to catch Danu staring at her with an inscrutable expression. Abruptly, Danu's gaze slid away, and then she jumped to her feet.

"I told Lilith that I'd evaluate this afternoon's latest surveillance reports—finish some tests for her about the integrity of the satellite data," Danu announced. "I'm off to the Leader's House now." Yanking on her own sweatshirt, Danu smiled, "See you tonight, Styx." Facing Tor briefly, Danu managed, "Meet you back at the room later."

"Right," Tor replied, thinking, *She can barely speak to me, sometimes. Does she really dislike me so much?*

With a mumbled good-bye, Danu threw on her heavy jacket and made for the door, leaving Tor feeling as if she had missed something—something important. *But what?*

Danu jogged down Cammermeyer Street to the Leader's House, delighting in the light snow that had begun to fall. Watching the flakes melt on contact with the street, she idly wondered if the snow would stick later in the evening, when the temperature dropped. She passed a group of little girls running and laughing, their arms stretched up to the whirling flakes, capering with glee at this first snow. With a sigh, Danu turned her face upward and felt herself mimicking with her spirit what the children dared to do in body. Moments later, still entranced with the weather, she nearly tromped right over Marpe and Samsi as they hustled out of the Leader's House.

"If you're looking for Whit and Lilith, you've just missed them," Samsi informed her, tying a vibrant blue scarf over her thinning white hair.

"There's an emergency meeting at the Cedar House," Marpe added excitedly, buttoning her coat. "Council is called to session! We must fly."

"What's the emergency?" Danu asked.

"Something about the satellites," Marpe answered, scurrying away, linking her arm through Samsi's.

Danu closed the door behind them, wondering, *Is that why Lilith seemed so tense? Are the satellites failing?*

She continued to the Watch Room at the back of the building. Keying the lock with a touch of her hand, she entered, pulled off her jacket, and plopped wearily into the compu-chair. After running a succession of satellite-scan programs and jotting notations for Lilith's review later, she found herself yawning. The room was pleasantly warm and so quiet. Her head began to nod, and though she struggled to resist the torpor, she finally closed her eyes. *It's only around four. I can rest a minute*, she told herself.

When she raised her head again, her neck ached. Checking her wristcom, she jerked upright in the chair. *It's almost six! Damn! This was my chance to scrutinize a wealth of data in complete privacy and I've blown it!* She'd actually fallen asleep—dead asleep— and lost over two hours. Tor would be looking for her, ready to go within thirty minutes. *How can I do anything in so little time?!*

For a moment, Danu sank back in the compu-chair, feeling defeated and stupid. Then, determination and a cool anger took over. *I will* not *give up. I owe it to Lupa.*

With flying fingers, Danu began manually punching in coordinates, conducting her own random analysis of the report. Her tests thus far had proven that the satellite scans were inaccurate and essentially worthless. So, instead, she would rely on the film from the jetcraft. She selected the most recent hourly jetcraft fly-overs, specifically each section of the North Cascade area. Then she examined the films grid by grid.

This afternoon's cloud cover made the search almost pointless, yet she pressed on, a hunch nibbling at her, as she lingered over the jetcraft film taken just before the storm had moved into the mountains. As the camera panned over the western crest of the Cascades, near Hart's Pass, Danu saw what looked like a vague, gray discoloration. It was too localized to be a cloud—a cloud would have skidded briskly over that white surface on sheer force of wind. A cloud would not hover like that over one particular coordinate. Amazed,

Danu leaned forward and ran the film backward, then forward again, examining the distortion intently.

Not a cloud, but steam. As if someone were venting warmed air from underground.

Intrigued, Danu quickly keyed the computer, requesting a herstorical file search for all recorded real estate titles in that mountainous area. The search produced an "Authorized Personnel Only" barrier. Holding her breath, Danu immediately entered a high-security clearance code. The code was old, but effective, for she had seen Whit use it in September to gain entrance to a high-tech weapons storage facility at the old Naval Air Station on Whidbey Island. As Whit had gained access to stockpiles of hand-held rocket launchers, so Danu now received clearance to all the information she needed about this piece of mountain property. The wallscreen lit up like a meteor shower, and SAC Early Warning Site 1982 flashed its access code onscreen.

Great! A military outpost!

With a crow of victory, Danu jumped out of the chair and grabbed a chip from the wall shelf. Within moments she was recording map coordinates, geographical approach routes, base code-keys, and the locations of the doors to the underground station. Fifteen minutes later, she was jogging through the dark, on her way to the hostel, carrying in her jacket all the data she would need to track down and confront Arinna Sojourner.

Not for a second did she consider telling the others what she had discovered. For Danu, there was no alternative to what she was about to do. This was the moment she had been waiting for. Here was her chance to make Arinna pay for the life she had so viciously torn from Lupa Tagliaro. Danu had decided on this course of vengeance long ago, and nothing would sway her from it now.

And if I die doing this, Danu decided, *it's worth dying for. And better me than Kali.*

❖ ❖ ❖ ❖ ❖

A few hours later, after eating heartily, they were all gathered around the long pine table at Whit and Kali's house. A fire in the hearth and candles on the mantel cast a gentle yellow glow about the dining room, highlighting and shadowing a cast of familiar faces. While the snow still fell gently outside, melting as soon as it touched the ground, the women within the granite house were surrounded by empty plates and wine glasses, the remains of a delectable meal.

Sitting back in her chair, Styx watched the others around her. Whit was listening to Lilith's account of the damaged satellites, quietly inserting bits of information here and there, as Kali and Tor leaned forward, completely absorbed.

"Will the Border disintegrate, then?" Kali demanded, grasping the long-term results faster than the others.

She knows better than anyone in this room the horror enclosed behind that invisible shield, Styx reflected.

The others, Neith and Albie in particular, stopped their separate conversations and paid close attention as Whit replied.

"Several of Artemis's grain transports are currently in Lang, delivering harvest loads. We've contracted to have them return to Isis loaded with parts for a spacecraft and new satellites," Whit elaborated.

From the corner of her eye, Styx noticed Danu's almost hungry interest.

Rubbing her forehead thoughtfully, Lilith related, "We've sent out a call on the comline, which is currently being transmitted all over Freeland. We're asking for anyone with specializations in astrophysics, satellites, rocket propulsion, and so on, to report to Isis, immediately. The sooner we get started on building, the sooner we have a spacecraft."

"Once we assemble the ship," Whit went on, "and figure out how to mount an expanded version of Lilith's crystal drive component, we intend to penetrate the upper atmosphere and enter space. Then, we hope to replace the damaged satellites with new, more advanced units made from the NASA components our sisters in Lang found left in storage."

"That sounds like it will take a long time," Kali worried. "Will the Border hold?"

"We don't know," Lilith answered. "It may be too close to call."

"Of course," Whit noted, "Arinna did this on purpose—to split our focus and get us off her tail."

"I'm not giving up on Arinna," Kali muttered. "I still know where my priorities are."

Whit gave Kali a long-suffering look, which Kali met with a resolute stare. Then Styx noticed Danu watching Whit and Kali, her affection for them evident, before she smiled a private, and altogether self-satisfied smile and looked away.

Now what's she up to? Styx pondered. Leaning forward, she concentrated on trying to read Danu's thoughts and found only a swirl of white mist. Perplexed, Styx turned and looked out the window. *She's thinking about the weather? But there's no fog tonight—only a light snow....*

At the end of the table, Albie and Neith had slipped into silent, lighthearted conversation, signing rapidly, virtually ignoring Danu and everyone else.

If I didn't know better, I'd think Albie was Neith's main interest these past few weeks, Styx concluded, watching Neith's eyes linger on the young utility forewoman.

Danu seemed to have noticed the exclusive interaction of her friends, too, and looked sad. After comprehending that each would rather talk to the other than to her, Danu had withdrawn from the group in general, and talked only when spoken to directly.

Does she regret rejecting Neith? Styx wondered, then decided, *No.* Danu seemed to have something of great import on her mind, something that made Neith's attempts to make her jealous very small in comparison.

When Whit shut the lights off and Kali walked in with a birthday cake covered with candles, Danu only stared at it blankly, until the cake was placed before her.

"Oh, yeah," Danu mumbled, as if reorienting herself. Then, with a wary glance at Kali, Danu took a deep breath.

As the redhead leaned forward, preparing to blow, Tor asked insistently, "Did you make a wish?"

Danu stopped, pausing, staring at the eighteen dancing flames. Then she blew them all out in one long exhalation.

"What did you wish for?" Neith inquired, looking slightly smug.

Danu pretended she didn't hear.

A short time later, after the cake was eaten, Whit was shooing them all out, saying she was worried that the snow would begin to accumulate, as predicted. But all those who were not driving had had a few glasses of wine, and the significant glances had begun to snag and hold between Whit and Kali, Neith and Albie, even Lilith and Styx. Lustful looks were being cast about the dining room table, as if only one particular dessert were on anyone's mind. Styx knew that Whit's attempt to hustle them out had more to do with her passion for Kali than with any accumulating snowfall.

As they all bundled into coats and jackets, bidding Whit and Kali thanks and good night, Styx noticed Danu wistfully studying Tor. And as Lilith tried to insist that Tor leave her new motorcycle at Whit's and travel with the rest of them in the large transport vehicle, Styx interrupted.

"Let them be, Lil," she said softly. "There's hardly any snow down, yet. They'll be fine."

Amazed that Styx was opposing her, Lilith merely raised her eyebrows and headed out onto the porch.

A few minutes later, Styx saw them pass her in a swirl of white flakes. Tor was gripping the handlebars, confidently directing her bike, while Danu clung on behind her, leaning against Tor in a way that seemed to solidify everything Styx suspected.

Gaea, it feels so good to hold her, Danu realized, tucking her face behind Tor's shoulder, out of the blistering cold wind.

They passed the big, six-wheel-drive transport vehicle the others rode in, and were bathed in headlights for several moments as they moved in front. Then Tor accelerated and they flew down the country road, into darkness and dizzying bits of white, the cycle's own single headlight illuminating the way home. Danu clung to Tor's firm body, absorbing the bumps with her, leaning into the curves. Even through the thickness of a black leather jacket, the intimacy of the ride was compelling.

How will I ever keep her at a distance, now?

Whit closed the door behind her guests and turned to find Kali returning to the dining room, intent on cleaning up dishes. Impatiently, Whit sighed, and then followed her.

"Do you think Danu enjoyed herself?" Kali asked, looking disturbed. "Her mind seemed to be off somewhere else...." Thoughtfully, Kali began collecting dishes, stacking them at the end of the table, near the kitchen. Behind her, the hearth fire had settled into a small affair, cheery, yet not overly bright.

Savoring this ethereal view of her lover by firelight, Whit walked about the room slowly, blowing out candles. As she came round to Kali's side and blew out the last one, Kali chided her, "Whit—I can barely see what I'm doing now."

Without reply, Whit reached for Kali, and slipped an arm around her slim waist. Kali let go of the dish she held, and it rattled into place atop the pile. With a drowsy blink, Kali allowed herself to be drawn in closer, until their lips were brushing. And then Whit's hands were roaming, caressing the familiar contours.

Whit nuzzled Kali's long blonde hair, then nibbled at her sweet-smelling, silken neck. She felt her senses spinning. For her, the entire world had become the woman in her arms, the woman moving with her, in this dance of arousal. She moved her cheek against Kali's jaw, and at last Kali gave a small moan, turned her head, and took Whit's mouth with her own. The kiss began with a gentle hunger, then quickly swept Whit into a compelling urgency. Within moments they were clutching each other, their mouths supple and consuming.

When she finally was released from the long, delirious kiss, Whit implored, "Let's go upstairs."

Instead, Kali pushed her back against the table. A silhouette against the orange embers of the hearth, Kali ordered softly, "I want you here."

Stunned, Whit just stared at her, paralyzed by the jolt of excitement those words had delivered. Kali stepped closer. She deftly unbuttoned Whit's long white shirt, exposing skin to the fire's fading warmth. Her eyes seemed to glow as they passed over Whit. Slowly, deliberately, she unbuckled Whit's belt, opened the trouser fastenings, then smoothed her hand provocatively across Whit's lower belly. Whit shifted with the touch, helpless, as Kali's fingers trailed still lower. As she tried to straighten up, Kali made contact with her moist yoni, and Whit gasped.

"Mine," Kali whispered.

Her breath coming fast, her heart pounding within her chest, Whit dropped back, letting her hips rest against the table edge. Snaking a supportive arm around Whit's middle, Kali pushed her back farther, so that she was off balance. With a smile, Kali used her knee to move Whit's leg out, gaining more room to maneuver. A second later those long, strong fingers slipped tantalizingly over Whit's clitoris.

Kali murmured, "You don't want to *always* be in control of things, do you?"

Gasping, Whit attempted to embrace Kali.

"Put your hands on the table," Kali instructed, her voice quiet, yet uncompromising.

As Whit's hands fell back to support her, Kali slowly began playing her. A ferocious desire steadily surged through Whit, electrifying every cell in her body. As her head dropped back, Whit stiffened, surrendering even as she willed herself to resist. *I started this. How did I end up pinned against the table?*

Leading Whit into the rhythm, Kali teased her lover's body into a faster pace. "Do you like this?" Kali crooned.

Trying to answer, Whit broke into an extended groan of pleasure.

"Isn't it nice to let someone else...plan things...do things?" Kali asked.

Whit was beyond the ability to speak, arching to meet the fingers of the woman who was ruling her at this moment. Gracefully ardent, Kali leaned forward and alternately suckled each of Whit's nipples to life, leaving Whit trembling, rigid with increasing desire.

"Who's in charge, Tomyris?" Kali whispered in Whit's ear, quickening her stroke. "Tell me." Sensing Whit's readiness, Kali concentrated on finishing her.

Whit bellowed, coming over and over in huge waves of passion. And still Kali pushed her on, varying the tactics, ensnaring Whit with one form of lovemaking after another. And through it all, Whit remained pinned against the table, shuddering, plummeting helplessly into deeper, longer spasms of pleasure than she had ever known. Finally, she crumpled into Kali's arms, spent, and was helped to the polished wood of the dining room floor.

Whit watched drowsily as Kali moved about, tossing a few logs on the fire, then going away for a time. Lying there, in a languorous stupor, Whit felt herself drifting toward sleep. Then a thick quilt fell over her and Kali appeared above her.

"How do you feel, my love?" Kali asked quietly.

In answer, Whit reached up to her with one arm. Kali gave Whit her hand and sat down, Indian style, facing her. Taking a deep breath, Kali began, "You know I love you."

"Gaea, yes, but show me again," Whit joked softly.

Kali stared at her soberly, almost apprehensively. Whit frowned as she watched her lover struggling to assemble phrases, readying to make some sort of case.

"What is it, Kal?" *After that incredible seduction, how can anything be wrong?*

"We need to come to an agreement about our roles in Isis," Kali stated. "You are the elected Leader, and so you have power over the citizens of this colony." Brushing back her long, flaxen hair, Kali sighed. "But I am something else again, Whit. And you have no power over me."

Wide awake now, Whit scrambled to sit up. "I *never...*"

Kali gave a soft snort. "When Arinna Sojourner is found—and it will be soon—I'm sure you intend to overrule any decision I make about leaving Isis."

"That's not true!" Whit protested. "I'm willing to discuss it!"

With a slight touch of her finger to Whit's forehead, Kali reminded her, "I can hear what you don't say."

Abashed, after opening and closing her mouth with ridiculous, transparent rebuttals, Whit decided at last to stay silent.

"I'm no longer the frightened, confused woman you brought out of Elysium, Whit," Kali continued. "I've trained and prepared for this task. Sometimes I think I was born for it."

Suddenly terrified for her lover, Whit clenched her hands into fists and turned away from her. *Oh, please, please just stay here! She'll destroy you—tear you to pieces!*

"I can't stay here," Kali said soothingly. "I won't stand by, helpless, and watch my home and the people I love annihilated. Not again. If you love me, please don't ask me to do that, Whit."

The quiet was an ache between them, until Kali reached over and stroked Whit's face. "I propose that we make a bargain." She waited until Whit took a quavering breath and turned to face her. "I will leave all government and military decisions to you, my Warrior Chieftain. And you will leave all things of the psychic realm for me to deal with, because I am your Wiccan Mage."

With a heavy heart, Whit nodded, and Kali drew her into a loving embrace. They sat together before the crackling fire, feeling the magnetic flow of yin and yang between them.

And then, determined to demonstrate how much she treasured this precious woman, Whit drew her down beside her, and they began love's eternal dance.

6

Tor slowed the motorcycle to a stop in front of the hostel. Reluctantly, Danu hopped off, removed her helmet, then stood on the steps, uncertain about what to do next. Without a second look at her, Tor cruised the bike over to the large toolshed across the wet street. Through the swirling snowfall, Danu watched her dismount, swing open the wide, pine-board door, then push the cycle into the darker reaches of the shelter. In a minute she reemerged with the black helmet tucked under her arm, and came walking, head down, back toward Danu. When she lifted her head and saw Danu waiting for her on the steps, her look of surprise was unmistakable.

Of course she's surprised, Danu chastised herself. *I haven't once waited for her in all the time we've roomed together. Guess I've been running from her for weeks.*

As Tor came up to her, into the full light of the porch lamp, they fell in step together and mounted the stairs. Danu watched the heavy braid swing across Tor's back, watched the confident gait of a body well-honed. Her black jacket emphasized Tor's strong shoulders, and the loose brown trousers still managed to give the impression of slim hips and firm thighs. But it was her face that captivated Danu. Tor's smooth, high cheeks were ruddy from the bracing ride; her normally shielded midnight eyes were haunted by some unspoken trouble.

As she gazed at her, wondering what was on her mind, Danu had a revelation. *Why, in Gaea's name, have I been running from this woman? She's beautiful.* For once, not restraining the desire to gaze at her, Danu sighed.

She had not initially thought that Tor was beautiful, but that was before she had gotten to know the thoughtful and affectionate nature that lived beneath Tor's tough demeanor. Somehow, during these past weeks of sharing a room, Tor had gotten beyond Danu's many defenses and entered her heart.

Why did I take so long to admit this to myself? Danu thought, her spirit heavy with a strange discomfort. *I've probably lost my chance.*

As they passed through the front door and headed toward their wing, a continuous throng of women brushed by them, all of them laughing and bantering with friends. It was Saturday night, the first snow was falling, and everyone in the hostel was on her way somewhere. The sound of booted feet thundered up and down the stairs that rose through the center of the three-story structure. Loud music and boisterous conversations flowed from the open doors of rooms they passed.

Looking rather bleak, Tor brushed the DNA plate before their door with her hand. Seconds later, she pushed the door open, leading the way inside. She tossed the helmet onto her bed, pulled off her leather jacket, then turned to face Danu.

After Danu closed the door behind her, she leaned against it and met Tor's eyes.

"Are you all right?" Tor asked.

Danu frowned, looked down, and thought, *Yeah, for someone with a hole in her head, I'm just fine.* Feeling incredibly self-conscious, she placed the helmet Tor had lent her on a bookshelf by the door.

"You hardly said a word at Whit and Kali's," Tor persisted. "You acted as if you were just barely enduring the small fuss they made over you."

Restless under Tor's steady scrutiny, Danu moved toward her, not exactly sure what she was going to do, but certain all at once that she wanted to try to do *something* with this woman.

How can I tell her that I just spent half the night trying not to think about what I'll be doing as soon as she goes to sleep? Danu wondered anxiously. *Keeping my plans from both Kali and Styx took every ounce of concentration I had.* Aloud, Danu mumbled, "Um...I've got a lot on my mind lately."

Slowly, Tor reached out, and in a gesture of infinite comfort, stroked Danu's cheek. Reeling beneath that delicate caress, feeling a warmth tingling all through her body, Danu momentarily closed her eyes.

When she opened them again, Tor was shoving an arm in her jacket. "I've got to go," Tor muttered, heading for the door.

Do something! Danu told herself. *Don't let her leave!*

In two quick steps, Danu had her by the arm, spinning her around. Amazed, Tor glanced from Danu's hand to her face.

"Don't I get a birthday kiss?" Danu improvised awkwardly.

A kaleidoscope of emotions crossed Tor's face, one after another—relief, delight, trepidation, confusion. At last, they both stared at each other, slightly overwhelmed at the suddenness of this development. And then, Tor stepped forward and placed a chaste kiss on Danu's cheek.

Just as Tor was about to retreat, Danu's hands caught the smaller woman's shoulders. Slowly, Danu leaned down, grazing her lips across Tor's. It was a light exchange, that began and ended, and then began again on another level. Feeling incredibly reckless, Danu really kissed her this time. A tiny, helpless noise escaped from deep in Tor's throat. Almost without conscious thought, Danu felt them gradually enfolding one another, and still the kiss went on, imperceptibly melting boundaries in a wave of heat.

When they finally parted, Tor took several deep breaths, shook her head, and then moved away from Danu, back into the center of the room. There was an odd, almost incredulous, expression on her face.

Did I overstep myself—do something wrong? Danu fretted.

Tor was taking off her jacket, her eyes studying Danu as if she were some complex puzzle. "Are you sure you want me?" Tor asked, her voice very low.

"Yes," Danu breathed. "Very much."

Casually, Tor draped her jacket over the back of the desk chair. "I saw Neith's chase and thought..."

"This is different," Danu interrupted.

"Different now," Tor remarked, "but maybe not so different later." Then with a shrug, Tor concluded, "No matter." She ran her eyes over Danu, responding to what she saw with a look that made the hair rise up on Danu's neck.

Tor suggested, "Why don't you take your jacket off?" With a slight smile, she teased, "You *are* staying, aren't you?"

In a wink, Danu yanked the jacket off and flung it on her bunk.

Decisively, Tor began unbuttoning the red-and-black-plaid flannel shirt she wore.

Danu felt her heart jolt into a pounding pace.

"I decided long ago," Tor announced, "that you were ready for loving, but not for love." She peeled off the flannel and revealed the thin shoulder straps of a snug undershirt.

Danu's mouth went dry.

Tor stated sensibly, "It's all part of Gaea's plan. The body hungers, even when the heart does not." And then, as she placed a boot on the edge of the chair and leaned over to untie the laces, her eyes flashed up at Danu with a poignant wariness that caused Danu to doubt Tor's apparent sophistication.

Methodically, Tor pulled off her boots, then removed the hidden holster and laser pistol from the back of her brown pants. After tucking the pistol into a desk drawer, she sat on the bed and began undoing her belt.

"Aren't you going to help me with any of this?" she joked, but the chuckle that followed had a distinctly nervous quality.

Feeling as if she were dreaming, Danu went to the bed and sat down beside her. Suddenly, all she wanted to do was get her hands into the shining, ebony mane that had tantalized her each morning and evening, as Tor brushed it. Fumbling with the small red ribbon at the end of the long, thick braid, Danu realized that her hands were shaking.

Tor laughed, "You're knotting my hair." Then she directed firmly, "Try something else."

Mesmerized, Danu found herself gazing at the smooth biceps and triceps in Tor's arms as she began unbraiding the long black braid. Then she noticed apple-sized mounds beneath the tight black undershirt. Her pulse quickening, Danu slipped her hands over the cotton material, pulling the shirt out of Tor's trousers.

The softness of Tor's skin was a shock—a visceral shock—that started something akin to a primal, instinctive glowing in Danu. Her fingertips moved slowly, compulsively over Tor, barely touching. Following the natural contours of Tor's body, she traveled over back and shoulders, over ribs and breasts and belly, feeling the rock-hard muscle beneath that warm, velvet skin tensing in reaction. All Danu knew was that she was starving for this—starving for a sensation she had not known existed. She just couldn't stop touching her.

She was undoing Tor's pants, leaning closer to her, wanting more, when she noticed that Tor's hair was loose about her face, flowing down her back. Tor was sitting there, trembling, her eyes heavy with desire, her hands gripping the bed covers.

"Oh Mother," Tor whispered. "I knew you'd be like this."

From there it seemed incredibly easy to just ease back onto the bed, pulling Tor down with her. She pressed her fully clothed body into that provocative black undershirt and those partially opened pants, and it made her wild.

And then they were kissing passionately, their hands coursing everywhere. Danu's elbow banged into Tor's motorcycle helmet and she shoved it aside, then heard it thump onto the wooden floor. They rolled back and forth on the bed, each one intent on topping the other, each one seizing the thrill of potential conquest and then abruptly exchanging it for the delectable delights of surrender.

All at once, Tor broke free and slipped off the bed. "Get naked, Danu," she ordered, breathing hard. And then she was shucking off clothes, and turning on her audio chip player, and lighting a candle—all in quick succession.

When Danu wasn't fast enough for her, Tor grabbed Danu's boots and yanked them off, then followed that by removing Danu's trousers with an authoritative tug. As Danu shivered, both with cold and anticipation, she allowed herself to fully see the nude woman before her. She had been turning away from Tor for so long, trying not to notice that splendid body as it changed clothing before her eyes each day. Now that she dared to look, she couldn't seem to tear her eyes away.

Dreamily, it registered in Danu's brain that a Mahler symphony was playing. Tor lay down next to her on the bed, snuggling closer, while they both laughed with nervous excitement. Then, in a heart-stoppingly sudden move, Tor was climbing on top of her, gliding a thigh between her legs and parting them.

Gasping, Danu couldn't believe how soft this hard-muscled woman was. She felt Tor's hands moving all over her, guiding her into a realm of sexual hunger that Danu had never experienced. Skillfully, Tor was fingering her nipples, caressing her from neck to yoni. Slowly, repeatedly, Danu was compelled to moan and squirm, as Tor's feverish body snaked over her. She felt the universe coiling up in her loins, and she shuddered with need. All the while, Tor was speaking to her, though as her senses went crazy, Danu couldn't for the life of her figure out what she was saying.

At last, as Danu's confusion registered on her, Tor stilled her constantly moving body and repeated, "This is your first time—am I right?"

With a shaky sigh, Danu managed, "Am I that b-bad?"

Grinning, Tor assured her, "No, you're great. A quick study—as in everything."

Danu swallowed hard, then ventured, "It doesn't bother you—the fact that I'm Think Tank?"

Laughing, Tor gave her a solid hug and said, "I love it!" Then, in a burst of exuberance, she went on, "I love..."

She never finished the statement. Instead, she just leaned lower, first brushing Danu's nose with her own, and then ardently initiating another kiss. It was only hours later, when Danu had time to replay, endlessly replay, these electrifying moments with Tor, that she remembered the broken-off quality of that statement and began speculating about what Tor had been about to say.

When Danu could barely endure one more scintillating moment of foreplay, Tor embraced her and moved into a purposeful rhythm. Instinctively, Danu gripped Tor the same way, her fingers digging into Tor's glutes, as Tor rocked faster. Dimly, Danu was aware of the wetness Tor was leaving with each thrust against her thigh. She was aware and amazed at her own body—which was arching and tightening—seemingly knowing exactly what it needed and how to get it. She felt a brief flush of triumph as she heard Tor's soft, helpless moans. And then all rational thought ended, simply overpowered by sheer sensation.

A towering wave of feeling rose, catching her, engulfing her. It radiated from where her clitoris met Tor's insistent leg, pushing outward into every fiber of her being. For a time all she could do was grasp Tor and ride absolute ecstasy.

At last, as the last sizzle flared through newly awakened nerve endings, she curled into Tor, feeling an exquisite vulnerability. She was raw with emotion, utterly defenseless, adrift in a euphoria of deep, unacknowledged feelings for the lover in her arms. Tor lay upon her, limp and perspiring.

This was not the relentless pressure, the inescapable sense of unfulfilled expectations that she had felt from Neith. There was at once a spontaneity and a fated quality to this lovemaking with Tor. And for the first time in months, Danu felt wondrously happy.

I can't believe I almost chose to forego this. How could I have been so dense?

Tor began kissing her again—kisses which seemed half an expression of thanks and half a demand for more lovemaking. And Tor was deliciously demanding. Within minutes, she was giving irresistible attention to those areas of Danu's flesh that seemed to crave being touched. Danu's usually rational mind had no chance to analyze or contemplate further. Tor's kisses were hot, Tor's hands were knowledgeable, and Danu found herself being led into another ecstatic round of lovemaking.

Quickly, passion overwhelmed Danu. Only this time, Tor seemed intent upon mimetic instruction. As she teased and enthralled Danu with one erotic revelation after another, she encouraged Danu to repeat the lesson on her. Soon they were on the brink of orgasm, moaning and pressing against each other in a hungry desire for completion.

And then, all at once, Tor flopped on her back and gave herself up to Danu, her face trustful and flushed with want. Wide-eyed, Danu savored the entire experience—watching as Tor quivered under her unrelenting strokes, arching, mindless with need. When Tor came, Danu knew that those moans of pleasure would be associated in her memory forever with sexual power.

And as Danu smiled and cuddled closer, Tor hugged her, nuzzled her neck, and kissed her softly all over her face. Danu suddenly realized that she was being seduced again, but she was not clear on when the cuddling had turned to fondling, or when nuzzling had turned into a series of small, electrifying bites along her neck. One moment she was relaxed and satiated, lying in Tor's arms, the next she was whimpering beneath Tor, completely on fire. Only this time, as Tor cleaved her open, the vulnerability Danu had felt earlier ambushed her. All her emotional defenses unraveled, and inexplicably, she was crying. A jumble of deeply buried feelings fought their way to the surface.

Tenderly, Tor gathered Danu close, murmuring, "Let go, girl—let it out."

And let go she did. Danu cried all the tears of grief and rage and loneliness that she had been stoically storing within her for months. She cried for Lupa, and she cried for herself. And finally, at the very end, she cried for Tor, because she already half-suspected that this was the woman she had been unconsciously searching for, the woman she could love. And now, the woman she would have to leave.

Lying in Tor's sheltering embrace, exhausted, she fell into a light sleep. A short time later when she woke, the candle was much smaller. For a moment, Danu stayed there, noting how her body had nestled into Tor's. They were like two puppies of the same litter, comfortable in the most ungainly positions, as long as they were touching.

I don't want to leave her, Danu realized, *but I've got to.*

For a bit, she allowed herself to entertain what a future with Tor could mean, but then, through her love-fogged brain, duty reasserted itself. She remembered the bitter vow she had made on Lupa's grave, the vow to track down Arinna Sojourner and make her pay dearly for her treachery and betrayal.

With care, she slid from Tor's arms and watched Tor moan and burrow deeper under the covers. *So beautiful*, Danu thought, then forced herself to move away, and concentrate instead on the plan she had made months ago.

Very quietly, she gathered the mountaineering clothes she had stored in the foot locker by her bed. She dressed herself in the thermal underclothes, water- and wind-resistant trousers, and a heavy wool sweater. Soon she finished tying her boots and went to stand by Tor, gazing longingly at her sleeping form.

"I think I love you, Tor," she whispered, aching to hold Tamatori one last time.

Instead, with her eyes on the sleeping woman, she went to Tor's desk drawer and removed the laser pistol. As she slid her own belt through the holster and cinched the weapon around her waist, Danu watched Tor, half-hoping that the soft, rustling noise would wake her. "I'm borrowing it," she whispered a compulsive explanation, although Tor would never consciously hear it. "I need something of yours—for luck."

Grimly, before she could weaken completely and change her mind, Danu grabbed up her alpine parka and stole noiselessly across the room and out the door. It was nearly three in the morning, now, and most everyone was in bed. The corridors and staircases were empty and the silence overwhelming. There were no curious women to ask where she was headed at this hour. She pushed open the exit door and hurried down the porch steps, only to discover that the storm was still blowing strong and a foot of snow had drifted against the building. She pulled the hood of her parka over her head as she looked up and down the street.

A big transport vehicle with a plow mounted on the front was scraping a path down the street. Hoping to make up for lost time and avoid the sentry patrols, Danu flagged down the driver and asked for a ride to the airfield. The young warrior in the cab was an acquaintance from the past summer, a former member of Albie's utility crew. She waved Danu aboard, and they engaged in a companionable chat about the loveliness of this first snow before Danu fell into a troubled reverie.

What's the matter with me? she wondered.

After all, she was more than ready for this. Long ago, she had stashed a backpack and additional supplies in a hangar locker at the airfield. In her trouser pocket, she had the secretly copied map coordinates and everything the Watch Room computer could give her regarding the classified details of the SAC outpost. And she knew Whit's brand new Swallow was fully fueled and parked in Hangar 3— she had checked on that important detail only yesterday. So what was wrong?

This is what I wanted. Why do I feel so awful?

Slowly, it came to her. In the terrible, crushing despair that had followed Lupa's death, she had found something in life worth dying for. But now, leaving Tor and that soul-shattering experience of love behind her, she realized that she had found something in life worth living for, as well.

What am I doing? I might not make it back from this.

The snowplow stopped before Hangar 3 and the young warrior commented, "Lieutenant Iphito said the airfield was closed until the worst of the storm passes."

"I'm just here to get a look at that prefabricated warehouse Whit ordered set up for the NASA spaceship," Danu replied, amazed at how easily the lie tripped off her tongue.

"In the middle of the night?" the plow driver asked incredulously. "In a blinding snowstorm?"

Immediately conscience-stricken, Danu could only blush.

Observing her, the driver laughed and stated, "I'll bet there's a woman in this mystery. You're meeting someone here, right?"

Shrugging, Danu avoided her eyes.

"Well, watch out for the sentries," the warrior counseled. "Since that spooky appearance Arinna Sojourner made at the All Hallows' Eve Ball, Commander Whitaker has put the airfield under heavy guard. Must be at least twenty sentries out here tonight. Don't let 'em catch you here."

With a sincere thank-you, Danu hopped down from the cab, then waved as the young warrior drove the big truck on, into the dizzying curtain of flakes. After a surreptitious glance around, Danu ignored the prefab nearby, and instead advanced on the aluminum-sided hangar with the number three painted boldly on its side.

A short time later, she collected her survival gear, backpack, and laser rifle from the hangar locker. She placed her synlight on the shelf of the locker, adjusted the light beam, and searched the bottom of her backpack for a small plastic case. It contained her newly designed wristcom, the weapon that would put an end to Arinna Sojourner and her campaign of terror. *With Gaia's help, my plan will work. All I need is to get close enough to her and block my thoughts.* Taking the deadly wristcom from the clear case, she set it, did a radio check, and adjusted several radio frequencies on it. *So far, so good. Now for the beam.* Pleased with her work, she strapped the wristcom to her left wrist, aimed it at a waste bin a few meters away, and pressed a newly added key above the reset switch. A fine beam of red light burst forth from a small opening on the outer rim of the wristcom. *Good*, she thought. Danu made another final adjustment for amplitude and frequency, and then aimed the harmless-looking wrist communicator at a metal storage cabinet against the wall. Instantly, a two-centimeter hole appeared in the door of the cabinet. Danu smiled. *I'll get you, Arinna.* She switched the safety toggle, and patted her new weapon. *The wonders of nanotechnology,* she mused, shaking her head.

Slinging her backpack and rifle over her shoulder, Danu picked up the synlight and quickly transferred her supplies to the Swallow, which sat in the center of the hangar. Her synlight beam explored the sidewall, searching for the overhead-door switch. As she opened the doors, she prayed the howling wind would mask the sound of them being opened. Then, quickly, she climbed aboard the Swallow and fastened her gear in place, making sure it was secure enough for even the roughest flight. Hurriedly, she closed the hatch, locking it. And moments later, she was settled into the flight chair, running a preflight systems check—ready for takeoff.

So far, so good, she thought, not believing her luck.

Danu had just learned to fly the craft in September, during one of Whit's successful attempts to break through the depression she had fallen into after Lupa's murder. And though Danu knew her skills as a pilot were limited at best, she felt she knew enough to accomplish her mission—to search for and destroy Arinna Sojourner.

Cloaked in darkness, the Swallow rolled through the open doors of Hangar 3 and onto the barren, snowswept tarmac. Through the expansive Plexiglas cockpit, Danu spotted the silhouetted figures of two warriors marching through the blizzard on the far side of the airfield. As the Swallow entered the yellow pool of light cast by a tall security light, one of the sentries noticed the reflective gleam on the metal wing of the craft, and turned to look. Danu abruptly ended taxi-mode and pulled back the vertical-lift lever. Rotors located in the center of each wing swiftly lifted the aircraft off the ground.

Grabbing her companion's arm, the surprised sentry watched the tilt-rotor lift straight upward into the blizzard engulfing Isis. Then, quickly, Danu shifted the power from the wing rotors to the forward-thrust engines. The sentries watched the Swallow soar into the storm and disappear as one of them activated her wristcom and called the command post.

An hour and seventeen minutes later, Danu was flying the Swallow over the great peaks of the North Cascade Mountain Range. She had activated the radar-blocking shields as soon as she'd left Isis, and knew her craft was beyond monitoring by both Lilith's highly sophisticated Watch Room scanners, and whatever SAC devices Arinna had managed to restore in her mountain outpost. No one in Isis would know where she had gone, and no one within the underground SAC installation would know she was coming.

Unless Arinna's psychic powers have advanced to the point where she can actually sense me arriving....

Apprehensively, Danu swallowed. This part of the plan had always been a calculated risk. Her strategy was simple: All she needed was to get close enough to Arinna, and carefully aim her new microlaser at her. The tricky part would be keeping her secret from Arinna. *If I can blank my mind with a wall of snow, as I did at the dinner party, I should be okay. Oh, Mother of the Universe, help me,* she thought, fearfully. *Just one good shot—that's all. Just one good blast.*

Checking her wristcom and running her index finger over it, Danu prayed, *Please, don't let her sense me....*

Between the blinding storm and the darkness of the night, Danu was relying completely on her aircraft's three-dimensional radar system. Anxiously, she sweated over the controls, concentrating on her approach to Hart's Pass. As she lined up her map coordinates with the onscreen grid, she leaned forward momentarily to peer through the window of the curved Plexiglas cockpit. She shifted power to the vertical rotors and was now hovering approximately two kilometers above her landing site—a small snowfield, a half kilometer or so from a rear entrance to the SAC installation. At least that was what the old U.S. military records indicated.

Suddenly, a flash of bright blue light caught her attention and caused her to look down at the earth below. What appeared to be a streak of lightning—blue lightning—arced upward from Hart's Pass below, heading directly for her aircraft. With a shuddering, explosive blast, the bolt of pure energy hit, engulfing the Swallow, hurling it sideways and pinning Danu against her flight chair. She heard a rush of wind and fought to stabilize the craft. The rotor on the left wing wouldn't respond, and the right-wing rotors were frozen halfway between the vertical and forward-thrust positions. Still, for a few minutes, the winged craft was buoyed on a mountain wind, while Danu struggled to keep it aloft and control the descent. Suddenly, the craft started to spin. All at once, the Swallow was out of control, plummeting toward the snow-covered mountains below.

Seconds later, and without much warning, the aircraft slammed hard into a bank of snow. Danu, still strapped into her flight chair, was knocked insensible. The Swallow lay in snowbound quietude. Except for the restless, howling night wind, nothing moved.

Gradually, Danu regained consciousness, opened her eyes, and glanced around the cabin, incredulous that she was still alive, or at least she thought she was still alive. Moving each of her legs, one at a time, and then her arms, she concluded that nothing was broken. Inside the Swallow, the orange emergency light still glowed, showing the jumble of her carefully packed supplies scattered all around. Before her, the Plexiglas front was riddled with impact cracks, but had proven its strength of design by not shattering. As she shook off her confusion, a surge of panic raced through her. She struggled to push up the left sleeve of her parka and prayed her wristcom was intact and the microlaser unharmed. Suddenly, the aircraft moved and she noticed that the craft was listing. *I'd better assess the damage and get moving*, she thought. Carefully, she released her flight harness and clambered across scattered survival gear. Trying to still her trembling hands, she gathered her gear and checked her rifle and sidearm. Suddenly, she remembered the fuel supply and began sniffing the air for methane gas or smoke. *None. Great, my luck is holding, thanks to Gaea's small kindnesses,* she thought.

She found her synlight intact, dropped it into her parka pocket, and spent the next several minutes shoving her shoulder into the door hatch, until the hatch gave way and swung open. She hesitated, then sat down on the lip of the door frame and put on the snowshoes she had brought along. There was no sense in getting herself immobilized in an impossibly deep snowdrift before she could even figure out where she was. She jumped from the aircraft into the dry powder below, sank a bit, then was able to clumsily tread across a surface that glowed even in the dim, overcast night. She took out her synlight, switched on the broad-beam setting, and aimed the beam at the wrecked craft. As she was buffeted by the gusting wind and the constant spray of white, Danu squinted at the dark lump embedded in an enormous mound of snow. After she took inventory of the damage, Danu wondered how she'd survived the blast, no less the crash.

Whatever had hit the left wing had left only a charred, melted stub where the rotor had once been mounted. The fuselage of the visible left side displayed long, scorched lines. What damage the right side of the craft had sustained—and Danu had no doubt that it was major—was hidden in the snowbank. It was only the considerable depth and softness of this snowbank that had saved the Swallow from total destruction. She circled the craft, searching for signs of a fuel leakage, and was relieved to find none.

It then dawned on Danu, *I crashed Whit's Swallow.* Worried and feeling oddly dazed, she thought, *If Arinna doesn't kill me, Whit surely will.* And then she paused and remembered the cause of the wreck. *Lightning? Has Arinna constructed some deadly new weapon?*

With a sigh, Danu pulled her compass out of her parka pocket. She spent a moment fiddling with the illuminated display, methodically getting her bearings. What little light was available from the pale moon was amplified by the reflecting capabilities of the snow all around. She pointed the compass toward the small, dark, snow-covered shapes in the distance, and realized she was on the edge of a pine forest. Snowshoeing over the drift, across the ledge the Swallow was perched upon, she reached the wall of a huge cliff face. There she discovered a narrow, flat ledge leading upward, climbing along the side of the mountain.

This looks like a trail, Danu decided, then shivered as a cold blast of wind suddenly shot through her. Abruptly, she pocketed the compass.

As she snowshoed over deep snow, heading back to her craft, she calculated the last coordinates she had seen on the map panel, just before the crash. If her estimation was accurate, the lightning—or whatever—had caused her Swallow to veer about thirty-two kilometers east of Hart's Pass. And that meant that what she had found was an old wagon road, a passage that was once used by gold prospectors crossing the spine of the Cascades, over two centuries ago.

Her thoughts were interrupted by a mournful howl in the distance. Danu's head snapped up and she stared out into the darkness that stretched beyond this small ledge of white.

Wolves, Danu thought, as her heart began pounding. *I never thought there'd be wolves.* Anxiously, she laid her mittened hand upon the lump at her waist, where Tor's laser pistol was holstered beneath her parka. Reassured, she tried to keep her wits about her as she hurried back to the aircraft.

I'll just have to get myself out of this fix, Danu decided, as she approached the craft that would probably never fly again. *Guess I'll have to hike up the mountain on that old wagon trail. It should only take me a day or so, and I've got plenty of survival rations on board....*

Another howl, much closer this time, split the rush of wind.

With bounding steps, Danu plunged into the deep drift by her Swallow and hauled herself through the door, up into the aircraft. She undid her snowshoes and placed them aside, then quickly shut the door on the cold, snowy night, deciding to shelter within the craft, since there wasn't much she could do in the dark. Trying to maintain her composure, Danu set about checking the Swallow's various systems, including communications. Nothing was operational. She felt very alone and frightened. Gratefully, she remembering the emergency backup batteries. She threw the switch, hoping they had not been damaged, too. She waited. Nothing. She turned the switch off and then on again. This time the environmental-control system kicked in, with a comforting hum. Relieved for the moment, Danu turned up the heat in the cabin, estimating she would have relative warmth for a few hours, if she conserved battery usage. She unrolled her thermal sleeping bag, climbed in, and set its internal heat unit to a comfortable level. She checked her wristcom for the time, and set the alarm. *I'll rest until first light, and then start up the mountain to Hart's Pass. Just a couple of hours sleep, and I'll be ready for Arinna Sojourner.*

For a while, she lay there, tense with fear, trying not to focus on the series of howls that penetrated the walls of the aircraft. She found herself thinking of Tor, reliving their lovemaking as body memory pushed through her anxiety. Within seconds, desire had resurfaced and claimed her. In a haze of remembrance, Danu gradually relaxed and contemplated what had happened between them. And then she recalled that phrase, "I love...," and the passionate kiss that had followed.

What did she mean? Danu wondered, torn by both hope and despair, suspecting that she already knew very well what Tor had meant.

When she at last slept, it was not very well.

The previous night's blizzard was long gone now, and even with sunshades on, Danu was squinting against the sun's reflection on the snow all around her.

To her right, the cliff rose in a straight, striped, gray-and-ocher-colored wall. To her left, was the edge of the trail, and a 1,000-meter drop. In the valley below, a forest of blue spruce trees stood, covered with snow. Danu surveyed the magnificent valley, thinking that the tall trees looked like cutout cookies on a huge sheet, covered with icing. It reminded her of the cookies her mother used to make for Winter Solstice each year.

I never even said good-bye to Mother, she thought regretfully.

Distracted by that thought, Danu stumbled as she swung her snowshoe forward. Quickly, she righted herself and glanced nervously at the cliff. The trail was approximately two and a half meters across, and with the heat of the afternoon sun, the surface was becoming slippery and treacherous. Unused to snowshoes, she had already fallen several times, and her cheeks bore ice abrasions to prove it. Though she had taken off her parka earlier and strapped it across the top of her pack, she was sweating profusely. The laborious trek up the mountain trail and the hot afternoon sun were sapping her strength.

Thirsty, she stopped, unclipped her canteen, and took a long drink. As she returned the canteen to her belt, her eyes swept over the pristine vista before her. Beyond the snowy, blue-green spruce forest, great canyon walls rose. In the distance, perpendicular to the canyon, several magnificent jagged and glaciered peaks jutted up sharply against a blue sky.

Tor would love this place, she thought. *Maybe when this is all over....* She stopped her daydream right there, and made her tired legs go forward again. It was ridiculous to think that she could ever successfully take on Arinna Sojourner and escape alive, so it would do her no good to fantasize about what she might one day do with Tor at her side. *I should just be grateful to have known her, to have rolled in the sheets with a woman like that in my arms.*

Disheartened, yet determined, she methodically lifted her feet, carefully placing the snowshoes upon the slippery surface of slush. This was not going to be easy.

After she had been plodding along for hours, she noted a sharp drop in the temperature. She stopped and unstrapped her parka, pulling it on again. When she lifted the pack and laser rifle once more to her shoulders, the weight seemed nearly unbearable. Breathing deeply, using the Zen exercises Tor had taught her, she continued upward along the icy trail. It seemed only a short time later, though her wristcom indicated it was actually over two hours, when she noticed that the position of the sun seemed to have changed radically. It had dropped toward the line of western mountains more quickly than she could believe possible. In a moment of panic, she realized she had barely a half hour of daylight left before total darkness descended. Ahead, the steady incline of trail was leading onto a small plateau. A windswept field stretched off to her right, a field with barely a surface dusting of snow. Beyond, a small forest of trees clustered at the foot of a mountain.

I'll camp here, Danu decided. *It looks safe back there near the woods.*

Much later, in the darkness of her small alpine tent, Danu awoke. Even beneath the cover of the scrubby pine forest all around her, she could feel the fierce wind cutting into her. She was buried deep within her thermal bag, with the heating unit on high, and she still couldn't get warm, even with her parka and boots on. Outside the tent, the wind sang a constant song through the evergreens and hurled bits of icy debris against the side of the tent. But that wasn't what had woken her—she was sure of it.

She strained to hear the night sounds. Then she heard it again—the other noise. Something large was thrashing wildly through the trees nearby. Branches were cracking, and a low, snarling sound was reverberating through the night. Straining her ears, Danu unfastened her thermal bag, ready to go out and investigate. But the wind shifted, and the noise was gone, lost in a rush of air across many-needled boughs. She lay there, stone still, a moment longer, uncertain.

All at once there was a deafening roar. Danu scrambled out of the thermal bag, just in time. Something ripped into the tent above her and her shelter was transformed into two flapping rags caught uselessly on thin aluminum poles. That same roaring whatever-it-was grabbed the end of the thermal bag, just as Danu had wriggled free of it.

Crawling frantically across the frosty stubble of grass, terrified, Danu glanced behind her and saw only a massive shadow shape against the pine trees. It was busily ripping her thermal bag to shreds, then tearing into her backpack. As she leapt to her feet and began to run, she glanced back again and saw the creature rise on its hind legs, beating her rifle into the frozen, rock-hard ground and then flinging the broken pieces into the night.

It's destroying the laser rifle, she thought, flabbergasted for a moment. And then, as the huge, inky creature pivoted toward her, against the bright spray of stars in the cold night sky, Danu recognized her attacker. *A grizzly!* She screamed into the darkness.

Running for her life, Danu made for a big ponderosa pine near the cliff's edge, with the grizzly lumbering behind her, giving chase. Rapidly, she climbed up the lower branches, out of reach. When she got to a fork in the tree about seven meters above ground, she brushed off the snow in the natural saddle and sat down. Undaunted, the beast began trying to make the same ascent, but the branches which had held Danu broke and snapped off beneath the bear, tumbling him to the ground. Enraged, the grizzly tore into the tree, sending large chunks of bark, and any limb within reach, to the ground. After this tantrum, the bear went into a long period of restless pacing. Every once in a while, it would rise up, reach for Danu, and roar in apparent frustration.

But Danu had already realized by then that there was another danger—she was freezing. Although she'd been sitting there in the cold, harsh wind for only a few minutes, she already had chattering teeth, a numb nose, and icy cheeks. *If I stay up here much longer, I'll never get Arinna*, she cautioned herself. *Blast this damn bear and be done with it.*

All of a sudden she remembered Tor's pistol strapped to her waist. "What a fool I am. Some warrior, I can't even remember I have a pistol," she said out loud. She reached for the pistol in her holster, all the while griping to the grizzly, "Why, in Gaea's sweet name, aren't you hibernating, bear?"

In answer, the huge grizzly grabbed the trunk below her and shook the tree with all his formidable might. Caught off guard, Danu nearly slipped from her perch, and just barely managed to hang on and ride out the animal's wrath. But as she stared down at him, badly frightened, she got a good look at the grizzly's eyes. Shocked, she found herself staring into a flat, passionless darkness. A void. It nudged some memory in her, and without explanation, an intuitive response rose to the surface of her awareness.

Arinna....

And then she knew that Arinna was using this bear, as Arinna had once used Danu herself in another attack, on another unsuspecting victim, in the meal hall last summer.

When the grizzly let go and went back to pacing, Danu slipped off her mittens and pulled out Tor's weapon. Quickly, she set the laser pistol to mid-range power, adjusting the barrel so that the beam would be dispersed in one hard, but blunt, blow. She didn't want to kill one of Gaea's creations, just knock him out long enough for her to get out of the area. As the bear rose up, snarling, then shaking the tree again, Danu took aim and fired. In a dazzling burst of white light, the animal whimpered and rolled onto its side.

She placed her weapon in its holster and waited a moment, just to be safe, then stiffly climbed down from the tree. She had to leap the last three meters, because all the lower branches were now torn off the tree. Taking the synlight out of her parka pocket and activating it, she skirted around the unconscious bear, and began to make her way back to the ruined campsite.

The bright beam from her synlight helped her assess the damage to her campsite and gear. She packed up what few supplies the bear had not ravaged, then grabbed her snowshoes. As soon as she tried to put them on, she saw the left one was damaged. Glancing repeatedly, anxiously over her shoulder at the still lump of fur barely thirty meters away, Danu quickly improvised by using the tent lacings to make the repair. After all, she wouldn't be using this tent again, or most of the freeze-dried food packets that had been ripped open by sharp claws. The thermal sleeping bag lay two meters away, ripped to pieces, heating-element wires sticking every which way, thoroughly emptied of its lifesaving insulation. She could not sleep now without the risk of never waking up again.

For a few minutes, she merely sat there, dumbfounded, buffeted by the cold wind. Then, trying to psych herself up, she thought about Lupa. Tough, unyielding, never-give-up Lupa.

So get moving, Danu told herself. *You have to put some kilometers between you and that bear.*

As she stood and shouldered a considerably lighter pack and directed the synlight beam ahead of her, she heard a hair-raising howl farther down the mountain. With a shudder, Danu headed back toward the mountain trail.

Meanwhile, back in Isis, an agitated Whit sat in the Watch Room compu-chair. She was flipping through a random set of satellite scans, cursing under her breath. Lilith stood nearby, her wise blue eyes watching Whit with concern. Kali and Styx worked with the auxiliary computer system on the other side of the room, trading suggestions and checking and rechecking the comline network. In the corner, her head buried hopelessly in her hands, sat Tor.

It was nearly midnight and still they had no idea where Danu had disappeared to.

"Since Arinna scrambled the satellite transmissions," Whit finally snapped, "this data is damn-near useless. I can't make any sense of it!"

"Well, we've eliminated one possibility," Styx said, approaching the compu-chair with Kali right behind her. "There's no record of Arinna making contact with Danu through the comline."

"It's an enclosed system," Lilith commented. "She couldn't break into the operation base...."

"Remember, this is Arinna," Kali warned, her brown eyes grave. "If she wants to, she can do just about anything."

Slamming her hand against the keyboard built into the end of the armrest, Whit ended the satellite-search program. With a sigh of frustration, she leaned forward and rubbed her eyes. "How on Gaea's sweet earth did Danu ever find a lead in that mess?"

"We don't actually know that she did," Lilith answered.

"I tell you, she spent all last night blanking her mind," Kali stated vehemently. "She ran the Watch Room scans and found something, then had to come out to our house and socialize." Sweeping her loose hair back from her face with her hand, Kali elaborated, "That's why she seemed so strange. It wasn't the fact that Neith and Albie were courting right in front of her. It was that she already *knew* something and didn't want to give it away."

Irritable, her nerves frazzled by the long day of worry, Whit growled, "I know she's a genius, but how could anyone—even Danu—make sense of these scrambled satellite reports?"

Tor was suddenly off the floor and in their midst. "She wouldn't," Tor explained. "She doesn't deal with laborious, troublesome things—she would find another way of doing it."

For a long moment, Whit stared at Tor, considering what she had just said. Then her gray eyes narrowed, as she considered the only other option. "There are the jet fly-over surveillance films from yesterday and today," Whit mused, "but we've already reviewed them. The Intelligence team checked them out twice, and then Lilith reevaluated the film without finding..."

Interrupting, Kali commented, "But at accelerated viewing speed, that's enough film to dull anyone's attentiveness." Then, seeming to realize that she was criticizing Lilith, she flushed and gave Lilith an apologetic look

Impatiently, Lilith urged, "What's your point, Kali?"

"Limit the film review to the North Cascades," Kali told Whit.

Immediately, Whit keyed up the stored records of Saturday's two fly-overs, one from early morning, one from late afternoon.

Kali explained to the others, "On All Hallows' Eve, Danu heard both Whit and me discuss the strange heat dispersions up in that region."

The morning film revealed nothing, and their hearts fell.

"Let's see the afternoon film, too," Styx requested.

They all watched the film of late Saturday afternoon, just before the snow front moved into the Pacific Northwest. A cloud cover obscured most of the land being filmed, and Whit growled with frustration.

"See it through," Lilith counseled quietly.

Then all at once, the cloud cover shifted and the mountain range was clearly visible. As the camera panned over one particular section, a white haze caught Whit's eye. A seasoned pilot, she studied the small blip, then stopped the film.

"What's that?" she asked excitedly.

Squinting, Styx guessed, "Looks like a little cloud to me."

Whit started the film again. Several other clouds around the mountain moved along quickly, while the haze Whit had pointed out shifted shape but stayed essentially in the same place.

"If it's a cloud, why is it pretty much limited to that one sector?" Lilith asked thoughtfully.

Whit stopped the film again, and again they studied the strange shape of the hazy area on the film.

"Please run one of today's air-search films, Whit," Tor requested, her voice low, but the uneasiness unmistakable.

Complying, Whit called up another late-afternoon film. The sun was shining brightly in this one, and as the jet came over the same area again, the white mist was visible in exactly the same place.

"Steam?" Lilith speculated.

"Where would steam be coming from?" Styx retorted. "There's never been anything up there—no houses, no villages—even before the AGH plague or the Great Schism. That's Hart's Pass—a treacherous, inaccessible piece of territory."

Lilith and Whit exchanged a significant look.

"Okay," Kali remarked, folding her arms over her chest. "What do you two know that we don't know?"

Whit answered, her gray eyes somber. "More than a hundred and twenty-five years ago the U.S. Air Force had a Strategic Air Command early-warning base up there, monitoring the entire North Pacific."

"And..." Kali prompted, certain, somehow, that there was more.

"There are underground missile silos on site, with armed nuclear warheads, as well as a mothballed fleet of fighter jets and bombers," Lilith supplied, then clasped her delicate hands tightly together. "They are still armed with nuclear warheads."

A ghastly silence reigned as everyone quickly processed this information.

Meanwhile, the film onscreen was continuing over another area, and Kali's sharp eyes caught the glint of sunlight on metal. Mouth dry, she pointed, and said, "Whit, could you enhance that object?"

Once more, Whit stopped the film, and then increased the magnification as she attempted to improve the image definition. But the picture was still too blurred. However, with enhanced computer imaging, they could reconstruct the lines of aircraft enough to recognize the tilt-rotor.

Closing her eyes, Tor breathed, "Oh, Gaea. The Swallow."

7

Dawn's first rays found Danu shoeing along slowly, her gait awkward in the hastily repaired snowshoes. Her backpack felt heavy despite the fact that it was considerably lighter after most of her supplies were destroyed. Her eyes burned with fatigue and her face stung from the cold wind. More frequently now, her thoughts seemed to wander uncontrollably, and she half-feared that she might be on the verge of hypothermia. After leaving the Swallow at the crash site, Danu had never quite been warm. She had been walking now for seven hours, trying to get to Hart's Pass and the SAC installation before the subzero temperatures and lack of food permanently disabled her. Since the bear's attack, she had kept moving constantly, and though she was too nauseous now to be concerned about food, she still felt terribly, terribly cold.

Hours later a sudden panic seized her. *Where am I? How much farther?* Digging in her parka pocket, she pulled out the compass to check her bearings, then accidentally dropped it in the snow. Even though she could hardly feel her fingers, she swished her mittened hand through the soft crystalline powder of this higher elevation. Finally, she found the compass and tried to still her shaking hands long enough to take a reading. *You're getting careless*, she admonished herself.

Draw on Tor's Zen teachings. Center yourself. Breathe deeply and clear your mind.... Tor, how I wish you were here. For a moment, she thought she could hear Tor's strong voice urging her forward, urging her to keep moving.

She trudged on in a sort of daze, climbing up and over the ridge before her, and then around an endlessly curving section of rocky road, then finally into Hart's Pass. Yesterday's sunshine had given way to a low, dark cloud cover, and Danu fought against the shivering and chills that began to rack her body.

At long last, ahead of her she saw the twisted, rusted ruin of a chain-link fence, almost totally submerged in snow. She hesitated, then stood there staring, suddenly feeling terror skittering up her back like a spider.

Arinna's here. For an instant, her accelerated heart rate felt decidedly painful. *You can't turn back. You'd never survive the climb back down,* she thought.

Then again, she thought she heard Tor's voice. *Come on Danu! Get a grip, girl!*

She took several deep breaths, trying to review the alternative plan she had been devising as she trudged through the night. *Find the entrance, override the security system. Once inside the tunnel entrance, avoid detection, go directly to the War Room, where she'll most likely be. As soon as I see her, get close enough to get a clear blast off. Arinna will never suspect the laser in my wristcom. A simple and uncomplicated plan. All I have to do is block my thoughts from her.*

More to satisfy a nervous compulsion for thoroughness than out of an actual need to check the blueprints already indelibly stamped upon her photographic memory, Danu pulled photocopies of the installation from an inside pocket of her parka. Once more, she examined the SAC blueprints she had taken from the Watch Room files. Satisfied, she returned them to her pocket and continued with her journey.

Fifteen minutes later she was standing in front of the fence which surrounded the SAC installation. The silence was deafening, except for the northwesterly winds that continued to howl and drive the afternoon temperature down. Danu looked around for signs of life—but there were none. It appeared that no humans had been here for at least a hundred years, or more. A few old helicopters sat rusting and tethered to the ground, probably over a landing pad that was not visible due to the snow accumulation. The threatening nimbus clouds overhead jerked her back to the present, for they promised more snow. With a determined grunt, she easily surmounted what was once a high barrier, and stepped over the rusted barbed wire that topped the fence.

Clumsily, she moved forward, stopping once to retie her snowshoe. Even though she longed to just drop into a snowbank and give in to the overpowering fatigue and longing for sleep, she kept going. She noticed that some buildings were still intact, but it was obvious that they were uninhabited; the windows were broken and most of the roofs had caved in on the structures.

What you're looking for is underground, she reminded herself, forcing herself to stand without swaying. She inspected the deteriorating installation, searching for the source of the elusive steam.

And then she saw the plume of white mist rising from a short, wide, plastic pipe positioned beneath a grove of tall cedars. And beyond the vent, Danu saw a large metal door fitted into the machine-carved surface of the mountainside. The cedars had provided a windbreak, so that only a small portion of the door was covered with snow.

Moving with determination now, Danu snowshoed as fast as she could to the entrance, and spent several minutes studying the huge, twentieth-century locking mechanism on the heavy steel door. After a moment of contemplation, she took off her mittens, examined her hands, and tried to warm her fingers with her breath, to no avail. She suspected several of her fingers had frostbite.

She slung off her pack, opened it, dug out her utility knife, and fumbled to pull out its screwdriver tool. Turning back to the lock box, she began working on it. Her normally precise, fine motor skills were somewhat impaired, and the tips of her fingers were burning. But she knew better than to rub them. At least now she had some shelter from the wind, but her teeth still chattered. A moment later, the wind suddenly died and an eerie quietness came over the area. She stopped her work on the lock mechanism and looked around—nothing. She closed her eyes, took three deep, long breaths, and continued with her attempt to dismantle the lock. Finally, she removed the cover plate and began working on the circuit boards. Even though the screwdriver repeatedly slipped off its mark, she eventually succeeded in tripping the locking device. The compression mechanism hissed and the door slid open with an ominous thud.

Danu unlaced her snowshoes and placed them against the wall, grabbed her backpack, and looked behind her once more. Stone silence. Nothing moved, not even the wind.

Ahead of her, lit by archaic fluorescent tubes overhead, stretched a narrow, concrete-walled passageway. A wave of fear washed over her as she stepped across the threshold of the installation.

Once inside, she removed her sunshades and placed her backpack beside the door. Glad to be indoors, she wearily unwrapped the gray scarf from her neck and pulled it off, noting for the first time the rips left in the fabric when the bear had torn into her pack. Still shivering, she shoved the scarf into her pack, thinking, *From the frying pan into the fire.*

With difficulty, she drew her laser gun, and holding it with both hands, cautiously entered the corridor. Exhausted and cold, she welcomed the shelter of the tunnel, but she was still chilled to the bone and shivering. She walked slowly downward, into the bowels of the SAC installation, her boots dropping snow with each step, when a horrible sense of foreboding gripped her. She stopped and looked behind her—nothing. After taking several more steps forward she heard it, the sound of the steel door sliding shut behind her. There was no turning back.

Moving on, she sighted two round objects twenty-five meters ahead of her on the floor. *What on Gaea's earth is that?* She squinted and stepped closer, then froze. For a moment, she stared, too stunned to move. *If I had any doubts, they're gone now. Arinna is definitely here.* Grinning the macabre grin of death, hollowed-eyed, and brown with age, two human skulls had been placed in the tunnel, like hideous sentries. They were probably the remains of a pair of U.S. servicemen who had perished here during the Great Schism, years ago. And rather than lay them to rest with a decent burial, Arinna had put the dead men's skulls on display. Arinna's grisly warning achieved its purpose—Danu was unnerved.

What am I doing? In the Mother's Name, how did I expect to pull this off? And then Danu caught herself. *Remember—blank mind, blank mind—wall of snow.* Hands shaking, Danu pulled her parka closer about herself. She checked the setting on her laser gun, and made sure it was set to kill. *This is the real thing, kiddo,* she thought grimly.

Her stomach was churning and she felt light-headed. Though she kept trying to remember the exact strategy she had formulated for this showdown with Arinna Sojourner, her brain was becoming muddled. Alarmed, she found herself staggering as she made a series of turns, each of which led her deeper into the mountainside. *According to the blueprints, there should be a corridor intersecting this passageway that leads to several storage facilities and an auxiliary power plant,* Danu thought.

Until now, Danu's youth and inexperience had shielded her from the real consequences of her decision to rid Freeland of Arinna Sojourner. Like most young people, Danu was not in touch with her own mortality. But now that she was finally here, she began to realize that her plan might have some serious flaws. Fortunately, her stubbornness kicked in and overrode the momentary panic. There was no turning back now. She checked her wristcom as if for comfort.

And then she heard the resonating hum of a large power generator. Cautiously, Danu inched forward along the wall, her pistol held in front of her. And then she saw a door set into the concrete wall on her right. A few steps more and she was leaning against the steel door, breathing shallowly, listening to the machinery behind it.

This is it. You can do it.

In a bone-chilling moment of clarity, she realized what a fool she had been to come crashing in here alone. But it was far too late now to do anything except go forward. *At least I can try to spare Kali*, she thought. *If I do this one thing right, I can save a friend.* There were no other options. Slowly, she pushed down on the door handle and opened the door enough to slip through. With her laser gun raised, she cautiously stepped into a dimly lit room steeped in shadows.

She kept her back against the wall, as she waited for her eyes to adjust to the dim light. Then she realized that she was in some sort of large power-generating facility. Twin power generators were on-line, their massive engines driven by small cold-fusion devices.

More evidence of Arinna's presence.

And there was heat in this room; she felt it on her cheeks and ears. *Gaea—it feels so good.*

As she moved across the room, she suddenly sensed someone emerging from behind the second generator, someone who apparently had been watching her. Immediately, Danu whirled, and pointed her pistol at the woman. She found herself gazing into Loy Yin Chen's jubilant ebony eyes.

"Mother's Blood!" Loy gasped. "I might have known you'd be the one to come!"

Keeping the laser pistol pointed at her, Danu glanced instinctively at the door on the opposite side of the large room, beyond Loy. "Where's Arinna?" she snapped unsmilingly.

Loy started to step forward and hesitated when Danu barked, "Don't move." But somehow, Danu's voice lacked conviction, and before she knew it, Loy was at her side, embracing her. Danu's gun arm dropped into a relaxed position, the gun now pointed at the floor.

Loy was gripping her shoulders, stepping back to take a good look at her. "You look awful," she remarked, her usual sarcasm tempered by her obvious joy at seeing a once-friendly face again. "Are you all right, Danu?"

Danu nodded, knowing very well that she was not all right. Her head was spinning, her fingers and toes were burning, and she felt ready to vomit. However, she also knew she couldn't reveal to Loy how vulnerable she actually was. She was not certain if she should trust Loy. Though Arinna had taken Loy off as a captive, the two had been thick as thieves before that, hatching all sorts of mischief while

Isis was under construction. And she remembered Kali had said that Arinna and Loy were lovers. There was a very real possibility that Loy had found it more convenient to join Arinna in her plans for world conquest, since resisting her would probably have led to an abrupt death. And it would not be the first time that Loy had sacrificed personal honor for personal gain.

Somewhere in Danu's depths, she remembered to shield her thoughts. *Block! Snow falling—a wall of snow. Block!*

"Do you have an aircraft outside?" Loy was asking. "Let's get going before Arinna picks you up on the surveillance scanners." Abruptly, Loy motioned to the very small, state-of-the-art camera strategically mounted high on the wall near them.

Furrowing her brow, Danu tried to remember if she had seen any cameras in the passageway she'd just left.

Loy seemed to read her mind, and said, "You've come in the back way. The cameras are hidden in that corridor. I ought to know— I put them there." Grimacing with anger, Loy continued, "You see, I'm Arinna's slave here. Most of this restoration work has been done by *me*. The past few weeks, she's kept me busy setting up a laboratory on one of the lower levels. That's why I think we could escape. She's working in the lab right now, and there are no surveillance monitors in there yet."

Eyes blinking with exhaustion, Danu asked suspiciously, "Why were you in here waiting for me?"

With a playful laugh, Loy pulled off Danu's navy wool hat and tossed it on the floor, then ruffled her red hair. It was an old, annoying gesture of Loy's, and Danu remembered with a sinking feeling how much Loy used to aggravate her.

"Hecate!" Loy grinned. "You sound like you don't trust me, Danu."

Danu winced at the shortened version of Lupa's favorite expression, 'Harrowing Hecate.' " Why should I trust you? And answer my question, Loy," she growled.

Assuming a more serious posture, and now regarding Danu with a grudging respect, Loy said, "Trust me, Danu. I wasn't waiting for you. I was taking my noon reading on the cold-fusion adaptor.

Neither Arinna nor I are sure how long these old generators will hold up, jerry-rigged as they are with the cold-fusion adaptors." Placing her hands on her hips, Loy swung her gaze to the generators. "Something could short out and blow at anytime. Know what I mean?"

Danu stared at the chart Loy had left near one of the generators, then nodded, satisfied. Somehow, she managed to make her legs move and they carried her to the door, which seemed kilometers away. With every minute that passed, Danu felt more physically ill; she was not certain how much longer she could stay on her feet. As she reached to open the door, Loy grabbed her arm.

"Don't go any further!" Loy ordered, whispering fiercely in her ear. "She'll squash you like a roach! Let's get out of here, *now*, while we still have a chance!"

Without a word, Danu wrenched her arm free of Loy's grasp, then collapsed against the door, breathing erratically.

"You're sick, aren't you?" Loy observed, her voice changing to a softer tone. Stroking Danu's cold, dry face tenderly, Loy guessed, "Hypothermia—am I right?"

Danu was having trouble focusing her eyes. "Just shut up, Loy, and point the way to Arinna," she snapped in a hushed voice, knowing she sounded irrational and just not caring. "And then get the hell out of here. You can take my parka, and my pack is by the outer door with my snowshoes. The only craft is a demolished Swallow about thirty kilometers south, down the mountain." Swallowing hard, Danu finished, "But you could hole up there until someone comes looking for me."

For an instant, Loy stared into her eyes, the facile manner completely gone. Immediately, Danu realized that Loy was now revealing her true self. All the barriers were down and the woman was actually making an entreaty. "Please, come with me," she murmured, her lips barely moving.

Go after Arinna, Danu urged herself, *while you still have the guts to do it. Block. Must Block. Don't forget to block.* She looked at her wristcom, as if to check the hour.

Pushing past Loy, she opened the door and stepped into another dimly lit passageway. The Regulator was pressed flat against the cinderblock wall, and for a second, it didn't register with Danu that what initially appeared to be an apparition was moving toward her. He came out of the shadows—huge and menacing—his green, short-waisted uniform jacket identifying him—seconds before he grabbed her and slammed her into the wall. The instant she hit the wall, the gun flew out of her hand. In disbelief, she heard it clatter across the concrete floor. She struggled, but it was a decidedly feeble attempt. And as the Reg lifted her bodily, pinning her shoulders against the unyielding wall, Loy slipped under his long arm.

Tears welled up in her eyes as Danu helplessly watched Loy snap a set of shackles on her. Swiftly, each wrist and ankle cuff was locked in place. At Loy's signal, the expressionless Reg set Danu back on her feet, then seized the lightweight chain attached to her handcuffs and tugged her along behind him. As Danu stumbled, trying to keep up with the big man, she threw a blistering look at Loy, who hurried along beside her.

Loy held her by the elbow, supporting her as the younger woman almost fell. "Slow down," Loy commanded the Reg, but the Elysian did not alter his pace.

"Get your hands off me," Danu hissed at Loy.

Her features impassive, Loy returned, "That Reg will *drag* you down the passageway and scrape your face right down to the bone if you lose your footing. Save all that righteous anger for your big entrance." Her face suddenly grim, Loy elaborated, "Arinna's been waiting for you since she shot your Swallow down, two nights ago."

They descended deeper into the installation, with the tunnel twisting and turning. Danu remembered the blueprint of the installation showing an elevator shaft, and she wondered why they were not taking it. She then remembered that the elevator would be near the main entrance to the facility.

She decided to stop resisting the Reg, and instead moved along compliantly. Looking straight ahead, she said, "You knew, didn't you, Loy?" Then it dawned on her— she had been duped. "So, you're working for *her* now...right?" Danu shot a quick glance at her left wrist. The shackle rested below her wristcom. *Wall of snow*, Danu repeated over and over again in her mind, and thought, *If I'm to die, let it be with honor.*

A few minutes later, the lighting in the tunnel brightened and the Reg began to slow his pace.

Giving Danu a distinctly compassionate look, Loy confided, "You may not believe me, Danu, but I'm just as helpless as you are." Loy kept looking at Danu as she adjusted her pace to match the Reg's. "Believe me when I tell you that Arinna is soulless and without compassion. She'll toy with you a bit—she's like that." Then, leaning closer, whispering, Loy urged, "Keep looking for a chance to escape. Someday, she'll make a mistake. I'm still hopeful that I'll make it out of here—alive."

And look where it's gotten you, Danu thought wryly. Frowning at the Reg, feeling desperate, she demanded, "How the hell did she get a Regulator through the Border?"

Loy's only answer was a tense exhalation of breath.

The Reg paused before another door, waiting for the thick steel panel to slide open. Several sharp tugs on the chain brought Danu into a very large, dome-shaped room.

This space clearly had been a War Room, built to monitor global military events. But someone had spent a great deal of time and expertise advancing the capacities of these surveillance systems. Every side of the room glowed with concave wallscreens, fitted into the walls and ceiling dome. Surreptitiously looking around the War Room, Danu glimpsed several electronic maps of Freeland, with color-coded glyphs showing where each colony located its military aircraft, heavy laser artillery, the Bordergates, research facilities, and arsenals. Another section revealed a continuous visual surveillance scan of the SAC compound and Hart's Pass.

Danu turned to Loy and asserted bitterly, "You *betrayed* me."

A flicker of guilt crossed Loy's face, but then she turned toward the platform in the center of the room. "I have done as you asked, Arinna," she declared simply in a subservient voice.

From the corner of her eye, Danu caught a graceful motion on the platform, where a beautiful woman rose from the impressive compu-chair mounted there. "Ahh yes, sweet betrayal," Arinna fairly crowed, as she sauntered down the ramp to floor level and motioned the Reg to bring Danu forward.

One yank on the chain sent Danu to her knees at Arinna's feet. Mesmerized, Danu found herself staring up at the woman, her thoughts an uneven spin of despair and admiration. *She was a good-looking woman before, but now...she's absolutely bewitching.* Unable to stop herself, she examined Arinna closely.

The long, wavy hair was a mix of gold and chestnut, and it fell over her shoulders in a shining mass. Her body was curvaceous, her bronzed skin radiant. Arinna's green eyes smiled into Danu's own, and Danu felt warmed and comforted. All the goodness in the world seemed to enfold her.

Bewitching...bewitching. With a jolt, Danu came back to her predicament and realized that yes—the woman before her was indeed bewitching—had, no doubt, just bewitched *her.* In the space of those few delicious moments, Arinna had probably searched her mind quite freely and discovered everything she wished to know. Disconcerted, Danu tore her gaze away from Arinna's emerald eyes, and fixed her attention on the big Reg by her side.

A Reg! Danu thought, immediately despairing again. Isis and all of Freeland were in grave danger if Arinna was importing Regs to carry out her treacherous plans. *But Regs hate women. How is it she can make this one obey her?*

Chuckling, Arinna touched Danu's hair, her manner very gentle. "I can make him obey my will," she answered, "because he is *mine*—just as you shall be."

Danu flinched away from her, and felt a shattering jolt of fear. The swift sequence of events—the jet crashing, the wearying trek up the mountain, the exposure to the elements—had insulated her in a series of problem-solving crises, until now. As she glanced up at Arinna's face again, she saw the sorceress's incredibly wicked smile, and her heart quailed. What had she gotten herself into? With a supreme effort, she reminded herself to remember the curtain of falling snow. *Snow! Snow all around me.*

Obviously gloating, Arinna beheld the massive Reg proudly. "What a splendid likeness he is, don't you think?" When Danu frowned, unable to follow, Arinna ordered the Reg, "Turn around." As the Reg pivoted, Arinna pressed a spot on the occipital lobe of the Reg's head. Immediately, a portion of skull lifted up, revealing a datatronic matrix, with pulsing lights of various colors dotting the circuitry. Stunned, Danu now understood that the Reg was an android, programmed to obey only Arinna.

Arinna smugly congratulated Danu and closed the matrix panel. "Well done, little architect. You always were the bright one, weren't you?" There was a joyous implication in the way she said it, as if Danu's mental abilities would soon be hers to control. It made Danu feel sick with apprehension. She knew she would have to act quickly if she was to complete her mission.

"I have many of these manly beauties," Arinna boasted. Then, addressing the Reg, "Alert mode," she casually commanded. The Reg swung back to face Danu, its facial features so like that of a human that Danu was impressed despite herself.

Airily, Arinna explained, "While Loy was helpfully dealing with the ancient clutter of this abandoned installation—disposing of skeletons and other debris from the past—I was picking up where I had left off last year." Smiling proudly, she disclosed, "I've designed and created the most sophisticated computer manufacturing facility in Freeland. I actually set it up here about seven months before I ever officially arrived in Isis to serve as Systems Director under your pathetic Tomyris Whitaker."

Danu narrowed her eyes in disbelief. *Seven months before the Leaders' Council ever even reopened Isis for settlement? Seven months before the Directors were even appointed? How could she have been so sure of being made a Director?*

Grinning at Danu's skepticism, Arinna elaborated, "It's quite true. Influencing others to do my bidding is a talent I've been developing for years, Danu. And I must admit, it has become quite an easy thing for me to do. As easy as it is for me to read your thoughts, I might add."

All at once, Danu was uncertain of there being *any* possibility of vanquishing Arinna. Despair and exhaustion finally came crashing in on her. Suddenly, she slumped into a kneeling position, as chills racked her body. *Walls of snow. Walls of snow...all around me.* She felt increasingly nauseous and disoriented. Her mind was spinning in a snow-filled world. Somewhere above her, Arinna's melodious voice continued to proclaim her achievements and invincibility.

"I built myself a mountain lair and subdued a few local wild beasts to protect my perimeters—I believe you met the grizzly," Arinna chuckled, amused by Danu's scowling reaction. "Then, my young one, I used one of the supply depots within this wondrous complex to manufacture a fighting unit. I've a regular Palace Guard now." Reaching out and forcibly turning Danu's head to the wallscreen, Arinna showed off her work via one of the security scanners. On the wallscreen, row upon row of Reg androids were standing at attention, mutely waiting to be summoned from a nearby storage facility.

Danu strained with all her might, trying to shake off Arinna's light grasp on her mind. Oddly enough, she couldn't seem to make herself do as she wished.

"And here," Arinna went on expansively, "is my arsenal, courtesy of the Aryan Federation, and that delightfully insane American male fondness for nuclear weapons."

Alarmed, Danu turned to see just what Arinna meant by that remark. She had heard rumors about armed nuclear missiles in some of the old SAC installations in Freeland. Originally the Strategic Air Command Centers were built kilometers away from any of the silos housing missiles. *But Goddess, in the hands of someone like Arinna....* Danu couldn't finish the speculation. For there they were, on the wallscreen, eight armed missiles, in their launch tubes. *One for each colony*, Danu thought, with a sinking heart.

Danu was beginning to panic. *Snow falling all around me. I have to make my move soon,* she thought, afraid that Arinna might pick up her thoughts. But Arinna was too engrossed in showing off her plans for world domination to pay any attention to what Danu was thinking, planning.

"I have established quite an impenetrable fortress here," Arinna concluded. "If I had been able to escape Isis *with* Maat's files on the Think Tank Project, my plans for this planet and the human race would be on schedule." The woman paused and glowered, her anger building, moment by moment, at having been stymied.

At that very moment, her entrancing beauty metamorphosed, and Arinna suddenly appeared ugly. Repulsed by the cruelty written on her face, Danu thought, *Gaea, protect us! This woman is a megalomaniac. How could Freeland have spawned her?*

Arinna was on an egotistical roll, and focused only on what she was thinking and saying at the moment. Her voice now loud and sharp, as if she were speaking to a large audience, she intoned, "Kali Tyler, daughter of Maat Tyler and the Think Tank Project, has proven to be a major impediment to my plans. But I, Arinna Sojourner, will have her kneeling at my feet soon enough."

Danu shot a quick glance at Loy, who was standing nearby, and was surprised to see her tense posture, her eyes wide and filled with fear. She looked completely cowed. Gone was her arrogance, the air of superiority that had once been her signature.

Standing above her, Arinna tugged Danu's chain and Danu obediently got to her feet, though for the life of her, she did not know why. "But *you*, Danu Sullivan, are the solution to all of my problems," she crooned. Tenderly, Arinna cupped Danu's cheek, and announced, "I think my ruse to get you here was quite brilliant. I knew you'd discover the steam vent, which, by the way, I've hidden quite easily for months from Tomyris Whitaker's ridiculous aircraft surveillance. She couldn't spot a thing I didn't intend for her to spot." Obviously impressed with herself, Arinna laughed a long, high-pitched laugh that reverberated around the War Room.

Danu was shivering uncontrollably again as she faced Arinna, eye to eye. She felt herself being sucked into the sinister green pools of this madwoman's eyes. Danu knew she had to make her move soon, but she was paralyzed with fear, powerless to act.

"Oh, yes, my powers are far greater than any of you ever imagined," Arinna murmured. "You've all been so busily preparing Kali to stand against me—such a stupid waste of time. My appearance on All Hallows' Eve was a warning to all of Isis—not just an entertaining display of my psychic abilities. It was child's play to channel the ambient energy forces from the assembly of women, which allowed me to override the security codes of your central computers. And needless to say, the psychic projection of myself was also a piece of cake," she finished smugly.

Fascinated, Danu couldn't pull her eyes away from this madwoman's beautiful face. The words seemed to wind their way in and around her will, pulling her along, readying her for something she sensed waiting above her like the rumbling presence of an avalanche.

"You should be honored," Arinna was confiding, "for you have two important roles to play here." She wound an arm around Danu's waist endearingly. "First, you are my bait. Now that you are here with me, Whit will be forced to set aside any plans she has of trying to keep Kali from doing battle with me. And as Whit knows, Kali is *not* ready to stand against me. In a matter of days, Kali, too, will be enslaved. A most powerful weapon to do my bidding, don't you think?" Arinna asked rhetorically, and laughed.

Inwardly recoiling, Danu shrank away from the slender woman next to her. *Oh, Mother, what have I done?* she asked herself in despair. "P-Please don't hurt Kali," she stammered in desperation. "You don't need her—someone as powerful as yourself shouldn't have to share the fame your deeds will..."

Laughing musically, Arinna chucked Danu's chin indulgently, remarking, "Very artful, Danu, my young slave, but you will learn quickly that I am not so easily duped. If I were you, I would have more concern for my own fate than for Kali's." The gleam in Arinna's eyes as she spoke these words chilled Danu to the bone.

"Fate? What...what are you going to do with me?" she asked, her voice filled with dread as the shackles cutting into her wrists reminded her of her mission. *Snow all around me.* Danu's teeth began chattering and her muscles twitched.

Arinna looked Danu up and down, and then asked, "Poor Danu, are you still cold?" Not waiting for an answer, Arinna continued, "Soon, my little one, I will have you warmed." And then, Arinna's psychic antennae suddenly perceived snow all around Danu. But after a moment, she dismissed it. This daughter of Freeland had simply been exposed to the early winter elements for too long.

Tapping her forehead with her middle finger, she said, "I've digressed now, haven't I, Danu? As I recall, we were discussing Kali and the fate of Freeland, were we not?" Arinna looked around the room at the wallscreens, and focused on the monitor which revealed the armed missiles. "Using those nuclear warheads is my last option," Arinna confessed. With a sly, sidelong glance at Loy, she finished, "After all, why destroy what you desire to rule? And rule I will."

At that moment, Loy met Danu's eyes, and again, Danu saw the terror there...and something else she couldn't decipher.

"I may not have the Think Tank files, or the data to work from, but my dear Danu, I do have you and your genes. And soon I will have Kali Tyler. Then I will be ready to make your clones and create an army of superwomen warriors for the new world order that I envision." Her green eyes narrowing, Arinna smugly contemplated Danu, like a hungry cat observing the mouse beneath its paw. "Yes! I *do* have *you,* dear, sweet Danu."

Danu swallowed hard as she stood helplessly before Arinna.

Very pleased with herself, Arinna grinned. "*You* are a veritable reservoir of superior bioengineered DNA material, and you will provide me with all the material I need for standard parthenogenetic procedures." Sweeping her eyes over Danu's weary stance and dirty, tattered clothes, Arinna announced, "You will be my bride of science. By joining your genetic design with my own, I shall create a generation of superior Freeland daughters—the likes of which the world has never seen."

Aghast, Danu tried to struggle against the grip Arinna had on her mind, determined to go down fighting. But she found she couldn't even turn her head away from those dazzling, hypnotic eyes.

"I shall force-grow my super-warriors with advanced growth hormones and feed them scientific information from Freeland's major data banks. My warrior daughters will be intellectually and physically superior to all life forms on this planet," Arinna explained. "And they will be programmed from birth to hate and destroy all those who oppose me, Arinna Sojourner, and the new world order. I expect that in five years I shall have an army of invincible warriors, who will do my bidding, unquestioningly." Pausing for effect, Arinna ruffled

Danu's hair again. "And they will all have your sweet face and curly red hair."

Confident in her power over Danu, and believing she had broken her will, Arinna disengaged the psychic grip she had on Danu's mind. She then pointed at Danu and laughed. "Yes, Danu, you are my slave and it is good that you accept your destiny."

Immediately, Danu realized that she could turn her head and move her arms, and she also knew it was now or never. This was her chance. In a flash, she mustered up all of her energy and jumped back away from Arinna, managing to land on both feet. A powerful anger welled up inside her, fueling her determination to kill Arinna Sojourner. Danu grabbed her wristcom and quickly pressed the safety release. Without much thought, almost instinctively, she aimed the wristcom so that the deadly miniature laser beam was pointed at her captor. In a split second, before the Reg, or Loy, could respond, Danu fired the deadly beam of light at Arinna's head. Then everything seemed to be happening in slow motion for Danu. The laser beam appeared to take forever to reach its target. Time itself seemed to be standing still. And then it happened. Danu watched in disbelief as the finely controlled beam of light simply scattered harmlessly around Arinna's body as it dissipated into nothingness. And Arinna stood there unharmed, laughing triumphantly, her arms folded across her chest.

Danu was stunned. Her mouth hung open as she looked from her wristcom to Arinna. She felt like a ridiculous failure, but she was not willing to give up, not just yet. Again she pressed the wristcom laser, and again the deadly beam of blue light scattered benignly around Arinna. For a few moments, Arinna floated several centimeters above the floor, with a golden-green aura surrounding her.

Very pleased with herself and her power, she looked down upon her captive. "Poor Danu." Arinna shook her head, noting Danu's disappointment. "What a pathetic effort. Did you really think that you could destroy me with that toy of yours?" she asked, with utter contempt in her voice. "Did you not know, young Danu, that I am invincible, that I am always protected by my own power?" With those words, Arinna psychically flipped the wristcom off Danu's wrist and sent it flying across the room. Loy gasped aloud at this new demonstration of Arinna's psychokinetic abilities, while she watched the wristcom sail across the room and land out of sight behind the computer.

Danu was bitterly disappointed in herself, but willing to die with honor. Again, she summoned what little energy she had left and streaked into action. With shackles clanking and hindering her movement, she charged forward, toward Arinna, intent on killing the woman with her bare hands if possible. *"I will kill you, Arinna Sojourner, if it's the last thing I do."*

She had only taken three steps before Arinna simply ordered, *"Enough*, Danu!" Immediately, Danu froze, unable to move. "It is time you learned that when you obey, you will be rewarded, and when you disobey, you will be punished."

Nothing moved in the War Room. It was menacingly quiet, except for the hum of the computers and the ventilation system. Fear snaked through Danu's very being as she waited for Arinna's wrath to take shape.

Off to the side the Reg stood at attention, face impassive, unfeeling. Next to him Loy stood with her head bowed, not wanting to witness what she knew Danu was going to experience. Danu realized there would be no help from Loy Yin Chen.

And then, with one arm pointed heavenward and the other pointed at Danu, Arinna shouted, "Do not forget this moment, Danu." And without mercy, she unleashed a white-hot bolt of raw energy. The searing pain permeated every cell in Danu's body—every neuron in her body ignited in fire, sending forth blistering pain to every cell. Her muscles contracted, twitching involuntarily, as she screamed in agony. This was pain the likes of which she had never known.

Finally, Arinna lowered her arms and smiled like an angel, as Danu went limp and collapsed onto the concrete floor. Curled up in a fetal position, she suddenly felt a comforting warmth pressing in on her. Arinna's gentle voice caressed her. "After all you've been through, you feel so tired—you feel so ill. You need to rest. Don't you, sweet Danu?"

And then Arinna seemed to enter her, engulfing Danu in a strangely sensual seduction. Arinna was everywhere—in her mind, in her body, strumming deep, inner chords of repose. Her senses reeling, Danu abruptly began to lose track of events. All she knew was that Arinna filled her, Arinna soothed her, Arinna embraced her very soul.

There was nothing else but Arinna.

That same afternoon, in the Council Hall of the Isis Cedar House, the Council had convened to discuss strategies for dealing with the growing dangers that faced them—Arinna Sojourner and the possible annihilation of Freeland at her hands. Whit had shown the surveillance film, pointing out both the steam and the damaged Swallow just south of Hart's Pass. As a military person, Whit firmly believed the only way to handle Arinna and the current crisis was with a military strike, spearheaded, of course, by herself. However, she postponed putting forth this proposal, a proposal which was designed to deal with another danger. Being the military strategist that she was, Whit decided to bide her time. For now, she merely opened up the debate.

Several hundred concerned citizens had crowded into the gallery of the Council Chambers. Seated around the circular table, Council members somberly discussed various plans, weighing the advantages and disadvantages of each. In the gallery section which lined the walls, women paid close attention, occasionally turning to whisper an opinion to a neighbor. Needless to say, every Isian had an opinion.

Initially, Kali had put forth her plan to fly out to the SAC installation and provoke a direct confrontation with Arinna. This option had been discussed, but was quickly voted down. In fact, the vote on Kali's cherished solo effort had been almost perfunctory, and now Kali sat in her seat beside Whit, her face a mask of polite interest. But Whit knew better than anyone that beneath Kali's polite exterior burned an anger the likes of which none of them could imagine.

Whit's mind drifted briefly, exasperated by Kali's stubbornness. *She keeps glaring at me as if it's my fault that her plan was rejected. Kali just doesn't realize how completely crazy her plan is!*

If she'd only trust my judgment and experience more, our relationship would be a hell of a lot better, too. Damn. Despite the fact that both Co-leaders were fuming, to all present, both appeared to be calmly paying attention.

When Whit returned to the present, Marpe, the elderly textile merchant, was emphasizing the need for an effective plan, one which would eliminate the necessity of ever having to face Arinna Sojourner again. With a respectful acknowledgment of Kali's psychic skills, Marpe stated that she felt Kali would require additional support, that there was too much riding on the success of this mission for one person to be solely responsible for it. Several Council members nodded in agreement.

To other Council members, "additional support" began to sound more and more like Boudicca and her hundreds of Celtic tribes, rallying to chase the Roman army from Britain. Samsi was even proposing that a battalion of warriors could parachute out of air transports. *And then we'll not only have Danu lost up in the mountains—we'll have at least a hundred or so others lost, too,* Whit thought sarcastically.

Whit just shook her head and clenched her teeth, impatient as ever, with the amount of nonsensical jawboning necessary for the democratic process. The din in the Council Chambers had increased significantly: women in the gallery were shouting out opinions to whomever would listen, and of course, some of the Council members had started private conversations. Whit slapped her hand on the table and stood up in annoyance. *Damn it.* She banged the wooden gavel on its block and called out, "Members of the Council, please come to order—now." She banged the gavel several times more. "Honored members, may I remind you, time is wasting and we *must* come to a decision." Gradually, the chatter subsided.

After an hour, Styx finally gained recognition and stood to speak. She waited for total quiet before she began. A sense of expectancy fell over the Council as Styx reminded them of the imminent danger that Freeland faced. Her dark Mayan eyes were making contact with one member after another. As she stretched forth both arms toward her audience, she spoke passionately, "My friends and comrades, must I remind you that this woman caused the needless death of Lupa Tagliaro, that she took the life of one of her own," her voice rose, "for no reason except that Lupa once nettled her? Must I remind you of her vindictiveness and lack of respect for life? I have not wanted to acknowledge what I am about to tell you—but I have sensed her power is growing, and we must act swiftly and wisely. We must..."

Styx never finished her sentence. Suddenly, Whit was on her feet, interrupting. "Styx, forgive me, my friend, but I must tell the Council of another great threat that Arinna poses, and no one here has yet addressed that threat." Styx yielded the floor to Whit, but remained standing, her arms folded across her chest.

"I must admit that what I am about to tell you will need further verification...." As Whit formed her thoughts, it occurred to her that now Kali would have to concede that a military strike on Hart's Pass would be the best way to resolve the current crisis facing Freeland.

In a somber voice, Whit elaborated, "Have the older women of Isis forgotten the threat that SAC installations in some parts of what is now Freeland posed a hundred and twenty-five years ago?"

Suddenly, Lilith raised her hand to her mouth. As if reading Whit's mind, she, too, realized what the additional threat would be.

Whit continued, "Have we so quickly forgotten the threat of nuclear war which the world before the Great Schism lived with on a daily basis? It is no secret that I oppose Kali going on this mission without military support. Perhaps after you hear what I have to say, you will reconsider some of the options you have heard today." Whit paused for a moment, running her hand through her hair, not daring to look at Kali.

All eyes were riveted on Whit.

"As some of you know, I have access to the old United States data banks of the old National Aeronautical and Space Administration, as well as the data banks of the Strategic Air Command. We are not only going up against Arinna Sojourner, but we are also faced with possible annihilation from twentieth-century nuclear weapons." Whit took a deep breath, paused to let her words sink in, and tugged at the collar of her uniform jacket. She realized that she was scared. But being the soldier that she was, she did not mince her words or try to soften the blow of what she was about to say.

"Most probably there are still missiles, armed with nuclear warheads, housed in the Cascades SAC installation. If there are armed missiles, the warheads must be disarmed and removed. We will need several explosives specialists and a nuclear physicist to do this. I reiterate, a military contingent is needed for this mission." With that, Whit shrugged her shoulders and abruptly thanked Styx for letting her speak.

A heavy silence fell over the assembly. Following this pronouncement, most everyone in the room was stunned. And then outraged cries of anger and shouts for justice rose in the Council Chamber. Simultaneously, the faces of the younger women, especially those well schooled in the history of the United States, became frozen in fear.

Styx waited for the reality of Whit's words to settle, and for everyone in the room to quiet down. Thoughtfully, Styx placed her hands on the Council table, leaned forward toward her colleagues, and said, "We are not just talking about the survival of Isis. We, brave women, are talking about the survival of Freeland and the future daughters of our nation. We cannot afford to put our heads in the sand. As Whit has told us, there is another grave danger besides Arinna. Now is the time for us to heed the guidance of our best spiritual, scientific, and military minds. We are not, I repeat, we are not going to get a second chance to do this right. And we may have to sacrifice some of our loved ones in the defense of Freeland."

Then Styx lowered her voice, putting every bit of wisdom she possessed into the words she said next. She knew everyone, including the younger citizenry, was hanging on her words. She especially wanted to reach these young women who had only heard the warrior stories of past years—who dreamed of glory without consequence—of glory without death.

"Listen carefully, women of Isis, we may have the means to defeat the evil personified by Arinna. But the numbers you contemplate sending against her will not defeat her...she will simply slaughter them." Styx paused and looked around at the Council members, letting that dire prediction penetrate their consciousness.

Council members had begun to stir uncomfortably in their seats. And behind them, in the gallery, alarmed citizens began shouting their opinions again. Armed sentries at exits and entrances attempted to hush their alarm. Quietly, Lilith touched Styx's arm to get her attention. The stately Mayan warrior bent down as Lilith whispered in her ear. Their exchange did not escape Whit's notice.

Standing tall, Styx again waited until the noise had died down, then continued, "How many we send will not matter so much as the expertise that each individual is able to contribute to the mission."

Whit noticed Kali sitting up straight, nodding agreement.

"Therefore, citizens of Isis, I suggest," Styx concluded, "that only those with training for this life-and-death mission, or those possessing special skills, be sent.... And do bear in mind, it is very likely that those who go...will not return. May Gaea guide us." Styx soberly looked around the Council Chamber and then sat down.

Silence reigned for a few moments as many of the women put a protective arm around some loved one. And then Kali was on her feet. In a loud, controlled voice she beseeched the Council, "I ask the Council of Isis to refrain from assigning warriors at all, since this will be a suicide mission...." She paused, and with eyes flashing, surveyed them all, both Council and gallery women. "Instead, I propose that we ask for a few *qualified* volunteers to go with me. Once I dispose of Arinna, there will be no need for explosives experts and nuclear physicists." As she spoke in a determined voice, her hands defiantly on her hips, a golden aura began to form around her.

At once, Styx stood, her hand on her sidearm. "I will! I will go with you," she shouted, before Kali had even finished, "and together we will defeat Arinna Sojourner."

Just as quickly, as Lilith half-stood with her hand covering her mouth, Kali addressed Styx, "Thank you, my Teacher, but no—you cannot. You must stay here, and if possible, form a second line of psychic defense, in the event that we fail to destroy Arinna Sojourner."

For a moment, Styx remained standing, her face a portrait of stubborn resistance. Then, after a long stare from Kali, she bowed her head and sat down again.

Now Whit was standing and smiling broadly at Kali. Since the Council did not seem especially enthusiastic about dealing with the nuclear threat, Whit pursued another tack. "It seems reasonable to send volunteers who can assist you, Kali.... And it is also prudent to send along several warriors. As Co-leader and Commander of the Military, I am recommending that Captain Razia select two special-forces warriors to accompany you. That is, if they are willing to volunteer." Whit looked at Captain Razia, who was standing with two warriors at the main entrance. The captain nodded her approval and saluted.

Feeling somewhat triumphant, Whit said, mostly to Captain Razia, "This operation should have a contingency plan, which we can discuss later."

Kali was furious at Whit's latest maneuver, but before she could respond, most of the Council members were on their feet, clapping and shouting approval for Whit's proposal. And from the gallery, several women were moving proudly down the aisles toward the Council table.

Whit again picked up the gavel and banged it. "Will the Council please come to order, so that we may conclude our business." Looking at the women who had come forward to volunteer, Whit ordered, "State your name and area of expertise to the Council, please."

Two determined voices called back.

"Neith Murray, Healer."

"Tamatori Yakami, Warrior, Wiccan, and Martial Arts Master."

And then the silence fell again, as the third woman stood tall and signed, *Alborak Hild, certified Mountain Guide.*

Mildly taken aback by the first few women to come forward, Whit commented aloud, "But...of the four volunteers so far, only Lieutenant Yakami is an active duty warrior...."

Calmly and politely, Kali retorted, "Albie and I are warrior reserves. If you think it's necessary, Co-leader, reactivate us."

Neith replied, "We were raised to defend Freeland and our freedom. All the women of Freeland are warriors, whether in uniform or not, Co-leader. And besides, it is always prudent to take along a Healer, don't you agree?" A smile crossed Neith's face, for she was pleased with herself.

All around the Council table and in the gallery, women were nodding in agreement, as Captain Razia and her team came forward without fanfare.

Whit was not pleased with the idea of volunteer civilians going on this mission. This had not gone as planned. Taking a deep breath, Whit asked for a show of hands acknowledging acceptance. Hands were slowly raised, as one by one, the Council members voted. Whit briefly met Lilith's blue eyes as Lilith raised her hand, too.

How can I allow this? Whit wondered helplessly. *They're going to their deaths, my friends....* Striving to conceal her distress, and to buy some time, Whit took an additional moment, making a show of counting hands. She hoped her face did not reflect her feelings.

Stoically, Whit looked at the volunteers, including Kali and Captain Razia's warriors, and announced, "Unanimously, the Council of Isis accepts your service as volunteers."

Lilith was now on her feet, and in her role as temporary Deputy Leader she announced, "Will the volunteers all meet with Albie to compile a list of necessary equipment and supplies, and then regroup at the Leader's House at twenty hundred hours to discuss strategy." She looked around the Council Chamber for Captain Razia. Finding her, she ordered, "Captain Razia, you and your warriors will also meet us at the Leader's House." Lilith then whispered something in Whit's ear.

Finally, Whit rapped the gavel and declared the Council Meeting adjourned. Suddenly, Whit searched the faces of the crowd for the Science Officer. Spotting her, she shouted for Colonel Ferris to join her and Captain Razia in her office.

Chairs all over the Council Room scraped back, and women from the gallery began pressing in around Neith, Albie, Tor, and Kali, shaking their hands, wishing them Gaea's blessings.

Brooding, Whit watched Kali join her little band of "experts," exchanging encouraging words and smoothly organizing them. How easily she slipped into the role of group leader. Torn between great pride in Kali's competence, and equally great misgivings about the nature of this mission, Whit could only stand aside and watch. For the first time since her early youth, she was being left at home, out of the action. And she was belatedly discovering how much she hated it.

Ten minutes after the Council meeting ended, Whit nervously paced the confines of her office, her boots clicking rhythmically against the hardwood floors. Though she had managed to get three warriors assigned to the mission, she still felt as if Kali had outmaneuvered her. Whit was worried. She believed that Kali was not prepared sufficiently to lead this mission, nor, for that matter, to successfully challenge Arinna Sojourner.

A sharp rap on the door interrupted her. Barking, "Come," Whit turned to see Captain Razia and Colonel Ferris enter and salute. "At ease," she sighed, hoping these two venerable career officers could turn the tide on this mission and help her.

Razia, in her tough, steely-eyed way, seemed to read Whit's tension. With a cool acceptance, she looked down and calmly waited for the orders that might lead to her death. Ferris, however, a tall, olive-complexioned Arab woman, behaved like the detached and curious scientist she was. She met Whit's troubled gaze and held it.

Running a hand through her hair, Whit confided, "I think you both know that I am not pleased with the shape of this mission."

Captain Razia gave a slight nod, while Colonel Ferris's mouth twitched, as if she were suppressing a grin.

"I don't think," Whit went on, "that we can negate the possibility that Arinna Sojourner was psychically monitoring the Council meeting. But my plans will take this into consideration."

Both officers nodded in agreement with Whit.

Whit stepped forward, and in a conspiratorial tone said, "I have a contingency plan that I want to run by you...."

The officers watched her, listening intently.

"At this time," Whit explained, "the future of Freeland is in jeopardy. We face annihilation in one of two ways—one is Arinna's power, the other is her possible use of the nuclear missiles. Which is why I asked you to meet with me, Colonel Ferris."

"I surmised as much, Co-leader," Zak Ferris replied, her smile at last breaking free. "Would you like me to arrange for the dismantling of those warheads?" Clearly, Ferris was one step ahead; she knew what Whit wanted and needed for the success of this mission. She also knew that she could deliver.

"Good, Zak! I knew I could count on you," Whit said, beaming back at her. "I want you to work with Captain Razia and her special forces. And by the way, it is not necessary for you, personally, to go on this mission...."

Quietly, Ferris interjected, "Come, now, Whit. We both know that it will be necessary for me to oversee the disarming of the weapons...."

In a firm voice, Whit countered, "But the satellite project is our next priority. You are our highest-ranking science officer, and we are currently in need of your expertise there, as well."

Zak exchanged a glance with Captain Razia, then offered an alternative, "My junior officer, Lieutenant Colonel Rosenblum, is also a specialist in space science, including satellite research and development. But I'm afraid I'm the best when it comes to twentieth century nuclear warheads. And besides, Whit, I very much want to go on this mission. Remember, my mothers also died during the burning of the first Isis colony."

"All right," Whit finally conceded. "I want you to select two of your best explosives experts and a nuclear physicist for this operation," Whit stated. "Do not tell them any details until the last minute. This is information on a need-to-know basis. The fewer who know about it, the better."

Colonel Ferris acknowledged the order by nodding her head as she adjusted her warrior jacket. Clearly, it was more difficult for her to place the lives of others at risk than it was to face that danger herself.

Rubbing her neck, Whit turned and sat on the edge of her desk. Captain Razia, you will lead the tech team that targets the missiles. However, I want you to assign two of your warriors to Kali's squad—just in case...." With an abrupt wave of her hand, Whit ended her speculation.

"Yes, Co-leader," Razia answered. There was an excited gleam in her eyes now, as if she were relishing the prospect of her assignment.

"Kali will be in charge of her group," Whit clarified, "and I'll make sure that Tor understands that it will be her job to protect Kali at all costs. After all, it appears that she is our only weapon against Sojourner." She leaned back, contemplating both officers. "However," she emphasized, "Kali is not to be told anything about the tech team's mission. Hopefully, Arinna's obsession with capturing Kali will cause her to focus her psychic powers exclusively on Kali and her team." With conviction, Whit ended, "And what Kali does not know, Arinna, hopefully, will also not know."

Whit walked around behind her desk and took a clear plastic tube of blueprints off the shelf. "Captain, I've made copies of the blueprints of the SAC installation for both you and Kali," she said. "The blueprints indicate that there are auxiliary ventilation shafts running from the surface to beneath Level 22 of the northwestern side of the installation. These ventilation ducts will allow you access to the missile silo. It seems that the Aryan Federation took over this SAC installation just after the fall of the U.S. federal government. These neo-Nazis then built a missile silo into the side of the mountain, thinking the facility would make them invincible. But they didn't count on the AGH virus."

"How fortunate," Captain Razia commented, flashing a canny grin. With the decisiveness of a seasoned officer, she came forward to help Whit anchor the corners of the blueprints she was unrolling on the desk.

With a frown creasing her face, Ferris asked, "Whit, didn't the Aryan command realize that it was not wise to house nuclear missiles at a strategic command center? The Pentagon was always very careful about separating the two."

"Guess they weren't as smart as they thought they were," Whit answered with an ironical smile. "But it certainly has created a problem for us now." Whit ran her hand through her hair. "Actually, if this mission is successful, we are going to have to decide how Freeland should handle the remaining missile silos in our territories." Suddenly, she felt overwhelmed by the gravity of the situation.

Whit began roughly outlining her plan. "So, the tech team will approach from the northwest. You are authorized to take whatever special aircraft and equipment you may need." She pointed to the blueprint. "You can see that these ventilation ducts lead to the surface over here. Gesturing above the blues with her hand, Whit explained, "This duct opening appears to be approximately one kilometer from the main installation entrance over here. And the missiles are located...right here." She stood slowly and looked squarely at both officers. " Your mission, my friends, is to disarm those warheads, at any cost."

Their gazes steady, Razia and Ferris nodded.

Whit rolled up the blueprints, placed them in the tube, and handed them to Captain Razia. "May the Goddess watch over you and her tech team."

Both officers eyed Whit soberly, saluted, and briskly turned on their heels.

8

Barely an hour after the Council meeting had ended, Whit and Kali returned to their home in the countryside to prepare Kali for the mission to the North Cascades. Upstairs, in their Spartan bedroom, Kali set about selecting appropriate clothing and dressing for the mission. And nearby, indefatigable, Whit sat on the edge of the bed. Knowing she could not broach the subject of her meeting with Razia and Ferris, she stubbornly tried a variety of arguments to dissuade Kali from going at all.

Annoyed, Kali finally said, "I guess wanting you to support my decision to undertake this mission is too much to ask." With a fierce look, Kali grabbed her backpack and strode out of the bedroom, not even bothering to look at Whit.

Whit was feeling resentful and exasperated and responded by immediately changing into winter hiking attire and boots. She finished by strapping on her laser weapon. Slamming the bedroom door behind her, she rushed into the hallway, dug her own backpack out of the storage closet, and headed down the madrone staircase two steps at a time.

Kali looked up as Whit charged into the small pantry off the kitchen. She watched silently as Whit jammed freeze-dried food packages into her backpack. "What are you doing?" Kali finally asked, knowing full well what she was doing.

"What I should have done from the very beginning," Whit replied evenly. "This is a military mission, and it needs a ranking officer—me."

For a moment, Kali simply stood and watched her in disbelief. Whit's behavior baffled her. Then, her chin set in an obvious declaration of displeasure, she fastened her own backpack and stormed past Whit.

Seconds later, just before the front door slammed, Kali barked over her shoulder, "I'll wait for you in the transport, Tomyris."

For a moment, Whit just stood there, her backpack slung over one shoulder, staring up at the ceiling and wondering how things had gotten so damn complicated. All she wanted to do was protect Kali and Freeland from harm. And now she felt like a fool for not having the courage to tell Kali about the two-pronged operation she had just devised with Razia and Ferris. She knew that Kali would not approve.

A half hour later, after stopping by the house on Earhart Street to pick up Lilith and Styx, Whit drove the transport vehicle toward the Leader's House. She was glowering, only half-listening to Styx and Lilith, as they provided Kali with some necessary information about the SAC installation.

"Whit," Lilith repeated, "I asked why you were dressed like that."

Glancing down at the wool turtleneck under her unzipped parka, and the insulated trousers and boots she wore, Whit purposely misinterpreted Lilith's meaning. "Am I not dressed appropriately for this mission, Lilith?"

Silent, Kali stared straight ahead, into the darkness beyond the headlights. Whit knew this meant that Kali was absolutely livid and didn't trust herself to comment.

"Surely you are joking, Whit. Please tell me you don't intend to go on this mission...." Lilith said sharply, trying to maintain her composure.

"If I don't go, there's no real leadership!" Whit said through clenched teeth. "It's a military mission and needs a capable leader," she defended, her eyes moving to the rearview mirror to see how this news was being taken. "And besides, I know Arinna Sojourner."

In the back seat, Lilith now looked troubled and disapproving.

Styx retorted, "Tor's military, Whit, and..."

"A lieutenant, for Gaea's sake!" Whit shot back.

"And Captain Razia and her party are highly trained...."

Whit started to interrupt Styx again. "Please do not interrupt me again, Whit. I have been patient with you all day because I know how much you fear for Kali and love the women of Isis, especially your friends." Styx stared at the back of Whit's head and paused. "You are the Co-leader of Isis. You are brave and highly skilled in many areas, but you must learn to delegate power and trust other women in our community, women who are also very brave and talented in their respective areas of expertise. You, Whit, have a lot to learn about leading." Styx continued, "As I started to say earlier, Captain Razia and her special unit will provide some military support. And you must trust that Captain Razia knows what she is going to do. Being a good leader, military or political, means not being a bully and thinking that you can, and must, do it all yourself."

A part of Whit knew that Styx was right, but she had a difficult time accepting this truth from the wise Styx. She simply looked in the rearview mirror and raised her eyebrows, conflicted.

Silence. All four women were deep in thought.

Moments later, Kali was the first to break the silence. Defiantly, she asserted, "*I* am the Mage, Tomyris, and *I* will command this operation against Arinna. Since the Council has seen fit not to send me alone on this mission, I will at least have final say in how the nonmilitary group approaches and enters Arinna's stronghold."

Lilith could not believe what she was witnessing between Whit and Kali. She was deeply disappointed to see how their personal struggles were impacting on this most important mission to save Isis and Freeland. But she also loved them both, and decided to simply let them say what they needed to say to each other, while they had the chance.

"Kali, you have no idea what you're undertaking!" Whit snapped back. "Arinna Sojourner has had years to perfect what you've only been experimenting with for the past two months!"

Enraged, Kali turned to face Whit. "I'm the only one in this damn colony with even a clue about how she operates!" Then she unleashed what they both knew was at the heart of this disagreement—the long-unspoken truth. "Why don't you have more confidence in *me*, for once? Why is it *you* who always has to be in charge—you who has to be the stronger one—*constantly*! *Why, Whit*?! Kali waited for an answer, but knew that none would be forthcoming.

Whit simply gripped the steering wheel hard with both hands until her knuckles slowly turned white. She could hardly help noticing that the women in the back seat were still deathly quiet.

Angrily, Whit pulled the transport to a screeching halt beside Tor's motorcycle and stomped on the brakes. The vehicle had barely stopped when Kali jumped out and marched around to the rear cargo hold. Opening the hatch, she dragged out her pack and charged into the Leader's House, leaving Whit, Styx, and Lilith behind.

Nodding at Styx, Lilith emerged from the vehicle and detained Whit with a hand on her arm. Styx followed Kali into the large building and left Whit and Lilith alone in the wintry night.

As they stood outside the Leader's House, an overhead electric light illuminated Lilith's sorrowful expression.

As she saw that look, Whit's stubborn frustration withered and fell away. "You know she's going to die out there, Lil," Whit choked, tears rushing into her eyes as she acknowledged the reality of her statement.

Gently, Lilith said, "Dear Whit, as Leader, you have been chosen by the women of Isis to undertake grave responsibilities, and to protect Isis. But going off on this mission is not the best way for you to serve Isis and Freeland. Whit, you are needed here. You owe it to the women of Isis. They need you."

"Lilith," Whit responded in frustration, raking a hand through her dark hair, "I've never in my life done what's expected of me!"

"That I well know," Lilith said, her piercing blue eyes leaving no room for discussion. "However, you once promised me that when the day came, you would accept Kali as your equal. You said you would help her, as she has always helped you."

"Not fair," Whit sighed. "This is all happening much sooner than I ever expected."

"Much too soon for me, too, Whit." Resignedly, Lilith's sad eyes fell away, and the older woman seemed to strive to maintain her composure. "Will you keep your promise?" Lilith asked.

With a heavy sense of foreboding, Whit nodded assent, then abruptly led the way inside. *There must be something I can do,* she thought.

Tor watched Kali storm into the conference room and fling her heavy pack on the floor. Turning her back on the rest of the gathered volunteers, she unrolled a map upside down and then stared at it a full minute before cursing and turning the laminated map right side up. Soon afterward, Styx, and then, finally, Lilith and Whit, came in. Tor was not surprised to see Whit dressed as if she would be joining them. She had wondered how long Whit would remain in Isis, pushing papers while Kali faced death in the North Cascades.

Albie and Neith surveyed Whit, then exchanged glances. Seeing this, Whit summarily dispelled any notion the group might have about her joining them. Signing as she spoke, Whit confessed, "I was going to go with you, but," she sent an apologetic look at Kali, "you already have a well-qualified leader." Her husky voice rich with respect, Whit asked, "Kali, would you please brief us all on your plans for finding Danu and confronting Arinna."

Tor caught the surprised look that crossed Kali's face, and how it was swiftly replaced by a candid gaze of forgiveness, aimed directly at Whit.

Then, turning toward the group, Kali stood as she reviewed them. Neith and Albie sat together on one side of the conference table, opposite Tor. Seeming to gather her thoughts, Kali began signing as she spoke. "We'll fly out to the crash site in a helijet, flying low to escape radar. But I should mention that there is the strong possibility that Arinna will sense us—especially me. No matter, I feel we should be cautious, just the same. I'm not willing to give her even the smallest advantage. So we'll play it safe."

Albie nodded and Neith shifted in her seat.

Kali continued. "I want to get a look at the Swallow Danu used, and see what brought it down. We may be able to learn something about Arinna's weaponry. And maybe, just maybe, the evidence at the crash site will provide us with more information about Arinna's power and her operation in the Cascades. This means we'll be landing about thirty-two kilometers southeast of our objective." Kali indicated a point on the map and ran her finger along it, saying, "After investigating the crash site, we'll fly up to within five kilometers of the SAC installation, here," her long, slender finger stopped, "and hike the rest of the way to a secondary entrance, over here. We will not enter through the main entrance." She looked up and around at her small group, and asked, "Are there any questions?" The women simply shook their heads, each one dealing with her own fears.

Tor was concerned about the readiness of Albie and Neith for this mission, but said nothing. *These two are young and have never been on a military mission*, Tor mused, eyeing Neith and Albie skeptically. *I wonder if they'll be able to handle it when Arinna unleashes her campaign of terror.*

Neith seemed to feel Tor's scrutiny and turned to stare in return. She pushed up the sleeves of her sweater, then sat up straighter and rubbed her brow. Beside her, Albie turned her attention to retying the laces of her high mountain boots.

A brisk knock sounded on the door, and Captain Razia and Colonel Ferris entered the conference room, followed by four warriors, all carrying extra weapons and supplies. Kali motioned the new group to be seated. Whit knew she had to talk to Kali in private—soon.

Surprised by Colonel Ferris's appearance, Kali cocked her head to one side, quizzically, and asked, "Zak, are you volunteering for this mission, because..."

Before Kali finished speaking, Whit stepped forward and whispered in Kali's ear. Somewhat annoyed, Kali turned abruptly from the group of women and followed Whit out of the room. Once outside, she warned, "This better be good, Tomyris...."

Tor glanced sideways at Colonel Ferris, but said nothing. She simply steepled her fingers in front of her and sighed. Something was up—that was clear.

On the other hand, Neith was not shy about speaking up. Colonel Ferris, why..."

Quickly, Lilith politely interrupted Neith, and said, "Zak, may I speak with you privately?" Neith was taken aback momentarily, but said nothing. Ferris quickly rose and joined Lilith in a corner of the room.

In the meantime, Styx thought it prudent to provide the group with all of the personal background information that she had on Arinna Sojourner and how they might, in some small way, protect themselves psychically.

A few minutes later Kali, with her jaw muscles set tight, returned to the conference room, followed by a poker-faced Whit. Everyone took their seats. "Colonel Ferris... Zak, Whit has told me of her meeting with you. I want to thank you for taking time out of your busy schedule. Hopefully, the satellite project, under your direction, will progress smoothly. I look forward to working with you when we return from this mission." Kali smiled wanly, trying to be positive about the future, and wondered if the mission group would believe what she was about to say. "Colonel Ferris has come here to fill us in on the expected weather conditions in the Cascades and how the subzero temperatures will affect the functioning of our aircraft, electronic equipment, and laser weapons. So listen carefully, my friends."

Zak Ferris briefed the mission group, providing them with information that might very well save their lives. She started by removing her own hand laser from its holster, and proceeded to show the women how the nanoscopic mirror might lock up, or how a microscopic layer of ice might form on the sapphire crystals, and what they should do to rectify the situation. Potential problems regarding the aircraft were saved until the end

Tor appeared very interested in what the science officer was saying, and when she finished, asked, "How will the freezing temperatures affect our wrist communicators, Colonel Ferris?"

Ferris patiently explained what problems might occur, ended her presentation, and wished the warriors Gaea's blessings. "May you all return safely." All the while, Zak knew that the chances of her tech team returning to Isis were nil. But she was a seasoned warrior, used to death-defying missions, and so a philosophical "that's life" smile crossed her face.

Time was of the essence, and Kali was eager to get this mission under way. She quickly reiterated her strategy for Captain Razia's warriors. "Are there any questions?" She waited a moment and then slapped her hand on the conference table, "Well, then, let's make herstory."

But no one moved. Kali's band of volunteers looked anxiously at their leaders. Whit was standing beside Lilith, her arms folded across her chest, lost in her own thoughts, when Albie suddenly stood, and signed, *Kali, Whit, Lilith, Styx...before we go, I want to say how lucky we are to have you as our elders and leaders. And our love of Freeland and each other will make us strong against Arinna Sojourner.* Then she blushed and quickly sat down, thinking, *I'm glad I said that just in case I...*

Moved by Albie's remarks, Whit was more determined than ever not to just stand by and do nothing while her friends risked their lives.

"Bring your packs forward," Kali ordered, "and we'll distribute the supplies and weapons."

For roughly fifteen minutes, the group silently organized their gear, then closed their packs and tied the thermal sleeping bags on.

With a tersely worded warning of, "Try to hang on to this one, Lieutenant," Captain Razia handed Tor a new, holstered laser pistol. As Tor strapped the gun around her waist, the four assisting warriors opened a sturdy crate of rifles. After a nod from Kali, Captain Razia distributed laser rifles to the women. But when Captain Razia handed the lightweight laser weapon to Neith, the young Healer merely shook her head, refusing it. Without a word, she continued to check the contents of the medical kit she had brought.

For a moment, Kali's brown eyes lingered on Neith, as if debating how to phrase what she wanted to say. At last, she said firmly, "We all need to be clear about what to expect." Shoving her hands in her pants pockets, Kali eyed her band of warriors. "Arinna has already killed without remorse." She let the gravity of that sink in a moment, for in Freeland, murder was an uncommon and heinous crime. "Danu may well be dead already, or...seriously injured...beyond anyone's ability to save her."

Neith made a small sound in her throat. There was an almost indiscernible shake to her shoulders, and then she was openly weeping. Quietly, Albie moved her square frame to Neith's side and placed a comforting arm around her.

"I will not grieve for Danu," Tor resolved. "She is not the inexperienced child you all seem to think her...although I do admit she is naive and sometimes behaves rashly."

"You don't even know her!" Neith flung back, distraught.

"You're wrong," Tor related softly, "I *do* know her."

In an instant, all eyes were on Tor. Everyone in the room seemed to understand the significance of that remark.

Abruptly, Neith stopped crying, her eyes accusing and at the same time, relieved.

That's guilt written on her face—because she's involved with Albie, Tor realized, then wondered, *Is Neith making this trip to honor the bonds of friendship, or is she still suffering from unrequited love?*

In an obvious effort to relieve the tension, Styx speculated, "It's more likely that Danu is trying her best to distract Arinna's powers of psychic observation. And if she also manages to disrupt what technical surveillance Arinna probably has in place, you'll be able to penetrate the installation successfully."

That's true, Albie gestured, ever the optimist.

"For now," Kali concluded, "our plans are no more than this: we check out the crashed Swallow and see what we can learn about Danu, and possibly Arinna. And then we'll fly up to the SAC installation. You'll receive your orders on a need-to-know basis. This way there is less likelihood of Arinna discovering our plans." She cast a brief sidelong look at Whit, as if expecting criticism.

Instead, Whit studied the floor.

Tor was a little shocked by Kali not providing them with more information about how this operation would proceed. *I'm not sure I like this, but she's the boss.*

Kali finished, "I'll go into more detail after we get a look at Danu's Swallow. Okay, let's get this mission in motion. Everything has been prepared for us at the airfield."

Collectively, Tor, Albie, and Neith lifted their packs and followed Kali and the other warriors out the door.

The airfield was ablaze with lights and bustling with activity. Both Kali and Styx suspected that Arinna was engaging in round-the-clock surveillance of Isis. In an effort to confuse Arinna and circumvent detection, all the trading vessels in this part of Freeland had received orders from the Eight Leaders Council to land in Isis, whether pursuing business there or not. And so aircraft of all sorts, from transport shuttles to grain ships, were landing, then soon afterward, taking off again. With so much air traffic during the course of this single night, Arinna was going to have a hard time staying interested in, and tracking, each individual launch.

Near the center of the airfield, in front of Hangar 4, Styx slowed the transport vehicle to a stop. As the mission team piled out of the transport and milled about on the cold, windy tarmac, a young corporal rushed up to Whit and saluted.

"Commander Whitaker! Reporting on the shipment from Lang, Ma'am," the teenager chirped excitedly.

Worried about Kali and the mission, Whit gruffly demanded, "Shipment? What shipment, Corporal?"

"The space-going craft, Ma'am. The one we're going to assemble from the old NASA parts and then use to place new satellites in orbit." Whit looked at the youngster sternly. Surely she was no more than fifteen years old. The corporal rushed on, "All the parts are indexed and crated, and those too large to crate are wrapped in plastic inflatables. Over there...." The girl pointed to a huge grain transport parked at the far edge of the airfield. "Lieutenant Iphito wants you to come take a look."

"In a few minutes," Whit replied, placing her hand over her heart and returning the corporal's salute. The girl ran off, and Whit joined Lilith, watching the mission volunteers stow their gear in the readied helijet fifty meters away.

Casually, Lilith said, "Cimbri from Artemis left a message on my comline. Said to tell you that any weapon or aircraft they have is yours to command."

Only half listening to Lilith, Whit found herself studying Kali, trying to memorize both her face and her distinctly graceful movements. At last, the aircraft had undergone a thorough preflight check and was cleared for takeoff. The ground crew and friends began exchanging good-byes, wishing the warriors good luck and a safe return. Impulsively, Whit took Kali aside, around to the other side of the aircraft.

Pulling Kali to her, Whit held her a moment, overwhelmed by a feeling of disbelief that this was actually happening. They were about to be separated for the first time since their chance meeting in Elysium, over a year ago. As Kali stepped back, obviously preoccupied, ready to get on with her departure, Whit whispered, "How is it we've never handfasted?"

Surprised, Kali searched Whit's eyes. "Marriage? We declared as partners...."

"Which is pretty much what everyone does initially, isn't it?" Whit stared into her lover's eyes, needing some reassurance, some small measure of hope, in order to continue believing that she would spend the rest of her life with this woman. "I want more, Kali. I want us handfasted."

Her deep brown eyes steady, Kali asked with a bit of sarcasm in her voice, "Is it because we're beyond the crazed rush of infatuation now, and seeing the reality of who each of us is—not just the illusion of who we want the other to be?"

Frustrated that nothing she tried to say to Kali ever came out as she intended, Whit gripped Kali's arm, and her husky voice grew fierce. "It's because I *love* you—love you so much I can't even begin to contemplate my life without you! *I need you!* And when you come back from this..." Whit's voice cracked and she faltered. For the second time in less than an hour, tears sprang helplessly to her eyes.

As Whit turned her face away, Kali reached out and gently took Whit's chin in her hand. For an endless moment, her eyes penetrated Whit's soul, and she said, "And I love you, Tomyris. When I come back, we'll ask Lilith and Styx to perform our handfasting. But there is something I want even more...."

Whit did not trust herself to speak. She merely nodded, waiting for Kali to continue.

Gathering her nerve, Kali gave her head a slight toss, sending her golden braid over her shoulder. There was a corn-yellow flash as it moved, even in the shadow of the helijet. Beyond the craft, the glare of powerful overhead security lights illuminated the airfield, and voices were calling for Kali, announcing that it was time to go.

"Have you thought of...." Kali began, then concluded with a whisper of breath, "a child?"

Her voice hoarse with restrained emotion, Whit replied, "Yes."

Taking her in a strong embrace, Kali kissed her with the longing and heat of a woman who had little wish to leave. Then she suddenly broke from the embrace, sighing, "Oh, Whit...."

Whit gripped her, desperate. "Promise me you'll come back."

Instead, consoling, Kali joked, "Can you imagine the child that would carry our genes? Stubborn, willful, defiant...."

"We'll make a little terror," Whit breathed, "that will turn Freeland on its ear." Whit kissed her, then, a long, soul-shattering kiss that unified and fused them as nothing else could.

Then, tears on her cheeks, Kali slipped from Whit's arms and strode around to the other side of the aircraft. Following on her heels, Whit saw her board. At the door, Kali turned and met Whit's eyes. Slowly, she placed her fingers over her mouth, then extended her hand toward Whit.

A kiss.

A feeling of déja vu swept over Whit. *Why is this so familiar?* Whit reached out, pretended that she had caught the gift, then stored the kiss in her heart. Kali gave her a tremulous smile. The door closed, and Lilith pulled Whit back to a safe distance.

There was a faint hum as the near-silent engines revved. Styx and Lilith stood with Whit, watching the helijet lift-off from the tarmac. For a brief moment it hovered as the rotors shifted position, then the craft darted forward, into the night.

Gone, Whit thought, for a moment, terrified.

"The Mother's Blessing on them," Styx prayed quietly.

Studying the Mayan face beside her, Whit asked, "During the Council meeting—after you volunteered to go with her—what did Kali mind-speak to you to make you stay?"

Her dark eyes serious, Styx replied, "She told me you'd be needing me."

Instantly, a desperate sense of foreboding stole over Whit.

And then the voice of the exuberant young corporal sounded behind her. "Commander Whitaker! Please, won't you come and inspect the spaceship components, Ma'am?" The adoring teenager pleaded with Whit. "Captain Iphito is still waiting."

"All right, Corporal, all right. I'm coming. By the way, Corporal, what's your name?" With a deep sigh, Whit left Lilith and Styx.

"My name? My name is Jack Rabbit.... Well, that's not my real name, but...." The girl bounced along beside Whit.

As she walked away, head down, into the darkness of the airfield, Whit wanted more than anything else to burst into deep, heart-wrenching sobs. But she was Leader, and she was needed elsewhere.

Gaea protect her, Whit prayed.

Using her three-dimensional radar imaging system, Kali piloted the aircraft over glacier-covered crests, then banked tightly, staying within one hundred meters of the peaks below them. It was difficult flying so low in this mountainous region, but if they were going to escape radar detection, this was the only way to do it. They swept south of Hart's Pass, making directly for the section of old wagon trail where Danu's wreck lay half-buried in a snowbank. After locating and verifying the site, Kali shifted power from jet engines to the rotors, and landed the aircraft in the small clearing, right next to Danu's downed Swallow.

Because they had decided to maintain radio silence before leaving Isis, Kali did not send a message to Whit, though she would have liked nothing better than to hear her voice one more time. Instead, Kali commanded, "All out."

They laced on snowshoes and then clambered outside, anxious to see if Danu might still be in the snowbound Swallow. Checking her wristcom, Kali noted that it was 24:35 hours. Above them, a three-quarter moon hung in the night sky, casting a blue-white glow upon the snowy meadow.

In the semidarkness, their synlights held before them, the small band of warriors cautiously made their way over to the snowbound Swallow. Kali motioned the two warriors from Captain Razia's security forces to take up sentry positions, while she and Tor pulled open the damaged Swallow's door several centimeters. Just as Kali started to step into the Swallow, Tor suddenly pulled her back. "Wait, Kali!" she whispered, "We don't know what could be waiting for us in there." Before Kali could respond, Tor shouldered her way past Kali, her laser gun out and ready. She stood close to the side of the door and carefully peered inside. With the beam of her synlight she examined the interior of the plane. Satisfied it was safe, she entered the craft, with Kali close behind her.

It was quite empty.

Moments later, Neith and Albie came aboard the craft, determined to find some clue to Danu's whereabouts. Relieved that Danu was not lying dead in the plane, Neith took a deep breath, then muttered, "When I get my hands on her...."

Just then, Tor spotted the paper stuck conspicuously atop the flight control panel in the cockpit. She began to untie her snowshoes as rapidly as she could, then scrambled up the incline of the leaning craft and grabbed the note. After a quick look, she announced, "Danu's handwriting." She slid back down the floor of the cabin and handed the paper to Kali.

Kali read the short note aloud. " 'Ship brought down by lightning emanating from the SAC installation as I attempted to land. I'm okay. Have gone up the mountain to complete mission. Am using old wagon trail.' "

As Kali read, Tor signed the message to Albie, who shook her head.

At once, Kali took charge. "Tor, check the ship's systems and see if the black box can tell us anything." Swiftly shedding her mittens, Kali signed to Albie, *You check the wing and fuselage. See what damage this "lightning" did to the aircraft.*

They spent the next forty-five minutes maneuvering in the snow and investigating the damaged Swallow, their four separate synlights winking here and there in the darkness. Inside the ship, Tor ran down a preflight checklist. After tying one end of a fine, nylon safety cord to the door and the other end around her waist, Neith wandered off, searching the surrounding area for possible clues that would shed some light on the direction Danu took off in. While Albie clambered over the remains of the charred wing, Kali's synlight shone on the scorch marks left on the fuselage.

Finally, stomping her feet and beginning to shake in the harsh bite of a cold, howling wind, Kali shouted for the warriors to return and report their findings.

"Extensive damage to the ship's systems," Tor reported. "Except for the black box and air filtration unit, the electrical circuits are completely shorted out." Holding the black box in both hands and looking at it, Tor continued, "The black box recorded a sudden and enormous electrical charge hitting the left side of the ship, then a wild, barely controlled landing which finally ended in this crash site." Shaking her head in amazement, she concluded, "It's incredible. I don't know how Danu walked away from this."

Albie quickly took off her mittens and signed, *This wreckage is like nothing I've ever seen before. Whatever caused the damage was very precise and very controlled. That blast—lightning or whatever—sent the craft off course, eventually forcing it down, without incinerating the entire Swallow or harming Danu.* Albie blew once on her hands and immediately tugged the mittens back on.

Facing Albie, so Albie could watch her face, Tor agreed with a nod. "Uncannily precise, if it was lightning. Maybe it was some new kind of laser."

Before Kali or Tor could respond, Neith, squinting against the cold wind, jumped in, "Of course it must be lightning. Some sort of weather phenomenon during the blizzard. After all, what weapon delivers an electrical charge of such magnitude? I've never heard of such a thing."

Running her mittened hand over the ice-cold fuselage, Kali cautioned, "The weapon could be Arinna herself." She shuddered with the thought of such power, and momentarily doubted her own abilities.

"Arinna—using lightning?" Intrigued, Neith lifted her knees and marched energetically across the snow to Kali's side. "What makes you think Arinna can—what? Throw it—shoot it? How does a person—even Arinna—cast a lightning bolt?" It was clear Neith was reluctant to believe that any human could possess such power, as she shook her head in disbelief and wonderment.

Kali frowned, baffled. "This is magic, that's all I know. I can still sense a...haze of negative energy suspended around this ship."

Then she turned and questioned, "Did you find any sign of Danu's trail?"

"Yes," Neith said, pointing toward the dark cliff. "There's a coded arrangement of stones near the cliff face over there. She seems to have followed the old way to Hart's Pass, the wagon trail from pioneer days."

Albie shed her mittens again, unable to forego jesting and injecting a little humor into the situation, *Trust Danu not to let a little thing like a plane crash stop her!*

They all grinned in response.

"Good work, everyone," Kali said, checking her wristcom again. Waving them all toward the ship, she announced, "It's zero two hundred hours. That's enough. Let's shelter on board the helijet for the night and we'll get started just before sunup. If you left any gear in the Swallow, better get it."

As Kali trudged forward, a howl cut the night wind. She turned, feeling the presence of numerous fleet-footed travelers; there were many elusive shadows in the nearby forest heading their way.

Suddenly, in unison, Razia's warriors, who had been standing guard outside, began shouting, "Wolves! Wolves!" as they started backing up toward Kali. Racing toward the women were dozens of wolves, their silver white coats shining in the moonlight, snarling lips revealing the sharp incisors ready to tear flesh. The sentries raised their rifles and began firing blast after lethal blast, only to find the downed wolves quickly replaced by more determined ones.

"Wolves!" Neith breathed, eyes wide with fear.

"Don't worry," Kali yelled. "Just run for the helijet. Move, Neith, move."

Snow flew as legs churned, Albie running just as quickly as the others, even though she had never heard the howls. Instead, she had actually seen the loping wolves emerging from the edge of the blue spruce forest a short distance away. Neith staggered and nearly fell, but Tor grabbed her arm and pulled her to her feet.

The first to arrive at the helijet door, Albie pulled it open, lunged inside, then turned to haul in Neith. Kali remained outside the aircraft with her laser drawn, as the wolves continued to race toward them. Suddenly, Tor was at her side, along with Razia's warriors. She turned her synlight to maximum brightness and aimed it at the glowing red eyes that circled nervously just a few meters away.

Then Tor and the rest of the warriors began firing their lasers. Over the howling wind Tor shouted to the others, "Put your synlights on maximum." Immediately stunned by the blinding light, the lead wolves froze. They stood there panting, their pink tongues lolling, whining in confusion. "Blast them to hell, damn it," Tor bellowed.

Then, unexpectedly, one wolf charged. Neith screamed, but Kali was prepared and dropped the animal with a lethal blast.

"Get in, Tor. Quick!" Kali ordered, never taking her eyes off the beasts. "These wolves are spellbound."

Slowly, Tor stepped behind Kali, still directing her synlight at the dozens of circling wolves before them. Taking hold of Kali's parka collar with her gun hand, Tor began backing up, pulling Kali backward with her as she moved. Another wolf charged and Kali fired another blast. In the next instant, Tor and the warriors were scrambling into the helijet. As all the wolves charged, Kali suddenly began shouting, invoking one of the Wiccan incantations Styx had taught her. The magical, strange-sounding words instantly stopped the wolves in their tracks.

Not wanting Kali to take unnecessary risks, Albie and Tor each grabbed an arm and yanked Kali up off the ground and into the cabin. As Kali tucked her legs up and rolled in, Neith yanked the door shut, and then they all heard the thud of bodies as the wolves senselessly hurled themselves into the side of the aircraft.

"Spellbound, huh?" Tor commented, surveying Kali's tense, perspiring face.

With a curt nod, Kali pushed herself up and made for her flight chair. "Try to get some rest," she instructed, trying to appear as if she did this sort of thing every day. "We're going to need it."

Just before the sun rose above the glaciers and granite mountaintops the next morning, the weary women began to stir and move about the helijet cabin. Tor, along with Razia's warriors, Anat and Crista, had taken turns standing watch, hoping the others could find several peaceful hours of sleep. Kali was the first to look out the cockpit window, knowing what she would see and steeling herself against the bloodied snowscape of the night before.

"Tor! Tor! Look outside.... I can't believe this." Everyone, including Tor, rushed to get a view of the small meadow adjacent to the cliff's edge.

Albie signed her reaction, but no one saw her. They were all too busy registering the incredible scene before them.

Without thinking, Neith rushed to the cabin door and pushed it open before anyone could stop her. "How is this possible?" she snapped to no one in particular, and she jumped outside without snowshoes. "Where, in Gaea's name, are the dead wolves? And the snow, it's pure white and untouched, except for our own tracks."

One by one, the others exited the helijet, each woman not believing what she saw, each woman, that is, except Kali. "I told you the wolves were spellbound, that this was Arinna's doing." The early sun cast a warm, golden glow on the peaceful meadow and a gentle breeze stirred the forest spruce a short distance away. Kali took a deep breath, shook her head, and said, "We'd better get moving. If any of you left any gear in the Swallow, get it now, and watch out for those snowbanks by the cliff's edge. And stay alert." *We were lucky last night,* she thought. *Arinna is toying with us and I've got to stop her before anyone dies.*

Outside the helijet, Kali visually checked the body of the aircraft, including the engines and rotors, just to make sure it was not damaged when the wolves attacked. Satisfied that everything was okay, she returned to the cockpit to check the various systems before they took off for the SAC installation. Time was running out. She pressed the ignition switch. To her relief, the jet engines kicked in and the rotors started spinning in spite of the frigid temperature. Remembering the black box, she thought, *I want to bring it back to Isis. Hah!*

That's a joke. I'm assuming I'll come out of this alive. She slipped out of her flight chair and yelled to Tor, "Where's the black box?"

Tor shrugged her shoulders, "Good question. I must have dropped it last night somewhere in the snow, during the wolf attack. I'll check around."

Kali jumped out of the helijet and figured they'd find the box faster if she helped.

Albie hurriedly trudged over to the Swallow and quickly retrieved her pack and rifle. She looked at Neith and signed, *I've gotta pee, I'm going to the woods over there. Tell Kali I'll only be a minute. Take my backpack, will ya?*

Neith smiled and signed, *Still shy?*

Albie shoed to the edge of the woods and looked back at the small band of warriors preparing to leave on the next leg of their mission. She smiled and looked around at the giant spruce and ponderosa pines. The sweet smell of the ponderosa filled her with a sense of peace. Walking several meters into the woods, she found privacy behind a wide-trunked tree. The snow wasn't as deep here as it was in the meadow. After finishing what she came to do, she pulled up her trousers. While buckling her belt, she chanced to look up. It was then that she saw the series of deep gauges in the trunk. *Claw marks made by a very large bear. Hmm, but there are no paw prints in the snow.* Quickly, she grabbed her rifle and started back to the helijet.

At the edge of the woods, Albie witnessed a sight that froze the blood in her veins. She tried to shout, but very little discernible speech resulted. Time seemed to stand still for Albie. Instinctively, she responded by firing her laser into the air, afraid that if she fired directly she might hit Neith. She prayed she could draw someone's attention.

As Albie had hoped, the flash of blue light in the distance did catch Tor's attention. She turned to Kali and saw that she, too, was looking in Albie's direction. It didn't take them but a moment to realize why Albie was firing her weapon.

Suddenly, a frightful scream pierced the icy air.

Tor and Kali jumped up and turned. Neith came racing past them, her arms pumping to increase her speed. They immediately saw the reason why. About ten meters behind her, a huge grizzly was chasing her at a trot. Both Kali and Tor dashed for the laser rifles leaning against one another in tepee formation less than a few steps away, but the bear was slapping the weapons out of reach before they had grabbed even one. Gasping, they both pivoted and sprinted, as the bear's immense front paws swept a rifle barrel into his mouth. With a fearful tearing of teeth and paws, the grizzly shattered the rifle, then grabbed another and another, systematically destroying all three. Growling, he lumbered forward.

As all three women clumsily shoed before the bear, Kali looked back over her shoulder and saw the grizzly stop and point his nose into the air, as if sorting through the bouquet of human odors for one particular scent. Then, with a roar that echoed back from the surrounding mountains, the beast broke into a faster run.

Kali, out of breath, yelled, "Anat, Crista, where the hell are you?"

Anat and Crista had jumped out of the Swallow after hearing Neith's scream. They attempted to get the grizzly in their rifle sights, but found that Tor and Neith were in the way. The warriors separated and ran to flank the bear.

Within the space of a breath, the bear seemed to have singled Kali out, separating her from the others, pursuing her to the very edge of the cliff. One minute she was running with the others, the next she was flanking them, and then they were behind her, shouting to her from a distance. There was a U-shaped valley of blue spruce below her, and the edge of the cliff was now less than a meter away. In a panic now, Kali swung about. Rising up on his back legs, the bear was moving in on her before she could think what to do.

Then Albie dashed in from the side, her laser pistol drawn. Suddenly, the bear dropped to all fours, and Albie's shot flashed over his head as the bear lunged forward. With two swipes of a golden-brown paw, the bear sent Albie spinning across the thin crust of snow, a spray of red in her wake.

Horrified at what was happening, Kali was conscious of Neith's scream, of Tor, laser pistol in hand, darting in to take Albie's place. "Don't, Tor!" she yelled, trying to breathe deeply and gather

her ki, certain she could invoke an incantation if she could only get a minute to focus.

"This is Arinna's work!" Tor shouted to her, "The bear's targeting you!"

Executing a low slide, Neith skidded to Albie's side and pressed both hands down on the fountain of red gushing from her friend's head and bloody, torn arm. Momentarily distracted by Neith's motion, the grizzly whirled, and seemed ready to launch an attack on the young Healer. Before she knew what she was doing, Tor heard herself shouting vehemently at the bear, waving her arms and making herself too exciting a lure to dismiss.

As the grizzly snarled and made for Tor, Kali raised her arms and chanted a series of incantations—including the one she had invoked so successfully against the wolves the evening before. Unfazed, the bear met Tor's sudden change of direction and pressed the lieutenant toward the cliff's edge, a few meters away. Quicker than any of them could believe, as Tor feinted and dashed from side to side, the bear trapped her at the edge. Seeing what was about to happen, Kali tried, in rapid succession, every Wiccan spell she knew. None of her spells seemed to affect the rampaging beast.

Mother! I can't save her! Kali shrieked internally. *Maybe Whit was right. She belonged on this mission.* Feeling helpless, she fired off what should have been lethal laser blasts at the beast, but he kept moving toward Tor, in spite of his wounds. *She's going to die.*

Fearlessly, Tor stood ready—knees bent, palms stretched up and outward toward her opponent. And as the bear moved to slap her with a massive paw, Tor dove past him to his left side, rolled to an upright position, jumped, and spun around, delivering a powerful kick to the bear's knee joint. This effectively shifted his center of gravity.

Already caught leaning to the side, the bear now lost his balance and rolled on the ground. In the wink of an eye, the bottom half of him dropped over the cliff edge. For a few seconds his front paws clawed frantically for a hold on the crusty snow. Then he simply disappeared over the edge. One second he was there, a rippling golden-brown mass of brute strength and potential death; the next second, the crystalline snow he had kicked up during his attack swirled in the air, the only remaining evidence that he had been on the cliff at all.

Except for Albie.

Kali ran to Tor, helped her up, then the two of them hurriedly joined Neith and the two warriors at Albie's side. Squatting in the pool of bright red blood on pristine snow, Neith kept direct pressure on the long, deep wound. The grizzly had sliced right through Albie's parka and into the well-muscled chest and arm beneath. Anat was frantically wrapping a scarf around Albie's head wound.

Her brown eyes shining with unshed tears, Neith moaned, "It's bad—*very* bad!" She paused, trying for self-control, then abandoned the effort. "She's going into shock. Let's get her into helijet where it's warm—*now, dammit!*"

The women quickly carried Albie to the aircraft, where Neith raised the cabin temperature. While Tor, Anat, and Crista stood watch outside the helijet, Kali and Neith spent the next hour working on Albie. Neith quickly scanned Albie's vital signs. "This is not good, Kali," she said simply. With the help of a micromedi-laser, and using all her skill as a surgeon, she treated Albie's wounds as best she could. But it was apparent to all of them that Albie needed to be taken back to Isis or she would die.

Kali stood close by, flexing her shoulder muscles, then began chanting a healing spell she remembered from her days in Elysium with Baubo. Soon she could feel the golden warmth surge through her.

Still kneeling beside Albie, Neith said sadly, "There's an infection developing in her shoulder, and I'm afraid sepsis is setting in. We've got to get her to the clinic."

Kali knelt opposite Neith and placed her hands on Albie's chest. In a murmur of breath, she continued chanting the healing spell. Within seconds, she felt the healing energy flowing—from her core, down the length of her arms, through her palms, and into Albie's still body. But after a few moments, Kali began to feel drained, then dazed. Reluctantly, she removed her hands and stepped away from Albie.

Neith ran the bioscanometer over Albie again. Somewhat amazed, she remarked, "That seems to have done the trick...for now, anyway." Neith brushed the hair back from Albie's face tenderly.

With Albie resting comfortably, Kali called the women in from the cold to tell them of the change in plans. Her energy a little strained from the healing spell, Kali said, "Crista, get yourself into the cockpit. After you drop me at Hart's Pass, you'll fly these women back to Isis. I want you all out of danger as soon as possible. Do you understand?"

Crista hesitated and looked at the other women uncertainly.

"Crista, that's an order. Now move!" It was clear Kali was determined to have her orders obeyed.

Then Tor stepped forward and met Kali's eyes. Kali saw in those black orbs a fierceness of will that matched her own. "I'm going with you, Kali." *Don't say no to me,* Tor thought, adjusting the holstered laser and maintaining fierce eye contact with Kali.

"I'm just a warrior, Kali," Tor breathed. "And ultimately, aside from those handy flashes of psychic power, so are you. But together, you and I are going to stop Arinna Sojourner. Or die trying."

Time was ticking and the silence in the cabin was deafening. Kali was conflicted, but took the measure of this woman. She knew Tor would prove a formidable ally. Finally, she said, "Okay, Tor. It's you and me. Everyone else goes back to Isis. Crista will fly Albie, Neith, and Anat back. Since it seems that Arinna already knows we're here, we might as well fly up to Hart's Pass and the SAC installation. Okay, everyone, take your seats and let's get out of here."

Each woman scrambled to her assigned place, except Anat. Her feet glued to the floor, her voice edged with a slight tremor, she said, "Co-Co-Co-leaderrr...I...I'm not needed in I...Isis. My life belongs to you and Freeland, and I'm going with you and Tor." Anat's olive skin took on a blush as she lowered her eyes and waited for a response.

Kali swung around to face Anat. "Why is it that no one wants to obey my commands around here? Look at me, Anat. You know that you'll probably die up there."

Anat looked up at Kali and said, "I'm prepared. I'm a Freeland Warrior."

Kali, with tears forming in the corners of her eyes, said no more and took her seat.

Crista took the pilot's seat and toggled all the necessary switches, while Neith secured Albie's stretcher for the flight, then buckled herself in. The helijet lifted off without incident and headed due east, into the rising sun. Kali and Tor strained in their seats to survey the ground below, to catch a last glimpse of the place where death had almost claimed them.

Quietly, Kali said, "Tor! Anat! We'll be landing in approximately ten minutes. Before we disembark, make sure you check your weapons and take anything else you think we may need, including sunshades. The last thing we need to deal with is snow blindness."

At Hart's Pass, nothing moved but the wind.

Kali stood tall and pulled a thermal hat over her blonde hair. She looked lovingly at all of the women as she bid them farewell. "If it is not meant for us to be together again, may the Mother bless us all."

9

Danu blinked several times as she gradually became cognizant of her surroundings. Dazed, she glanced around, recognized Arinna's War Room, and realized that she was still deep within the mountain stronghold. Above her, on the platform, Arinna lounged in her leather compu-chair, steepling her fingers as she contemplated Danu. Loy stood by Danu's side, her eyes clearly trying to give Danu some sort of warning.

As she shifted her position, automatically taking an inventory of how she felt, the overall sluggishness of her body registered. Then she felt a sharp, fiery pain across her lower abdomen. Wondering, *What on Gaea's sweet earth is that?* she began a cursory self-examination. To her surprise, she wasn't wearing her mountaineering clothes anymore. Instead only a loose, belted white robe covered her nakedness. *My clothes?*

"Congratulations," Arinna's silky voice proclaimed. "You've made your first donation to my cause. While you slept, I harvested ova from your left ovary. You've provided me with enough eggs abundant in genetically enhanced DNA to make a grand start. Your future daughters, or should I say mine, will be the super-warriors of my new world order."

Roughly pulling the robe apart, Danu found a bandage taped along the left side of her abdomen, and immediately felt faint.

"I took the ova from you yesterday morning and then spent hours last night preparing a series of enzyme baths for the DNA. While you've been resting, my Delphi Unit has been initialized and now supports the first batch of our mutual conceptions."

Oh, Goddess, I'll be the mother of demon daughters.... Bile surged into Danu's throat.

"You should be *proud* of your role in my plans!" Arinna hissed. In an angry rush she left the compu-chair and swept down the ramp from the platform. The android Reg left its post by the door and fell into step beside her.

As Danu tried to back away, Loy's hand shot out and caught her by the arm. Before Danu could get off a kick, the Reg had subdued her, pinning her arms behind her back. Arinna hovered nearby, wearing a cruel smirk. Danu knew this was just the beginning of her torment.

"Shall I tell you who came to call while you were resting?" Arinna taunted.

Against her will, Danu's heart leapt up with hope, and she purposely turned her face from Arinna, trying to blank her mind. *I won't give her the pleasure....* A wall of snow appeared in Danu's mind's eye. It seemed to work, as the blocking had with Kali and Styx at the birthday dinner—*when was that? I'm losing track of the time. How long have I been here? My wristcom?*

Danu could not seem to keep Arinna from penetrating her mind, no matter how hard she tried.

Arinna came closer to her. "Now, Danu, wouldn't you like to know who followed you?" A lovely, long-fingered hand plunged into Danu's thick, red hair, pulling Danu's head back, bringing her eyes up and even with Arinna's own. "Or what happened to our visitors?"

Suspended in the depths of dark, green eyes, Danu didn't even bother trying to reply. *Oh please, no. She's hurt them.*

"I keep telling you, Danu," Arinna crooned. "Save the concern for yourself." On a signal from Arinna, the Reg shifted his hold, pressing his hard fingers against the abdominal incision.... *Pain, excruciating pain.* In agony, Danu cried out as the Reg loosened his grip on her. The room spun, her knees buckled, and Arinna's insistent voice was thrumming near her ear, through her body.

"Stand up, I said," she ordered, and Danu did her best to oblige. She could feel herself swaying, could feel Arinna's hand moving through her hair again. At a distance, Loy stood stone still, simultaneously watching Danu and keeping an eye on the Reg. *She's endured something like this, too.*

"Tell me who came for you?" Arinna coaxed.

Danu stared at her. *Why is she doing this?* But remembering the Reg's hand digging into her flesh, she was reluctant to fence with Arinna again. She gave the question careful thought, then blurted, "Kali." It seemed fairly harmless; Arinna already seemed to know that Kali was preparing for a psychic duel. Then, dizzy with pain, she glanced at Loy, wondering if this was how betrayal began.

"Very good, Danu. I'm pleased that you did not lie," Arinna enthused, genuinely pleased. "And who else?"

Suddenly wanting to be done with it, Danu reared back and spit in Arinna's face with all the force she could muster. She heard Loy gasp, and then she was slammed to the concrete floor, pinned on her back by Arinna's boot on her neck.

Above her, Arinna was shrieking, "I know what you're trying to do, my little genius! But you won't die yet—no—not for a long, long time!"

Savagely, Arinna kicked her.

Danu curled up into a fetal position, feebly trying to protect her ribs and throbbing belly.

"You see, I am already well aware of anything I choose to know!" Arinna declared. "I can sense whatever I wish—whether within this installation or hundreds of kilometers away!" With a sneer, Arinna leaned closer. "This is the beginning of your training, Danu. And before I am through, you will answer any question I put to you...."

A gasp of pain escaped past Danu's tightly clenched teeth.

"Your friend Alborak is dying," Arinna hissed, "a victim of the same bear I sent against you!"

Another kick, this time to the kidneys, left Danu moaning helplessly, refusing to believe that Albie was dying. *Gaea! I've been so naive about Arinna's powers.*

"And the rest of your friends—Kali, Neith, and your Samurai lover—have abandoned efforts to 'save' you. At this very moment they're carrying Alborak back to their helijet, and returning to Isis as quickly as possible." Arinna punctuated the harsh words with another kick.

This time, the boot landed on her wound and Danu felt the stitches give way. A rush of blood oozed over her abdomen.

"You *said* you'd give her to *me*," Loy was protesting. "That she was my reward for loyalty."

Though aching and bleeding, Danu was more distressed by what she had just heard than by anything else that had transpired. Looking up to see Arinna's wicked smile, Danu realized that Arinna had registered her abhorrence.

Arinna paused for effect, looked Danu over, then addressed Loy. "Should I be jealous, my love?"

Both frightened and wary, Loy met Arinna's eyes and attempted a weak smile. "Absolutely not."

Arinna walked languorously over to Loy and kissed her lightly on the lips. "I remember how intrigued you once were by this one's innocence," she murmured. Possessively, Arinna sent her fingers over Loy's denim jumpsuit, lingering on her breasts.

Eyes slowly closing, and then opening again, Loy seemed to become enmeshed in the weave of some spell. A flush spread up her neck and into her face.

"Should I be jealous?" Arinna repeated.

Her voice thick, Loy returned, "I am yours. You...are my mistress." She said it like a mantra—like something she had said a thousand times.

"Good," Arinna whispered, stroking Loy's neck. "I'd regret having to return you to obedience training." With a sureness, Arinna's hand moved down Loy's torso, lower, and still lower, until the palm finally paused, resting on Loy's pubic mons, the fingers pressing into the space between Loy's legs.

Loy stared straight ahead, her body rigid.

Smiling in triumph, Arinna granted, "You may take her."

Swiftly, Loy stepped around Arinna, leaned down, and grabbed Danu by the arm. With a tug, she brought Danu to her feet.

Through a haze of pain, Danu noted the smear of blood on the floor, the blood seeping through the bandage. She clutched at her half-open robe and tried to close it. "No, Loy. Please, no...." she pleaded weakly.

And as Loy dragged Danu toward the door, Arinna announced, "I'll be in the lab," and then chuckled malevolently. "And I'll expect you in my bed this evening, Loy."

Mercilessly indifferent to Danu's staggering gait, Loy crossed the War Room with Danu in tow. She stopped at the steel door, waiting for it to slide open. Impulsively, Danu tried to fight against her, and then nearly collapsed. She felt so weak; her legs had become rickety poles, and she could not keep her balance.

Following behind them, on her way to wherever the lab was, Arinna called to Loy, "Do you need the Reg?"

Loy viciously cuffed Danu on the ear, snarling, "Behave!"

Danu was rubber-legged to begin with, and the blow sent her to her knees. Aggravated, Loy grabbed her elbow and yanked her up again.

"No," Arinna laughed, pleased, "I don't think you need any help. You appear to be handling this yourself very nicely." Then she cautioned, "Remember, she is *my* property and I need her alive. See to the abdominal incision first."

With a nod, Loy began pulling Danu down the dimly lit hall.

Behind them, Arinna entered an elevator and disappeared into its steel enclosure.

Muddled with pain, Danu wasn't sure where they had gone, but all at once Loy had her leaning against a cinderblock wall next to a wooden door. She swept the door open, then dragged Danu inside a small chamber. Strangely, Loy's manner abruptly changed, and she wrapped an arm around Danu, guiding her gently to a narrow bed against the wall.

Instantly, Danu was off the bed, rolling painfully to her feet, only to have Loy tackle her down to the covers once more. "Cooperate, dammit!" Loy hissed. "I don't want to hurt you!" But by now, battered and confused, Danu only knew she had to resist, had to fight until they accidentally killed her—or she would end up like Loy—a traitor to her people. And so she fought on until Loy landed a punch to her jaw that knocked her senseless.

The next thing she clearly knew, Loy was beside her on the bed, re-stitching the incision on her lower abdomen. While Danu squinted, wondering why her wound felt so numb, she noticed that the robe was gone and she was nude. And then, as she tried to move her arms and legs, she realized she could not. A fast check revealed that there were soft cotton restraints on each ankle and wrist, attached to the bed frame and tying her in place. She tensed, then yanked against the ties, trying to break free.

"Stop it," Loy barked, annoyance sharp in her voice.

"W-what are you going to..."

"Young idiot," Loy breathed, then added in a querulous, louder tone, "I tied you to keep you still, so I could sew you up before you bled to death."

Danu listened distrustfully, merely staring at her. She realized that she was steeling herself for the next onslaught of abuse. If things were what they seemed to be, what was coming next was the form of abuse she feared most—sexual abuse. It was becoming clear to her that Loy intended to make her a plaything for the evening. *If that's not what she wants, why did she bring me here?* Danu thought with a shudder.

After a few moments, Loy finished her work. Using fresh bandages, she carefully dressed the wound, then untied Danu, warning, "Stop hitting me—it hurts."

Danu frowned suspiciously and watched Loy pull out a rough, woolen blanket from a small foot locker in the corner, then shake it out. Shivering, Danu saw the words U.S. ARMY imprinted across the bottom third of the blanket.

"Your incision is under a local anesthetic for now, but it'll hurt like hell later," Loy warned.

Danu scornfully wondered if she was supposed to be grateful.

Sighing wearily, Loy sat down on the bed, facing her. She ran her hands through her gleaming black hair, and Danu noticed for the first time how the once-stylish cut had gone ragged. But Loy was still an attractive woman—and seemed more fascinating to Danu than she had during the previous summer. There were expressions around her eyes that Danu had never seen before: compassion and humility, and the look of a long, draining struggle. Arinna had been teaching her lessons all right. More than obedience, Danu was sure. And Loy had learned some bitter ones; it showed in her face.

Leaning back against the rough cinderblock wall, Loy said softly, "I'm sorry I treated you like that...tricking you, shackling you, dragging you to Arinna...the grabbing, the hitting...I hated it." Danu waited, as Loy pinched the bridge of her nose. "Unbelievable as it may seem," Loy finished, "I've been trying to help you, without getting both of us killed."

"I believe you," Danu mumbled, and she did, for some reason. Closing her eyes, she suddenly noticed how much they burned, how incredibly tired she felt. Now that fear and fighting seemed to have ended for a time, the only thing she wanted to do was fall into an exhausted sleep. However, Loy was talking again, and Danu obligingly opened her eyes, trying to seem attentive.

"I don't want her to do to you what...what..." And then she sat there, scowling, her eyes like hard coal. "I'm going to try to keep her away from you," Loy told Danu earnestly. "Maybe, since she needs you for her parthenogenetic conceptions, she'll just take eggs from you every once in a while, but for the most part leave you alone."

Shuddering, Danu shook her head. "Kill me first, Loy. I won't be the source of Freeland's ruin."

Loy wrapped her arms about herself, sadly rocking back and forth on the bed. "Don't you think I've tried to escape that way myself?"

Danu peered at the stricken woman before her, dismayed.

"Of course I failed," Loy whispered, then in a stronger voice confided, "She hates you, you know, almost as much as she hates Kali and Whit." A loud silence filled the room, and Loy said, "And I really fear for you, Danu. Please try not to antagonize her...for both our sakes." She kept her eyes lowered as she spoke.

Swallowing, Danu said softly, "She knows I'm here to avenge Lupa. Perhaps she's afraid of me." Then she laughed ironically at her own words. *Arinna afraid of me? That's a joke.*

Loy looked distressed. "Arinna told me about that." Then, sighing, she offered, "I know Lupa was your friend. I'm sorry."

Danu was determined to concentrate on gathering information, readying herself to face her foe. Firmly, she put aside the weight of sadness. "Was the explosion that blew up the Leader's House last August magic?" she asked.

"No. Plastic explosives she found here and took to Isis with her." Loy glanced over her shoulder at the door.

It was an automatic response, the result of deep fear, and Danu wondered again what terrible methods Arinna had used to train Loy in obedience.

Daring to go on, Loy whispered, "She can't use magic all the time, or she ends up with very little power." Dark eyes still on the door, Loy divulged, "I get the impression it's like anaerobic exercise—you know—like running a sprint. It's a short-term, major energy expenditure, and then she has to rest."

"Hmmm," Danu mused. Despite her best effort, her own eyes were closing. She felt Loy get off the bed, heard faint, rustling noises, and then drifted into a doze.

She sensed a warmth and softness that could only be another woman's body pressed against her. Danu nestled into it, murmuring a name. But something wasn't right. The scent...that was it. This woman had another scent. Instinctively, Danu rolled back, and saw Loy's surprised, somewhat guilty face.

"Who's Tor?" Loy asked quietly.

"What are you doing?" Danu demanded groggily, the beginnings of outrage flaring through her.

"It's my bed, and Arinna expects me to be in it, having my way with you." With an annoyed chuckle, Loy stated, "Don't worry, I only intend to be found sleeping with you. If she finds anything less, we're both going to be punished." And then the expression on Loy's face turned grave.

"Are there cameras in here?" Danu whispered, squinting as she tried to focus on the walls and ceiling. "Are we under surveillance?"

"No cameras," Loy muttered, "but...she seems to know whatever she wants to know about what I do...what I think...." Her face became tense with fear.

After a moment, Danu asked, "How did she train you, Loy?"

There was a long silence, so long that Danu thought Loy would not answer. Then Loy rasped, "She tortured me. Her hands, her fingers, can emit...electrical charges...and she can fluctuate the voltage at will."

Impulsively, Danu held her.

Loy was trembling from just talking about it, but the woman pushed on. "She's evil, Danu. Gaea only knows why she's the way she is, but she lives to conquer, to destroy."

"We have to stop her," Danu affirmed.

"We will," Loy promised, "but not by ourselves. We wouldn't stand a chance. Wait for Kali."

"But she's leaving—with the others," Danu protested.

"No, Kali wouldn't leave us," Loy countered. "She's as bad as Whitaker when it comes to this hero stuff. And thank the Goddess she is, for she's probably the only force standing between Arinna and all of Freeland, at this point."

Kali's coming? I have to figure out a way to help her, Danu thought, her mind whirling, unable to concentrate.

Loy whispered, "Perhaps you and I can tip the scales of power a little more in Kali's favor, eh?"

In the middle of trying to take this all in, the possibility of rescue, of hope, of working with Loy to help Kali vanquish Arinna, Danu yawned. Her body had endured all it could these past several days, and it was dragging her inexorably toward oblivion.

Slipping an arm around her, Loy pulled Danu closer. "Just for appearances," Loy grumbled. "I've gotten enough unwanted fondling from Arinna to end all my bad habits, I think. I'll never touch a woman without being invited to again."

Somehow, knowing that Loy badly needed open affection put a different face on this. Danu snuggled into her. "This is a narrow bed, anyway."

A short time later, Danu was in a deep slumber, dreaming that she and Loy were safe in the arms of a woman with long golden hair, a woman who rocked them like babes and sang them to sleep.

That same day, Lilith stood beside Whit, watching her tiredly rub her eyes, then refocus on the air-surveillance films playing on the wallscreen. They had spent the last few hours of the afternoon in the Watch Room, examining and reexamining the morning and afternoon fly-over data. Lilith knew that, besides being generally worried about Kali, Whit was now convinced something had gone desperately wrong during the planned-for trek up to Hart's Pass.

"These films are taken from so high up that they're worthless!" Whit finally snapped. "Damn! What I wouldn't give to have an enlarged satellite image."

Trying to distract Whit, Lilith prodded, "I hear you haven't been to see the prefabricated warehouse the warriors are throwing up down near the airfield." When Whit made no reply, Lilith teased, "I would think that you'd give anything to see all the NASA components they've uncrated and stored in the hangars down there."

"I saw the cargo being unloaded yesterday," Whit muttered.

"Yes, but now it's unpacked and able to be really..."

With a terrified sob, Whit leaned forward, clasping her head in her hands. "Oh, Lilith! I'm so afraid of losing Kali!"

Her heart breaking for her, Lilith placed a hand on Whit's shoulder. At the touch, Whit leapt out of the compu-chair and cursing, made for the door. Her mother's instinct made Lilith grab Whit's long black coat and her own heavy poncho from the pegs by the exit. Almost at a trot, she followed Whit out of the room, into the hall. Whit slammed the DNA panel, locking the door, then marched through the hall, wiping her eyes.

"I won't cry, dammit," Whit was muttering. "I feel like all I've been doing lately is crying."

"Come down to the airfield," Lilith coaxed, "and help me on the satellite parts. It'll get your mind off Kali. Hopefully, with our scientific expertise, it shouldn't be more than a few months before everything is assembled and ready to go. With Colonel Ferris coordinating the project, I'm sure it'll be a success."

Whit looked doubtful, and said, "Yeah, provided we can terminate Arinna Sojourner." Reluctantly, Whit grabbed her coat and slung it over her broad shoulders. "Just for a little while," she conceded. "Early this morning I placed a bulletin on the comline that will run all month. The Eight Leaders Council has authorized me to recruit and put on government payroll all the aeronautical engineers and astrophysicists we need."

Together, they left the Leader's House and moved into the cold November wind outside. The last remnants of Saturday night's snowfall flew about them in powdery white dust whirls as they marched down Cammermeyer Street. They moved with confident strides, one tall, dark-haired Leader moving proudly beside an older, silver-haired one. Neither was aware of the looks of admiration they garnered from the women they passed. They were too busy trying to come up with some miraculous solutions to their problems.

And their problems were huge. Arinna Sojourner, besides being a threat to Kali, seemed invincible. And the satellites were spinning, crippled, high above them in deteriorating orbits in space. At some unpredictable point in the future, the satellites were going to fall out of orbit and the Border separating Freeland and Elysium would disintegrate. Whether because of Arinna or the Regulators, Freeland would soon be engulfed in a battle for survival.

Lilith breathed deeply of the bracing mountain air, trying to settle her mind. When she spotted a flash of red from the corner of her eye, she stepped toward it, flagging the vehicle down. The electro-bus came to a stop, and Whit seemed to shift out of her reverie.

As the young driver opened the door for them, Lilith asked, "Can you drop us at the airfield?"

Giving a curt jerk of her head toward the crowd already on-board, the driver retorted, "They're all headed there, Co-leader. All day, since early this morning, I've been hauling women out to see the space shuttle."

Lilith climbed the steps of the bus and scrutinized the crowd of thirty or so women—young teenagers, elders, and mothers with small children, middle-aged businesswomen, shopkeepers—all of them sitting in seats, chatting merrily. Whit followed after Lilith, and when Lilith turned to see her reaction to this crowd, she found Whit's face a study in puzzlement. A young teenager jumped up to give Whit her seat, and Whit gestured for Lilith to take it. As Lilith sat down, the electro-bus started forward again, and Whit stood beside her, swaying with the ride, gripping a hand rail overhead.

"Are you all so interested in space travel?" Whit asked, seeming to really need to know.

All of them replied at once, all with glowing eyes and excited voices. The general jumbled response seemed to be most definitely, "Yes!" Each woman tacked on a personal editorial to convince Whit about why they were so intrigued with the possibility of space travel. The result was a confusing din of voices.

As the noise died out, and they laughed good-naturedly at themselves, one woman beside Lilith spoke out. "It's the dream that counts, Tomyris." It was a voice from the distant past, a voice tinged with age, frail and yet vibrant, all at the same time. The old woman pulled her hood closer about her face, keeping her face in the shadow. "The dream, Tomyris, never give up the dream," she repeated. "Not only for the science, nor the benefits of facing the unknown."

"What?" Whit asked, grasping a hint of what she meant, but not quite all of it.

"It builds national character to reach for the moon, you know." With a nod, the elder embellished, "Back in the last century, those Kennedy brothers knew what a dream could unleash. But they were Celts, don't you know, and those people always dream big."

Skewered to the soul with the truth of it, Lilith watched Whit peer at the woman who was so carefully hiding her face.

"Have we been playing it safe, then?" Whit asked the elder. "Is rebuilding Isis not enough?"

"We've survived the AGH plague, and kept freedom alive in the midst of the Second Dark Ages," the elder granted gently. "That's quite a lot. But shall we merely aspire to recreate what was once a great but very flawed civilization? Or shall we aspire to reach beyond that—on the earth as well as in the heavens?"

No one spoke.

Her gray eyes suddenly alight with hope, Whit asked, "You think we are capable of such noble endeavors?"

With a long sigh, the old woman stated, "Maat used to say, 'We are capable of anything we dare to dream. The Age of Woman-kind is upon us.'"

The older women in the bus broke into a quiet murmur among themselves, remembering those words, remembering the first Leader of Isis. A little girl picked that moment to earnestly announce to her mother, "I want to fly the ship to the stars, Mom." Everyone joined in pleased laughter, then fell back into excited discussion.

Whit bowed to the elder, then gazed through the electro-bus windshield, her brows lowering as she drifted into deep thought.

Lilith's eyes moved back to the elder, examining the hood over her hair and the thin, straight shoulders beneath the black cloak. *There is something about this woman that is so familiar. I seem to recognize her essence,* Lilith pondered. *Who is she?* Seeming to feel Lilith's stare, the old woman kept her face carefully angled down.

Suddenly, Lilith brought her fingers to her brow and sheepishly said, "Excuse me, elder-one." Lilith began, "I do not wish to appear rude, but do I know you?"

"I am a traveler from another place," the woman whispered enigmatically, and then, despite the gentleness of Lilith's questions, would say no more, other than, "and I have been sent to tell you that the spirits of the mothers will do all they can to protect the daughters of Isis."

Lilith was stunned by the elder's remark, yet attempted to ask another question. But the old woman turned away. The vehicle came to an abrupt stop and jarred Lilith back to the moment.

At the airfield, everyone piled out and moved toward the row of hangars where the space shuttle and satellite parts were on display. Lilith fell into step beside Whit and decided to tell her about the elder's cryptic message. Whit stopped and stared at Lilith, saying, "Lil, if you're saying what I think you're saying...no...that's crazy. This is the 22nd century." Whit pulled her collar up against the wind and linked arms with Lilith as they crossed the snow-strewn tarmac. They could see the new warehouse that was half-constructed a short distance away. Being a prefab, this building would go up fast, and Isis scientists and volunteers from all over Freeland would soon be at work assembling a spacecraft.

Lilith worried about the hundreds of new visitors due to arrive, and finally she asked, "Whit, where are we going to house all these scientists?" Lilith quickly forgot about the elder's message as they began to discuss this new problem.

"I've lined up a woman—Sagana Semiramis—who's been working down in Old California territory with a topnotch crew, building for the men of Harvey," Whit returned, shoving her cold hands into her pockets. "I figure we'll hire her to construct another barracks, then turn her loose as a freelancer. Gaea only knows how many of these visitors will end up as permanent residents."

Filing through the side door into the first hangar, Lilith and Whit joined the crowd wandering around assorted opened crates and strange-looking metal forms. Farther along, there were masses of small, unidentifiable pieces as well as engine parts and heat shields. Warriors stood throughout the building, hands comfortably clasping laser rifles, their feet spread shoulder's width apart, and ready for any eventuality. A hushed silence reigned, and only the hum of engines every once in a while broke the respectful quiet. Decibel-squelch devices on Freelandian jetcraft had eliminated most of the noise of flight, but as the comings and goings were directly overhead, the crowd heard them.

They filed through the second and then the third hangar, before Lilith again noticed the old woman she had sat next to on the bus. The elder waved to her, then pointed at Whit, signaling for Whit to approach.

"I believe she wants you to come over," Lilith told Whit.

With a shrug, Whit glanced at the old woman. She waved back before starting to move in her direction, through the crowd. Whit's curiosity was definitely getting the better of her.

Lilith followed with a puzzled look on her face.

About halfway across the hangar, Whit said, "Where did she go? I've lost sight of her."

Very perplexed now, Lilith looked around the hall, then spotted the young warrior posted at the exhibit where they had seen the elder. "Let's ask the sentry," she proposed.

They walked across the hangar, elbowing their way through the throngs of women, at last arriving at the spot where they had last seen the elder.

"There was a woman standing here," Whit began, addressing the warrior who stood beside several large, shiny pieces of polished steel. "Where did she go?"

"Which woman, Ma'am?" the warrior returned. "There have been hundreds of women standing here."

"An elder in a black cloak, with a black hood over her head. She just waved to us from this very spot," Lilith interjected helpfully.

The warrior's eyebrows went up and she gave Lilith an incredulous look, before answering, "Sorry, Ma'am. I never saw such a woman."

Exasperated, Whit snapped, "You *had* to have seen her!" She whirled around, searching the converging crowd milling about all around them. "She was right beside you!"

Shaking her head, the warrior reiterated, "Leader, I never saw any woman in a black hooded cloak." Meeting Whit's eyes forthrightly, she finished, "I'd have noticed someone dressed like *that*."

Lilith could see that Whit believed the young warrior. Confounded, Whit glanced at Lilith, then began inspecting the crowd again, intent on finding the mysterious elder. Slowly, her gaze returned to highly polished metal sheets, where she saw the reflection of the elder-one. Stunned, Whit spun on her heels, ready to reach out to the old woman, but she was not there. Whit ran her hand through her hair, totally bewildered.

"Lilith! Did you see her?" Whit asked as she kept looking from the polished metal to a point behind her where the woman should have been and was not.

"No." Frowning, Lilith shot an uneasy gaze around, too, then found herself scrutinizing the mirrorlike polish on the metal sheets leaning against the crate. It was easy to see that the pieces were designed to be fit together, creating a huge, cone-like shape. Turning to the flustered guard, Lilith asked, "What exactly is this, Sergeant?"

"I believe it's what they called the nosepiece, or the nose cone, Acting Deputy Leader." Touching the extraordinarily shiny metal with her hand, the warrior elaborated, "The high polish is supposed to deflect the massive radiation and heat of the sun that exists in the upper stratosphere."

Whit was nearby, listening, but looking very perturbed. She shoved her hands in the pockets of her well-tailored pants, then gave Lilith an abrupt nod of the head, indicating that she was ready to leave.

Looking tense, the warrior gave a crisp salute, and though Whit merely sketched one in return before heading for the exit, Lilith brought her hand to her heart and said graciously, "Our sincere thanks, Sergeant."

Outside, as they walked across the tarmac toward a newly arrived electro-bus, they both kept their silence. Lilith noted that Whit seemed to be as deeply disturbed as she felt herself. As they waited for passengers to disembark the red bus, Whit kept looking around, examining the multitudes of women all over the airfield.

At last, Whit muttered, "It's as if she were a ghost."

And Lilith's shiver had nothing to do with the cold wind.

10

"**Where's** Whit?" Lilith inquired of the group of teenagers clustered together at a table by the meal hall door. Because many of them harbored secret crushes on Whit, Lilith had found they could be relied upon to know her whereabouts at any time.

A pretty one turned and indicated the group of older professionals gathered near the back of the vast hall.

Immediately, Lilith spotted the Leader of Isis, obviously engaged in an informal discussion with representatives from the Small Businesswomen's Association. As Lilith watched, Whit raked a hand nervously through her dark, tousled hair. Her eyes were narrowed and her lips were a straight line of tension. Even from this distance, the strain on her was easily visible.

She'll be a wreck before this is over, Lilith thought, wishing somehow to protect Whit from the news she was about to deliver.

The noise of plates and silverware clattered in the background as Lilith crossed the timbered hall. The stained pine walls and high ceilings did little to muffle the noise, but she noticed that it was not nearly as loud or crowded in the meal hall now as it had often been during the summer months. Since many of the original settlers had moved out of the hostels and into private residences, the numbers using this place to eat had been greatly reduced. However, the warriors stationed in Isis for construction duty still ate here, and the warriors were always a rowdy bunch.

As if in illustration of that rowdiness, as she passed a table of the gray uniforms, she overheard a particularly lusty remark about herself and couldn't help blushing. *Well, if I can still provoke talk like that at sixty-four*, she thought, *the least I can do is acknowledge it.* She turned abruptly, sought out the eye of the speaker, and stared her down. And thus, amid a chorus of whoops and whistles, Lilith finally pivoted and approached the businesswomen.

"What in Gaea's name was that all about?" Whit asked, grinning.

"Overactive hormones," stated one of the businesswomen, with a dismissive glance at the table of warriors.

"Would you like an introduction?" Lilith asked. "They're harmless, you know. I think most of them are just far from home and getting a little lonely."

"Really?" another woman asked, her eyes on the boisterous crew, alive with interest.

With a wink at Lilith, Whit crossed the scarred hardwood floor and had a word with the twenty or so warriors lingering over the remains of their dinner. As Whit was about to return, they stood, hastily neatened their uniforms, and came with her. After a long series of self-introductions, Whit ordered several jugs of hard cider from the kitchen, then left the women jabbering among themselves.

That done, Whit turned to Lilith, but saw a look that worried her. Trying to appear composed, she asked softly, "What's wrong?"

"And I thought I was being so crafty."

"It's your eyes—they show your every emotion—like Kali's do...." Whit hesitated, examined Lilith closely, then said in a rush, "It has to do with Kali, doesn't it?"

"Yes. Now don't panic, people are watching." Waving and casually smiling, as if the social mixer now under way was the most prominent thing on her mind, Lilith took Whit's arm and said, "Come outside with me." When Whit began to stride quickly toward the door, Lilith checked her. "Appearances, Whit," she murmured.

With an impatient snort, Whit slowed down, managing a stiff, tight smile to the group as she left. "Have to check on something," she called apologetically. She grabbed her black, knee-length Leader's coat off a peg by the door and shoved her arms in the sleeves.

Once outside, Whit faced Lilith. "Tell me."

"One of Razia's warriors, Crista, landed the helijet a half hour ago. The Healers didn't want us notified right away, not until they took care of Albie." Lilith put her hand on Whit's shoulder. "Kali's squad was attacked by a spellbound grizzly...."

Whit took in a great gulp of air. "And Kali? Is she..."

"...Albie was mauled and has lost a good deal of blood. She's critical. Kali, Tor, and Anat elected to continue their mission. They're fine."

Fuming, Whit swore, then raised her fists to the cloud-covered full moon. "Oh, for a chance at Arinna Sojourner!"

The moon suddenly broke through the clouds and Lilith was startled by the bloodlust apparent on Whit's grim face. Illuminated in a silvery light, her eyes fierce, her lips drawn back in the feral outrage of a woman who has finally borne too much, Whit looked the image of a banshee.

"Be careful what you wish for...." Lilith cautioned.

"I *want* this, Lilith. More than anything!"

They began to walk side by side again, and dark, ominous clouds swept over the moon. "I thought you'd want to talk to Neith," Lilith went on helpfully.

"Thanks, yes, that's exactly what I want—for now."

They set a fast pace and strode down Cammermeyer Street to Neith's Clinic. Before the colorfully painted Victorian building, several bicycles and an Emergency Medical Team vehicle had been parked. Returning the salute of the stocky sentry posted at the door, Whit lengthened her stride and almost left Lilith behind in the hallway.

She opened the door to Neith's office and rushed in, with Lilith close behind. They found themselves in the company of four Healers, all of them buzzing around Neith like bees around a clover blossom. The sweet-faced, dark-skinned young woman was sitting on an examining table as various people asked her questions and others removed her bloodstained parka. Her soft, brown eyes were red-rimmed with fatigue, yet they also flashed with irritation at the way her colleagues were badgering her.

"Quiet, please," Whit commanded, and the chattering gradually ebbed.

Neith's eyes moved gratefully to Whit. "I'm just tired. I don't need all this attention," she entreated.

"Well, how about choosing one Healer, then," Whit suggested.

"Roxana," Neith mumbled. A stout, grandmotherly African stepped to Neith's side and the rest all moved reluctantly to the door.

One of the departing Healers, a slim, fortyish Native American, took Whit aside and whispered, "Albie's in the life-support unit down the hall."

The Healer introduced herself as Weetamoo, newly arrived from the colony of Lang, then dropped her voice still lower and confided, "According to Neith, Kali performed a healing spell on Albie, which seemed to help. By all rights, Albie should be dead." Weetamoo turned a pair of compassionate brown eyes on Neith, then swung back to face Whit. Softly, she stated, "All the same, there's been major blood loss, shock, and sepsis—blood poisoning." Frowning, Weetamoo sighed, "Albie still may not make it."

Anguish at this news flickered across Whit's face.

"We'll keep you apprised," the Healer finished. Then, with a nod at Lilith, she followed her colleagues into the hall.

Roxana had meanwhile taken off Neith's boots and thick socks, and was making a cursory check for frostbite.

Whit came forward and placed a hand on Neith's shoulder. "Glad you made it out all right," she said, allowing the relief to show in her face and voice.

Neith simply nodded. When Lilith embraced her, a few tears escaped, streaming down the young Healer's brown cheeks.

"I know you're beat, Neith—but I need a report," Whit stated.

Roxana admonished, "She needs a change of clothes and a hot meal first, Leader."

Whit and Lilith turned politely away as Neith moved slowly off the table and began to pull her thick wool shirt over her head. Roxana swept busily by them a few minutes later, her arms loaded with Neith's clothes.

As she placed the clothing on a countertop for later collection and cleaning, the maternal Healer decreed, "And now she needs a nice, hot shower."

Neith herself overruled that, stating, "Later. Just get me some scrubs, and something to eat, please."

The elder muttered her displeasure at this. Nevertheless, she drew a set of fresh surgical scrubs from a drawer beneath the counter and swept imperiously past Whit and Lilith.

At last, when Neith was dressed in scrubs and soft cotton surgical shoes, with a white terry-cloth robe draped around her shoulders, Roxana was ready to relinquish her patient.

"I'm going to have some soup fetched from the meal hall and then look in on Alborak," Roxana stated. Addressing Whit, Roxana instructed, "And while I'm gone, don't wear her out with your questions." Delivering a final, no-nonsense look, the portly elder strode out of the room.

A moment after the door closed behind Roxana, Neith broke down, weeping silently, impatiently wiping her eyes. Despite this, she said, "Let's get on with it."

"No...we can come back...." Whit hesitated.

But the young woman would not be dissuaded. Her voice breaking with exhaustion, Neith launched into the tale. She told of landing and inspecting Danu's abandoned Swallow, repeating Kali's puzzled comment about the damaged wing.

Whit interrupted, "Lightning? D'ya mean Kali thought Arinna was able to control lightning and used it as a weapon to bring down Danu's craft?"

"Yes. Don't ask me how, though—we never got a chance to discuss that part because the wolves attacked."

"Wolves?" Lilith asked, turning pale. "Wolves wouldn't come *near* people...."

"That's what Kali said, just before the attack," Neith commented dryly, resuming the account.

Then, wearily, she described their escape from the wolves the night before. As she came to the part about the grizzly, and Albie's being mauled, she began sobbing uncontrollably. Tenderly, Lilith pulled her into her arms and held her. After a moment, her head on Lilith's shoulder, she picked up the thread of the narrative and continued all the way to the point where Anat dropped off the three other women at Hart's Pass.

Aggravated, Whit muttered, "What idiots," then saw Neith's face and reined herself in.

"They're brave as hell, Leader!" Neith protested. "And they're only finishing what they started. If Albie hadn't been hurt, we'd still be with them."

Pushing her hand through her hair, Whit remarked, "It's obvious that Arinna's power has evolved beyond what anyone ever imagined. I see no point in....."

"We have no choice," Neith challenged. Sojourner is demonic. On our return flight to Isis, we seemed to enter a time warp. The aircraft's engines were engaged and the rotors spinning, but we weren't moving. There was no moon and the clear night sky was starless.... It seemed as if we were in a black void. Our wristcoms indicated that time was not passing. We should have been back in Isis hours ago." Neith took a deep breath and shuddered, attempting to shake off the fear that held her in its grip. "We seemed to be stuck in another dimension for hours. Then, suddenly, the moon and stars appeared and flight continued. We figured Arinna was toying with us." She wiped her sweaty palms against her pant legs and looked from Lilith to Whit. "We can oppose her and risk death, or not oppose her and still risk death. She's fiendish."

Struck by the truth of Neith's impassioned words, Whit stared at the young Healer, feeling ashamed of herself. *If I really love Kali, I must support her in this. Even if it means that she's recklessly risking her life. Even if it means losing her....*

Angry, Neith stared back, then dropped her gaze. "I don't mean to be impudent," Neith sighed wearily. "I know how much you love Kali. It's just that...Albie is near death. She was mauled while firing at point-blank range, trying to save your Kali." Pausing, Neith clasped her hands together. "I've never seen anything like what I saw up there, Whit. Raw courage. Kali, Albie, Tor." Neith bent her head, crying again. "Warriors—all of them."

"And as courageous as you," Lilith asserted, stroking Neith's tight, dark hair. "And you've done your best for Freeland today. Let's get you to bed."

An icy wind blew through Hart's Pass, chilling the backs of the three warriors from Isis as they snowshoed toward the SAC installation. Though the sun shone brilliantly earlier in the morning, it was now draped with heavy, fast-moving nimbus clouds. Finally, the women came to the chain-link fence at the perimeter of the old installation. As they carefully stepped over the barbed segment of the fence, Tor turned to Kali and Anat, saying, "Danu probably came this way."

They exchanged uneasy looks, then quickened their pace.

A light snow began falling as they stomped across a half kilometer of snowfield, past a dilapidated cluster of buildings. Once, as Kali's sharp eyes left the broken path of white and swept the overcast sky above her, she spotted a pair of golden eagles flying overhead, their bronze feathers glittering against the gray clouds. *If my totem has chosen to appear, then the time of testing has surely come.*

When Kali dropped her gaze, she saw a puff of white steam drift upward from beneath a stand of cedars. "Tor, look. The steam vent," Kali announced softly, indicating the direction with her hand.

And then they saw it at the same time—the large steel door set into the mountainside. Judging by the trampled snow in front of the door, Kali surmised that Danu, *or someone else,* had also found the door. They assumed the snowshoes left leaning against the rock face, directly beneath the lock box, were Danu's. The women began a slow, clumsy run, lifting their knees, swinging their own snowshoes toward the door as quickly as possible.

As they reached the spot, Tor grabbed up one of the discarded snowshoes, inspecting it quickly. "It was broken. Look at these repair knots," she informed Kali quietly. Then, casting a searching gaze around the exterior, Tor whispered uneasily, "So what's the plan, Kali? Seal off the air vents?"

"No, Tor!" Kali returned, a little annoyed. "That would take forever. I'm surprised at you." With a brief grin, Kali shook her head. "Besides, I told everyone the plan would be revealed on a need-to-know basis...remember?"

Meanwhile, Kali had tossed her mittens on the ground, turned her back to the blowing snow, and pulled a utility knife from her pack. She selected the screwdriver edge, and with the deep, even breaths of trancing, she began working on the lock box. "Danu must have tripped this mechanism, but I don't understand why she would've closed it back up again."

"Wait," Tor urged. "We have no idea what's behind that door.... And maybe the lock is booby-trapped."

Ever vigilant, Anat stood a few meters away, her laser rifle switch on lethal. She kept scanning the area all around them.

"Yes, we do," Kali returned. "Danu and Arinna." She paused a moment, studying the wiring of the ancient automatic lock. "And I know you dislike Danu's being in there with Arinna as much as I do."

"This could be a trap," Tor worried, glancing about the silent, desolate military outpost.

"Of course it's a trap," Kali sighed. "She's used Danu to lure me up here, and it worked," she muttered, squinting at the wire combinations, then using her screwdriver to rework several sets. "Trust Arinna not to understand that I was coming after her anyway, no matter what Whit or any one else had to say about it. She could have left Danu completely out of it."

Holding her breath and praying, Kali placed a short piece of black wire across two terminals, and watched the steel door rumble open, hiss, and slide into a recess. Almost immediately, Tor leapt inside and pounced on the gray warrior backpack just inside the entrance. With her rifle comfortably balanced across her forearm, she hastily opened the fastenings and checked out the contents of the backpack. She pulled out a scarf which was slashed down the middle with several parallel slits.

Eyes wide, Tor held the scarf up for Kali to see, concluding, "Bear."

With a nod, Kali peered down the well-lit, broad tunnel ahead of them. It stretched as far as she could see, a long shaft that sloped and curved downward, into the bowels of the mountain.

Looks like we're about to march into the mouth of some monstrous snake, Kali thought, and then shuddered. Unzipping her parka and reaching into an inner pocket, she withdrew the map of the SAC installation.

With her finger, she quickly marked their current position on the map and followed the line of the tunnel to various lower levels. All at once, her shoulders were tense and she could scarcely breathe. Slipping the map back into her parka, she took a deep breath and exhaled.

Tor narrowed her eyes, trying to guess what the new plan would be.

Kali removed her snowshoes and her backpack, and then placed her rifle against the inside wall of the tunnel entrance. She cleared her mind and removed her laser pistol from its holster. *Okay, I'm ready.*

Aloud, she ordered, "Tor, Anat, stay here and guard this entrance from the inside."

Tor merely sent her an inscrutable gaze, then motioned to Anat to stand guard, which she was already doing. Tor couldn't believe she was actually thinking that they could escape death.

Slowly, Kali began walking into the tunnel. She was concentrating and reaching out, searching the various dimensions of reality with tentacles of psychic energy. Surprised to find Tor's presence was much closer than anticipated, she whirled around, and saw Tor moving down the tunnel toward her, silhouetted by the daylight from outside.

"I told you to guard the entrance," Kali protested as quietly as she could.

"It's okay. Anat can take care of the entrance," she assured her. Then, casually said, "My job is to protect you, Kali. Those are my orders."

"Just a minute! Neither Whit *nor you* is my keeper!" Kali flared.

"But Arinna sure will be," Tor grumbled, "if you insist on taking unnecessary risks."

Kali hissed, "I order you to stop. About face. Double time—are you listening to me, Lieutenant?!"

"Frankly, no."

Torn between fury and exasperation, Kali snapped, "Gaea, you're ornery! I've never seen such bad conduct in an officer."

"Why do you think I'm still a lieutenant?" Tor conceded.

Kali stopped, catching Tor's arm and pulling her to a standstill. Her eyes wide, she whispered, "Wait."

Directing her gaze ahead, Tor saw what had caught Kali's attention. On the floor, on either side of the concrete tunnel, a pair of human skulls shone dully in the fluorescent light. "What's this?" Tor muttered.

"I don't know," Kali admitted. "Since I entered this tunnel, all my usual psychic senses are gone. I can't sense a thing. But let me pass by these ghoulish toys of Arinna's first—in case they're an anchor for some sort of spell."

No sooner had Kali finished speaking, than Tor darted forward, past the eerie-looking skulls. With a small, apologetic shrug, she paused and waited for Kali on the other side of them.

"What in Gaea's name is the matter with you?" Kali snapped in a hushed voice, catching up. "Are you going to purposely disobey every command I give you?"

Accepting the rebuke calmly, Tor merely waited at Kali's side.

After a moment, realizing that Tor was not going to explain or defend her actions, Kali mumbled a soft curse and continued her descent. *Probably wasting my breath trying to give her orders,* she decided.

They were well into the tunnel by this time, having just passed Level 4. Each woman was feeling more and more apprehensive. Their steps slowed; conversation ceased. Though Kali continued her psychic reach, she was unable to sense Arinna's presence. Then they both heard it and paused—the hum of generators.

Around the next bend in the tunnel they came to a steel door. Noiselessly, Tor approached the room and rested her ear against the door. With a nod, she indicated that the source of the hum was behind the steel door.

Each woman stood to one side of the door with laser pistols ready. Kali tried to steer Tor into a less perilous position, and said, "You open the door and I'll go through first—you cover me."

Tor nodded and smiled. She opened the door, and quickly slipped through just a step in front of Kali.

Taking only a second to frown in displeasure at being outmaneuvered yet again, Kali immediately scanned the dimly lit room. Back to back, and moving in unison, she and Tor entered what appeared to be an energy-generating facility. Two huge generators stood side by side, obviously powered by the small cold-fusion units mounted on the generator casings. On the other side of the large room was another door. With a sharp wave, Kali directed Tor to follow her as she made for the exit.

They hesitated by the door.

"I still can't sense a thing," Kali whispered in frustration. "I'm psychic-blind. Arinna must be blocking me. There's no other explanation." And then Kali was beset by a wave of panic. *How can I defeat her, when I can't even get past her psychic shields?* Pulling herself together, she realized that this was exactly what Arinna wanted her to feel.

"Time for some warrior-sense, then," Tor supplied. "Where is the most likely place to encounter an ambush?"

"You mean, besides right here?" Kali cracked, giving a hint of a smile. She impatiently tried to push a few strands of hair away from her eyes, back into her French braid.

"Well, I'd say we've temporarily ruled out our present location," Tor returned, arching an eyebrow. "And by the way, in case any future plan changes involve splitting up, Whit gave me orders before we left Isis. I'm to stay by your side, no matter what *you* say—until we both return home." *Listen to me, return home.*

For a moment, Kali didn't know whether to strangle Tor, hug her, or laugh hysterically. And so she merely stood there, her gaze fixed on the black laser gun she held before her.

As she clenched the weapon, her hand began to shake. Hearing this last, wholly unexpected confirmation of Whit's love for her, she felt a wrenching ache. The closer she came to Arinna, the more acutely she was aware of all she had left behind: safety, friends, love.

I'm going to die here, she thought. *Far from Whit, far from home—just like Baubo died in Elysium.*

Gallantly, Tor reached out and grabbed Kali's shaking hand and held it. The grip was warm, steady, reassuring. They stood there together for a moment, silently rallying each other, affirming their faith in each other. Then Kali murmured her thanks and Tor freed her hand.

Once more, Kali drew out the map. Opening the laminated folds so Tor could see, she indicated their progress.

During the next few moments they quietly discussed Kali's plan. It was a plan she had told no one, a plan that had been purposely kept in Kali's mind—behind psychic barriers—away from Arinna's relentlessly probing powers.

"Arinna will probably be in these lower-level office areas," Kali indicated the section on the map, "or in this large domed chamber. See? It's labeled as a monitoring facility."

"She's probably monitoring us right now," Tor said. "But I don't see the connection. Why the office area?"

"Look at the way the row of offices are linked by both the connecting doors between rooms and the corridor outside. And the corridor itself twists and turns—easily defensible." Kali pressed her fingers to her forehead, trying once more to reach with her mind and grasp some inkling of where Arinna might be.

Observing her, Tor asked, "She's blocking you?"

With a nod, Kali returned, "As I expected."

"What about Danu? Or Loy? Can you sense them?"

Again, Kali concentrated, and again, felt only a psychic barrier all around her. "She's so strong," Kali breathed, all at once adrift in self-doubt. "I thought I had augmented and strengthened my latent powers enough to do this." She met Tor's eyes, growing alarmed. "Maybe I was wrong."

With a calm air of acceptance, Tor shrugged and placed her hand on the lever that worked the door mechanism. "Kali, it's enough that you are willing to try. Stop doubting yourself."

Kali startled Tor with a quick, sisterly embrace, and said, "Thanks again." Then, taking several deep breaths, she shook her arms out and wiggled her fingers. "I'm ready. Open the door."

Tor pressed the lever and pushed, then slowly stepped into the hallway, using her body to block Kali in the threshold.

"I should be in front, Tor," Kali protested.

"In a minute," Tor promised, carefully scoping the poorly lit corridor. She was ready to intercept any laser blasts or paranormal barrages meant for Kali. Satisfied that the hallway was empty, she moved enough to make room for Kali.

"You're *not* my bodyguard, dammit," Kali fumed.

"According to Whit, I am, and she outranks you," Tor retorted, daring an impish grin. Then, growing serious, she confided, "Let me protect you if I can. You're our best prospect for getting Danu out of here—not to mention defending Freeland."

Kali began moving down the hall, running a hand along the rough cinderblock, examining the smooth cement floor. She had the laser gun ready, and for some reason she found herself paying particular attention to the aged, yellowed ceiling tiles overhead.

Glancing uneasily over her shoulder, Tor had fallen in step beside her.

They moved cautiously, staying close to the right wall. Halfway down the corridor, Kali held up her hand. "I've got something." She tilted her head to the side, listening with her inner sensors. "There's a life vibration—several life vibrations—up ahead, in an enclosed space. Probably the monitoring facility."

"And, of course, *we're* who they're monitoring...." Tor commented sourly, glancing behind her again. The corridor was still empty, but Tor's Zen training warned her that this was a very vulnerable place to be. "What's our plan?"

"Our plan is the fact that we have no plan," Kali stated in a low, calm voice. Now that she once again had a degree of psychic sensitivity, her calm assurance resurfaced. "Arinna can't read me, and subsequently thwart me, if I'm living from millisecond to millisecond, now can she?"

Tor understood the logic, but was not thrilled with the idea of not having a plan.

Something caught Kali's eye. She focused on the overhead ceiling tiles, raised her hand, and made a soft clucking noise. At once a small detonation sounded, and with a burst of smoke, a microscopic camera lens fell through the broken tile and smashed on the floor. The fiber-optic lens, the size of a human hair, had been threaded inconspicuously through the seam of the tile, recording their movements, and, no doubt, their words.

Suddenly, at the far end of the hall, a door swung open and four huge, green-jacketed men came charging toward them.

Regs! Kali's mind trumpeted.

Paralyzed, she stood there for several seconds, her heart rate skyrocketing. Then, a flood of adrenaline sent her running back toward the generator room, running faster than she knew she could move, with Tor close on her heels.

Skidding to a stop, Tor yanked the door open and shouted, "Inside! Inside!"

An instant after Kali had passed into the darker room, Tor was right behind her, swinging the door shut and jamming the lever up, in an attempt to lock the door. Seconds later the door was abruptly pulled open and a shocked Tor was dragged a meter or so into the hall before she let go of the handle and leapt backward, just centimeters ahead of the huge hand that grabbed for her.

After firing her laser at the Reg, Tor quickly dashed to Kali's side. Though the lethal blast of blue light struck the Reg mid-chest, it didn't stop him. There was no hole or smell of burning flesh. Instead, he led the other three Regs into the generator room, where they surrounded the two women. Tor snatched a quick look at her laser, then said in bewilderment, "Kali, the laser blast didn't even faze the Reg."

Human? Kali thought, the horrified fear suddenly diminishing as her rational mind snagged on that concept. An instinctive doubt was making itself known. *I'm not registering them as flesh and blood beings? Why?* She studied the strangely passionless eyes of these Regs; something was wrong. *Hold on—there's no life vibration from any of these guys. What the...*

Before she could think any of it through, one of the Regs moved on Kali. She fired her own weapon. Nothing. She looked at the gun and then at the Reg with disbelief. Expressionless and completely unfazed by the laser blast, the Reg knocked the pistol from her hand with one quick kick. As he lunged for her, she grabbed his wrist, directing his motion past her and into the hard, unforgiving metal casing of one of the generators. He hit head-first and slid to the floor—immobilized.

Our lasers aren't even leaving scorch marks! The Regs are protected—but how? "Hold your fire!" Kali shouted to Tor. "Hand-to-hand combat!"

Beside her, Tor holstered her gun and within seconds was fighting two Regs at once, while the third Reg circled Kali, his arms moving smoothly through kung fu fighting patterns.

When did the bastards start learning martial arts? Kali fretted, then dodged as the Reg initiated a strike.

From the corner of her eye, she saw Tor whirl through a combination of attack moves that dropped one of the Regs and staggered the other. Deciding to finish this quickly, Kali blocked her own attacker's punch, and carefully regulated her breath, sliding into dim muk—the death strike. After a sideways feint, causing her opponent to overreact, she sent a hard, two-handed blow to the back of his neck. The Reg fell forward and lay still.

"Tor, target their heads. That's their Achilles' heel—I think," she yelled.

Sure she had done fatal damage, Kali turned to help Tor dispose of the one remaining Reg. Yet as she kicked the lone fighter's legs out from under him, she became aware of motion behind her and quickly dropped to a crouch. She barely avoided a large booted foot sailing through the space where her head had been. Rolling left, she realized that this was the Reg she had just taken out with a *death blow*. Two and two clearly was not adding up to four.

This is crazy! How's he back up? she wondered frantically, jumping back several times to stay clear of each of his successive kicks.

Then, from the side of her, a hard kick caught her in the ribs, raising her up off her hands and knees and heaving her over on her back. In a blur of pain, she identified him as the Reg she had earlier sent headfirst into the generator. Here he was again, towering above her, his slightly dented face creepily impassive while he hovered there, not even really looking at her.

"Capture only.... Capture only," the other Reg intoned, stepping around the Reg who had kicked her.

And capture her he did, by merely leaning down and grasping her arm, slinging her effortlessly over his back like a bag of laundry. Kali squirmed against him, her feet flailing in the air. As she tried to push herself clear of him with her free left arm, she saw Tor battling nearby, dark eyes narrowed with concentration. Both of the Regulators Tor had been fighting with were back on their feet and circling her. In a brilliant double spin-kick, Tor sent both of her Regs to the floor, then turned, breathing hard, to deal with Kali's captor.

"Let her go," Tor wheezed, moving to position herself between the Reg and the door. With a distance of perhaps four meters between them, the Reg who was carrying Kali ignored Tor with a casual disregard.

In the center of the room, the other Regulators were getting clumsily to their feet.

"Look out!" Kali yelled to Tor.

Tor crouched down readying herself, but Kali saw how fatigued she was. Quickly, she searched her mind for a response, but before she could come up with one, the Regulators all simultaneously wrenched to a stop, including the Reg carrying Kali. Like puppets on jerking strings, they collectively twitched and swayed on their feet. Suddenly, they stilled. There was a long, suspended hush in which nothing happened. Then all four Regulators abruptly collapsed, falling in four separate heaps to the floor. Kali twisted herself away from the Reg who had held her, then pressed a hand against her aching ribs. Still unsure the danger was past, Tor stayed in her combat crouch, watching the fallen Regulators.

"What happened?" Kali demanded, flabbergasted.

"Gaea knows!" Tor gasped. Bending over, her eyes still scanning the Regs, she added, "I may not have known the woman, like the rest of you who spent last summer working with her, but...but..." Tor breathed deeply, "I'm getting a healthy respect for the creative talents of Arinna Sojourner."

"I can't believe it!" Kali declared, "Who would have thought she'd make androids?! *Reg* androids!"

"More than that," Tor acknowledged. "What materials did she use to construct them? They're completely unaffected by laser fire."

"Why didn't our lasers drop them?" Kali wondered aloud, staring down at the Reg who had seized her moments ago. "I tried to hit where I thought it would be most vulnerable."

Wiping her sleeve across her brow as she loosened the gray warrior's scarf at her neck, Tor guessed, "A good laser shield and maybe a little magic.... Gaea, who knows with someone like Arinna?"

With great care, Kali prodded a Reg with her boot. "I think they're permanently disabled."

"Beats me how that happened, unless they're under Sojourner's control," Tor offered.

Spotting her laser gun across the room, Kali walked over and reclaimed it. "Well done, Lieutenant," Kali said as she returned to Tor. "Thank the Goddess you held them off for as long as you did." As she turned toward the door, her hand still against her ribs, Kali grimaced.

"You're hurt," Tor said.

"I'm all right. I don't want to waste any psychic power with a healing spell," Kali returned, stepping over the Reg by the door."

Alarmed, Tor caught Kali's arm. "You're not OK. I can tell by how you're moving, Kali."

"We have to go on—she *may* not know we've evaded capture," Kali pleaded, her brown eyes earnest.

Tor was doubtful. "Maybe we should retreat. But that would just delay what may be inevitable. No! I'm willing to go down fighting."

Kali peered at her from behind several strands of blonde hair. Her French braid was unraveling, her cheeks were fiery red from the fight. For a moment, just a tiny moment, Tor knew Kali was actually entertaining the possibility of withdrawing. Then, with a slight shake of her head, Kali whispered, "Right, Tor. Now let's get on with it."

Tor whispered a blessing beneath her breath. "Gaea be with us and all other fools."

11

Whit aimlessly stirred her potato soup as she sat at a table in the Isis meal hall. Across from her, Lilith was secretly studying her friend, worrying. Traces of gray lay in dark half-circles under Whit's eyes.

"I had the strangest dream last night," Whit reflected. She looked across the meal hall; her smoke-gray eyes took on a faraway look that Lilith had only rarely seen in them before.

"Tell me about it," Lilith prompted.

"I dreamed I was traveling throughout our solar system on this fantastic Freeland spacecraft. And as I traveled on and on, through the emptiness, I knew I was on my way home to Isis." Whit paused and drew a deep breath. "Only, as the ship descended toward what I thought to be Earth, I knew Kali wouldn't be there, waiting for me."

As Lilith stared at her, Whit felt her lip begin to tremble.

"I flew through clouds," Whit went on, "then dropped out of overcast winter skies, and there she was—Isis—only not as she is now. Larger, more beautiful, not just a small mountain colony trying to establish a foothold in Freeland, but a thriving metropolis—one of scores of Freeland city-colonies."

Lilith watched her face, saw the flush of enchantment turn to puzzlement.

"And then, as I was bringing the ship down, I saw that old woman in the black hooded cloak."

"What old woman?" Lilith asked, as the hair at the back of her neck was standing on end, and she feared she knew very well what woman Whit meant.

"The woman who was on the bus," Whit explained, "the one who told me about the value of dreams."

"And?" Lilith leaned forward, scarcely breathing.

"As in our ships now, I had a wallscreen which presented visuals of port, starboard, fore, and aft. She was standing off to the side, on the tarmac below me, waiting in a safe zone with a group of other women. No one else was dressed like her—she caught my eye right away...." Sending a hand slowly through her dark hair, Whit continued. "And as I brought the ship lower and lower, she stretched her arm out toward me and...what looked like blue lightning...shot from her fingers."

Perplexed, Lilith pushed her bowl of soup away and rubbed her forehead.

Whit was frowning, staring hard at the table. "The lightning hit the metal nose-section of my ship and ricocheted off, heading right back at the woman in the hooded cloak. When the lightning returned to her, she exploded in a fiery blue flame."

This is making no sense at all, Lilith thought, growing more skeptical by the second of the vision-potential of this dream.

"And then," Whit stated, half-smiling, "as the flame diminished, I could see Kali standing there, where the elder had been before. And though she was still as lovely as ever, Kali was much, much older. Three young girls flanked her—and I knew their names, Lilith— though I promptly forgot them as soon as I woke up. They were all waving excitedly at my ship."

After a long silence, during which Whit carefully avoided Lilith's gaze, Lilith at last inquired gently, "What do you think it means?"

Lifting her eyes to Lilith's, Whit whispered, "When I saw Kali and those girls, Lil... There was such love—on their faces, in my heart—*such love!*" Whit clenched her fists. "It *has* to mean *something....*"

While Lilith and Whit puzzled over the dream, Captain Razia directed her pilot to bring the helijet over the last ridge. As they crossed over the icy crest, a snowy clearing came into view below.

"Take her down," the captain ordered, then turned and scrutinized the hand-picked team behind her.

Her two special-forces warriors, Sergeants Dimarco and Newport, were already crouched by the door, laser rifles cradled in their arms. Ferris's nuclear physicist, C.A. Wolfe, was peering out the window, her lips parted with anticipation. Beside her, the explosives experts, Williams and Marino, were whispering together. As Captain Razia listened, she realized they were reviewing their warhead dismantling procedure with one another, performing a readiness exercise for what had to be one of the most frightening operations of their careers.

And then she turned to find Zak Ferris's dark, calculating eyes on her. "Always meant to ask you," the colonel said, keeping her voice low, as if to prevent the others from hearing.

"What? Razia prompted curiously.

"How about having a late dinner with me when this is all over?"

Momentarily taken aback by the bold invitation, Razia flushed. Then she retorted, "You have this problem with timing, my friend."

While Zak was laughing, they landed softly and the door slid open. The two warriors leapt out and assumed defensive positions on either side of the opening as the other women exited. One by one, the tech team jumped out into the knee-deep snow.

Captain Razia poked her head back inside and instructed the pilot, "Go back over the ridge and set her down. Wait for my signal on the comline, then return for us." Squinting into the bright snowfield, Razia added, "And be ready to lay down a barrage of heavy fire to cover our butts."

The automatic door slid closed and the helijet lifted off. Ferris grinned at Razia, as the captain ordered, "Move out!" And then she was panting steamy breaths into the icy air as they all ran across the glistening snow. Their immediate destination—the boulders at the bottom of the cliff before them.

There, on the northwest side of the mountain, directly opposite the southeastern approach of Kali's group, they found the ventilation ducts just where the blueprints had said they would be. Concealed among the boulders, two aluminum ducts slanted down into the mountain at a twenty-five-degree incline. The tech team was about to penetrate Arinna Sojourner's fortress. At Captain Razia's signal, Sergeant DiMarco's laser rifle made quick work of the grill bolted to the left vent.

"Ready your synlights," Razia told the others.

"According to the blueprints," Razia said, "we need to get to the fifth level. This vent connects with each level via grilled panels on the north end of each corridor. Tersely, Razia continued, "And be on the alert for any surveillance devices that Sojourner may have set up, especially infrared eye beams. DiMarco, you take the point, and put on those special glasses." Eyeing each of the women, she emphasized, "Stay quiet and step lightly. These vents will carry the sound of a careless footstep or word."

Razia turned and checked the barren snowfield behind them, then held up her hand and signaled them forward. Cautiously, the two Sergeants climbed into the duct, aiming their synlights ahead of them. C.A. Wolfe and Ferris followed, both scientists looking excited. As Razia motioned the explosives experts, Marino and Williams, to enter before her, she noticed they were holding hands, their lips moving in silent recitation. With one last glance about, Captain Razia stepped into the ventilation duct.

Their descent into Arinna's domain had begun.

With a diving roll, Tor shot through the doorway of the domed room, then moved quickly to take shelter by the side of a large platform in the center. Immediately afterward, Kali bolted in, keeping low, sliding for cover under a conference table spread with what looked like tea sandwiches and two dusty bottles of champagne. Kali paused, glancing about expectantly. Tor kicked aside some shattered glass on the floor with her boot, then inched her way around the rectangular center platform.

It took them both several minutes to investigate the room and satisfy themselves that the large space was safe.

Pointing to the blank white screens fitted into the surrounding walls and the concave ceiling, Tor speculated, "I think they used to call these huge monitoring facilities 'War Rooms.' "

"Why would Arinna abandon this War Room?" Kali wondered aloud. "This was a definite advantage...."

Tor gave up her search of the cartons nearby after finding only an assortment of modern electronic equipment. Glancing over at Kali, she saw her climbing the platform ramp, obviously intent on examining the compu-chair and control panel there. At the same moment, Tor noticed the strange burnt smell, the vague haze of smoke still in the room.

"There was a fire...." Tor guessed.

"And it was up here," Kali added, pressing a hand against her aching side. Careful to avoid the liquid puddle on the floor, Kali approached the huge computer. She leaned over a charred panel and carefully examined the burnt holes in the computer's casing. After a moment, she stepped back and gave a low whistle. "I wonder how this happened? Helluva way to lose the valuable data I'll bet this system could provide."

"It seems kind of bizarre," Tor commented. "I mean, what a lucky break for us that this computer crashed when it did."

The remark hung in the air.

Instinctively, Kali knew this disabled computer was the result of sabotage, not luck or an accident. From her overseeing position on the platform, Kali carefully surveyed the room. "What's that?" she demanded, pointing out to Tor the cluster of spots off to one side of the floor.

Kneeling down on the concrete floor, Tor touched her finger to the dark, thick liquid. "Blood," she answered, her voice tight with restrained panic.

"Come on, Tor," Kali ordered, running down from the platform. "I think Danu's in big trouble."

In Isis, in the hearth room of Lilith and Styx's comfortable townhouse on Earhart Street, four women solemnly conferred.

Her legs folded Indian-style, Styx sat on a large, braided rug before the fireplace, listening to Whit recounting the dream she'd had. Neith sat next to her, sharing the rug. The Healer stretched her hands out to the fire, considering what she heard. On the cushioned sofa next to Whit, Lilith sat nervously clasping her hands together.

Dido, Lilith's orange tabby cat, reclined regally atop the couch, behind Whit. She, too, listened, her eyes half-closed, while she rhythmically flicked her tail.

As Whit ended her dream-story, Lilith asked Neith and Styx, "What do you think it means?"

After a lengthy pause, during which the only noise in the room was the pop and hiss of the wood in the hearth, Neith evaluated, "Let me get this straight." She faced Whit, baffled. "You said first that as you were flying this ship through space, you knew you were on your way home."

Whit nodded.

Scratching her short, tight black hair, Neith pursued, "And you knew Kali wasn't there."

Her mouth tightening, Whit nodded one more time.

"But then, after the lightning hit your ship," Neith went on, "and ricocheted back to the ground, striking that woman in the black cloak, Kali appeared in her stead."

"Yes," Whit affirmed.

Very slowly, her brows lowering in an effort to understand, Neith said, "But you said Kali would not be there...."

In an abrupt move, Styx got to her feet, demanding of Whit, "When you and Lilith went to see the display of NASA components, where did you say you lost sight of that hooded woman?"

"Well, it was near these gigantic, shiny, metal nose-cone pieces...." Whit rambled.

"Show me!" Styx ordered, grabbing Whit by the hand and tugging her toward the hall.

With the sudden motion, Dido jumped off the back of the couch and fled upstairs.

"Have you figured something out?" Neith called to Styx, vaguely annoyed that her conversation with Whit was obviously over, and she was still confused.

"No—*you* figured something out—and thanks!" Styx shouted back, then snatched her jacket from a closet, yanked up Whit's coat from a hall chair, and propelled Whit out the door.

"*I* figured it out?" Neith murmured, completely at a loss.

For a second, Lilith stood there, mouth agape, while Styx and Whit disappeared down the front steps. The open door stayed open, and to Lilith's mind, it was clearly an invitation.

"Well," Lilith told Neith, "I'm certainly not going to miss any of whatever is going on!"

They fetched their coats and hurried after them.

✧ ✧ ✧ ✧ ✧

Colonel Ferris aimed her synlight ahead of them, announcing in a whisper, " Looks like another grill—we must be at Level five, our objective."

Motioning everyone to stand still, Captain Razia turned off her own light and edged forward. Her heart pounding, she peered into the cavern that yawned beyond the wire grill. In the soft yellow glow of emergency lights, the noses of eight missiles pointed above the steel catwalk deck that lined the perimeter of the silo. Razia felt a wave of relief. As planned, they were entering the silo at a point that would allow them access to the warheads. They would approach their objectives via the portable ramps that hung from the steel catwalk a few meters beneath them.

The once-gleaming missiles were now covered with more than a century of dust. Large stars and stripes were still visible on the sides of each missile. For an instant, Razia reflected on the men of the past who had created these horrible weapons of mass annihilation.

Checking the cavernous silo, Razia noted a surveillance camera on the opposite wall. "Hmm." She thought it strange that the camera was not directed toward them. Ferris's synlight should have triggered the camera lens to zoom in on them, but it didn't move. Razia's gaze followed the steel walk around. In disbelief, her eyes focused on a strange sight. "Ferris. What do you make of that below?" she whispered, as she pointed to the bodies of four Regulators.

"They appear to be dead, Zak. But what are they doing here?" She shook her head. "I don't remember any reports indicating that the Regs had taken over this part of the old U.S., no less this installation."

The rest of the team inched closer to the wire grill as they attempted to get a look.

"Something very odd here," Captain Razia breathed. "Could be a trap, so stay alert," she said in a loud whisper. She then motioned to Sergeant Newport. "Incinerate this grill."

"Permission to run recon, Ma'am," Sergeant DiMarco whispered earnestly, coming forward to scope the scene before her.

"Granted," Razia answered.

Cautiously, Newport and DiMarco jumped on the catwalk below, eyeing the bodies of the Regs expectantly. Newport began walking around the catwalk, her laser rifle switch set to lethal. After several minutes they reported the area safe, and the surveillance camera nonoperative.

Quickly, the rest of the team joined the sergeants on the catwalk, their weapons at the ready.

The tech team raised the ramps and connected them to each of the missile platforms. Soon Marino, Williams, Wolfe, and Ferris were each standing by a missile and searching their packs for the appropriate tools. Razia turned away. She loosened her warrior scarf and used a corner of it to wipe the beads of perspiration from her forehead. She realized that she couldn't even watch them remove the exterior panel of the warheads. In the background, C.A. Wolfe's soft voice was dispensing unsolicited advice about the nuclear components and certain volatile chemical materials that might be present.

Ferris called out to her technicians, "Disarm the warheads without taking any unnecessary risks...and be alert for possible booby traps." With her trademark chuckle, she reminded them, "No second chances at this test."

Hours seemed to have gone by before Ferris walked over to Razia and whispered, "Four down and four to go."

There was a large freight elevator that went to the lower levels of the SAC complex, but after noting the amount of blood on the floor near the control panel, Tor told Kali she would rather take the stairs. Readily agreeing, Kali led their panther-like descent through the nearby stairwell to the office area.

It was easy to pick up the bloody trail next to the elevator door on the floor below—the blood shone in the murky light—dark, gleaming spots upon the gray concrete floor.

As Kali raced, zigzagging from one wall to the next, she realized that the corridors on this lower level were designed like a maze and could easily conceal a patrol of Regs from view until she and Tor had literally collided with them.

She glanced down and saw another spot of blood, this splash larger than the others that had led them here. *Oh, Danu! You're leaving us a trail and possibly losing your life while doing it.*

Sweating, tense, she raced to the next intersection, paused, then peeked around the corner. Tor dashed up next to her, her eyes checking their rear, her hand clenching a laser gun tightly, even though they already knew it would do absolutely nothing against an android Reg.

"Door ahead," Kali whispered. "Right side. Let's check it out."

They darted down the length of hall and reached the door. Tor flattened herself against the cinderblock wall, while Kali tried the knob and found it unlocked. As she pulled the door open, Tor smoothly inserted herself between Kali and the doorway, once more managing to enter first.

"Oh, for the love of the Goddess...." Kali breathed.

In silence, Tor blocked the path, inspecting the room before her. Then, cautiously, with Kali only a few steps behind, she eased inside the dimly lit space.

Kali was immediately aware of the ceiling. *High for this far underground*, she thought. Dark steel girders crisscrossed the structure, supporting the shadowy ceiling and the higher level above. Rows of towering shelves angled away from Kali, all stocked with dust-covered crates and boxes. The overall impression was similar to a charcoal sketch expressing lines of perspective.

"Warehouse," Kali informed Tor.

"Also some sort of automated manufacturing site," Tor commented, peering at the computer panels and dangling robotic arms suspended above a squared section of conveyor belts.

"That equipment looks pretty modern—even from this distance," Kali observed. "This must be where she built those Regs we met."

"Look over there," Tor whispered, awestruck.

Following the direction of Tor's stunned gaze, Kali focused on an open area in the distance. When she saw the crumpled bodies, she involuntarily started. Even in the gray light she knew them.

Regs! Hundreds of them!

Though Tor held her laser gun before her, she glanced around for another weapon. She glimpsed a broom resting against the wall to their left and grabbed it. Swiftly holstering her pistol, she cracked the brush end of the wooden pole across her raised knee; the section which secured the brush fell to the floor, echoing loudly through the vast storage room.

Not a Reg stirred.

Meanwhile, Kali concentrated on slowing her pounding heart, reassured by the lack of life-vibration from these prone figures. *They're not real Regs,* she told herself. *You can handle this.*

Tor started forward, clenching the long pole in both hands like a Samurai sword. Kali swallowed nervously, and once more tried to rub some of the pain from her ribs. Then she made herself follow. As they neared the jumble of green-jacketed Regs, she was able to discern a pattern in the seeming disarray. Apparently, these giants had once stood in two neatly regimented rows. But for some reason they had fallen, and now they were lying there like so many stringless marionettes.

Although she was close enough to touch them, Tor chose instead to extend the pole, nudging a foot, then a leg, then levering the pole under the back of one of the Regs With some effort, she flipped him over. Carefully, Tor leaned over the Reg and lifted the lower edge of his jacket. They both recognized the dull sheen of skin-like plastic even in the indistinct light available.

"More androids!" Tor pronounced, then breathed a sigh of relief. "And all seemingly out of commission."

"Why?" Kali wondered quietly. Now that her fears were allayed by the obvious loss of function in these units, her next priority was to figure out exactly why these potentially lethal weapons were also coincidentally inoperative.

"Perhaps they were tied into the main computer upstairs," Tor guessed, "the one that got a blasted and crashed."

Shaking her head, bewildered, Kali surmised, "It's as if someone took it upon themselves to level the playing field. Someone has made damn sure that it will be just me against Arinna."

"Except she has two hostages—Danu and Loy," Tor declared, stepping back from the Reg. "And we're not even really sure *what* Loy is—hostage or foe."

"Loy's on our side," Kali stated confidently.

"How do you know?" Tor muttered, dubious. "From what I've heard of her, she's always played a game of political expedience."

"But deep down," Kali replied, "Loy is a Freeland Warrior." With a worried frown, Kali remembered the blood in the hall. Heading for the door, she concluded, "And the Loy I knew could be pretty damn troublesome when she wanted to be."

Arinna stood in the center of the brightly lit room. She faced the double doors, waiting expectantly.

Through slitted eyes, Danu watched her, knowing from the rigid stance that Arinna was relying solely on her paranormal abilities now. From where she sat resting against a large, cylindrical, steel-and-glass-enclosed case, Danu made a rapid assessment of her situation. She was still shackled. In fact, chained by a lead leash to a handle on the humming piece of equipment she leaned against. Still disoriented, she squinted at the unit.

After a moment, she comprehended that this was a parthenogenetic womb—a Delphi Unit—no doubt the current repository of the ova Arinna had stolen from her. *We must be in the lab....*

From what Loy had told her earlier, Danu knew the double doors Arinna observed so closely separated this, the last section of the lower level, from the warehouse space and office section that occupied the other two thirds of the floor plan. Situated as it was at the end of the corridor of offices, this lab was the furthermost part of the entire installation.

As she gazed at the cherished, indispensable Delphi Unit, Danu puzzled over why Arinna had chosen to make her stand against Kali here, of all places. Idly, she wondered how Arinna planned to conduct an unprecedented psychic battle while her first batch of superwomen were so close to the fray.

In a rage, Arinna whirled on her, and Danu winced as the icy green eyes targeted her. "Don't you worry, little genius!" Arinna declared. Coming nearer, Arinna hissed, "I'll dominate this contest from the moment Kali Tyler walks through that door." Grabbing Danu by the hair, she pulled her head back and leaned down to whisper, "And then I'll make Kali my bride of science, too. Between the two of you, I'll garner enough eggs for countless superior parthenogenetic creations."

Chained hand and foot by the shackles she wore, feeling impossibly weak, Danu could only look back at her, breathing raggedly. She was striving to keep her mind blank, not to allow fatigue and pain to dull her wits and let Arinna see into her mind. She needed to formulate a plan of escape, but for the moment she was simply trying to hold onto her sanity.

Still gripping her by the hair, Arinna yanked Danu's head around, so that she could see Loy—arrogant, proud, beautiful Loy Yin Chen—lying on the floor, face-up, eyes closed, only a meter away. Her right arm was brutally deformed: from below a rolled-up sleeve, both Loy's radius and ulna protruded—two gory sticks of shattered white bone. Meanwhile, the left wrist was slashed and seemed to be the source of blood beneath Loy. But it was her face that made Danu cry out. Loy's cheek was slashed with three deep, diagonal cuts.

"Just so you know," Arinna instructed, her voice cold, "what I do about betrayal." She held up her hand for Danu to see the blood still dripping from an old-fashioned steel scalpel. With a rough shove, she let go of Danu and stood above her, seeming to feed off her terror.

Desperately trying to recollect events, to remember what had happened, Danu searched Loy's still form, looking for some sign of life.

She remembered going to the War Room, shackled and in quiet agony from the unrelenting pain of her incision. Subdued, clad in a denim jumpsuit like Loy's, Danu had been led along the dimly lit hall by Loy herself. Tugging gently on the lead chain, Loy had warned her that, for security purposes, Arinna would no doubt take control of her mind as soon as the confrontation with Kali began.

Once they had entered the War Room, Danu remembered looking up and seeing Kali and Tor on the wallscreen. They had just entered through the steel door in the mountainside, and were arguing as they came down the corridor. It took her breath away—the surge of affection and fear for them—as she saw their faces. A short time later, they were conferring in the generator room, then coming down the corridor that led to the War Room itself. And then Kali had sensed the presence of the camera, reached toward the ceiling tiles, and the wallscreen had gone blank. At that point, Danu abruptly lost track of events.

She took control of my mind—as Loy said she would.

Except that she also remembered something odd unfolding just before Tor and Kali came down that last corridor. Loy had been preparing a sort of small victory feast, complete with diminutive sandwiches and a couple of bottles of champagne. Loy had subtly winked at her, then poured two glasses of the ancient vintage.

Ingenuously, Loy had walked up the ramp, respectfully approaching Arinna as she stood on the platform above them. In her hand, Loy had carried two glasses of champagne. Though Arinna had laughed and accepted one, wickedly pleased by Loy's toast of "Hail to the Conqueror," she had waved Loy aside, too engrossed with observing her opponents to finish her glass. And so Loy had taken the glass back, then set both drinks down on the housing of the mainframe computer responsible for the control panel.

What happened then? Danu mused, unable to resurrect another moment.

Glancing up, she found Arinna's venomous eyes riveted on her. "The bitch got hold of your wristcom and blasted my mainframe," Arinna provided, her voice controlled, lethal. "That *shit* blew out the entire system and rendered both my War Room and my Regs inoperable—but only temporarily."

Stunned, Danu again checked Loy's starkly pale face and the steady flow of blood from both her left wrist and her flayed cheek. If Loy wasn't dead yet, she soon would be.

How on Gaea's sweet earth did we even get down here?
Danu wondered, her weary mind rebelling against the fact of them
being so far from the War Room. She was beginning to have trouble
blocking her thoughts from Arinna.

"While you were spellbound," Arinna disclosed, her smile
chilling, "you held Loy for me."

I held Loy....No! Bile rose in her throat as Danu tried to break
the gaze and could not. Arinna grinned maliciously, as if delighting in
Danu's revulsion.

"You wanted to know how we got down here, didn't you?"
Arinna taunted. "Well, listen to the grisly tale, my curious little
genius." The nemesis of Freeland inhaled deeply. She stood tall and
looked pleased with herself, taking pleasure in Danu's obvious discomfort. "I first slashed her wrist while we were all still in the War
Room." Her face now fiendish, Arinna elaborated. "I *had* to leave a
trail for your friends to follow, you see."

Closing her eyes, and slowly reopening them, Danu vaguely
worried that she was going to throw up.

"On my orders, you quite obligingly dragged her down here.
After all, I couldn't take time to resurrect the Regs," Arinna continued. "I know that she still cares for you—neither one of you fooled me
with that performance yesterday—supposedly sharing a bed when all
either one of you did was *sleep*! I knew she wouldn't risk hurting you
in trying to free herself." With a harsh laugh, Arinna proclaimed,
"That's Loy's weakness. She likes to think she's a hard-boiled
cynic—when in fact she's flawed clear through with compassion!"

It sounded so ridiculous that Danu almost laughed with her,
then caught herself, and gazed at Loy's mutilated face. *What a price
to pay for compassion—compassion for* me*!*

"I gave her the facial cuts as we entered this room," Arinna
tossed off casually, then mused, "But she didn't scream as I wanted
until I broke her arm."

Dazed and sickened by this cold-blooded enumeration of
horrors, Danu could only shake her head.

"I never should have trusted *anyone*!" As if to emphasize her
point, Arinna stepped up to the unconscious Loy and viciously kicked

her in the side. "Well, I've had my revenge, haven't I?" she screeched at Loy. "I've made your blood my final lure!"

Spinning to face the entrance to the laboratory, her eyes crazed, Arinna commanded loudly, "Come to me, you pitiful fools! I'm waiting!" A shimmering green aura began glowing around her, as her rage mounted. "I'm hungry for the precious flesh of Kali Tyler, my partner-to-be!" Her voice resonated beyond the walls of the lab. "And I'm thirsty for a Samurai's blood!"

Shuddering helplessly, Danu involuntarily glanced at Loy again. All at once she was engulfed in an overpowering swell of anger. Feeling as if she were on the edge of hysteria, she tugged desperately, futilely, at the lightweight steel link that chained her to the Delphi Unit.

As Kali and Tor neared the lab, they could hear Arinna's voice echoing down the hall. Though the words were too muffled for them to catch the meaning, the madness in the voice rang out loud and clear. Kali, however, was radically affected. Staggering, she gripped her head with both hands, giving a small moan of pain.

Tor acted quickly. She grabbed Kali's arm and they returned to the shelter of the warehouse. Briefly, Kali stood in Tor's arms, bewildered, then pushed herself clear.

"No, Kali," Tor began. *I can't let her sacrifice herself for the rest of us—and that's what I think she's had in mind all along.*

"Please, don't try to stop me, Tor," Kali pleaded quietly. "This is going to be hard enough without fighting you, too."

Knowing the truth of it, Tor still couldn't help grabbing her arm, delaying her. "Make her come after you. Make her fight us both in here," Tor pleaded. "There's more room to move—more places to duck behind and gain temporary protection."

Her jaw set, Kali shook her head, then all at once seemed to reconsider. "Okay, I'll get her to come in here—and you get Danu and Loy out. Get them up to the surface and away from this place."

"No," Tor countered, determined not to leave her to this struggle alone, "I'll come back for *you*."

Rubbing her ribs, expelling a painful breath, Kali shook her head. "Don't. I'll either survive or I won't. There's nothing more you can do to help me—you know it." Looking deep in her eyes, Kali entreated, "Help Danu and Loy instead."

Tor swore softly.

Sensing that this was as close to a halfhearted compromise as she was going to get, Kali pressed, "Go back down the hall to the first turn in the corridor. Stay out of sight and remember—your mind has to be empty or she'll hear you."

Frowning, Tor asked, "Empty?"

"Yeah. Have you ever been in a bad fog?" Kali inquired, her mouth twitching up on one side. "Maybe stood on the shore of Puget Sound, surrounded by white mist?"

Perplexed, Tor nodded.

"Well, think of that. Hide yourself in the mist," Kali urged. "It seems to work very well for your friend Danu."

"Is that how she kept you in the dark after she discovered this place?" Tor asked, genuinely curious. "That night of the birthday party?"

"Exactly, except she used snow," Kali confirmed. "And it's a trick I think will fool Arinna the way it fooled me."

A few minutes later, purposefully thinking of white fog, Tor hustled down the hall to the first turn in the corridor, flattening herself against the wall on the opposite side.

Then she heard Kali boldly issuing a challenge to Arinna. "There's an electric cable that runs across the ceiling of this warehouse, Arinna. And guess what?" Kali's voice echoed. "I can shut off the power that runs this whole place. Or, for that matter, I could blow up this entire mountain and half of North America. Then neither of us would win...." Kali paused for effect. "So Arinna, why don't you come down here and convince me NOT to do that?" While Kali waited for a response, she realized to her own surprise that before she would allow Freeland to become enslaved, she would carry out this threat.

Gaea, listen to her, Tor involuntarily thought. *She sounds just as bold as Whit!* Then, remembering Kali's instructions, she quickly shrouded herself in a heavy, white, swirling mist.

A palpable stillness seemed to settle over the hallway, and Tor suspected that Arinna had been properly provoked, and was now psychically searching the building, pinpointing the exact location of her tormentor. For what seemed like an eternity, Tor concentrated on white fog. A confident click of boot heels sounded in the distance, growing steadily nearer, then stopping. Tor strained her ears, and finally heard the door of the warehouse gently close.

She waited, filling her thoughts with a white mist, then poked her head around the edge of the wall. A long, empty corridor stretched in front of her. With as much stealth as she could muster, Tor dashed to the double doors at the far end of the corridor.

As Kali fine-tuned her psychic antennae, she heard Arinna breathing, felt the warmth of her body heat, and knew that Arinna was in the warehouse. Arinna had come for her, and the battle she had sought for so long was at last about to unfold.

Instinctively, Kali hunkered down, for she knew she was still temporarily safe from Arinna's vision, though not from her psychic feelers. She was hiding in the midst of army-green steel crates and barrels, four stacks of them arranged in a towering square around her.

Swiftly, Kali fortified her psychic shields and regulated her breathing. From the beginning of her Wiccan training, she'd always excelled at this—diffusing her presence, cloaking herself in illusion. Now, as she hid in the recesses of row upon row of warehouse shelves, she carefully blanked her mind.

Arinna was already attempting to penetrate her defenses. The soft click of ghostly boots echoed in aisles where no one walked, as Arinna tried to spook Kali into reacting and showing herself.

Just buy Tor some time to get Danu and Loy out, she told herself. *Do nothing for as long as possible.*

And so she crouched between the tall stacks of steel crates, biding her time. Sooner or later, Arinna would come into range and the real battle would begin. For now, Kali was most definitely the mouse, playing with a very diabolical cat.

Danu grunted as she jerked with all of her might at the steel chain that locked her to the Delphi Unit. Just hearing Kali's challenge to Arinna had reenergized her. When she heard the double doors behind her open, she was certain Arinna had returned, victorious. Whirling, fists clenched before her, Danu fought the wave of light-headedness that threatened to engulf her.

Terrified, but mobilized to fight, Danu took a full minute to recognize the woman in the doorway. She then burst into tears and dropped to the floor.

Within the space of a breath, Tor was there, kneeling beside her, holding her, rocking her, murmuring in her hair. Danu cried so hard she choked on the sobs. In the shelter of Tor's arms, she was given a series of kisses, which began as comforting brushes against her wet cheek and ended with conviction on her lips. As Danu quieted, Tor eased away from her.

Her breath still catching in small, tearful rushes, Danu watched as Tor examined the steel chains that held her captive. Without warning, Danu's fear came surging back.

"There's no time. Leave me, Tor," she urged.

Tor gave her a sideways glance. "The hell I will," she muttered.

"She'll capture you, too!"

"Not me," Tor stated coolly, focusing on the lock. Holding up her laser gun, she modified several settings, adjusting the length and magnitude of the beam. She looked earnestly at Danu and said, "When I tell you to, take a depth breath, hold it, and don't move a muscle." Tor proceeded to hold the chain attached to each steel cuff taut. "Okay, hold your breath." Then, carefully, she aimed and fired the laser gun at each of cuff locks. "There—done. Now let me change the settings on the laser back to lethal, before I forget. And then, dear friend, we'll get the hell out of here, while we can." Tor's words were braver than she actually felt.

Danu raised both arms above her head, happily wiggled her fingers, and flexed each of her ankles. She looked at Tor lovingly, and thought, *That's confidence.* For a moment she basked her battered spirit in Tor's self-assurance. "Thanks, Tor, thank you," she said as she leaned against the Delphi Unit, incredibly exhausted.

The Samurai Warrior stared hard at her. And then, as if registering for the first time how unnerved and spent Danu was, Tor tenderly stroked her cheek. Her dark eyes discerning, she asked softly, "What in Gaea's name did she do to you?"

Quivering, Danu ran her eyes over the glittering steel-and-glass culture cabinets of the Delphi Unit, and found she was unable to tell Tor what those mitosis tanks held, how her eggs and the eggs of Arinna Sojourner were used to fertilize each other. She couldn't bring herself to tell Tor how Arinna planned to use her progeny...not yet.

Instead, Danu looked hopefully at Tor and asked, "You really think we can get out of here?"

Tor smiled and shrugged her shoulders. "It's worth a try."

As Danu rubbed her chafed wrists, Tor quickly turned to Loy, who lay unconscious, and said, "She's still breathing, but barely." She checked her vital signs. "In shock," Tor announced, "but we can't treat her here. We've got maybe another two minutes before Kali and Arinna start battling." Hastily, Tor unwound her loose, gray warrior's scarf and made it a temporary pressure bandage. She tied it firmly around Loy's slashed left wrist.

"That'll have to do for now," she muttered. Squatting down, Tor gathered Loy close and hoisted her upper body over her own shoulder. Using a firewoman's carry, Tor stood up with Loy draped over her back. "Kali says think of a white mist," she gasped to Danu. "We must cloak ourselves in a mist. It might just help us escape."

Slowly, shakily, Danu stood.

Her eyes narrowing, Tor saw the fresh stain on the side of Danu's navy jumpsuit. "You're bleeding."

Danu was silent, but placed a hand near the stain, trying to protect her lower belly. Cautiously, she made herself walk to the lab table at the far end of the room.

"What are you doing?" Tor called in a hoarse whisper. "We gotta get moving."

After a careful scan of the chemicals on the shelves nearby, Danu grabbed a bottle of concentrated hydrochloric acid and walked unsteadily back to the Delphi Unit.

"What are you doing?" Tor repeated, her tone determinedly patient and understanding, as if she suspected Danu had lost a bit of her sanity in this ordeal.

Noting Tor's suspicions, Danu thought, *Yeah, maybe I have gone a little over the deep end.* With meticulous, calculated deliberation, she uncapped the bottle, lifted the lid above the nutrient bath, and dumped in the entire container of deadly acid. *I'm murdering my own children, and if that isn't crazy, I don't know what is. The only thing I could do that's worse is allow them to be born to live as monstrous mutations, conceived to serve as agents of death for Arinna.*

As Tor stared at her, comprehending something of Danu's anguish, Danu closed the Delphi tank lid and placed the empty bottle of hydrochloric acid on top of it. Her face twisted with suppressed emotion, she turned from the Delphi Unit, and staggered to the door.

Then Tor was by her side, whispering, "We're together now, Danu. Just follow me. You can do it."

Gulping, Danu nodded.

"Remember, now. White fog."

Blinking wearily, Danu made herself envision long, curling tendrils of white mist. She surrounded herself with it, wrapped herself in it, and felt a merciful peace descend. She was barely conscious of Tor taking her hand and leading her through the door, down the corridor.

12

While Arinna was closing in on her prey, the tech team was furiously at work disarming the missiles. The atmosphere was tense as Razia, Ferris, and the nuclear physicist, C.A. Wolfe, gathered around the last missile that had not yet been disarmed. Carefully, the women examined the crude black letters on the main panel. Behind them, three meters away, Marino and Williams waited nervously with Sergeants Newport and DiMarco.

"Okay," Wolfe muttered, "Sojourner scribbled 'Isis' on this one. So what? Let's just get on with the job and get the hell out of here." She took a step closer to the missile and ran a trembling hand over the lettering. Shaking her head from side to side, she selected a wrench and carefully placed it over the bolt head in the upper left corner of the panel.

"No, wait!" Razia hissed. "I don't like this." She stepped forward and put her hand on Wolfe's shoulder. "So far, so good. Let's not get careless or underestimate Sojourner's hatred for us all."

"Wolfe! Razia is right," Ferris said sharply, as she, too stepped forward. "Arinna is treacherous. The fact that she designated this particular missile for Isis might have some twisted significance."

The silence of the past century roared in their ears. Finally, Razia said, "In the twentieth century this situation would have been described as a 'royal mind-fuck.'" No one moved. They just stood there, immobilized by the deadly dilemma facing them.

Wolfe's voice increased in pitch and began to echo in the silo. "There's no way we can leave here without disarming this missile. "Come on, I just want to get it over with and get the hell out of here, Zak." She removed the wrench from the panel bolt and looked up and over her shoulder, scanning the catwalk above. A tiny muscle over her right eye began to twitch. She half expected to see Arinna materialize above them. The others followed her gaze. Nothing.

Razia noted the beads of sweat on Wolfe's brow and began to fear that she was losing her nerve. Turning to Colonel Ferris, she said calmly, "Zak, we need to talk." Giving a nod in the direction of the catwalk, she ordered Wolfe to join the other women there. A frustrated Wolfe cursed under her breath as she headed for Sergeants Newport and DiMarco.

When Wolfe joined the sergeants, she turned and said something to Marino and Williams. Razia saw the brief exchange, but thought nothing of it as she took Ferris by the elbow and walked to the opposite side of the missile platform. "My gut and my years of experience tell me this baby is booby-trapped, Zak," Razia confided, frowning as she rubbed her chin thoughtfully. "And Wolfe is not giving too much thought to this possibility. I'm really surprised at her behavior. It's not like her."

Zak Ferris stared at the steel grating beneath their boots. "I agree, Razia. How do you want to proceed at this point?" she asked. With their backs turned to the missile, the two women did not see Williams and Marino advance toward the last nuclear missile.

"I'll do this job myself," Ferris abruptly decided.

"No, Zak!" Razia said sharply.

"You know it must be this way, my friend," Ferris said as her eyes met Razia's. "Now, get everyone else out of here... not that it will help," she chuckled ironically. "If I fail, we'll all go up, including Arinna." Suddenly, Ferris realized the significance of her own words. "That's it, Razia ! That's it!" Her eyes widened as she blurted out, "If she has tampered with the warhead, it would be in such a way so as *not* to detonate. Otherwise, she, too, would be incinerated. So the booby trap..."

From the corner of her eye, Razia caught sight of Williams leaning forward, disengaging and lifting the wrench as she removed the last bolt. Suddenly Razia's face took on a look of disbelief, and she was shouting, "No!!" even as Williams freed the panel and swung it open.

Startled, Williams looked over at Razia. For an instant, nothing happened, and Razia thought that perhaps her fears were unjustified. But seconds later, the young technician raised her hand and stared at the bolt she held. All of a sudden, her face paled dramatically, and the wrench in her other hand, along with the bolt, dropped on the steel grating, making a sharp, clanking noise. With a painful groan, Williams staggered backward onto the platform railing.

"Jan! What is it?" Marino yelled as she ran to her side.

Marino clutched her lover's hands in a panic. Instantly, she, too, gasped in pain, "Colonel...Ferris...her hand...I feel it burning through me."

Razia moved toward the two women, but Ferris lunged and grabbed her before she reached them. "DiMarco! Newport! Back off!" she shouted to the sergeants as they ran forward, horrified at what they were seeing. "Stay clear—that's an order."

Williams slumped heavily against Marino, blind with pain, and began to convulse. "Col... don't know wha's happen...ing...poi...son...." She struggled to breathe and at the same time vomited. Marino watched helplessly as Williams slipped from her arms, and lay sprawled at her feet. Then Marino felt her own knees buckle, and as she convulsed, collapsed next to her lover.

Razia ordered the others to stay back, while she and Ferris cautiously stepped closer. Ferris removed her bioscanometer from her belt and crouched down close to the two women. With tears beginning to form in the corners of her eyes, she scanned their bodies, even though she knew they were dead.

"They're dead," Ferris said in a low voice, to no one in particular. "Extensive nerve damage."

"Which means what?" Razia demanded. "What killed them?"

"I don't know for certain, but most probably some poison that is quickly absorbed through the skin, and then attacks the nervous system." Ferris paused, and shook her head sorrowfully. "We won't know the specific poison until we do a toxic scan of some tissue samples...provided we make it out of here." She stood slowly, not taking her eyes off the young, dead warriors. And under her breath she whispered, "May you rest peacefully in the arms of the Mother, daughters of Freeland."

Ferris and Razia turned and looked at the deadly missile and the opened warhead panel. "The underside of the panel cover, and perhaps even the bolts, were probably coated with the poison. And Williams absorbed it when she touched the panel." Ferris's voice cracked a bit and became hoarse with emotion, "And all Marino had to do was touch Williams' hand.... Whatever it is, it did its job effectively."

The warhead panel hung half open, and the remaining women came closer, disbelief written all over their faces, tears in their eyes. The silence in the silo was deafening. No one spoke.

Then C.A. Wolfe groaned, "Oh, Gaea. It's my fault!"

Razia turned sharply, anger filling her dark eyes. She grabbed the front of Wolfe's jacket, pulling her close, and snapped, "Did you tell them to go ahead and open the panel? Did you?! Did you?"

Wolfe was quivering and shaking her head. "Captain—I...I didn't know.... I thought you were overreacting. Please," she pleaded, "I had no idea...."

Razia shoved C.A. Wolfe away from her and yelled, "This is not one of your damned laboratories! It's a military mission—and you will act only on my orders! Is that clear, Wolfe?"

Ferris brushed by her, yanking on a pair of white latex gloves.

"Ferris!" Razia barked, shaken by what she knew Zak was about to undertake.

Ferris paused by the missile. Looking over her shoulder, she said, "Razia, you know this warhead must be disarmed. These gloves should provide the necessary protection, but if not," she smiled wryly, "I suppose I'll never get to have that dinner with you." She turned back to the warhead and began studying the internal circuitry.

Razia stood there, unable to speak, as Ferris reached into the compartment and began the dismantling process. Overwhelmed with fear for her friend, Razia forgot her fury with Wolfe, and watched, almost unable to breathe, as Zak's capable hands worked their magic. The other two warriors remained on alert, weapons ready, just in case Arinna had any more surprises.

Much later, Zak Ferris heaved a sigh and announced, "Last warhead disarmed." A satisfied grin crossed her face. "Now, let's get the hell out of here."

"Okay, tech team, move out."

"Wait, Captain," C.A. Wolfe cried out. "Are we just going to leave them here—Williams and Marino?"

Razia and the others looked at the bodies of their fallen comrades.

"They shall not be forgotten, by me or Freeland," she said solemnly. "Once we defeat Arinna Sojourner, we'll have their bodies brought back to Isis for a proper burial."

The women quickly picked up their equipment, scanned the silo, and began their hasty ascent to the surface.

Once more, Kali heard the click of phantom boots passing by the spot where she was hiding among the three-meters-tall stacks of steel crates. Breathing evenly—in, out, in, out—she hid her trepidation beneath a smooth veneer of psychic magic.

She was also using her psychic powers to shield Tor, Loy, and Danu as they passed through the hall just beyond the warehouse door. Arinna's perception was now so focused on ferreting out Kali that she seemed not to be bothering to monitor her other concerns. The Delphi Unit, her hostages, the general security of the underground complex, all of them registered no trace of Arinna's oppressive psychic presence.

Damn her! We're already unevenly matched, Kali thought angrily. *Arinna concentrates on one thing—hunting me—while I split my power to protect my friends.*

In addition to tracking Tor, Loy, and Danu, Kali was also aware of something toxic permeating the embryos that were being nurtured in the Delphi Unit down the hall. She sensed a hundred small souls departing this life in the wake of some cosmic moral decision Danu had just made. Though the details were hazy to Kali, she felt strangely compelled to keep this event from Arinna.

Slightly dazed, Kali shook her head. Splitting her power was depleting her strength. She could physically feel it: a slow, subtle draining that showed itself in how much strain she felt while holding Arinna's search at bay. But since she could think of no better means of handling this crisis, she continued her blocking strategy.

Maybe after Danu and Tor put some distance between this place and themselves, I'll be able to center my power on Arinna alone, Kali thought.

Then she heard it.

"Kali," that sweetly feminine voice was calling. "Let's end this foolish game of hide and seek." Echoing through the dimly lit warehouse, the voice was thick with the charms of a master Wiccan. "Come out and join me," Arinna invited, cajoled.

It was all Kali could do to remain behind her shields, safe within her barricade.

Arinna went on seeking her, calling to her in a seductive voice, as she gradually increased the intensity of her psychic probe. As time passed, Kali broke into a sweat, expending more and more effort in controlling her responses to Arinna's thrust. *I'm on the defensive,* Kali worried. *She's wearing me down.*

Within minutes, Kali had her hands over her ears, trying to block Arinna's melodious voice. But to no avail. The honeyed tones, the dulcet promises, were in her head, flooding the psychic link they shared. Arinna's deadly enchantments were tugging at Kali's soul, enmeshing her will. Kali's power to resist was rapidly fading, her desire to crush this cruel woman dissolving.

How can I keep her out of my head? Kali thought, nearly panicking at the terror of falling prey to Arinna's domination. Immediately, the answer sprang to mind. For Kali, only one event ever obliterated awareness of anything and everything else in the world. *Imagine you're in Whit's arms, making love*, she told herself.

The separation from Arinna's mind-grasp began gradually. Then, as Kali purposefully relived some of her more torrid moments with Whit, the break at last became complete. Daring to test her stamina further, Kali stretched her psychic net and stole a brief glimpse of Tor. There she was, climbing the stairs to the second floor, with Loy over her shoulder, and Danu's hand clutched tightly in her own.

Keep going! she urged them. *Get away!*

Again, she felt Arinna's delicious mind-touch engulfing her, and again she strengthened her psychic shields. She was sweating, trying to keep her breathing regulated, deep and even and noiseless. *Whit*, she reminded herself. *Think of Whit. Together in a white mist.*

Mmm...that playful nuzzle against my ear that makes me wild. Those large hands claiming me, caressing every nerve in my body to exquisite life. Those sensuous lips branding my mouth, hardly giving me a moment to consider whether or not I want to be handled like this; whether or not I want to be first teased, then paced, then gradually transformed into gasping, writhing ecstasy.

Oh, Goddess! Why did I spend so much time fighting with her—when all I usually ever want to do is drag her into bed and make love to her?!

Exasperated with herself, Kali shook her head, and caught another mind-picture. Tor was making a dash for freedom, staggering past the War Room, following the corridor, Loy's limp form across her broad, strong back, while Danu stumbled along beside her.

Once more, Arinna's sweetly dangerous voice penetrated Kali's block, nearly trapping her in an evil web. Once more, Kali dove into memories of Whit's touch, Whit's husky, arousing voice in her ear. Again, she was able to fend off Arinna's charm, though she was violently shaking with the effort now. Soothing herself with remembrances of Whit, Kali allowed herself to drift into a near trance, so intent was she on trying to physically recall those last, tender exchanges of love between them.

I'm weakening, she realized, dismayed. *I've got to hold on—or Freeland will fall.*

Then, in her mind's eye, she saw Tor and her wounded companions pass through the generator room. Tor entered the last tunnel with Loy still over her shoulder, Danu still being tugged by the hand. She seemed to be drawing upon every bit of endurance she had. Legs pumping, back straining, she was a champion driving for the finish line. Up the long incline toward the surface she struggled, toward the open door, her eyes fixed on a point of light in the distance. As she closed the space between herself and freedom, Kali saw the tunnel ahead of Tor filling with the strong rays of a late afternoon sun.

Is it still only afternoon? Kali thought, surprised. She was tiring badly. Her ribs ached, her head was ready to explode, and she began to feel as if she had spent forever down here.

And then, as Tor charged past the two skulls resting on the tunnel floor, Kali felt a ripple in the psychic current that seemed to permeate the entire SAC installation. Something evil had been released, triggered into motion by Tor's imminent escape.

Tor! Kali yelled with her mind, simultaneously shielding her message from Arinna. *You're in danger!* But Tor already seemed to be blocked from Kali's mind-speech, and did not respond.

As Tor, Loy, and Danu neared the exit, Kali felt the dark, ethereal menace lurking there, near the door itself. All at once, the view of the snowy mountain meadow beyond the tunnel threshold disappeared. The sunlight was gone. Gasping from her exertions, Tor chugged to a stop, staring in surprise at this transformation.

An ominous, roiling, dense black cloud seemed to pour out of the very walls near the entrance.

Beside her, Danu demanded, "Wh-what is it?" Pale and obviously shaken, she peered at this sudden, swirling barrier before the door.

"A spell, I think," Tor panted, "designed to kill us...or keep us here." Kneeling, she carefully lowered her shoulder and gently rolled Loy to the concrete floor.

From outside the entrance, Tor could hear Anat calling her name and Kali's.

As she stood up, Tor surveyed the frightening death cloud. "We have no time, Danu. And there's only one trick I can think of." Abruptly, she leaned into Danu, and surprised her with a fiercely tender kiss. Just as quickly breaking away, Tor directed, "You'll have to get Loy out.... Anat is on the other side of the entrance. Once you're out of here, cloak yourselves and get as far away as you can."

Danu pleaded with Tor not to leave, but to no avail.

Kali could do more than grimace as she viewed this scene in her mind's eye. Tor dashed toward the door, plunging herself into the smoky enchantment Arinna had woven across the entrance. As she entered the blackness, the death-spell discharged and penetrated her very being with incredible speed, surging into every cell. Her life-flow was choked off, and Tor writhed in the grip of the icy cold darkness enveloping her. With a tortured cry, she finally fell to the floor in mid-stride, in an agony of pain.

No! Kali pleaded, lanced through the heart by this psychic vision.

"No!" Danu screamed, staggering after Tor, her arms out-stretched.

Then, as quickly as it had arrived, the ominous black smoke disappeared, and sunshine poured once more into the tunnel, bathing Tor's still form in golden light.

With a mournful wail, Danu scrambled to her friend's side. Gripping Tor's arms, lifting and pulling her, Danu forced herself to think, to take control again. Kali could actually hear her imploring, "Sweet Mother, help us!" as she hauled Tor's unconscious body outside.

Now! Kali thought, drawing on the intensity of Danu's pain, Tor's sacrifice, and the impending destruction of Freeland, compacting it down, deeper, harder, with each blast of responding anger that rocked through her. *It's time Arinna learned about retribution!*

Standing, Kali stretched her arms up and out, then let the energy pour through her. At her will, the two tall columns of steel crates directly before her began to slide away from each other. Her psychic power was building, and a golden radiance surrounded her. Noiselessly, the stacks parted, allowing her to step into an area of the warehouse not far from where the fallen Regs lay in a pile.

And there, smiling malevolently, arms stretched upwards, Arinna Sojourner waited for her.

Once the roiling cloud disappeared from the SAC entrance, Anat helped Danu drag Tor outside, into the snow, and then went back for Loy. Minutes later, they had the two injured women lying near each other, safely clear of the entrance. In spite of the danger and confusion, Danu remembered to tell Anat to cloak her mind in a white mist.

In a near panic, blinded by the sudden sunlight, Danu knelt beside Tor in the snow. She placed her fingers against the unconscious woman's neck, and searched the sides of her trachea for some pulsing sign of life in the carotid artery. *No pulse*, Danu thought, inwardly reeling at the discovery. Swallowing hard, she lifted one of Tor's eyelids and saw the pupil beginning to dilate. She bent over her friend, her cheek a centimeter above Tor's slightly open mouth. *No respiration*, Danu noted. *Oh, Gaea—no respiration!*

Instantly, she initiated CPR, then shot a worried glance at Loy, lying nearby, helpless. *Hope she doesn't go into shock.* Anat laid her rifle aside and covered Loy with her own parka in a meager attempt to maintain Loy's body temperature. Torn by guilt, Danu gasped for breath as she tried to maintain an even breathing pattern into Tor's lungs. She begged aloud, "Oh, Mother...help us...save them... I can't...do this...alone.... Please...help us!"

And then, above the howling wind, she thought she recognized the mechanical thud of rotors echoing within the canyon walls that dominated Hart's Pass. She squinted against the sun's glare, and searched the blue sky overhead.

Kali strode boldly into the open space, her arms spread wide overhead, a golden aura radiating all about her. The final confrontation was here at last. Although her stomach quivered, in a strange way, Kali was glad the moment had finally come.

With a sugary chuckle, Arinna crooned, "And so we meet again, Kali Tyler."

Silent, infuriated, Kali breathed a steady Zen rhythm, moving the ki through her, readying to do battle.

Arinna grinned. "I have an advantage, you know, so long as you worry about your friends. Which, I might add, will do neither you nor them any good." Her hands moved through a pattern of hypnotic gestures, as she attempted to distract. "I felt that death-spell discharge, the same as you," Arinna smugly informed her. "Two are down... a few more to go, before all of Freeland is mine...before my new world order is in place. All will bow down before me." She laughed maniacally.

Oh, Hecate. What an evil fiend you are! Kali thought, enraged. She kept her power dispersed into the shields she had woven around herself.

Her face transforming into the savage snarl of an animal, Arinna raised her hands over her head, then flung them toward Kali, casting a psychic lightning bolt that flickered and sizzled across Kali's invisible shields. Kali closed her eyes against the brilliant blue light. For the first time, she realized just what she was up against. This was more than psychic strength; this was sheer demonic power—evil personified.

How the hell is she doing that? Kali thought, feeling vaguely overwhelmed.

Throwing her head back with glee, shaking her curly brown hair as she laughed, Arinna declared, "You won't be able to block my barrage for long, Kali. Who will you ultimately sacrifice—your friends or yourself?" And raising her hands over her head, Arinna stretched her fingertips toward the door. Blue fire seemed to jump from her hands, zigzagging across the room and incinerating the heavy steel door. Kali watched as Arinna turned and left the storage facility, laughing. She wanted Kali to follow her.

And as Kali scanned Arinna, easily reading her intent, she also discovered a major flaw in Arinna's defenses. Arinna's confidence in the superiority of her psychic abilities had made her careless. With surprise, Kali realized that Arinna's mind-blocks were not nearly as complex as she had originally thought.

Now's my chance! With all her will, Kali concentrated. For an instant, as she stared at Arinna, she managed to pierce Arinna's mind-blocks. One glimpse was all it took. She suddenly intuited how her own fury could be transformed into pure energy, and hurled from her fingertips. Arinna's secret weapon was no longer a secret.

Sensing Kali's penetrating mind-probe, Arinna gasped in surprise, and reinforced her own psychic shields.

But it was too late. Kali raised her hands, and the space around her began to glow with the brilliant yellow light which reflected her anger. Stepping forward onto the battlefield, she flung her fury at Arinna. The glowing arc of yellow-white light soared into Arinna's shield at an astonishing velocity, exploding in a blazing sunburst. The force of the blow nearly penetrated Arinna's shield. For an instant, Arinna's mind-shield glowed, as if hit with a power surge. Kali had found a chink in her armor.

Startled and alarmed, Sojourner turned and glared at her mortal enemy. Her eyes filled with hate. "Another hard-earned skill which you have simply stolen from me, you conniving little bitch!" she bellowed.

In quick succession, three blasts of blue-and-white lightning struck Kali's invisible shield. Now on the defensive, she dodged quickly, taking cover behind a pyramid of large steel barrels which, seconds later, were struck by yet another bolt of blue lightning. With a series of deafening crashes, the pyramid formation collapsed, causing the barrels to fall and bounce across the concrete floor. Shouting her frustration, Arinna zapped the barrels that still blocked her from Kali, and sent them careening toward her opponent. Kali continued to dodge around and to the side of the stacks of steel crates.

Her ears ringing with the noise, her eyes blinded by the dazzling blue light of Arinna's energy bolts, Kali frantically scrambled for cover.

I've got to stop this! she thought, cringing as three more energy blasts slammed the steel crates aside like toy blocks. The next fusillade sent blue fire crashing directly against Kali's psychic shield. *I can't keep getting pummeled like this! She's draining me and I've only gotten one good hit in!*

And then, as Kali tried to center and regain her sense of balance, she suddenly saw Tor standing beside her. Stunned, Kali asked, "What the hell are you *doing* here?!" In a hoarse whisper, she declared, "I saw you fall...*die.*"

Tor looked down at her body, bewildered.

"You agreed to stay with Loy and Danu!" Kali reminded her.

Across the room, Arinna stopped in mid-attack, watching them. She looked slightly rattled.

Tor, however, said nothing, only stared at Arinna.

"Answer me!" Kali insisted.

"I promised to stand by you," Tor said, although, oddly, her lips never moved.

"That was a promise to Whit—not me," Kali protested. "I release you...."

Still staring at Arinna, expressionless, Tor asked matter-of-factly, "Arinna, have you checked your laboratory recently?"

"What?" Kali glanced at Arinna, wondering distractedly why she wasn't using this opportunity to launch an attack.

"The Delphi Unit...." Tor intoned.

Perplexed, Kali watched the interchange between Tor and Arinna. With a slight hand motion, Kali lifted the block she kept over that end of the complex, though she still did not fully understand what had transpired there. When she heard the gasp from Arinna, followed by a shriek of demented rage, Kali knew that Tor had just helped her find another chink in Arinna's psychic armor.

"My babies!" Arinna screamed. "She killed my warrior babies! You'll pay...."

Taking advantage of the moment, Kali lifted her hands and threw another bolt of fury at Arinna, as hard as she could. And then, with a groan, Kali sagged to the floor, one arm about her middle.

This time, the yellow-white explosion had pounded through Arinna's shield, knocking her to the floor and leaving her dazed.

Glancing over to Tor as she readied another fusillade, Kali was surprised to find her friend heading toward the door, signaling Kali to follow her. After letting another power blast rip, Kali pressed her hand against her sore side and dashed toward Tor. She trusted this woman, even though her amazing recovery and reappearance in the installation seemed inexplicable.

As Kali ran, she kept glancing back at her opponent. A few moments later she saw Arinna struggle to her feet, prepared to defend herself against the next assault.

Before her, Tor paused on the threshold of the doorway, looking back at her with an intensity that riveted Kali's attention. Then, in the next seconds, Tor's image wavered before Kali's eyes, and in a heartbeat, was gone. At first, Kali told herself that it was a trick of the light, as she tried to deny the truth of what she had seen.

A wraith! A shiver ran up her back as Kali slowed, and grief overtook her. *Tor can't be dead! Oh, dear, sweet Mother, no!* And then the irrefutable truth mercilessly asserted itself.

Suddenly, in the space where Tor had been, an old woman appeared in a black cloak. Slowly, she pulled the hood back from her face. Kali gasped, and brought both hands to the sides of her face. She stood frozen, not believing her eyes. It had been so many years. Tears sprung to her eyes as she kept shaking her head in disbelief.

"Maat? Oh, Mother..."

Kali walked toward the elderwoman, hands outstretched, ignoring Arinna. She reached for the woman, embracing her. "Mother, Mother. I'm so sorry...I've missed you...."

The elderwoman smiled lovingly. "I am always with you, my daughter." With that, Maat disappeared. And Kali stood there looking at her empty arms, tears staining her cheeks.

Shaking her head fiercely, she said, "What is happening? How can this be?"

Suddenly, Arinna's voice broke the silence, "You're not leaving now, are you Kali?" Snarling malevolently, Arinna stretched her arms above her, and said gleefully, "We're just getting started!"

Arinna's arms came down, casting her deadly wrath across the room. The first strike of blue lightning hit hard enough to rock Kali within her sphere of her shields. Trembling and sweating, Kali clutched her side and ended up on her knees. The second strike flattened her, and the shields shimmered to an amber shade, almost, but not quite, collapsing.

Kali lay there, breathless, vulnerable. Surely the next blast would destroy her psychic shields completely. She shuddered to think what would follow. Determined to resist to the end, Kali shakily drew her laser gun, preparing to finish herself in the last freethinking seconds that remained.

Across the room, Arinna laughed maniacally and shouted, "And you thought you could stand against me!" She pounded her thigh, chortling with mad triumph. "You 'trained' with your pathetic friends—you worked so hard to prepare, but all in vain. Poor Kali." Sobering suddenly, Arinna hissed, "But even that Samurai specter showing up and traipsing through here cannot interfere with my plans."

Despairing, Kali curled up and pressed the barrel of her gun against her heart. And then she realized that Arinna had not seen Maat. Kali was seriously doubting her own sanity now. Feeling defeated, she dropped her chin to her chest.

Arinna raised her hands, crooning, "Oh, my dear, you don't want to hurt yourself. After all, you belong to me, now...beautiful Kali. You are so tired and need Arinna to care for you. Now don't you, my Kali?" Arinna's voice was mesmerizing.

The magic wove around Kali's weakened defenses, then managed to penetrate. For the moment she lost her desire to die and the gun wobbled in the sweaty grip of her hand.

"Drop the gun, Kali, darling," Arinna ordered.

The laser fell to the cement floor with a clatter.

Arinna glared at Kali contemptuously, her hate consuming her. "And now, Kali, to destroy forever any power that you may have.... Yes, you *will* be mine—your mind, your spirit...." She laughed and shouted triumphantly, "And your body, my dear, dear Kali. Forever. Never again will you resist me, Kali. Yes, you and Freeland and the entire planet will be mine."

Jubilant in her perceived victory, Arinna threw her arms heavenward and slowly brought them down, unleashing a series of blue lightning bolts that would finally destroy Kali's psychic shields.

Without warning, there was a sudden blur of motion at the edge of the doorway. Something, or someone, slid in front of Kali, raising a large, highly polished metal shield between Kali and the bolts of blue lightning emanating from Arinna's fingertips.

Everything was happening so quickly. Kali was stunned and dazed by what she saw. Brilliant blue-and-white electricity sparked all around them, followed by a sizzling snap and then a second explosion. Miraculously, the deadly lightning bolts were being returned to their source. And then, unexpectedly, there was a body pressed against Kali, cradling her. And in spite of the heavy smell of ozone in the air, this woman smelled amazingly familiar.

"Whit," Kali sighed, and then the world slipped away as she fell into the realm of unconsciousness.

When Kali opened her eyes, she had difficulty identifying her surroundings. All she knew was that she was being carried up an incline and being jostled about as Whit tried to distribute her weight more evenly. Whit lengthened her stride and cradled this most precious woman closer to her. Bleary-eyed, Kali tried to focus on Whit's face, then seemed to give up. She closed her eyes and murmured, "Tor needs me."

Struggling for each breath, Whit moved rapidly along the dimly lit corridor. Nervously, she looked back over her shoulder, checking her rear, half-expecting to see Arinna unleash another death bolt. Despite the incredible blast, she was not sure that Arinna had been destroyed.

Whit reviewed the amazing turn of events. The blue lightning bolts had bounced off her insulated metallic shield at the speed of light. Thanks to Styx's ingenuity, Whit and Kali had been insulated from the conducting capacity of the metal by the special nonconductive material Styx had fitted on the inside of the shield. Whit still couldn't believe it had worked. But she'd seen it with her own eyes. Arinna's lightning bolts had hit the outer sheet of that highly polished piece of shuttle nose cone and deflected back to their source.

As Styx had predicted, even the strongest of shields had to be dropped during the instant of spell-casting. And so Whit had last seen Arinna wide-eyed and open-mouthed as the blue fire slammed back against her. When the smoke cleared, all that remained where Arinna had stood was charred concrete.

Still, Whit worried. *Did she manage to escape somehow? Or was she incinerated by her own hand? Maybe it was all an illusion?*

Eyes still closed, Kali moaned against Whit's shoulder, and Whit broke into a run.

Quivering beneath the parka Whit had thrown around her shoulders, Danu watched Neith working on Tor, while a second Healer knelt beside Loy.

"Weetamoo, she's still not responding," Neith called urgently to her colleague. "I'm getting flat lines for heart and brain function."

Tersely, the copper-skinned Healer replied, "I'm stabilizing this one—be right with you." Giving Danu a quick, assessing look, the woman demanded, "Here...can you hold this unit for her?" Raising her hand, Weetamoo held aloft a blood transfusion pouch and a coil of plastic tubing. At Danu's blank stare, she impatiently waved her closer.

Danu stood unsteadily and crossed to the spot where Weetamoo stood. The Healer grabbed her arm just in time to break Danu's fall. "You're injured," Weetamoo said with concern, turning the bioscanometer in her hand on Danu.

As new tears slid down her face, Danu grabbed the pouch of blood and pushed the woman toward Neith and Tor. "I can wait. Save *her*...." Her voice breaking, Danu begged, "Please, save her."

Both Healers bent over Tor, working frantically to induce cardiac response. Weetamoo took over squeezing the Ambu-bag attached to the endotracheal tube that ran through Tor's mouth to her trachea. With a measured rhythm, Weetamoo would stop, and then place the heel of her hand on the inferior segment of the sternum, pressing down in a steady rhythm. Meanwhile, Neith had shifted positions. She opened her med-pak and pulled out an epinephrine injection unit.

After tearing open the package, Neith removed the first preloaded syringe. Danu watched Neith set the rest of the preloaded hypodermic needles within reach, then detach the cap from the syringe she held.

With one hand, Neith deftly opened Tor's shirt. The young Healer murmured to Weetamoo, "Administering epinephrine directly into cardiac muscle." Neith looked up at Weetamoo, then placed the needle against Tor's flesh and drove the needle down. Her hand steady, she injected the lifesaving stimulant.

Danu sat beside Loy, holding the saline unit up above her head with a trembling arm, while Anat held the blood pouch. Still nauseous, Danu gazed fixedly down the tunnel that led into the SAC installation. All at once she saw her—saw Whit running quickly up the last stretch of the tunnel, with Kali in her arms. Taking a sharp breath, she realized what Whit's coming out of there alive had to mean.

She's beaten Arinna! Unable to speak, Danu dashed the tears from her eyes and tried to sit up straighter.

As Whit cleared the entrance, she barked, "Evacuate! Let's go, let's go!"

Running the bioscanometer over Tor, Neith retorted, "She's still not responding! We shouldn't move her!"

Crazed and frightened, Whit shouted, "I don't give a damn!" Danu had never seen Whit panic. "Get them on the medicopter, now! That's an order."

The obstinate Weetamoo was not about to be ordered by anyone, especially when the life of a patient was at risk. "It's *my* medicopter, Leader!" Weetamoo snapped, her dark brows lowering. "And I say we're not leaving!"

With a terrified glance behind her, Whit hissed, "We're still in danger, dammit! I'm not sure if Arinna's dead."

"Well, if she's not," Weetamoo began, "this has all been for..."

Kali roused herself and weakly interrupted, "We have time, Whit."

Happy just to hear a lucid remark from Kali, Whit hugged her, then confessed anxiously, "I'm not sure if I got Arinna, Kali.... Can you sense anything?"

Rubbing her eyes, Kali muttered, "I don't sense her around here anymore, but I'm not sure what that means." Pushing against Whit's chest with both hands, Kali ordered, "Put me down, Whit. I can call Tor back...."

Frowning, Whit countered, "She's gone, Kal, she's dead."

Danu let out a scream and began to sob openly.

Weetamoo snapped, "Kali's the Shaman, isn't she Tomyris— not you?" With a no-nonsense nod of her head, she finished, "Then for Gaea's sake, get out of the way and let her call Tor back, before it's too late."

Giving Weetamoo an angry look, Whit opened her mouth, but it was Danu who spoke. Her voice raw with restrained emotion, Danu entreated, "Whit, please! I love her."

Whit looked at Danu, then at the tunnel, then back at Danu. Her gray eyes suddenly shifted to Kali, and when they returned to Danu, this time they were filled with empathy. Taking a few long strides, Whit set Kali down beside Tor. Gracefully, she moved behind Kali, placing her hands on Kali's hunched shoulders, steadying her.

"How can I help?" Whit asked, in a soft but determined voice.

Impulsively, Kali turned and kissed Whit's hand. "Keep physical contact with me." She took a deep breath, then finished, "I'm going into the nether world and I'm so...so tired. I'll need your life-vibration to stay anchored, to know how to thread my way back."

Placing a hand against Kali's cheek, Whit nodded. Danu saw her shiver, though whether it was from standing without a coat in the cold or from apprehension, Danu would never know.

As Kali laid her hands on Tor and rapidly descended into a trance, Danu's arm gave out, and her hand with the saline infusion pouch dropped into the snow by her knee. As she stared at this numb extremity, bewildered, she felt herself pitching forward, falling into the snow next to Loy.

Anat called for Weetamoo.

For a moment, Danu lay there, insensible. Then somehow she was above the scene, looking down. She felt so good—at long last—so free of fatigue and pain. As if from a high branch in the blue spruces nearby, she viewed Kali, Whit, and Neith kneeling by Tor's still form. She saw Weetamoo scramble over to Loy and what looked like a crumpled, redheaded girl.

Mother's Blood—that's me, Danu comprehended.

As Weetamoo opened the body's denim jumpsuit, beginning a full-scale, hands-on medical examination, Danu saw her body twitch with the first onslaught of a seizure. Within seconds, the body below her—surely not her own—was thrashing wildly, kicking powdery crystals of snow into the pure mountain air. A worried Weetamoo was murmuring things to her, easing her safely away from Loy. Then the Healer rooted through her med-pak pouch, cursing herself for lack of foresight.

Whit turned to Weetamoo anxiously and asked in a hushed voice, "What's happening?"

"Major dehydration, loss of blood, system shutdown," Weetamoo said, her eyes desperate. "I got a hint of this on the bioscanometer readout earlier, but I thought we had more time...."

Let me go, Danu thought. *I want to go....*

From the sky above her, Danu heard the cry of raptors and saw the golden eagles coasting above on slow currents of wind. Suddenly, in the air beside Danu, Tor floated, her wise eyes seeming wiser than ever.

They studied each other, smiling, the feelings they had so carefully hidden from each other on full display now. Tor's hand took Danu's own and Danu felt a sense of belonging and connection that she had never before experienced. Then, a dim, glowing figure appeared next to Tor, reaching for her. And all at once the peace and glory Danu felt enfolding her abruptly disintegrated.

Something sharp jabbed into her arm, and the weight and the ache of all she had so recently endured avalanched back over her.

"I.V. line in. Saline solution started," someone nearby was quietly recounting. "Let's get an EKG—quick."

And by her ear, another, more familiar voice was commanding, "Don't you dare die, little sister. Don't you dare die!"

Whit?

And after that, she knew nothing.

The med team worked furiously, and a short time later, Danu, Loy, and Tor were secured in the rear of the medicopter, safely sheltered in anti-shock bags. Nearby, Neith knelt, keeping a vigilant eye on the biomonitors. Whit harnessed Kali in a flight chair, and was not surprised to see her love fall deeply asleep before Whit had even managed to strap herself into the pilot's chair. Weetamoo quickly slid into the navigator's chair next to Whit.

Anat announced, "All hatches secured, Leader."

"Update patient status," Weetamoo called to Neith.

"All three are still unconscious. Heart rates are shallow, but stable. Respirations, the same," Neith replied, her voice composed. But as Whit glanced back at her, she saw the anxiety in her eyes.

Leaning forward over her controls, Whit engaged the engines and two large overhead rotors began spinning. Moments later, the medicopter lifted off. In a low, tight voice, she told Weetamoo, "If Arinna is alive, she'll try for us now."

Her gaze on the three-dimensional radar display, Whit paid careful attention to the ground they were leaving behind. Beside her, Weetamoo kept a similar vigil, peering at the monitors of the aircraft's fore, aft, port, and starboard cameras. Slowly, they rose, the shadowed snow and cedars of the meadow disappearing and being replaced by sheer cliff walls. After several tense moments, the craft attained enough altitude to swing clear of the canyon walls that formed Hart's Pass. Whit and Weetamoo exchanged glances and each released small sighs of relief.

The comline buzzed intermittently until Whit tapped the on-line switch and said, "Tomyris Whitaker, Co-leader of Isis. Transmit all stored messages now." Immediately, a short coded message appeared onscreen, and a pleasant voice intoned, "The ducks are on the pond. Repeat, the ducks are on the pond. Four geese have gone south for the winter."

Weetamoo shook her head, bemused.

"It's in code," Whit explained with a grin. "That's Captain Razia telling me the eight nuclear warheads are disarmed, and she's taken her tech team back to Isis." Sadly, Whit finished, "But she's lost two warriors. Again, Arinna exacted a high price." She shook her head, not quite believing all that had happened in such a short time. "Freedom is never cheap."

"I did not know that a woman could be so...brutal," Weetamoo admitted. "Loy and Danu bear physical injuries that are clearly the result of torture."

Staring at the glacier and granite mountain peaks they approached, Whit retorted, "Why should it shock you that women can be as cruel and brutal as men? Given the right set of circumstances, we, too, can be reduced to savagery."

Weetamoo looked at Whit with renewed respect, and countered, "But you are not like Arinna Sojourner."

With a shrug, Whit met her eyes. "If what I intended succeeded down there, then I killed someone today. And by the way, it's the second woman I've killed in as many years." Shoving a hand through her dark hair, Whit commented bitterly, "Tell me I'm not a savage."

The weathered planes of Weetamoo's face shifted. "You are a Freeland Warrior, sworn to defend freedom and protect those in need." With a somber smile, Weetamoo concluded, "And thank Gaea, you're good at it."

Accepting the acknowledgment with a grim countenance, Whit gave her full attention to piloting the medicopter over the great Cascade Range. As they crested the last peaks and turned toward Isis, Neith called from the back, "Watch how sharply you bank this thing, Leader! I've got patients back here, not sacks of oats!"

Wearily, with a soft chuckle, Whit nodded. Occasionally glancing at Kali's sleeping figure, she tried to maintain a smooth flight back to Isis. Weetamoo toggled the radio-control switch and contacted Lieutenant Iphito at Isis Airfield. Only half-listening to the highly technical report Weetamoo began giving to the medical officer Iphito had on standby, Whit felt her attention begin to drift. A relieved glow of accomplishment was stealing over her. She leaned back into the flight chair and gazed appreciatively at the panorama on display through the cockpit window. Spread out like a golden dream in the waning, late-November sunset, Freeland gleamed and sparkled all around her. With a glow of satisfaction, she acknowledged that she had made a difference.... Tomyris Whitaker, along with her comrades-in-arms, did save Freeland from yet another nemesis; this time one of their own—Arinna Sojourner.

They flew silently over green-and-white alpine meadows, and then, as they traveled lower over the western flank of the Cascades, came the kilometers of dark green fir forest. Soon, Whit saw the glint of rivers running east to west, and farther off, the sparkling blue of Puget Sound.

Years ago, the trees had reclaimed what houses and suburban streets had survived the chaos and fires following the Great Schism. Still, closer to the ghost city of Seattle, the ruins of long-abandoned homes and highways were evident from the air. The two aging flotation bridges across Lake Anne Bonney stretched across the calm autumn waters, and the weak orange sun on the horizon sent its colors across the scene like a pale wash of gold.

In the distance, Mount Tahoma loomed against the deepening blue of the east, a snowy giant already fading into the swiftly oncoming night. Whit pointed the craft toward the mountain, thanking the Goddess that Kali, Danu, Tor, and even Loy had survived this mission, so far.... She had no idea if it had been skill, or luck, or even a touch of the Goddess's plan, and some help from the spirits of their mothers, that had allowed them to come out of such a harrowing experience alive. What was more important was the fact that all four had managed to work as a team, even though they had each faced the worst of their own personal struggles against Arinna alone.

It's as Weetamoo says of me—they're warriors, Whit finally decided.

She shifted her gaze to the mountains as she climbed into the foothills near Mount Tahoma. Below, in the golden light of the late-autumn sunset, the thick fir and hemlock forest covered ridge after ridge, a seemingly unending expanse of wilderness. And then, down in a lovely valley, Isis glowed with the lights of a thousand households, all settling down for the night.

Home, Whit thought, her eyes filling with tears. *Home*.

13

Whit ran her finger around the stiff, starched collar of the white cotton shirt and craned her neck away from it. The shirt was uncomfortable, but she was also trying to subtly steal a peek out the huge bedroom window. From this, the second story of the Leader's House, she knew she should be able to see if the handfasting entourage was parading down Cammermeyer Street yet.

Marpe promptly slapped her hand away from the collar and tightened Whit's western string tie. "Do you want to look like a Leader on your handfasting day?" Marpe fussed possessively, "Or do you want Kali to have second thoughts?"

In response, Whit snorted. *Second thoughts? After all we've been through together?*

Whit stilled herself, watching her reflection in the full-length mirror which stood before her in the center of the large room. All around were the racks of dress wear and pompous apparel which she had already tried on and discarded. She should have selected her outfit weeks ago, but things had been as hectic as ever since she had returned from Hart's Pass with Kali snoring, a pair of contentious Healers, and three badly wounded women in anti-shock bags.

For one thing, she was still dealing with the satellite crisis. She had thought that getting that NASA ship built was going to be relatively easy, but while the anti-g thrust of the crystal unit looked good on paper, no one was quite sure what would happen during the real lift-off.

She also had a devil of a time convincing Marpe and Samsi that she would not go to her handfasting ceremony looking like an advertisement for some of their more radical clothing designs. Despite what anyone said, she would not endure epaulets on her shoulders or an array of gaudy colors. And so, on one side of her, Marpe adjusted a black sash around Whit's waist, while on the other side of her, Samsi brushed invisible lint from Whit's tight, dark-gray pants. The overall effect was simple, yet suitably elegant, Whit thought, though she still would have preferred her dress warrior uniform. Too bad Lilith had made it convincingly clear that as a democratically elected Leader, it would be wiser to forego military trappings on this occasion. Finally, Marpe brought the long, dark-gray jacket, and as Whit slipped it on, the ensemble was complete.

Anxiously, Whit studied her image in the mirror, wondering what Kali would think of her. Annoyed at her own insecurity, she made herself look away. *Mother, I can't wait till this affair is over with and we can get everything back to normal around here!*

As Samsi grabbed a brush and shifted her attention to Whit's gleaming black boots, Whit announced firmly, "I have been passing parade-ground inspections for years, Ma'am, and I will not allow anyone—let alone a respected elder—to shine my boots for me."

Covering her mouth with her hand and tittering coquettishly, Samsi put the brush aside and gave a slight bow. "I'll go see to the guests downstairs, then." With a trail of laughter and a swish of emerald chiffon, she scurried to the door.

Eyeing herself dubiously in the mirror, Whit pulled up her shirtsleeves and then ran a nervous gaze around the room.

A far cry from the large but sparsely furnished bedroom of her country house, this room filled with tapestries and pillows and beautifully carved wooden furniture still seemed strange and uncomfortable. Perhaps it was because she herself had only officially moved into the Leader's House yesterday. She had spent last night in that broad, brocaded bed alone, while Kali stayed in their country home, engaging in her private, Wiccan preparations.

Kali had insisted upon it, saying she needed to purify herself and give thanks to the Goddess. Instinctively, Whit had understood that Kali was using ritual to signal the end of one part of her life and the beginning of another. Her years of merely trying to survive from one day to the next were over. At long last, Kali was fully in control of her destiny, and was declaring herself as a full-fledged Shaman. As if to announce the fact to the entire colony, golden eagles had been circling above their country house ever since the medicopter had returned to Isis three weeks ago. Kali's growing psychic abilities had markedly expanded during the climactic battle with Arinna, and now there was no longer a question of what Kali's role in Isis would be. Weetamoo's tales of that afternoon on the mountain already had half the city calling Kali their "Shaman."

Two days after coming home, Kali had resigned as Deputy Leader. A new election for the post would be held next week, but everyone already knew that Lilith would end up in that position. Since several new herstory students were helping with her archival work, Styx didn't seem to mind Lilith's departure from their original plans. Styx could happily continue her work of saving the printed paper books still salvageable in the ruins of Old Seattle. And as for Whit herself, she was delighted that Lilith's counsel and insight would still be available to her.

As she thought over the hectic events of the past few weeks, and Kali's new position, Whit wondered, *How will this shaman business affect my relationship with Kali? As full equals, in bed and out, are we going to continue fighting as much as we have these past few months? Am I wrong to want a tranquil relationship?*

Marpe tugged a comb through Whit's thick, dark hair, trying to arrange it into some sort of graceful fall over her collar, while Whit clenched her teeth against the sensation of having her hair torn out by the roots. At last, Marpe caught sight of Whit's glowering face in the mirror and stopped, muttering, "I don't suppose you'd let me style it for you...."

Almost in answer, Whit sent a nervous hand through the glossy arrangement, then realized what she had done, swore, and clasped her hands behind her back. *Why did I ever promise Lilith I'd go along with this!*

Unexpectedly, Marpe gave her a thoughtful look and said, "Yes, it does look better that way, I think. There's always been a bit of the rugged rogue to your beauty, Tomyris."

Astonished by the use of the word "beauty" in association with her looks, Whit stared at the reflection of the gray-haired woman hovering behind her shoulder.

There was a peremptory knock on the chamber door, and with a wink, Marpe announced, "I'm done, and I think this must be Lilith." As she passed Whit on her way to the door, Marpe added, "May you enjoy your handfast with Kali as much as I have enjoyed mine with Samsi. And don't worry so much about it." Laughing, Marpe disclosed, "You two were cut from the same cloth!"

That's what bothers me! Whit fretted.

Marpe swung the door open, greeted Lilith with a kiss on the cheek, ushered her in, and then left. The door closed behind her and Lilith paused. Dressed in a long, white dress with an equally long white over-robe, Lilith strode over to Whit, looking her over as she came closer.

"Those colors are rather severe," Lilith commented, seeming very amused.

"I thought they looked...dignified," Whit murmured uncertainly, glancing down at herself.

Taking a bright, royal-blue coat from one of the racks, Lilith coaxed, "Let's see what this one does for you."

Grudgingly, Whit took off her dark-gray coat and handed it to Lilith. Seconds later, she slipped on the bright-blue coat and was amazed at the transformation she saw in the mirror. Smiling, she turned, watching the well-cut, flashing blue flow against her thighs. The coat made her feel sophisticated, and somehow braver than she had a moment ago.

Raising her eyebrows, Lilith teased, "You'll be lucky if Kali lets you dance with anyone else tonight."

Blushing, Whit mumbled her thanks.

Lilith linked arms with her, and led her toward the door. "I must congratulate you, Whit, on your growth in the arena of love." As Whit made ready to protest, Lilith stopped walking and faced her. "Oh, I know better than anyone how much loving someone terrifies you, so don't try to deny it."

Whit felt skewered by Lilith's perceptive blue eyes, and was not sure if she wanted to hear this or not.

"When you chose Kali as your partner," Lilith continued, her voice and manner tolerating no disagreement, "she was not the capable and confident woman you are living with today."

Accepting this truth, Whit nodded, then remarked softly, "She needed me. I suppose that was part of the attraction...."

"And you needed her," Lilith pointed out.

"Yes," Whit breathed, remembering the blonde stranger who had made love with her in an autumn field last year, when Isis consisted solely of the Cedar House and a city of decade-old, blackened ruins. "No one has ever loved me like that...so selflessly, so single-mindedly."

"And has that changed?" Lilith prodded softly.

Relief and comprehension flooded Whit at the same time. "No," she declared softly. "Kali has grown stronger, and along the way she's developed some abilities and knowledge that I'll never be able to master, but...she still loves me."

"Then, what causes these problems between you?" Lilith pressed, her eyes scanning Whit's face.

Feeling ridiculous, Whit first shrugged, then guiltily murmured, "Sometimes I guess I try to order her around."

Lilith's voice was compassionate. "Why?"

"I want to...keep her safe."

Lilith grasped Whit's hand and asked, "And does it keep her safe?"

"No," Whit sighed. "It just makes her mad."

"I see," Lilith said.

After a moment, Whit finally admitted, "So do I. What an idiot I've been."

"Not such an idiot," Lilith objected, gazing at her with heartfelt admiration. "You saved her life a few weeks back."

Suddenly remembering the topic she had been meaning to pursue with Lilith, and had not, Whit demanded, "Who *was* that old woman in the cloak, anyway—the one who pointed out the reflective properties of the NASA nose cone I eventually used as a shield? Has anyone been able to identify her?"

Flicking Whit an uneasy glance, Lilith turned and reached for the door handle.

Whit took Lilith's hand and insisted, "You know more than you're telling me, Lilith."

"I thought I recognized her voice," Lilith offered cryptically.

"And whose voice was it?" Whit urged, her eyes intense. *I need to know who helped us beat a seemingly unbeatable enemy. I want to find that old woman and thank her.*

With a sigh, recognizing that Whit was not going to let this drop, Lilith allowed, "I spent years with that voice, though the woman died long before her crone years ever claimed her. She's buried up on the mountainside, with all the others who died in the Fall of Isis, ten years ago."

"You don't mean..."

"I know this must sound absurd...but, yes, I think it was Maat." Lifting her chin and taking a slightly combative posture, Lilith finished, "And if I recall, you've met her ghost once before—during another occasion when Kali and Freeland were in danger."

Her dark brows meeting in a V of concentration, Whit gave a single, forthright nod and then pulled open the chamber door. "All I need now," Whit muttered dourly, "is for my mother-in-law to make an appearance at the handfasting."

From her spot near the large front door of the Leader's House, Danu watched Whit and Lilith walk along the balcony toward the freestanding staircase that dominated the Great Hall. The noise of a hundred or so women gossiping only increased as Whit in her vivid blue coat and Lilith in her white robe and long dress paused at top of the staircase. Every eye in the hall was riveted on them. Above the two leaders, across the domed ceiling and the walls of the Great Hall, Ida B. Wells, Bowdash, Roberta Achtenberg, Boudicca, Sally Ride, Phyllis Wheatly, and many other brave women of herstory were painted in the colorful murals. To Danu, it seemed appropriate that Lilith and Whit looked almost a part of that regal backdrop of Amazons.

She could see little else but the scene overhead right now, for on the main level, the place was packed with colorfully dressed women who blocked her view. By the shouts she heard from the doorway, she understood that Kali was now in sight, walking down the street amidst a parade of schoolgirl bands and warrior regiments.

Then Neith passed by her in a striking red jacket and gown. She snagged Danu's elbow, jerking her along. "You've been skipping your checkups at the clinic," Neith accused, heading for the back of the building and dragging Danu with her.

Danu tried to pull her arm free, afraid she might miss Kali's entrance. "I'm okay now," she defended, twisting to look behind her.

Relentless, the smaller woman not only maintained her grasp, but continued to push her way through the crowd, casting an appraising look at Danu's black overcoat and forest-green bodysuit.

Guessing that Neith's perusal was critical, Danu supplied, "Maybe I'm too informally dressed."

Shaking her head, Neith stated, "You look terrific."

And then, accelerating her purposeful gait, Neith steered them into the empty corridor that led to the Watch Room, dragging Danu along till they stood before the familiar steel door.

"I need your help," Neith announced abruptly.

Confused, Danu waited for her next words.

"Whit programmed your DNA. You can open the door," Neith elaborated, "and I can't. Earlier, Styx and I parked a couple of med-clinic escapees and their autochairs in here, to keep them out of the crowd scene down there...." Neith gestured down the corridor, toward the assembled dignitaries they had just left.

Understanding, Danu interjected, "Out of Weetamoo's sight, you mean. I thought she told them they couldn't come."

"Oh, for Gaea's sake," Neith complained, with a grin, "when do any of you warrior types ever do anything you're told!"

Danu broke into a laugh and Neith clamped a hand over her mouth. "Shh! Weetamoo's patrolling like a sentry. If she finds you and me down here, she'll *know* we're up to something."

"Since when did you start aiding and abetting med-clinic breakouts?" Danu asked, pretending to be shocked.

"Since Albie hopped in her autochair, pulled me onto her lap, and drove us out of the clinic and down Cammermeyer Street," Neith remarked. "I had very little to say about it."

"Oh, sure," Danu returned, "and since Albie's arm is still held together by sutures and she's not even scheduled for physical therapy for another week, that is *such* a plausible story."

Neith showed Danu her fist and then thumped her lightly on the arm. "Don't make me hurt you," she threatened.

Somehow, the joke triggered a memory, and for an instant, Danu heard Arinna's voice saying those words. "Don't make me hurt you...." Danu froze.

A long, agonized memory pulled at her, taking her back to Arinna's underground fortress, back to the terror she still visited each night in her dreams. Before her eyes, the hallway was transformed into Arinna's cold, austere War Room and she found herself shackled, at the end of a leash, standing before her green-eyed captor.

Someone was tapping Danu's arm and calling her name softly. Returning to the present, Danu found Neith standing close, taking her pulse. With a shaky sigh, Danu leaned against the wall, feeling faint.

"How often does that happen?" Neith asked, her professional manner back in place.

Mortified, feeling the heat rising in her face, Danu shrugged and made herself straighten up. "I'm okay."

"You're not," Neith refuted. "That bitch experimented with your psyche, and Gaea knows what else!"

"It's just nerves," Danu assured her, firmer this time. "Arinna was...a pretty frightening character. Sometimes I can hardly believe I got away from her...." Danu finished the quiet confession with a shudder. "That any of us got away...."

Surveying her, Neith pronounced. "You need to see a therapist."

"Can we get to the handfasting, first?" Danu asked.

"Sure, but don't forget to make an appointment, my friend," Neith responded, cocking an ear as a roar came from the Great Hall. "Now, open the door and let's get the fugitives rolling. There's an elevator at the end of the hall—we'll use that to get upstairs."

As Danu raised her hand to the DNA lock plate, Neith said, all in a rush, "By the way—I want to thank you for being so sensible when I was chasing you like that in September—you were right. You just weren't ready, and it wasn't fair of me to expect you to want what I wanted, just because I wanted it." Neith paused and frowned. "Did that make sense?"

Looking at Neith with soft eyes, Danu confessed, "I wasn't being sensible. I was scared."

"Scared of me?" Neith asked, incredulous.

"Scared of...falling in love...of losing control of myself," Danu admitted, then swallowed. "But it turns out that...I like it."

Smiling, Neith asserted, "So do I!"

And then they stood there for a moment, grinning at each other.

"So it all worked out, right?" Neith asked. "We're still friends?"

"The best!" Danu laughed, and hugged the small, wiry Healer.

Seconds later, Danu brushed her hand across the DNA lock plate. The metal door of the Watch Room slid back, revealing Albie, Loy, and Tor, all in various stages of mending. They were all sitting in their high-backed autochairs, eagerly awaiting Neith and Danu.

✧ ✧ ✧ ✧ ✧

As the warrior regiments marching in front of Kali and Styx approached the Leader's House, they broke into flanking lines. Within seconds, they formed a border of burgundy jackets on each side of the walkway that led to the large, heavy wooden doors of the Great Hall. Behind them, Kali could see and hear the cheering women of Isis. The wide expanse of garden before the Leader's House was filled with hundreds of women, many of whom had been waiting through the cold December morning, anxious to participate in some part of this herstorical handfasting ceremony.

Kali walked beside Styx, her pale-blue cloak and dress flowing behind her, her loose golden hair swirling in the wind. Though she draped her hand with a look of casual ease over Styx's extended arm, Kali's heart was thundering within her.

This isn't just an informal exchange of promises, Kali worried. *This is a legal covenant, binding us together, before Gaea and Freeland. I want to commit myself to Whit forever—but we can both be so bullheaded and short-tempered. I feel so confused, so scared....*

Leaning closer to her, Styx observed, "And you're working yourself into a near panic."

Chagrined to have had those particular thoughts so easily read, Kali bent her head and blushed.

With a low chuckle, Styx asked, "When you were on the brink of losing that battle with Arinna, I think you discovered more than a hitherto-unknown array of psychic skills." Examining Kali's profile, Styx speculated, "I think you found out how you truly feel about Tomyris Whitaker."

Remembering those glorious moments of certainty, Kali broke into a grin. She could still feel Whit's arms around her, holding the omnipresent evil of Arinna at bay. *The mere memory of our loving was stronger than all Arinna's power,* Kali reflected.

Warriors on each side of the opened oak doors saluted, hands over their hearts, and then Styx led Kali through the doors, into the Leader's House. As the crowd parted before them, the roar of welcome seemed to shake the foundations of the building, and Kali glanced around and smiled at all the familiar faces.

A little over a year ago, Whit brought me here, a starved, wounded survivor of Elysium. I never dreamed then that I would one day be received like this. She reached out to touch the hands reaching toward her. *My people,* she thought lovingly, then amended, *Our people.*

And with that, she lifted her eyes, searching for that one face. Her gaze journeyed up the stairs, then stopped and lingered on a dark-haired woman in a knee-length, royal-blue coat. Her gray, intense eyes very serious, her broad shoulders back, Whit waited beside Lilith for Kali to be escorted upstairs.

A rush of emotion surged through Kali. *Oh, Gaea—I love her. How could I ever have doubted it?*

It seemed to take an eternity to reach Whit's side, to get that large hand in her own. Amazingly, Whit's hand was trembling, and as Styx and Lilith followed behind them, Whit and Kali paraded across the balcony together, to the main hall beyond.

The walk down the wing of government offices gave them each a chance to glance shyly at each other, grinning with a dazed delight, as they advanced to the final scene of the ceremony. Turning left, Whit led Kali through a large banquet room, one of many that was set up and waiting throughout the colony on this day. On the opposite side of the room, another two warriors opened large double doors. Moments later, Whit and Kali stood together on a great balcony, overlooking the multitude of citizens in the great garden below.

Around them were gathered their closest friends.

From Artemis, Deputy Leader Nakotah Berry and Leader Cimbri Braun stood side by side, both looking incredibly regal and fit.

Nakotah tossed a long black braid over her shoulder and kidded Kali, "Still time to change your mind and try for me."

Cimbri kissed Whit on the cheek and blinked back a few tears. "Who'd have thought you'd ever settle down, Tomyris?"

Behind them, Captain Razia and Colonel Ferris saluted. Whit returned the salute, while Kali murmured, "Blessings on you. And many, many thanks. Freeland will never forget your brave deeds."

As Whit and Kali moved closer to the platform at the edge of the balcony, they saw Neith and Danu standing guard over three women in autochairs. Bundled in blankets against the cold day were Tor Yakami, Albie Hild, and Loy Yin Chen.

"I thought Weetamoo said..." Whit began.

"Shh!" Neith shot back. "She's in the garden below, looking for us." Neith glanced at Kali and explained, "It's only for the ceremony, and this *is* a once-in-a-lifetime happening."

Noting that Danu was holding Tor's hand, Kali commented, "She's a good one, Danu. Don't let her get away."

Danu nodded emphatically and announced, "Tor will be on medical leave for most of the winter. We want to talk to you and Whit, later, about renting your house in the country."

With a quiet laugh, Whit inserted, "It's yours." Bending lower, to look into Tor's dark eyes Whit added, "As long as you don't blow out the windows with Blaster Rock."

Tor smiled back and said, "Which reminds me—here's your handfasting gift." She handed Whit a lucite music chip box.

Reading the label aloud, Whit groaned, " 'The Maenads' Greatest Hits.' "

Everyone around them exploded into laughter. As Whit pocketed the small box, giving a giggling Danu a mock glare, Kali pulled Whit away, toward the small altar at the front of the balcony.

As they passed Loy, Whit paused again, leaning over to touch the top of Loy's forehead with her lips. "Thank you for what you did for Kali," Whit whispered.

One side of Loy's face was heavily bandaged, the other displayed a wry little grin. Twinkling black eyes shone up at them both. After all the facial reconstruction and plastic surgery of the last week, Loy was under strict orders not to talk. And for once, Kali was surprised to see Loy following a direct order. A thin hand scribbled a note on a small note pad, then showed the note to Whit. As Kali angled closer, trying to catch a glimpse, Whit steered her away.

"It was obscene," Whit muttered, rolling her eyes.

"I'll bet," Kali responded, laughing.

And so they stepped onto the raised platform together, a radiant couple filled with hope and love. The population below caught sight of them and roared. As Whit and Kali waved in response, Lilith and Styx marched proudly up on either side of them, bearing the Horns of Artemis and the cup of wine.

The schoolgirl bands began playing a handfasting ballad Whit had requested, and slowly, the voices of everyone present joined in, singing the verses. The melody sweetly echoed throughout the city and out over the quiet mountain valley, encircling the colony. Voices rose in unison, in harmony, heralding their allegiance to the ideal of one woman's devotion to another. And as they came to the end, the clouds overhead parted. For an instant, in hushed wonder, the excited crowd all watched separate rays of sunlight pour through the shifting December cloud cover, bathing the Leader's House in a pale, apricot-colored glow.

Raising her arms, Lilith presented the hallowed objects she had carried to the crowd below. Two thin, gold headbands, each with a crescent moon affixed to the front, glinted in the sunlight. Projecting her voice, Lilith called, "I raise the Horns of Artemis, and ask the Goddess's blessing on the promise about to be exchanged."

Lilith set one band carefully on Kali's shining yellow hair and then moved to Whit. Whit was so tall that Lilith had trouble settling it over the thick, dark hair, and quietly asked Whit to bend lower. Deftly, Lilith pushed her hand through Whit's unruly locks and pressed the band into place. Moving back, Lilith critically studied the crescent moon resting high on Whit's forehead.

As Whit straightened up, she winked at Lilith and whispered, "Thank you, Mother."

It was all Lilith could do not to grab her face and kiss her.

Stepping closer to Kali, Styx raised the large gold cup she carried. "May this red wine signify the pledge of blood, the uniting of flesh, the covenant of your two hearts." And with a solemn bow, she handed the cup to Kali.

Taking the cup, Kali faced Whit. "My love, I am yours," she stated, her eyes locked with the gray ones above her. She raised the cup to her lips and drank.

Slowly, Whit reached out as Kali handed over the troth cup, purposely pressing her fingers over the slender ones already holding the gold cup. Kali shivered and nearly dropped the cup. Rescuing it before it fell, Whit caught Kali's brown eyes and whispered, "My love, I am yours, forever," with an earnest conviction. Then, truly thirsty, Whit downed all the wine that remained.

After handing the cup back to Styx, Whit turned to Kali and extended her left hand. Kali reached with her own left hand and clasped Whit's, palm to palm; seconds later, they joined right hand to right hand, forming the mannaz symbol, the ancient runic sign for "humanity," with the figure-eight of their crossed arms.

Whit took a deep breath, and promised, "Till death do us part."

Her eyes filling with tears, Kali echoed, "Till death do us part."

And then they both leaned forward, over their clasped hands, and kissed.

From the shaft of sunbeams falling over the Leader's House, two golden eagles emerged, screeching as they soared low across the balcony.

The roar that went up from below was like nothing either woman had ever heard. It reverberated against the buildings nearby, then rang through the streets of Isis, and then rolled out over the cold mountain meadows of brown grass and small, determined pockets of snow. Far up into the mountains, the joyous noise sounded only as a wash of surf against a sandy shore, and then the wind caught the last vibration and swept it away, as if it had never sounded at all.

But in Isis, Kali and Whit stood together before their people, joined by hands and spirits, legally bound to each other for life. And the celebrating had just begun.

The End

MORE EXCITING FICTION FROM RISING TIDE PRESS

RETURN TO ISIS
Jean Stewart
The year is 2093. In this fantasy zone where sword and superstition meet sci-fi adventure, two women make a daring escape to freedom. Whit, a bold warrior from an Amazon nation, rescues Amelia from a dismal world where females are either breeders or drones. Together, they journey over grueling terrain, to the shining world of Artemis, and in their struggle to survive, find themselves unexpectedly drawn to each other. But it is in the safety of Artemis, Whit's home colony, that danger truly lurks. And it is in the ruins of Isis that the secret of how it was mysteriously destroyed waits to be uncovered. Here's adventure, mystery and romance all rolled into one.
Nominated for a 1993 Lambda Literary Award
ISBN 0-9628938-6-2; 192 Pages; $9.99

ISIS RISING
Jean Stewart
The eagerly awaited sequel to the immensely popular *Return to Isis* is here at last! In this stirring romantic fantasy, Jean Stewart continues the adventures of Whit (every woman's heart-throb), her beloved Kali, and a cast of colorful characters, as they rebuild Isis from the ashes. But all does not go smoothly in this brave new world, and Whit, with the help of her friends, must battle the forces that threaten. A rousing futuristic adventure and an endearing love story all rolled into one. Destined to capture your heart. Look for the sequel, *Warriors of Isis*.
ISBN 0-9628938-8-9; 192 Pages; $9.95.

WE HAVE TO TALK: A Guide to Bouncing Back From a Breakup
Jacki Moss
Here's the first interactive guide specifically designed for lesbians who have been left by their lovers. You will recognize many of your own thoughts, feelings, and fears, and learn new ways of dealing with the small problems created by a breakup, which left unchecked, develop into big ones. With gentle humor and keen insight, *We Have to Talk* will help you survive the pain so you can rebuild your life. You will even find reasons to laugh again.
ISBN 1883061-04-0 $9.99   (Available 1/95)

FACES OF LOVE
Sharon Gilligan
A wise and sensitive novel which takes us into the lives of Maggie, Karen, Cory, and their community of friends. Maggie Halloran, a prominent women's rights advocate, and Karen Weston, a brilliant attorney, have been together for 10 years in a relationship which is full of love, but is also often stormy. When Maggie's heart is captured by the young and beautiful Cory, she must take stock of her life and make some decisions.

Set against the backdrop of Madison, Wisconsin, and its dynamic women's community, the characters in this engaging novel are bright, involved, '90s women dealing with universal issues of love, commitment and friendship. A wonderful read!   ISBN 0-9628938-4-6; 192 Pages; $8.95

LOVE SPELL
Karen Williams
A deliciously erotic and humorous love story with a magical twist. When Kate Gallagher, a reluctantly single veterinarian, meets the mysterious and alluring Allegra one enchanted evening, it is instant fireworks. But as Kate gradually discovers, they live in two very different worlds, and Allegra's life is shrouded in mystery which Kate longs to penetrate. A masterful blend of fantasy and reality, this whimsical story will delight your imagination and warm your heart. Here is a writer of style as well as substance.

ISBN 0-9628938-2-X; 192 Pages; $9.95

ROMANCING THE DREAM
Heidi Johanna
This imaginative tale begins when Jacqui St. John leaves northern California looking for a new home, and cruises into the seemingly ordinary town of Kulshan, on the Oregon coast. Seeing the lilac bushes in bloom along the roadside, she suddenly remembers the recurring dream that has been tantalizing her for months—a dream of a house full of women, radiating warmth and welcome, and of one special woman, dressed in silk and leather....

But why has Jacqui, like so many other women, been drawn to this place? The answer is simple but wonderful—the women plan to take over the town and make a lesbian haven. A captivating and erotic love story with an unusual plot. A novel that will charm you with its gentle humor and fine writing.

ISBN 0-9628938-0-3;176 Pages; $8.95

YOU LIGHT THE FIRE
Kristen Garrett

Here's a grown-up Rubyfruit Jungle—sexy, spicy, and side-splittingly funny. Garrett, a fresh new voice in lesbian fiction, has created two memorable characters in Mindy Brinson and Cheerio Monroe. Can a gorgeous, sexy, high school math teacher and a raunchy, commitment-shy ex singer, make it last, in mainstream USA? With a little help from their friends, they can. This humorous, erotic and unpredictable love story will keep you laughing, and marveling at the variety of lesbian love.

ISBN 0-9628938-5-4; 176 Pages; $9.95

DANGER IN HIGH PLACES
An Alix Nicholson Mystery
Sharon Gilligan

Free-lance photographer Alix Nicholson was expecting some great photos of the AIDS Quilt—what she got was a corpse with a story to tell! Set against the backdrop of Washington, DC, the bestselling author of Faces of Love delivers a riveting mystery. When Alix accidentally stumbles on a deadly scheme surrounding AIDS funding, she is catapulted into the seamy underbelly of Washington politics. With the help of Mac, lesbian congressional aide, Alix gradually untangles the plot, has a romantic interlude, and learns of the dangers in high places.

ISBN 0-9628938-7-0; 176 Pages; $9.95

DANGER! Cross Currents
Sharon Gilligan

In this exciting sequel to *Danger in High Places*, freelance photographer Alix Nicholson is looking forward to teaching photography at Pacific Arts, a college idyllically located on California's North Coast. But as she quickly discovers, there are ugly goings-on beneath the surface beauty of her surroundings.

When her landlady, a real estate developer, turns up dead, and the police arrest Leah Claire, the woman's much younger lover, Alix is rapidly drawn into a complex web of intrigue and murder.

As she frantically searches for a way to free Leah, Alix unexpectedly finds herself at the dawn of a new romance ... and on the brink of her own destruction. A satisfying, well-crafted mystery.

ISBN 1-883061-01-6; 192 pages; $9.99

CORNERS OF THE HEART
Leslie Grey

This captivating novel of love and suspense introduces two unforgettable characters whose diverse paths have finally led them to each other. It is Spring, season of promise, when beautiful, French-born Chris Benet wanders into Katya Michaels' life. But their budding love is shadowed by a baffling mystery which they must solve. You will read with bated breath as they work together to outwit the menace that threatens Deer Falls; your heart will pound as the story races to its heart-stopping climax. Vivid, sensitive writing and an intriguing plot are the hallmarks of this exciting new writer.

ISBN 0-9628938-3-8; 224 pages; $9.95

SHADOWS AFTER DARK
Ouida Crozier

Wings of death are spreading over the world of Körnagy and Kyril's mission on Earth is to find the cause. Here, she meets the beautiful but lonely Kathryn, who has been yearning for a deep and enduring love with just such a woman as Kyril. But to her horror, Kathryn learns that her darkly exotic new lover has been sent to Earth with a purpose—to save her own dying vampire world. A tender and richly poetic novel.

ISBN 1-883061-50-4; 224 Pages; $9.95

DEADLY RENDEZVOUS: A Toni Underwood Mystery
Diane Davidson

Lieutenant Toni Underwood is the classic soft-hearted cop with the hard-boiled attitude, and she is baffled and horrified by her newest case—a string of brutal murders, in the middle of the desert, bodies dumped on Interstate I-10. As Toni and her partner Sally search for clues, they unravel a sinister network of corruption, drugs and murder.

Set in picturesque Palm Springs, California, this chilling, fast-paced mystery takes many unexpected twists and turns and finally reveals the dark side of the human mind, as well as the enduring love between two women. A suspenseful, explosive, action-packed whodunit.

ISBN 1-883061-02-4; 224 pages; $9.99

HEARTSTONE AND SABER
Jacqui Singleton

You can almost hear the sabers clash in this rousing tale of good and evil and passionate love, of warrior queens, white witches and sorcerers.

After the devastating raid on her peaceful little village, Elayna and her brother are captured and nearly sold into slavery. Saved from this terrible fate by the imperious warrior queen, Cydell Ra Sadiin, Elayna is brought to the palace to serve her. The two are immediate foes.

But these two powerful women are destined to join forces. And so, when rumblings of war reach the palace, Cydell, ruler of Mauldar, and Elayna, the Fair Witch of Avoreed, journey to Windsom Keep to combat the dark menace which threatens Cydell's empire and Elayna's very life. But along the way they must first conquer the wild magik of their passionate dreams, learn the secrets of the heartstone, and accept the deep and rapturous love that will transcend the powers of evil.

ISBN 1-883061-00-8; 224 Pages; $10.99

EDGE OF PASSION
Shelley Smith

The author of Horizon of the Heart presents another absorbing and sexy novel! From the moment Angela saw Micki sitting at the end of the smoky bar, she was consumed with desire for this cool and sophisticated woman, and determined to have her...at any cost. Set against the backdrop of colorful Provincetown and Boston, this sizzling novel will draw you into the all-consuming love affair between an older and a younger woman. A gripping love story, which is both fierce and tender. It will keep you breathless until the last page.
ISBN 0-9628938-1-1; 192 Pages; $8.95

How To Order:

Rising Tide Press books are available from you local women's bookstore or directly from Rising Tide Press. Send check, money order, or Visa/MC account number, with expiration date and signature to: Rising Tide Press, 5 Kivy St., Huntington Sta., New York 11746. Credit card orders must be over $25. Remember to include shipping and handling charges: $4.95 for the first book plus $1.00 for each additional book. Credit Card Orders Call our Toll Free # 1-800-648-5333. For UPS delivery, provide street address.